PRAISE FOR EARLENE FOWLER'S
BENNI HARPER MYSTERIES

IRISH CHAIN

"A TERRIFIC WHODUNIT! The dialogue is intelligent and witty, the characters intensely human, and the tantalizing puzzle keeps the pages turning."

—Jean Hager, author of
The Redbird's Cry and
Blooming Murder

"A BLUE-RIBBON COZY . . . This well-textured sequel to *Fool's Puzzle* . . . intricately blends social history and modern mystery." —*Publishers Weekly*

"CHARMING, BEGUILING, AND ENTRANCING . . . *Irish Chain* is a total joy."

—Jackson (MS) *Clarion-Ledger*

"THE CHARACTERS ARE TERRIFIC . . . the dialogue is amusing, and the plot is different and interesting. GRADE: A+." —*The Poisoned Pen*

"A DELIGHTFUL AND WITTY MYSTERY full of endearing characters. It offers insights into quilts . . . folk art, and historical events that add depth to its multi-layered story." —*Gothic Journal*

"KEEPS YOU INTERESTED AND GUESSING UNTIL THE END." —*Mystery News*

Kansas Troubles is an agitating pattern consisting of small and large triangles resembling bear claws. It evokes the image of rapidly spinning windmill blades or the twirling center of a tornado. All sharp points and angles, it will not produce a calming effect no matter what color fabric is used.

And don't miss the next Benni Harper Mystery
GOOSE IN THE POND
Coming May 1997 from Berkley Prime Crime!

FOOL'S PUZZLE

"BREEZY, HUMOROUS DIALOGUE OF THE FIRST ORDER . . . Quilt patterns provide a real and metaphorical background as a reader absorbs the names for different styles."　　　*—Chicago Sun-Times*

"I LOVED *FOOL'S PUZZLE* . . . [Earlene Fowler] made me laugh out loud on one page and brought tears to my eyes the next . . . I can't wait to read more."
　　　—Margaret Maron, Edgar Award-winning author of Bootlegger's Daughter

"A CRACKERJACK DEBUT."　　*—I Love a Mystery*

"A RIPPING READ. It's smart, vigorous, and more than funny: Within its humor is wrenching insight."
　—Noreen Ayres, author of A World the Color of Salt

"I THOROUGHLY ENJOYED *FOOL'S PUZZLE* . . . Fowler's characters are terrific . . . a super job."
—Eve K. Sandstrom, author of The Devil Down Home

"A NEAT LITTLE MYSTERY . . . her plot is compelling."　　　*—Booklist*

"LIVELY . . . More Benni mysteries are in the works and will be welcomed."
　　　—The Drood Review of Mystery

"A GREAT BEGINNING OF A NEW SERIES. The characters are charming and their interactions lively."
　　　—Mostly Murder

MORE MYSTERIES FROM THE BERKLEY PUBLISHING GROUP...

CAT CALIBAN MYSTERIES: She was married for thirty-eight years. Raised three kids. Compared to that, tracking down killers is easy...

by D. B. Borton

ONE FOR THE MONEY	TWO POINTS FOR MURDER
THREE IS A CROWD	FOUR ELEMENTS OF MURDER
FIVE ALARM FIRE	SIX FEET UNDER

ELENA JARVIS MYSTERIES: There are some pretty bizarre crimes deep in the heart of Texas—and a pretty gutsy police detective who rounds up the unusual suspects...

by Nancy Herndon

ACID BATH	WIDOWS' WATCH
LETHAL STATUES	HUNTING GAME
TIME BOMBS	C.O.P. OUT

FREDDIE O'NEAL, P.I., MYSTERIES: You can bet that this appealing Reno private investigator will get her man..."A winner."—Linda Grant

by Catherine Dain

LAY IT ON THE LINE	SING A SONG OF DEATH
WALK A CROOKED MILE	LAMENT FOR A DEAD COWBOY
BET AGAINST THE HOUSE	LUCK OF THE DRAW
DEAD MAN'S HAND	

BENNI HARPER MYSTERIES: Meet Benni Harper—a quilter and folk-art expert with an eye for murderous designs...

by Earlene Fowler

FOOL'S PUZZLE	IRISH CHAIN
KANSAS TROUBLES	GOOSE IN THE POND

HANNA BARLOW MYSTERIES: For ex-cop and law student Hannah Barlow, justice isn't just a word in a textbook. Sometimes, it's a matter of life and death...

by Carroll Lachnit

MURDER IN BRIEF	A BLESSED DEATH

KANSAS TROUBLES

Earlene Fowler

BERKLEY PRIME CRIME, NEW YORK

KANSAS TROUBLES

A Berkley Prime Crime Book / published by arrangement with
the author

PRINTING HISTORY
Berkley Prime Crime hardcover edition / May 1996
Berkley Prime Crime mass-market edition / March 1997

The Penguin Putnam Inc. World Wide Web site address is
http://www.penguinputnam.com

ISBN: 0-425-15696-6

Berkley Prime Crime Books are published
by The Berkley Publishing Group,
a member of Penguin Putnam Inc.,
200 Madison Avenue, New York, New York 10016.
The name BERKLEY PRIME CRIME and the BERKLEY PRIME CRIME
design are trademarks belonging to Berkley Publishing Corporation.

PRINTED IN THE UNITED STATES OF AMERICA

10 9 8 7 6 5 4 3

For Retha and Clarence Fowler,
my favorite Kansas couple

and

For Ann Lee,
who never stopped believing

ACKNOWLEDGMENTS

Gratitude and humble thanks to:

God, the only true Creator. All I have is from You;

Mary Atkinson and Ann Lee, insightful readers, faithful friends;

Deborah Schneider, simply the best agent in the world;

Judith Palais, an editor with enthusiasm, talent, and a wonderful sense of humor;

Joyce Goldberg and all the other great people at Berkley, thanks for your hard work;

Darrell and Joyce Albright of Pretty Prairie, Kansas, for their hospitality, friendship, and for rendering help whenever asked;

Mary Lou Wright of Lawrence, Kansas, for her generous hospitality and support;

Stephanie Harris (and Barbie and Tony), superior horsewoman, instructor, and generous dispenser of equine information;

Chief Delbert Fowler and Officer Larry Hudson of the Derby Police Department, for assistance above and beyond the call of duty;

Debra Jackson, Laurie Fowler, Tom and Bonnie

Fowler, Renea Frazier, and Gail Rose, for help in their particular areas of expertise (I'll always remember the escalator, Laurie);

Earl Worley, my father, and Retha Fowler, my mother-in-law, for their love and support;

Mary Arnell Worley, my mother, and Clarence Fowler, my father-in-law, for what they gave me while they were here on earth;

And always, to my husband, Allen. As far as I'm concerned, he can rope the moon.

AUTHOR'S NOTE

If you check a map of Kansas, you'll find that the towns of Derby and Pretty Prairie really do exist. They are both wonderful towns full of friendly, law-abiding citizens. The crime rate in both communities is extremely low. I want to thank the citizens of both towns for good-naturedly letting me use their place of residence for my creative purposes. Miller is based on a real town in Kansas, but I chose to fictionalize it out of respect for the privacy of the Amish who live there. I made every attempt to write about Kansas as accurately as possible and especially appreciate the help I received from all my new friends there. All characters in this novel are created strictly from my imagination and are not based on any real people. Any errors are, of course, my own.

KANSAS TROUBLES

Variations of the Kansas Troubles quilt pattern have been traced back to the early 1800's, and it was officially recognized by the Ladies Art Company in the latter part of the nineteenth century. An agitating pattern consisting of small and large triangles resembling bear claws, "Kansas Troubles" evokes the image of rapidly spinning windmill blades or the twirling center of a tornado. The pattern, all sharp points and angles, will not produce a calming effect no matter what color fabric is used. In all, Kansas Troubles has over twenty-five variations. Some of the more popular ones are called Indian Trails, Climbing Rose, Bear's Paw, Little Lost Ship, Rocky Road to Kansas, Slave Chain, and Endless Tears.

ONE

KANSAS. LAND OF sunflowers, golden wheat fields, occasional roads of brick (though none yellow as far as I could see), and the more-than-occasional tornado. Tornados were specifically on my mind that sunny but cool California Central Coast Saturday morning in July, since I'd just awakened from a dream featuring one. It was a large, menacing dust devil with blue-gray eyes at its widest part. Eyes that followed my every move like those crazy Mona Lisa paintings in slapstick horror movies.

The bed sagged on one side. A large hand enveloped my shoulder and gently shook it. I woke up and stared into eyes the same steel-blue as those in my dream. They gazed back at me in concern.

"Benni, sweetheart, are you okay?" Gabe asked. "You were whimpering in your sleep."

"What color did you say your mom's eyes were?" I asked, blinking rapidly.

"Kind of grayish-blue. Like mine. Why?"

"No reason." I didn't believe in prophetic dreams. Really I didn't. As he nuzzled my neck with his scratchy mustache, I tried to forget the image and just enjoy his warm lips tracing my collarbone. He was slightly damp and smelled of soap. I groaned inwardly. That meant a cold shower was somewhere in my immediate future. The hot water tank in my tiny Spanish-style house was more than adequate for one person. Two, if they took a reasonable length of time in the shower. Which he didn't. After a little over four months into this second marriage, the shortcomings of a shared domestic life were beginning to come back to me.

"He says you can even use the eyelashes," I yelled ten minutes later over the cascade of tepid water in the shower. I twisted the hot water spigot as far as it would go. My skin took on that always lovely plucked-poultry look.

"What?" Gabe yelled back.

I stuck my head out from behind the shower curtain and repeated my comment. He stood nude in front of the oak-framed bathroom mirror, the lower half of his olive face covered with snowy white shaving cream. I studied him in the mirror's reflection, relishing the domestically sensuous picture of a man shaving. His thick black mustache was tipped white like frosting on a chocolate cake. My eyes wandered down the back of the dense, hard muscles of his runner's thighs, pausing briefly on the pale spider-web scar on his left hip. A scar he refused to discuss the first time I noticed it. I repeated my eyelash comment.

He glanced at me in the mirror, his serious, deep-set eyes crinkling in amusement. "Keep staring, and I'll be joining you in there. Now, whose eyelashes are we discussing?"

"Ostriches."

His eyebrows went up in question.

"It's the latest thing that Uncle Arnie wants Daddy to invest in. It's not as crazy as it sounds. They even have a category now at the Houston Livestock Show for ostriches and emus."

"Eyelashes," he prompted.

"Keep your spurs on. According to Arnie, no part of

these birds is wasted. You can sell the meat and the feathers, then make the skins into boots or sofas. Their toenails are ground up and sold to jewelers as an abrasive, and even the eyelashes are used for paintbrush bristles or ornamental design.''

He rinsed off his face, his smooth brown back flexing attractively. I seriously considered his offer to join me in the shower. ''Sounds disgusting,'' he said. ''What do they decorate?''

''You got me.'' I stepped out of the shower and grabbed one of the fluffy, sand-colored bath towels a couple of his patrol officers had given us as wedding presents. ''But you can bet dollars to doughnuts that Daddy will turn in his cattle brand and raise birds when you start eating red meat again.''

''Anything's possible.'' He reached for my towel. ''Let me help dry your back.''

''Not a chance, Chief Ortiz,'' I said, wrapping the towel around me. ''We've only got an hour and a half before our plane leaves, and your help always slows things down.'' I pointed toward the bedroom. ''Get dressed.''

Sitting on the bed, he pulled on his favorite pair of faded Levi's and a moss-green polo shirt. I grimaced when he stuck his bare feet into scuffed leather Topsiders.

''One of these days, I'm taking those shoes to the dump,'' I warned.

''You do and maybe you and Arnie's wife can get a two-for-one deal with her divorce lawyer,'' he said with a serene smile. He shook his head and grinned. ''I like Arnie. He can always make me laugh.''

My Uncle Arnie can be a fun guy, but as Daddy likes to say, he's never been in any danger of drowning in his own sweat. Thirty years ago, when my mother was dying, Arnie and my gramma Dove moved from Arkansas to San Celina, on California's Central Coast, to live with my father and me. I was almost six years old, and my grieving father could barely care for his expanding cattle herd, much less an active, growing little girl. Arnie was thirteen at the time, so he's always been more like a brother to me than an uncle. His wife recently threw him out of the house, and he'd already worn out his welcome at the ranches of his three other brothers and two sisters, which were spread across the western United States. We were his last resort.

I slipped on a pair of wheat-colored Wranglers, boots, and a sleeveless denim shirt. Early July weather here on the Central Coast was the best in the country—sunny, breezy days flowing into cool, clear nights—but I'd been warned that summers in Gabe's hometown of Derby, Kansas, seven miles south of Wichita, were sometimes so hot and muggy that conversions in the local churches went up thirty percent whenever a minister presented a sermon on the physical existence of Hell. But, Gabe warned, wait five minutes, and the weather will change. Apparently Kansas weather was similar to what people were saying about our marriage—unexpected and bound to be stormy.

"Well," I continued, "I can't imagine him and Dove and Daddy driving all the way to Kansas without some big blowup. This ostrich thing has Daddy about ready to chomp a bit in two. They should have flown, but Daddy can't get Dove on an airplane to save his life."

"They'll be fine," Gabe said. He tucked his black leather shaving kit into the matching suitcase opened on the rumpled Irish Chain quilt covering our pine four-poster bed, the only piece of furniture we owned in common at this point. I compared his neatly packed suitcase with the haphazard muddle of clothes I'd thrown into my J.C. Penney canvas bag. Even our style of luggage was as different as night and day. With me being widowed only a year, Gabe divorced for seven, and knowing each other barely three months before getting married, family and friends were literally placing bets on how

long our marriage would survive. I couldn't blame them.
I would be the first person to say it didn't make sense.
But then, when did being in love ever have anything to
do with sense?

"I don't know," I said doubtfully. "It's a long way
to Kansas. A lot of desolate places to leave a dead
body."

He wrapped his arms around me in a warm hug.
"Quit worrying about them. We're on vacation. A vacation we both need."

I couln't argue with that. My position as curator of
the Josiah Sinclair Folk Art Museum and Artists' Co-op
might not involve as many life-and-death decisions as
his chief of police job, but it certainly caused me more
than enough stress. Keeping the shoestring budget
pumped with donations and maintaining a semblance of
peace among the forty often temperamental artists were
jobs I wouldn't miss for the next two weeks. But there
were at least a hundred places other than the Sunflower
State on my wish list of belated honeymoon destinations.
Not that I have anything against the state itself, mind
you. I mean, who can totally dislike a state whose official song is "Home on the Range"? And *The Wizard of
Oz* has always been one of my favorite movies, though
like most people, I'm always a bit disappointed when
Dorothy opts to return to black-and-white Kansas rather
than stay in Technicolor Oz. And I'm sure the state that
produced both William Inge and Superman has many
wonderful cultural and recreational sights. It just happened to also contain one cultural sight I was not looking
forward to. Namely, Gabe's family. Specifically, his
twin sisters and his mother.

Though I'd seen pictures of them, talked to them over
the phone, and heard quite a few stories in the last few
months, they still didn't seem real to me. Nor did the
life Gabe lived in Kansas until he was sixteen years old,
which was when his father died, causing Gabe's life to

totally change. After a few delinquent escapades that almost landed him in jail, his mother sent him to Southern California to live with one of his dad's brothers in Santa Ana. Even with the photos and the stones, I couldn't really picture this man, whose whispered Spanish words could melt me into soft wax, driving a tractor on his Grandfather Smith's wheat farm, any more than I could imagine him crawling through the soggy jungles of Vietnam or working undercover in the barrios of East L.A. The only context in which I'd ever seen Gabe was in his all-business Chief of Police (or as I like to call it, his Sergeant Friday) personality or his easygoing at-home demeanor. Sometimes it almost seemed as if he appeared from nowhere, sans history, and plopped down in San Celina just for my benefit. It was different from anything I'd ever experienced, being intimate with someone I barely knew. Life with my late husband, Jack, who had known me since I was fifteen and was raised on a ranch as I was, hadn't prepared me for the disparate backgrounds and complex emotional baggage people bring into middle-age relationships.

"They're going to love you," Gabe said, dropping a kiss on top of my head and picking up his suitcase.

"I hope you're right," I muttered as he walked out. I picked up the photo album we'd looked through the night before. The last formal portrait of his mother, Kathryn Smith Ortiz, was taken two years ago when she retired from forty-one years of schoolteaching. She was tall and broad-shouldered like Gabe and wore a prim, pleated-front grayish dress with pearl buttons and a gauzy lace collar. Under a cloud of lavender-tinged white curls, the somber eyes she'd passed down to her son reprimanded the photographer, probably for his bad posture. Being talkative as a kid and, to quote Dove, born with a mouth as sassy as a squirrel's, I sent up a quick thanks that she hadn't been *my* fifth-grade teacher.

His twin sisters, fraternal not identical, were six years younger than his forty-three years, and two years older than my thirty-five. Rebecca Ortiz Kolanowski and Angela Ortiz. Becky and Angel. In their latest Christmas card photo, Becky with her husband and children appeared the quintessential Middle American family. Her golden-brown hair, ivory skin, and almost-indigo eyes revealed more of her mother's Pennsylvania-Dutch background than her father's Hispanic one. She was pretty in a fresh, milk-commercial kind of way. Her two tow-headed daughters appeared to be about eight and twelve. Her husband, Stan Kolanowski, sported a crew cut so blond it appeared almost transparent, and looked like the safe, dependable insurance broker he was.

Angel was the image of her nickname, though Gabe said she'd done everything she could to live it down. One telling snapshot placed her next to a sparkling river, a girlish fist playfully threatening the photographer. Sunshine backlit her blond-streaked brown hair and dark almond-shaped eyes challenged the camera with a reckless, earthy expression that had probably caused more than one barroom brawl.

Gabe appeared in the doorway. "All packed?"

I zipped up my bag. "Yep. You know, it's weird having a new family. Worrying like a teenager over what I'm wearing, what stupid things I'll probably say, whether they'll like me or not." It hadn't occurred to me until after our whirlwind marriage that this man came with family already attached. I hadn't even met Sam, his eighteen-year-old son yet. Shortly after we were married in late February, Sam dropped out of UC Santa Barbara, withdrew all his savings, and took off with a friend for Hawaii, searching for the perfect wave. Gabe just about burst a blood vessel after getting Sam's postcard from Kaunakakai. That uneasy meeting still lurked on the horizon.

"If I can do it, you can do it," he said, with what I felt was not a great deal of sympathy.

"Thanks loads." I didn't voice the apprehension I felt about Dove meeting my new, apparently steel-spined mother-in-law. I would have preferred to face the Kansas clan on my own, but Dove insisted that unlike *some* people, she was going to meet Gabe's family even if she had to hitchhike. That was a direct barb at my dad, who had not traveled further than seventy-five miles from the ranch since I was a teenager. Dove had been nagging him to take a vacation for years, and she'd finally seen her opportunity. And she wasn't kidding about hitchhiking. As she so picturesquely put it, she'd trust a snaggle-toothed redneck in a flatbed Ford before she'd bet her life on a dope-sniffing yuppie flying one of those steel coffins. Leaving the ranch in the care of his trusted foreman, Daddy and Dove and Arnie were driving to Kansas in Daddy's new Ford pickup, stopping along the way to assuage Dove's wanderlust by visiting some of America's finer tourist attractions. They would meet us in Derby in two weeks for the Saturday afternoon wedding reception Becky and Angel had planned.

An hour later Gabe and I were standing at the ticket counter of the tiny San Celina airport, checking our bags for the American Eagle connection to Los Angeles International Airport.

"Have a good flight, Ms. Harper, Mr. Ortiz," the clerk said cheerfully.

Gabe growled deep in his throat and picked up my leather backpack.

"Are you going to do that every time someone says my name?" I asked, walking toward our assigned gate.

"Do what?"

"Make that noise in your throat. Sounds a lot like a big old bull choking on a hunk of cud."

He made the noise again and kept walking. He had taken my decision to keep the Harper name, and not become an official Ortiz, as an insult on three levels— as a man, as a traditional Latino man, and as a conservative Midwestern man. I sort of guessed it was one of those man things. But I was determined to keep my identity. Changing your name at nineteen when your vision is blinded by stars and an overload of hormones is one thing. Though at thirty-five I still had the hormone overload, I didn't *want* a new name, not even a hyphenated one. I loved Gabe and didn't want to put any more obstacles on the rocky road of our marriage, but something in me wouldn't give in on this no matter how much grumbling and pouting he did.

By the time we reached LAX, I'd teased him out of his irritable mood. "Tell me about your friends again," I said when our flight to Kansas was over the Mojave Desert. I unwrapped the snack sandwich that came with a container of yogurt, a cellophane-wrapped brownie, and an apple.

Pressing his head against the narrow plane seat, Gabe's face relaxed with memory. "We were inseparable from kindergarten to the summer I turned sixteen and went to California. We had some wild times, those guys and me."

"Just how wild?" I took a tentative bite of my dry sandwich, then abandoned it for the brownie.

"As wild as four teenage guys can get with an old '56 Chevy and three dollars worth of gas. We spent most of our time kicking up gravel outside of town, racing whoever could get their dad's new car."

Shoving my brownie aside, I dug through the side pocket of my backpack and pulled out the last picture Gabe and his three friends had taken together, seven years ago, right after Gabe was divorced. They were leaning against an old barn somewhere. Gabe, wearing a Dodger baseball cap and a white T-shirt, didn't look a lot different from the way he did now. He smiled at the camera, but his eyes seemed sad.

"I'll never keep them all straight," I said.

He pointed to a skinny, bearded man with a protruding Adam's apple and large plastic eyeglasses. "Lawrence Markley. He's part owner of a country-western nightclub called Prairie City Nights in Wichita. Does pretty well from what I hear. His wife's name is

Janet. I think she works in some kind of craft store in Derby.''

"Any kids?"

"A daughter. Grown up by now. Hard to believe.''

I pointed to the extraordinarily handsome man with dark blond hair punching Lawrence's shoulder.

"Rob Harlow. He works in Derby at one of his dad's feed stores. Jake Harlow owns a chain of them all over Kansas. Harlow's Feed and Grain. When we were in high school, his dad would leave Rob in charge of the store while he went down the street to the cafe, and Rob would talk one of us into taking care of the customers while he made out with girls behind the hay bales. They just couldn't leave him alone.''

"I can see why." Rob's grin was polished, his wavy hair stylishly cut—clipped short on the sides, longer in front. His face had lean, clean-cut features, a perfect cleft chin, eyes the unbelievable green of a 7-Up bottle. He was tanned a flawless Marlboro cowboy shade of brown.

"Remind me not to leave you alone with him around any hay bales.''

The flight attendant stopped next to my seat and picked up the remains of our meals. I clicked the tray back in place, leaned over, and kissed Gabe, nipping his bottom lip gently. "You don't have to worry about me, Friday. I tend to go more for the dark and brooding, pistol-packing ethnic types. So, I forgot—does gorgeous Rob have a wife and kids?''

"No kids. No wife either. At least, not anymore. He just divorced his third one. According to Becky, his latest love is a country-western singer. Or an aspiring one anyway. Sounds pretty odd. Grew up Amish.''

"You mean she left the Amish to become a singer? That *is* odd. I wonder if he seduced her from the fold.''

"If anyone could do it, Rob could.''

I looked back down at the picture. "And last but not least, Dewey Champagne.'' He wore a white straw cowboy hat pulled low over his oval face, obscuring his eyes. Unsmiling, he leaned back against the gnarled barn wall. He was a good six inches shorter than Gabe's six feet. "You were in Vietnam together, right? And he's a cop, too."

"Right. He worked for the Wichita Police Department for eight years, then came back home to become, as he likes to say, Derby's chief of detectives. Actually he's Derby's *only* detective. He says the hardest part of his job is supervising himself."

"Married?"

"Got divorced last year. And apparently he has a thing for singers, too. His latest love is named Cordie June Rodell, and she sings with Rob's girlfriend. She's also a good twenty years his junior."

"Kids?"

"Had two. A boy and a girl. The boy should be about twenty-one now. He's a bull rider."

"What's his name?"

"Chet Champagne."

I shrugged. "Doesn't sound familiar, but I haven't really been keeping up lately. What about Dewey's daughter?"

"There's a real tragedy. Her name was DeeDee. She was only sixteen when she was thrown off a horse and killed, about a year and a half ago. Dewey and Belinda broke up shortly after that."

"How awful for them."

"Dewey hasn't had it easy this last year or so. I hope this new lady friend of his doesn't take him for a ride." Gabe opened the book in his lap and frowned at the highlighted pages.

"Such relaxing summer reading," I teased.

"I'm never going to get this done." He was reading the diary of Søren Kierkegaard, determined to finish the masters thesis in philosophy he'd originally come to quiet, uneventful San Celina to complete. I, and an unexpected rash of murders in San Celina, had kept him from it.

"I'll leave you alone, then," I said and looked out the window. The air was clear for what seemed a hundred miles, and the fields we flew over looked like the clichéd image of a patchwork quilt. To be more accurate, they looked like an orderly Corn and Beans pattern or a strip quilt in shades of rich goldenrod and mustard yellow with an occasional sage-green square thrown in just to keep it interesting. Furrows like quilt stitching decorated the plowed fields in crooked abstract patterns that Gabe said helped keep the soil from being blown away by the strong summer winds. Silvery grain silos gleamed like new dimes in the bright sunlight.

Much sooner than I preferred, the seat belt sign flashed. The pilot welcomed us to the Wichita Mid-Continent Airport and went through his landing spiel, including a weather report I would hear repeated often during the next two weeks—"Mostly sunny with thunderstorms expected later tonight." He ended his speech with a hardy hello and a joke about tornados and milk cows, the punchline of which was lost in static.

From my perspective, Wichita didn't look at all like the Emerald City but just another skyscraper landscape against a sky that actually did appear bigger and bluer than California's. Bright green fields as round as archery targets dotted the ground.

"Why are some fields round?" I asked.

"A more efficient way of irrigating," Gabe explained. "It's done automatically, by a pivot arc. On the ground you can't really tell the fields are round."

The pattern of circles within squares would make a spectacular quilt. "Above Kansas" would be a good name. I mentally pieced it together, attempting to keep my mind off my least favorite part of flying—landing.

The plane hit the runway with a sharp bounce. "Half an hour until inspection," I said.

Gabe took my hand and kissed the soft skin on the underside of my wrist. "They're going to adore you. Look at the effect you had on me."

"Initially?" I said doubtfully. We met when I'd been involved in a murder at the folk art museum, and our relationship at first had been less than friendly to say the least.

He chuckled. "Well, they'll learn to love you."

We claimed our rented give-me-a-ticket red Camaro and started down the freeway toward Wichita. We passed the huge home store and warehouse of Shepler's Western Wear, a mail-order house I'd ordered from at least a few hundred times in the last twenty-five years. Eventually we pulled on to a two-lane highway heading south. Train tracks paralleled the road, shaded occasionally by huge, dusky-green cottonwood trees. There was no question we were in wheat country when we sped past old concrete grain silos, billboards advertising Farm Bureau Insurance, and a couple of yellow and black highway signs warning "Mowers ahead."

"There are trees," I said with surprise.

Gabe laughed. "Of course there are. Mostly cottonwoods, but some pines and box elders, and I don't know what else. What did you expect?"

"Things to be flatter, I guess. You know, wheat fields like oceans as far as the eye can see. Amber waves of grain. Corn as high as an elephant's eye."

"You're more likely to find the corn in Iowa and Nebraska, though we have our share. The flat Kansas you're thinking of does exist over in the western part of the state, but we do have our oceans of wheat around Wichita." He tapered his eyes, scanning the passing landscape with a farmer's measuring gaze. "Things are usually drier this time of year. They had good rains last year, so everything's stayed green."

"Except for no hills, it doesn't look a lot different from home."

He reached over and squeezed my knee affectionately. "We Kansans have stumbled into the twentieth century, Benni, no matter what the media would have you believe. Why, I've heard a vicious rumor that they've even got cable television in Wichita these days.''

"Not to mention flush toilets," I said.

"No wisecracks. You know we got those in the sixties.'' He fiddled with the rearview mirror, then let out a delighted laugh when a police siren screamed behind us.

"I told you it was only a matter of time," I said, glancing at the speedometer.

As usual, Gabe had been driving twenty miles over the speed limit. He always bragged about never getting a speeding ticket. Because he'd carried a police officer's badge since he was twenty-two, and knowing the brotherhood among cops, I didn't find that particularly remarkable and told him so. Often.

We pulled to the side of the highway, and a young officer with tanned Popeye forearms and mirrored aviator sunglasses walked up to Gabe's open window. "It's a joke," Gabe said in a low voice. "Dewey's behind it.''

"Driver's license and registration, please.'' The young man's voice was deep and polite.

Gabe handed him the information and waited, an amused half-smile on his face. The officer took the papers and walked back to his white and blue patrol car. After a few minutes, he came back and returned them to Gabe. He tore a ticket from his pad and passed it through the open window. "I clocked you at twenty-one miles over the speed limit, sir. This is a real pretty little Camaro, and I know these sporty cars can sometimes get away from you, but try and take it a little slower. We'd like you to enjoy your stay in Kansas without hurting yourself or someone else. Have a nice day.'' He flipped his ticket book shut and strode back to his car.

"This is a real citation," Gabe sputtered. "That lowdown son of a gun.'' I leaned over, looked at it, and laughed.

"It is," I said gleefully. "I can't believe it. Your first

hour in Kansas, and you already have a criminal record.''

"It has to be a joke," Gabe said. He looked in the rearview mirror and grinned. "He's coming back. Okay, Dewey, you really had me going there.''

"Excuse me, Chief Ortiz," the young officer said. "I have a message from Detective Champagne.''

"Yes?" Gabe prompted, holding out the ticket.

"He said to tell you that no one keeps their ch—'' He glanced over at me and blushed. "Pardon me, ma'am. Uh . . . no one stays a virgin forever.''

I giggled. Gabe growled at the officer's retreating back, then pointed a finger at me. "One more sound out of you, and you walk the rest of the way.''

I held up my hands in protest. "Hey, this is between you and your buddy. I'm just an innocent passenger.''

"He's going to pay for this," Gabe grumbled. I judiciously turned my head and smiled out the window.

In the next few minutes, we entered Derby. Gabe pointed to a busy Taco Bell on our left. "That's where my dad's garage was. Back then, it was the edge of town. There was nothing but wheat fields and a few houses until Wichita.'' He sighed deeply and nodded at the McDonald's, Kentucky Fried Chicken, Hardee's, Blockbuster Video, and Braum's Ice Cream that had mushroomed insidiously near the city limits sign. "I hate seeing this. It's not the town I grew up in. It could be anyplace now.''

Once past fast food row, the original Derby, with the muddy Arkansas River bordering the town to the west, had wide, clean streets that showcased many small independent businesses that had withstood the assault of the encroaching corporate food and retail giants. Gabe's face softened when we drove past the old Derby Cinema tucked into a strip mall called El Paso Village.

He let out a small grunt of annoyance as we passed the red brick building that housed the Derby Emergency Medical Service and the police department. Atop the square, neat building, an American flag and a blue and gold Kansas state flag whiffled in the brisk breeze.

As we drove through the center of town, Gabe pointed out landmarks. Next to the police station stood an abandoned brick building with the inscription "El Paso Water Company" over the door. "El Paso was the town's original name," he told me.

"El Paso? As in Texas?"

"From 1871 to 1888, until the Santa Fe Railroad changed it to Derby to end confusion with the one in Texas, but it wasn't changed officially until 1956."

We passed a small tan building on our right. A tilted green derby over the *D* in *The Daily Reporter* gave the newspaper's name a jaunty air. A large banner with a turkey-red Bear's Paw quilt pattern in each corner stretched across the building advertising the Bear's Paw Quilt Guild's First Annual Quilt Show: "From Our Hearts To Yours—Quilting From The Kansas Heartland." When I'd spoken to Gabe's sister Becky on the phone last week, she was excited about us being here during the show. She was current president of the three-year-old guild, and with the list of activities she reeled off, it sounded as if I'd have plenty to keep me busy while Gabe was off with his friends. That relieved my performance anxiety somewhat. I couldn't picture spending two weeks trying to make conversation with a new mother-in-law who, I suspected, was not thrilled with her son's impulsive decision to remarry.

We made a U-turn and came back to the middle of town where we turned left on a small street, crossed the railroad tracks and the Arkansas River, and drove down a narrow dirt road with houses on the left and open fields on the right. Most of the homes had deep front yards, dense with trees and vines. Boats and campers crowded many of the narrow gravel driveways.

"You can't tell from here," Gabe said, "but these houses sit right on the river."

"The Arkansas River, right?" I said, showing off my topographic knowledge of his home state.

"No," he said solemnly. "The Ar*kansas* River. Remember where you are." He turned into a narrow driveway, pulling up in front of a white, two-story wood-frame house with a steep gray roof and a red brick apron. The shady front porch held a natural wood porch swing, a yellow bird feeder, two white wicker chairs, and a padded redwood chaise longue. As Gabe turned off the engine, the screen door opened, and his mother stepped out. She stood as tall and sturdy as an elm tree, resting large hands on her narrow hips. She wore an iris-blue skirt, a white tailored blouse, and sensible navy loafers. Her pale skin had the translucence of nonfat milk.

"Mom," Gabe said, walking up the steps and throwing an arm around her shoulders. "You look younger every time I see you."

"Oh, get on with you," she said, slapping him lightly on the chest. Her stern expression softened to one of indulgence. Next to her creamy complexion, my dark-skinned husband looked like a foundling until mother and son turned and regarded me with the same mercurial eyes.

"This must be your new wife," Mrs. Ortiz said, her face holding the same I'll-make-up-my-mind-when-you've-proved-out look I'd seen so often on her son.

He smiled widely. "Must be. This is Benni."

I held out my hand. "Nice to meet you, Mrs. Ortiz."

She shook it firmly, her expression appraising now with the experienced evaluation of a public school teacher. "I'm glad you could come." Her voice was as cool and dry as the palm of her hand. I had no trouble picturing her clapping her capable hands briskly and bringing a rambunctious group of fifth-graders to attention. "Please call me Kathryn."

I nodded, thinking how different it was when Gabe was heartily welcomed into my extended Southern-born family. Half the time Dove, whom Gabe affectionately calls *Abuelita*, takes his side over mine in disputes. I had a feeling that wasn't going to be the case with Kathryn and me.

She looked up at Gabe, her granite face again turning gentle and liquid. "Are you hungry? Supper's waiting. I made your favorite chicken and rice casserole. When was the last time you had a good, home-cooked meal?" She linked arms with her son and led him toward the front door.

"I don't know," he said. "Let me think." He peered over her head and gave me a broad wink. I showed him a clenched fist.

Okay, I thought: cooking. Always high in the competition between mother-in-law and daughter-in-law. She had the home team advantage of giving birth to Gabe and raising him. I had the visitor's edge of daily exposure to his habits and that not-to-be-taken-lightly leverage of sleeping with him. I took a deep breath and followed them into the house.

Let the games begin.

TWO

I STEPPED OVER the threshold, feeling a bit like Dorothy, and was stopped in my tracks by a snarl. Actually it was more of a wet snuffle, but what the flat-faced creature with the skunk markings and stubby tail lacked in visual impact, she more than made up for in enthusiasm.

A Boston terrier with a rhinestone-studded collar and an attitude. Just what I needed.

She studied me with bulgy dark eyes, then growled deep in her throat, took a big wheezy breath, and coughed.

A Boston terrier with an attitude, a cutesy collar, and asthma. Great. Well, she obviously belonged here, so I figured we'd better make friends. I stooped down and held out my hand in a friendly gesture.

Now, let the record reflect that I like dogs. All dogs. Some I've even loved. There was one, a tough, solid-rumped old Australian shepherd named Pick who was my best friend until I was fourteen and he died of cancer. I would have taken a bullet for that dog. I'm telling you, there are few things in this world that beat sitting on the front porch of my dad's ranch, dawn breaking over San Celina's hilly horizon, all blood-orange and yellow, a hot cup of coffee in one hand, a cool canine nose in the other. And dogs like me. As with horses, I talk low and slow, and don't try to rush them. Works every time. Well, almost every time.

"Good girl," I crooned. She took one panicked look at my outstretched hand, let out a terrified scream, and dashed into the other room.

A minute later, Gabe and his mother came back into the room. Kathryn held the trembling dog in her arms.

"What on earth did you do to Daphne?" she asked. The dog whimpered.

"Nothing," I stammered. "I just—"

"Heavens, I've never seen her act like this before. Daphne just loves people. Are you by any chance afraid of dogs? They can sense that."

"No, I—"

She turned away before I could defend myself. "Now, now, princess, she's not going to hurt you. Want a treat?" The manipulative little mutt yapped in excitement. Kathryn walked into the kitchen, calling over her shoulder, "Supper's on the table. You two better wash up."

"Daphne?" I whispered to Gabe when we were alone. "Try Cujo."

His grin was as big as the Great Plains. "Watch it, Princess Daphne is Mom's pride and joy. She's the granddaughter of two national champions. To get on Mom's good side, you'd better make friends with the princess."

"I was trying. That dog took an instant dislike to me."

"Dogs don't make emotional judgments. They react by instinct. You must have done something to scare her."

"I didn't do anything!" I exclaimed. "Quit taking the dog's side."

"I'm not taking anyone's side," he said, chuckling. "Just give Daphne another chance. Maybe she just needs to get used to you."

During dinner, every time I shifted my feet, a low growl came from under the table. Only my respect for Daphne's canine compatriots in general kept me from acting out my fantasy of a football-sized ball of black-and-white fur flying over a goal post.

"Where did you say Becky and Angel were?" Gabe asked after dinner. We had moved to the front porch and were eating cherry cobbler and homemade vanilla ice cream. Gabe and his mother shared the wooden porch swing while I reclined a short distance away on the red-wood longue. I was thankful that Daphne had grown weary of her vigilant watch over my dangerous presence and had retired to a corner of the porch where she startled herself awake every so often with her wheezy snores.

"Becky's in Wichita," Kathryn answered, the squeak of the swing punctuating her sentence. "Paige and Whitney are having a dance recital tonight. She said she'd see you at her house tomorrow."

"If she thinks I'm dressing up in bell bottoms and love beads, she's out of her mind," Gabe said. He had warned me about Becky's penchant for theme parties. According to Kathryn, the Sunday afternoon barbecue Becky had planned for Gabe's first get-together with his old friends had a sixties motif.

"I think she'll just be happy to have you there, dear," his mother said evenly. "Angel's over at the bowling alley. She'd planned on being here, but two of her employees called in sick. She works too many hours, but she won't listen to me. Maybe you can talk to her. Get her to cut back some."

With her recent divorce settlement, Angel had bought Derby Bowl and was apparently running it very successfully.

"It's better than that bartending job in Kansas City," Gabe said evenly.

"Still, she works much too hard."

"I'll talk to her," he promised.

"Isn't that kind of like the rooster crying fowl to the chicken?" I commented. Gabe certainly wasn't the person to dispense advice about how to overcome workaholism.

"Gabe, you're as bad as Angel," his mother said with a sigh.

He grinned at her. "No one's that bad." He stretched his arms out in front of him and let out a loud groan. "I can't tell you how good it feels to be a civilian for a change. For the next two weeks, the biggest problem I plan on tackling is what to eat for breakfast."

I closed my eyes and let the rhythmic creak of the porch swing, the whirr of the crickets in the thick vines, and Gabe and his mother's murmured conversation filled with names of people unknown to me lull me into a light sleep. It seemed only minutes later when I opened my eyes. In that time dusk, damp and heavy, had settled around us, and the summer locusts vibrated like tiny buzz saws in the dense treetops.

"Welcome back," Gabe said, straddling the end of the chaise. "I'm going over to the bowling alley to see Angel. Want to come?"

I sat up and pulled at my cotton shirt; it stuck uncomfortably to my back like wet tissue paper. "No," I said, taking one of his big hands and sandwiching it between mine. "See her alone first. I'll meet her tomorrow."

He placed a kiss in my palm. "Don't wait up."

On the way upstairs I paused at the wall outside Gabe's old bedroom, where he and I would be sleeping. A gallery of family pictures covered the ecru wall, the patina of age giving the older ones a blurry, dreamlike appearance. My eyes traced Gabe's life from pudgy-faced toddler through the toothsome gawkiness of pre-teen years to a slim, hard-faced young man in full-dress Marine uniform.

One photograph in particular fascinated me. He and his father, Rogelio, stood in front of a faded blue Chevy pickup with a rounded hood and old-fashioned grille.

Gabe must have been about fifteen or sixteen; he had that slope-shouldered, sullen look boys that age seem to perfect to a science. His father, probably then in his early forties, with thick, wavy black hair as shiny as water, rested a possessive hand on Gabe's shoulder.

"I took that picture right before my husband's heart attack," Kathryn said, coming up behind me. She handed me two thick navy blue towels. Daphne stood loyally by her side, her upper lip quivering over tiny fangs, ready to defend her mistress against any evil I might be planning. "It's the last picture we have of him."

"He was a handsome man," I said. "Gabe looks a lot like him."

"Yes, he does. Good night, Benni. Let me know if there is anything you need." She started down the stairs, then stopped and called over her shoulder. "There are some photo albums you might like to look at in the bottom drawer of the dresser." Daphne growled a good night.

"Thanks." I hugged the towels to my chest and stared at Kathryn's retreating back, trying to imagine us ever getting beyond this polite guest routine. Though I was raised in California, I was unquestionably used to the Southern way of doing things. When someone married into a Southern family, he or she became just that—family. With all the aggravating trappings that sometimes went along with it. This polite but definite Midwestern reserve would be a challenge to say the least.

After a long cool shower, I put on my favorite bedtime attire, one of Gabe's extra large T-shirts, and opened the dresser drawer. Setting his four high-school yearbooks on the bed, I quickly poked through the rest of the drawer's contents—boy scout badges, old catechism lessons, a black penknife engraved with his initials, GTO. In the back of the drawer was a flat, hinged box with a photograph attached to it with a fat rubber band. I slipped it out and studied it closely. It showed

Gabe and Dewey and a short, wiry Hispanic man standing next to a bunker of sandbags. Dusty green fatigues
with baggy pockets hung low on their sharp hipbones;
their bare chests glistened with sweat. Gabe had a gaunt,
jumpy look to him, his blue eyes a stark contrast to his
deeply tanned skin. He wore an olive-green cloth head-
band tied around his head gang-banger style. ''Piss on
Death,'' it boasted. A gold crucifix nestled against his
dark chest hair, next to his silver dog tags. A long,
menacing rifle rested casually across his arms. This
young, hard-faced Gabe was frightening, but also appealing in an earthy, sexual sort of way. Dewey didn't
look much different from his photograph of seven years
ago. He apparently had one of those faces that settles
into itself at eighteen or so and never changes much
except for a bit of wrinkling around the eyes. He stood
spread-legged, thick, sinewy arms folded across his
chest. The other man was the same height as Dewey,
but thinner, with a flat, wide nose and deep acne scars
carved into his cheeks. He smiled with widely spaced
front teeth and pointed a skinny finger-pistol at the
camera. ''Perro Loco'' was written in black felt pen
across the front of the Hispanic man's helmet; ''Cowboy,'' on Dewey's.

I opened the hinged box and gazed down at the mil-
itary medal suspended from a red, white, and blue ribbon
and lying on a bed of cheap-looking blue velveteen. A
brass-colored star with a tiny Silver Star in the middle.
I turned it over and read the inscription: ''For Gallantry
in Action—Gabriel Ortiz.'' I set it down next to me and
pulled out his 1964–1965 yearbook—the year he was a
freshman. I was propped up against the flat maple headboard, yearbook across my knees and, as Dove would
say, checking my eyelids for holes, when a movement
on the bed woke me.

''What are you doing still awake?'' Gabe stretched
out next to me. I leaned over and kissed him, wrinkling

my nose at the stale scent of cigarette smoke clinging to his clothes.

"I wasn't. You smell awful. What time is it?"

"Past midnight. Angel and I got to talking." He sniffed his shirt sleeve. "You're right, I guess I'd better take a shower. Apparently bowling alleys are one of the last strongholds left to the smoking public."

"Did you get your sister's life all straightened out?" I asked.

"Angel can take care of herself. Most of the time, anyway. Mom tends to be a little overprotective with her bear cubs." He bounced gently on the bed. "This feels pretty comfortable. Sure beats the twin bed I slept on the first sixteen years of my life. So, what do you think of Kansas so far?"

I didn't answer right away, but instead looked up into his face—the sharp, high cheekbones I'd caressed so often, the black hair with just the slightest silver at the temple, the eyes that could go from slate-blue to iron-gray according to his emotional thermometer. I burrowed under his arm and kissed his neck, inhaling his heavy, gingery scent, almost as familiar to me now as the Zest soap I'd used all my life. Even with the intimacy we'd shared, there were times when he felt a complete stranger to me, when I awakened tangled up with him, smelling our mingled scents, and wondered what brought us together, what would keep us together. He'd lived forty-three years, and only six months of them had been with me. In this land of vast blue skies, green and gold prairie, and slow-talking people—where I was the stranger, not him—I was overcome by a sudden longing for San Celina's misty, oak-covered hills, its tart air redolent of cattle and horses, the comforting sound of Dove's raspy, scolding voice, and I felt like crying. I trembled slightly in his arms.

"Hey, what's wrong?" he asked. "It's not Daphne, is it? Don't let that old mutt get to you. She'll warm up."

"It's not that. I'm just tired, I think. The change of

time and scenery and all that. All the new people I'll be meeting. I miss San Celina already. I guess I'm not the most flexible person in the world.''

"Oh, I don't know," he murmured, running his hand over my bare thigh. "You've always seemed remarkably flexible to me.''

I laughed, pulled up his shirt, and lightly scratched his stomach. "Well, I'm glad your mother replaced your twin bed with a queen-size.''

"Me, too. I experienced some pretty lonely nights in this room, but those days are definitely over." He rolled on top of me, kissing me deeply, his hands reaching under my hips and pulling me against him.

After a few enjoyable minutes, I flattened my hands against his chest and pushed. "Well, Mr. Lonely, you can just dip that branding iron in a bucket of cold water. Not here. Not on your life.''

"What? Wait a minute, we're going to be here two weeks . . .''

"It won't kill you.''

He moaned dramatically. "You *are* kidding.''

"Am I laughing? I've explored this house thoroughly. Two of the three bedrooms are upstairs. That leaves one downstairs. One very significant one that we are, at this moment, smack dab over.''

"So?" He pushed up and gazed down at me, his mustache twitching.

"So, you know what I'm saying. These are wooden floors, and that's your mom's bedroom, so you are outta luck, buddy boy. I'm here to make a good impression. I have the rest of my life to bounce the bedropes with you.''

"Bounce the bedropes? Okay, Calamity Jane, just what am I supposed to do for the next two weeks?''

I kissed him quickly and shoved him off me. "Hit the showers, Friday. Use the spigot marked C.''

After some unsuccessful cajoling on his part, he finally rolled out of bed. The box containing the medal fell on the floor with a jangling thump.

He bent over and picked it up. "Where did this come from?" he asked, his voice tight.

"The dresser drawer." I handed him the picture. "This was with it."

He studied the photograph, an indecipherable look on his face.

"Gabe, that's Dewey, isn't it? Where was that?"

He hesitated, then said, "An Hoa."

"Who's the other guy?"

"Sal." The name came out as sharp as boot heels clicking. "Salvador Quintera."

"Who . . . ?"

A veil dropped over his face, and he turned away as if I hadn't spoken. "I have to take a shower." He opened the nightstand drawer, threw the picture and box in, and left me staring after him.

When he came back to bed, I curled under his arm, swallowing the questions tickling the tip of my tongue. Gabe's tendency to keep whole parts of himself wrapped up in secrecy had been a touchy subject between us from the beginning. I was trying to be patient, but I'd always been a person who, once I decided I wanted to know about something, jumped right in and learned everything I could in the shortest time possible. Though I tried not to compare our marriage with my first one, I couldn't seem to help it. One of the most comforting and fulfilling aspects of my relationship with Jack had been the complete openness between us, something I realize now I'd taken for granted. That kind of emotional intimacy came much easier when you were fifteen and eager to share every little feeling and experience. When connecting with another person at the halfway point in your lives, discoveries were made more slowly, and with more hesitation. That went against everything that seemed natural to me, and sometimes I felt like an impatient barrel-racing pony being forced to walk the cloverleaf course.

I sighed and kissed the bottom of his chin. "Good night, Friday."

He tightened his arm around my shoulders and echoed my sigh. "Dream sweet, *querida*."

The next morning, a sharp rat-tat-tat on the bedroom door woke me.

"Gabe," I murmured into the pillow. "Someone's at the door." The rapping continued. He groaned and turned over.

"I'm on vacation," he grumbled.

"Benni, are you awake?" Kathryn called through the door. "There's a telephone call for you. Long distance, I think."

"I'll be right there," I called out, jumping out of bed. The bedside clock radio said seven o'clock. Who would be calling me in Kansas at this hour of the morning? I pulled on the pair of jeans I'd left in a crumpled heap on the floor the night before and tried to fingercomb my tangled curls.

Already neatly dressed, Kathryn sat in the breakfast nook sipping a cup of tea. Daphne reclined across her mistress's fluffy house slippers and aimed a halfhearted snap in my direction. I ran my tongue over my teeth, feeling like a stall that hadn't been shoveled out for a week.

"Uh, good morning," I said. "You said I had a call?"

Wearing her habitually aloof expression, Kathryn pointed to the brown wall phone. I picked it up and gave a tentative hello.

"What did you do, stop to bake a cake? I've had it!" Dove's familiar gravelly voice blurted out. I felt my homesickness ease. Then panic set in.

I turned around and faced the wall papered in rust and brown coffeepots. "Dove, what's wrong?" I asked in a low voice.

"They're driving me to drink, Benni. I swear they are. It's all your grampa's fault. If he hadn't looked so all-fire handsome behind those matched bays fifty-nine years ago, I would have never gotten married.''

''What's going on? Where are you?''

I could hear her yelling to someone. ''Hey, you. Yes, you, young man. Where are we? What do you mean, what do I mean? Clean out your ears, boy. Where are we?'' She came back on the line. ''Elfrida, Arizona. Ham's Cafe in Elfrida, Arizona. We stopped in Tombstone and saw the World's Largest Rose Bush, Benni. Lord, you should have seen it. Aphid heaven is all I got to say.''

''Dove,'' I said, keeping my voice calm and patient. I could feel my mother-in-law's eyes boring into my back. ''Why are you calling me?''

''Just wanted to inform *someone* that I am getting fed up clean to my ears of all this squabbling, and I swear to Betsy that I'll not put up with it another day.'' In the background, I heard Daddy say, ''Now, Mama . . .''

''Don't 'mama' me,'' she snapped. ''Y'all are walking a thin line.''

''Dove,'' I said. ''I have to go. This call must be costing you a fortune. Just try and get everyone here in one piece.''

''It's okay,'' she said. ''I'm putting this call on that number you gave me a while back. Works great. Don't need no money at all.''

''My AT&T card? That's supposed to be for emergencies.''

''Honeybun, if this isn't an emergency, I don't know what is. Got to run, my biscuits and gravy are here. Oh, Lord, this stuff looks like paste. I can't eat this. Hey, you, young man. Yes, you . . .'' She hung up. ''Goodbye,'' I said to the dial tone so our conversation would appear somewhat normal to my mother-in-law. ''See you soon.''

''Is everything all right?'' Kathryn asked.

''Fine,'' I said quickly. ''My grandmother's on her way. She's having a great time.'' I inched my way backwards out of the kitchen. "I think I'll go take a shower." Daphne's caffeine must have kicked in at that point because she followed me all the way up the stairs, growling softly under her breath until, in her deranged little mind, she convinced herself that she'd chased me into the bathroom.

Later that morning while we drove around Derby exploring Gabe's old childhood haunts, I told him what was going on with Dove and Daddy. Kathryn had gone up to the Methodist church, where the Ladies Altar Guild was putting the finishing stitches on the opportunity quilt to be raffled off this coming Saturday, the second day of the Bear's Paw Quilt Show.

"Something terrible's going to happen before they get here," I said.

"You worry too much," he said. "Let's stop here for a minute." He pulled into the side parking lot of the brick police station.

"Does Dewey work on Sundays?" I asked him in the lobby.

"No." The dispatcher behind the glass window just happened to be an old classmate, so getting into Dewey's office was a snap. Gabe sprinkled a layer of salt in the bottom of Dewey's clean white Derby Police coffee cup.

"That's mean," I said, but laughed.

"Small potatoes next to my hundred-dollar speeding ticket."

At four o'clock we were back at his mother's house getting ready for the party. Kathryn had bowed out, saying she was tired from a day of quilting and that this was a young people's party anyway. Copying Gabe, I ignored Becky's sixties theme and opted for familiarity. I wore new dark blue Wranglers, a sleeveless white cotton shirt, and leather sandals. Gabe dressed California-casual in khaki chinos, a pale pink polo shirt, and his ever-faithful Topsiders.

Becky and Stan lived about three miles outside Derby's city limits, on a five-acre lot in an unincorporated part of Sedgwick County. As we drove toward their house on a narrow, curving highway, it became obvious that Derby and its surrounding area was a community in transition. Though many of the large lots still boasted old wood-frame houses like Kathryn's, there were just as many new and expensive contemporary homes, complete with matching horse stables and shiny satellite dishes.

"We used to call this Deadman's Curve," Gabe said as the road made a sharp bend to the left. Dark clouds were beginning to fill the stark blue sky; each breath I took seemed to require more effort, verifying the KYQQ disc jockey's pronouncement of thunderstorms later that night. "Hot and steamy country," he drawled. "Just like this next song by Tish Hinojosa."

We turned off on a dirt road bisecting two seemingly endless fields of bushy-headed milo. At the black-and-white cow mailbox labeled "Kolanowski," we turned and drove up a gravel driveway, parking behind a dozen or so cars and trucks. The house was a two-story red brick with four white pillars, a long front porch, and window boxes full of gold and rust marigolds. Sunflowers, their brown faces just starting to droop, lined the edge of a vegetable garden planted at the side of the house. We stepped out of the car, and the brisk warm breeze blew a scent of pine around us. I looked across the road at a forest of pine trees planted in neat rows and read the sign "Spears' Christmas Trees. Opens December 1." Peeking through the trees was the pointed patchwork roof of an ancient two-story farmhouse, the corner of a wooden barn faded gray, and part of a metal corral.

Without knocking, Gabe pushed open the front door to Becky's house. We walked into an airy foyer that held only an antique walnut hall tree and a long navy-and-burgundy braided rug. "Becky's probably in the kitchen," he said. I followed him through the open double doors on our left into the living room. A large, red-brick fireplace dominated the room. The furniture, hunter-green and navy plaid, was an expensive Ethan Allen country style.

Becky's love for quilts was apparent everywhere, from the navy and white Monkey Wrench crib quilt on the wall next to the fireplace to the Sunshine and Shadows quilt made of cheerful, Depression-era feed sack material to the quilt-patterned pillows scattered across the sofa and matching wing chairs.

"Clever," I said.

"What's that?"

"Her theme. Only another quilter would recognize it." I pointed to each of the four pillows. "Rocky Road to Kansas, Kansas Dugout, Kansas Dust Storm, and I can especially appreciate this one." I picked up the pillow and ran my fingers over the jagged windmill-like pattern. Gabe waited, his eyes questioning.

"Kansas Troubles," I said, grinning.

"Gabe! Is that you?" a feminine voice squealed. The swinging door to the kitchen opened, and Becky walked out wiping her hands on a spotless white baker's apron. She wore blue jeans and a red tank top with a matching ribbon around her brown ponytail. She hugged Gabe fiercely, then pulled away and faced me.

"You must be Benni. It's so great to finally meet you." She held out a tanned hand. "How was your trip? Isn't it awful there are no direct flights to Kansas from California? I hate landing in Colorado, don't you? Always that turbulence. When are your grandmother and father going to get here? Gabe says you're quite an expert on quilts. Your job sounds fascinating. You must tell me all about it. It's so great to have another quilt lover in the family. They all think I'm crazy. I mean, I'm an addict, you know? Keep me away from a fabric store for *any* length of time, and I go into withdrawal. And I won't even mention my antique quilt habit—Stan has no idea the money I've spent." She squeezed my arm. "Oh, I'm so glad you're both here. It's going to be such fun." She paused to take a breath.

Gabe laughed and ran his large hand up and down her back. "Benni, this is my sister Becky. She has an Off switch here somewhere."

"Oh, shut up," she said, her cheeks flushing a pale rose, and gave her brother a shove. "Ignore him. If it were up to him, the conversation would consist of 'How do you do—what's to eat?' "

"Good question," Gabe said. While we were laughing at the threatening fist she held in front of his nose, the door to the kitchen swung open, and his other sister, Angel, walked in.

"It's about time you two got here," she said. She wore tight men's Levi's, tan hightop work boots, and a white cotton-gauze shirt thin as a handkerchief and tied in a knot under her breasts. She slipped her arm through Gabe's. "It was so good talking to you last night, *hermano grande*. I wish you'd move back here."

"Not a chance, Angel." He put his arm around my shoulder and pulled me to him. "There's too much keeping me in California. This is Benni."

She looked down at me, an inscrutable expression on her face. Five seconds of awkward silence ensued, and it was instantly apparent which parent she'd taken after. I stuck out my hand and looked her square in the eyes. "Nice to meet you."

"Likewise," she said, shaking my hand quickly, her tone cool.

Slightly irritated, I turned back to Becky. "Your quilt collection is impressive. I like the Kansas theme of your pillows."

She looked pleased. "You *do* know your quilt patterns. I'll give you the fifty-cent tour before you go back to California. There's not a room in this house without quilts. But now, let's go down to the basement. We just had it redecorated last fall. Gabe, you'll love how Stan hooked up the jukebox to the new sound system. It's so loud, you can taste the music.''

"And how are my nieces going to sleep through all the noise we're going to make?'' Gabe asked.

"They're staying over at friends' houses,'' she said. "Tonight, in honor of you and Benni, we're all going to get wild and act like teenagers again.''

"Sounds good to me. When do we start?'' he said.

The basement family room was decorated in a red, white, and blue patriotic motif. A long oak bar with six red vinyl bar stools claimed one end of the huge room. Stan, Becky's husband, stood behind a professional-looking bar tap and pulled beers for the guests. Behind him hung a red, white, and blue Feathered Star quilt, a pattern I recognized from one of the quilting magazines our co-op subscribed to. A Dick Tracy pinball machine flanked one side of the bar, and one of those Wurlitzer jukeboxes with the bubbling neon occupied the other side. "Little Red Riding Hood'' by Sam the Sham & the Pharaohs blared from speakers hung in the room's four corners. In the back, people crowded around a carved walnut pool table, their exhilarated whoops and loud wolf howls sung along with the refrain of the song telling me most had already made more than one trip to the bar. Three dark blue love seats and some scattered easy chairs upholstered in a bright red-and-white-plaid fabric circled the small wooden dance floor in the center of the room.

"Let me introduce you to Stan,'' Gabe said as both his sisters melted into the crowd.

"Gabe, you old son of a gun,'' his brother-in-law said, holding out a long-fingered hand. He wore a red-striped shirt, a straw boater, and a blue satin garter around his arm. "Old Milwaukee still your favorite?''

"I'll just have a Coke,'' Gabe said, shaking his hand warmly. "What's with the barbershop look? I thought this was supposed to be a sixties party.''

Stan pulled a tall frosted glass from under the counter and scooped ice into it. "As you can see, no one here paid any attention to the queen bee's dress code. She gave *me* an ultimatum, though—it was this or a gold lamé Nehru jacket she found in a Wichita thrift store." He turned to me and lifted his hat. "You must be Benni. Welcome to the Ortiz clan. First and only piece of advice from a fellow prisoner of love—they are much more amusing after a couple of double Scotches." Gabe tossed a pretzel from the bowl in front of him at Stan. Stan caught it one-handed and popped it in his mouth.

At the other end of the bar, Gabe's buddy Dewey Champagne stood quietly watching the two men. He seemed, not bigger than the pictures portrayed him, but sturdier, more . . . substantial. He wore sharply creased Wranglers and polished brown Ropers. The sleeves on his navy blue Western shirt were rolled back, showing tanned, muscled forearms and square hands with white-scarred knuckles. He and Gabe pointedly ignored each other. Stan gave me a conspiratorial wink.

Dewey ran a finger down his dripping beer mug. "Stan, you old peabrain, don't you have *any* standards for your parties? You havin' to go down to Navy recruiting and pick up *swabbies* to fill in the guest list? Why not just go to the nearest silo and flush out a few fat old grain rats?"

Gabe faced him and said something in Spanish, his expression as revealing as a concrete slab.

Dewey slowly grinned. "When pigs fly, *compadre*."

Then they burst out: "Semper fi, do or die, gung ho, gung ho, GUNG HO." They fell into each other's arms, laughing and hugging and pounding each other on the back in that simian way men show affection to each other.

"Hey, cowboy, this is Benni," Gabe said after they'd finished their reunion ritual. "My wife." I smiled, still enough of a newlywed to enjoy the sound of the word.

"So you're the lady who actually captured *El Diablo*." Dewey's dark brown eyes narrowed. He rubbed a rough thumb across his bottom lip. "What kind of bait did you use?"

"El Diablo?" I looked up at Gabe and raised my eyebrows.

"Just an old nickname," he said, giving me an embarrassed grin.

"Benni, at one time, your old man here was one mean son of a . . . well, I'll just say no one messed with the Diablo or any of his buds. There was this one time when he and Crazy Dog and me were on R & R in Saigon, and these Army jerks were pretending to talk Spanish and—"

"For pity's sake, don't get him started, or we'll be hearing his dang war stories all night." The voice interrupting Dewey was sharp and nasal, pure Oklahoma Panhandle. The woman behind the voice appeared to be in her early twenties with the starched platinum-streaked long hair of a rodeo queen. She wore a cropped yellow satin top with guitars embroidered around the plunging neckline and butternut-colored jeans so tight you could see her panty line. If she'd been wearing any, that is. Her raspberry-tinted mouth pursed in a pout that would have been annoying on anyone less pretty. She rolled her turquoise eyes at Gabe, then leaned over and patted Dewey's cheek. "Not everyone is interested, darlin'. Some people weren't even *born* then."

"I'll hold her down, you smack her," Dewey said good-naturedly, reaching over and pulling her to his side. "In case you hadn't figured it out yet, this is my new lady friend, Cordie June Rodell. The next queen of country music, mark my words."

"Oh, Dewey, hush." Cordie June giggled and trailed her long sparkly gold nails through his dark hair. He ran his hand over her rump, his brown eyes gleaming with amused indulgence.

"Gabe, you look great!" A fortyish woman with silver-streaked black hair and a wide, friendly smile walked up and threw her arms around Gabe. Next to her, his friend Lawrence grinned from behind a reddish-gray beard. He was still as lanky as a teenager and wore the type of plaid sport shirt and gray slacks that made Mr. J. C. Penney a multimillionaire.

"Janet, you haven't changed a bit," Gabe said, hugging her and shaking Lawrence's hand. "Hey, buddy, how's the nightclub business?"

"Don't ask." Lawrence grimaced. "Cocktail waitresses, cooks, bouncers, the liquor license board. Musicians and girl singers. It's enough to drive a man to drink. Fortunately I can count whiskey as a business expense."

"Oh, pipe down," Cordie June said, sticking her tongue out at him. "You know you love it."

Janet gave me a friendly look. "Benni, right? I can't believe you captured our elusive Gabe here. After his divorce, we didn't think *anyone* was capable of that."

"I'm just now realizing what an apparent coup it was," I said, glancing up at Gabe and rolling my eyes.

"I keep telling her how lucky she is, but she won't believe me," Gabe said. A collective groan erupted from his friends.

"Then she's smart *and* pretty," Dewey said.

"Well, look what happens when Kansas opens the borders. All kinds of riffraff blows across the prairie." Rob Harlow eased around Dewey and Cordie June. His dark blond hair had turned just gray enough to take the edge off his boyish handsomeness. He flashed an audacious grin capable of seducing any woman in the room from eight to eighty. He was the kind of guy your mother dreamed about having as a son-in-law—until he turned out to be a serial killer.

"You must be Benni," he said, bestowing his smile upon me.

"Must be," I said, wondering why in the world my thoughts crept to serial killers upon meeting this perfectly nice man.

"Nice to meet you." He held my gaze just a couple

of seconds longer than necessary before turning to Gabe. "You haven't changed a bit, buddy. Still busting low-lifes in the mean streets?"

"I'm a suit now," Gabe answered mildly. "The only thing I bust these days is patrol officers who take too many sick days."

"You wrangled this depraved old *hombre* off the streets?" Rob said to me, his mouth turned down, impressed. "I didn't think anyone could do that with the wild man here. His first wife sure couldn't. What did you lure him into your lair with?"

"Lucky me," I said sweetly. "He was already semi-tame when I captured him." I was getting more than a little annoyed at the continued references to a nefarious past I knew nothing about.

Becky walked up and clapped her hands for attention. "Everyone find a seat. Cordie June and Tyler are going to sing for us."

Next to the jukebox, Cordie June stood talking to a petite woman dressed in tight black jeans and a black silk tank top. The woman had pale blond hair cut tomboy-short and spiky. They started fiddling with the switch on a microphone hooked into Stan's stereo system. The blonde turned and called for Stan's help. Lawrence got there before Stan and took care of the problem. She rewarded him with a flawless smile.

"Is that the Amish woman?" I whispered to Gabe. I set my Coke down on the small table next to the red plaid easy chair he'd claimed, and perched on the chair's padded arm.

"Appears so." He picked a stuffed cherry tomato off my plate of food and popped it in his mouth.

"She's beautiful."

"No surprise there. Homely women were never Rob's forte."

Not much taller than my five feet one, her only accessory was a pair of long silver and turquoise Navajo earrings. I searched her fluid, small-featured face and sensual gray eyes, trying to picture her clothed in the shapeless dress and white apron of an Amish woman.

To warm up, they did a twangy country version of Bonnie Raitt's "Let's Give Them Something to Talk About." Then they moved quickly into Wynonna's "Girls with Guitars" and Trisha Yearwood's "I've Been Living on the Wrong Side of Memphis." They continued through a repertoire of popular country-rock songs I guessed came from their act at Lawrence's club. They harmonized easily, Cordie June singing an energetic if slightly reedy soprano and Tyler belting out a voice that didn't match her delicate looks at all—a deep, throbbing alto. Cordie June sang a spirited rendition of "I'll Always Love You" trying, I imagined, for Dolly's sincerity and Whitney's soul. Her voice was young and clear and vibrant. But it was when Tyler ended the impromptu concert with Alabama's melancholy ballad "We Can't Love Like This Anymore" that it became obvious who had that elusive quality that makes a person a star. Accompanying herself with only a battered acoustic guitar, Tyler held us breathless with a smoky voice that was a heart-rending mixture of tough and tender. When the last note of the song resonated through the warm room, we were struck silent, captured by the spell of her remarkable voice. A voice that, for that instant, caused each of us to relive a time when love walked away from us before we wanted it to. I glanced at Cordie June, and for just an instant a look of anger darkened her face, then disappeared like a swift Kansas storm cloud.

"Anyone besides me need a cold beer right now?" Stan suddenly called out. Everyone laughed, and the party started up again. I stood up, and Gabe grabbed my hand, pulling me down into his lap.

"Want to go across to the Christmas tree farm and make out?" He buried his face in the hollow of my neck.

"Here's a cold drink, Friday." I pointed to my Coke. "I told you, you're on C-rations for two weeks."

"What's this about C-rats?" Dewey walked up, a bottle of Beck's in his hand. "Stan's got a secret stash for us purists. Better get one before they're gone."

"Coke's fine," Gabe said, picking up my glass and taking a sip.

"What's with him?" Dewey asked me. "Gabe here used to drink us all under the table. You got him on a short leash or something?"

"Don't look at me," I said. "I've never even seen him drink."

"Hey, bud, you doin' the twelve-step boogie these days?"

"Nah," Gabe said, nudging me to stand up. "I've finished everything on your plate. Let's go see what else Becky fixed for this bash." He walked away without looking to see whether Dewey or I followed.

Dewey gave me a curious look. "What was that all about?"

"I have no idea," I said. "Excuse me, I need to find the ladies room." I walked away, uncomfortable about discussing Gabe even with someone who'd been his friend as long as Dewey. And I was embarrassed that there was yet another piece of Gabe's life I knew virtually nothing about.

After a couple of hours of the incessant jukebox and the loud, raucous voices of people already halfway to horrendous hangovers, I wandered upstairs for some peace and quiet. I'd met so many people that evening, their names and faces had already softened to a huge blur. Fortunately the living room was empty. I walked around the room, enjoying the quality and variety of Becky's quilt collection. I was standing in front of a large turquoise, red, and black Amish Shoofly quilt next to the fireplace, losing myself in the serenity of its bold, simple pattern and intricate stitching when the sound of angry voices drew me over to a front window. I stepped to the side of the window and unabashedly eavesdropped. Looking through a gap in the curtain, I could discern a tiny figure in black etched against the moonlit front porch.

"Quit following me," Tyler said, her sultry voice harsh. "You have no rights in my life anymore." Her earrings swung and flashed, catching the pale light.

A man's voice gave a low, urgent reply. He stood back in the shadows, out of my viewing range. Though I strained to make out sentences, I could only hear single words—"home now, *Hochmut*, Hannah, *Gott*." His voice had a foreign sound, almost guttural. Like German. An Amish man?

"I don't care, I don't care." Her voice sounded desperate now. "Go away. There are police officers here, you know. They could arrest you."

"You would have me arrested, Ruth?" the man spat out. Then he muttered a short sentence in the foreign language again, turned, and ran down the porch steps. His figure was a dark outline, his hat and his clothing cut in the style of an earlier century. He was Amish. Obviously someone from Tyler's past. He threaded his way through the parked cars to a small white car idling out on the dirt road in front of the house. He climbed into the passenger seat, and the vehicle sped away, kicking up dust.

The front door opened, and I moved hastily back to the Amish quilt and resumed studying it. Picking up a corner of the quilt, I started counting the stitches, hoping Tyler wouldn't guess I'd overheard the argument.

"Twelve," she said behind me. "And I should know. I put every one of them in myself. Though I'd catch heck from my father for bragging about it."

I turned to face her. Her voice sounded husky, as if on the edge of a sob. Her pink-rimmed eyes blinked rapidly, but the practiced smile of an experienced performer prevailed.

She held out her hand. "I don't think we were officially introduced. Tyler Brown. Isn't this party for you and your husband?"

"Benni Harper," I said, taking her hand. Her hand-shake was firm and confident. "The party's more for my husband, Gabe. He's Becky's brother and grew up with most of these people."

"Homecomings," she said, her voice ironic. "A mixed blessing, aren't they?"

"Yes," I agreed. "I'm impressed with your stitching. I've never been able to do more than eight per inch."

"Actually, I've seen fourteen. My sister, Hannah, is incredible. But then she works at it a lot more than I do these days."

"You don't quilt anymore?"

She stared up at the quilt, an almost pensive look coming over her face. "I don't piece, but I still quilt occasionally. If gigs are slow and I need the money." She picked up the edge of the quilt. "This was my last quilt before I left the community. I sold it to Becky to help pay for studio time to record a song I wrote about a barrel racer who cheats on her husband with a bull rider. Her husband was the rodeo clown."

"Who did she end up with?" I asked, not knowing what else to say.

Tyler gave a self-mocking smile. "Her horse. Who else?"

I turned back to the quilt. "I guess you probably expend your creative energy in your music now. It's a shame to lose you as a quilter, though. Your stitching is incredible."

She fiddled with one of her earrings. It made a soft, tinkly sound in the quiet living room. "Most people look at quilts and see beauty and order. I see that, but I also see a prison."

She seemed open enough about her past, so, remembering what the man on the porch had called her, I said, "Tyler doesn't sound like an Amish name."

"It isn't. I decided new life, new name. My . . ." She paused and raised her chin a fraction of an inch. "A good friend helped me choose it. Someone who used to come by the cafe where I worked in Miller.''

"Oh.'' Her story fascinated me. I couldn't imagine what it must be like to completely discard one kind of life for another. ''How long ago did you leave the community?'' I asked.

"A year ago last January. I lived in Wichita and got a job as a waitress at a Shoney's Restaurant. I started going to little clubs, singing in their talent contests and bugging the different owners to give me a try. It was really hard at first.'' Her delicate cheeks flushed. ''Then I hooked up with T.K., and it got a little easier.''

"T.K.?''

"I met him at one of the clubs I sang at. He plays lead guitar in Snake Poison Posse. He was going to come tonight, but a friend of his asked him to fill in on a gig up in Kansas City. T.K.'s been a good friend to me. He's the one who brought Snake Poison Posse together and asked me to sing lead. We've been at Lawrence's club for about two months now. I'm getting a lot of good experience, but really, the only place to be is Nashville. I've got the money to go, but T.K. needs this gig, and I really owe him, so I promised I'd stay through the end of July. Then I'm heading south to Music Row to join all the other hopefuls. I'm hoping to get some studio work so I don't have to waste time waiting tables.'' She smiled thinly. ''At least for a while, anyway.''

"How did you meet Becky?'' I asked.

"I answered an ad she placed in the Wichita newspaper about buying authentic Amish quilts. She was a real lifesaver. I was desperate for money at that point, and she bought all the quilts I owned. Then I told her about my sister, Hannah, and she's helped Hannah make some extra money by consigning her quilts in some stores in Kansas.'' Tyler pulled absently at a strand of hair next to her cheek. ''It was just coincidence that she knew Lawrence. But that's how it is around here; someone you know eventually knows someone else you know. Sometimes that can get a little stifling.''

"I know," I said. "The town in California where I'm from is like that. But sometimes it's nice."

She raised her eyebrows. "I suppose. If you never do anything that people disapprove of."

"Do you ever see your family?" I was curious, knowing enough about Amish customs to assume her choice had caused her to be shunned, that no communication, no relationship, was allowed between her and the Amish community, including her family, for the rest of her life.

"No." Her tone told me that it was not a subject open for discussion.

I moved to a more comfortable topic and picked up the edge of the Shoofly quilt. "I've never seen this stitching pattern before."

"I took the design from the patterns that are blind-tooled around the *Ausbund*, our hymn book, but added my own touch. Believe me, my father is a minister, and he just about pulled his beard off when some well-meaning lady in our church pointed it out to him." Behind her smile was an unmistakable resolve and a hint of steel.

I glanced back at the tiny, perfect stitches. You had to peer at them very closely and adjust your eyesight, the way you do when you look at an optical illusion, but once you did, inside the simple leaves, in elaborate stitching, the words seized your heart with their passionate plea—NONONONO . . .

I was stunned silent for a moment. Then I asked, "Why country-western music?"

She thought for a moment. "The first time I heard it, it struck something in me. It seemed so free and happy, even the sad songs. Have you ever heard the songs in an Amish church service?"

I shook my head no.

"They are extremely slow and very structured. To an outsider, it would probably sound like chanting. On some songs it takes thirty seconds just to sing one line of one verse. To sing four verses can sometimes take twenty minutes or more. Sunday evening singing, when the young people get together, is a little better, but not much. For an Amish person singing is supposed to be a reminder of all that is worldly and sinful. From the first time I remember singing, I didn't feel that way about it. Singing made me feel happy. I would ask my father, Doesn't God want us to be happy? He would say sternly, '*Gott* wants us to serve Him.' But can't we serve Him *and* be happy? I would ask. He would get so angry with my questions that my sister would break in and ask me to fetch some eggs or go milk the cows.'' Tyler gave a deep sigh. ''I think I was about thirteen the first time I heard a country song. My cousin Levi had a transistor radio hidden in the barn. The song was 'I Saw the Light' by Hank Williams. Ironic, isn't it?''

I nodded.

''And the first time I sang in front of an audience . . .'' Her face flushed with emotion. ''I can't really explain it. It's like I'd never been born until I heard that applause. For a moment, when things are just right, it feels like . . . like love. I don't know how to explain it, but it's like you're really *loved*.'' She leaned toward me, her eyes bright and desperate. ''I can't let anything take that away from me. I just can't.''

Before I could comment, we were interrupted by a commotion downstairs. Angry male voices echoed up the narrow basement stairway. Like teenagers to a schoolyard fight, we rushed toward the frenzied sounds.

At the bottom of the stairs we watched Lawrence and Rob wrestle with each other in that awkward fighting dance that never looks as polished and masculine in real life as it does in the movies. Gabe pushed his way into the skirmish and pulled Rob back. Dewey and another man grabbed Lawrence. A trickle of blood trailed down from Rob's nose; Lawrence's glasses were lost somewhere in the scuffle. Without them, he appeared younger, his eyes wide and white-rimmed, like an owl's.

"I mean it," Lawrence said, stabbing a finger at Rob. "Stay away from her. I mean it." He shook off Dewey's arm. "Let me go. I'm fine."

"Apparently she likes it," Rob said. "Let her live her own life."

Lawrence lunged for Rob, but Dewey and the other man caught him. "Get him outta here," Dewey yelled at Gabe. Gabe grasped Rob's upper arm firmly and led him up the stairs. Tyler and I stepped aside to let them pass.

"Are you okay, Rob?" Tyler asked, reaching out to him. He irritably shoved her hand away. I widened my eyes at Gabe, who shrugged.

"Too much beer," he said in a low voice.

"Too much testosterone," I countered. He winked at me.

"Maybe I should go with them," Tyler said.

"Let Gabe walk him around outside," I said. "He'll cool down, and they'll forget all about it."

Becky ran up the stairs past Tyler and me, her face white with anger.

"Looks like Becky's upset," I said. "I'll go up and see if I can help."

In the cherry-red and white kitchen, Becky stood frowning in front of the open refrigerator.

"Is there anything I can do?" I asked.

"No, thanks." She took out a pitcher of iced tea. "I'm just trying to remove myself from the commotion before I lose *my* temper."

I hopped up onto the white-tiled counter and took the glass of iced tea she offered me. "What was it all about?"

She poured herself a glass and leaned against the refrigerator. "Same old stuff those two have been squabbling about for six months now. Lawrence's daughter, Megan, works for Rob." She paused and took a sip. "Apparently there have been quite a few nights that she's come home late. Working overtime, she says."

"So?"

"So, apparently she's not really working overtime. Or maybe she is in a way. Rumor is she and Rob are sleeping together, and Lawrence is mad as a hornet about it."

"How old is Megan?"

"Twenty-two. Certainly old enough to make her own decisions, as stupid as they might be. Heaven knows, getting involved with Rob Harlow is about the stupidest thing I can imagine any woman doing, but to tell you the truth, I think that girl's a spoiled brat and she's messing with Rob just to cause her parents grief. I'm surprised she isn't here so she could enjoy this little scene firsthand. I have no idea how two people as sweet as Lawrence and Janet could produce a daughter like that." She shook her head and dug into an open box of Ritz Crackers sitting on the counter.

"I thought Rob and Tyler were together."

She held out the box of crackers. I shook my head no. "*That* has never stopped Rob before. Not as long as I've known him, anyway," she explained.

We sat silently for a moment, the only sounds the murmur of the wind outside and Becky eating crackers. She set the box down and leaned her head back against the refrigerator. "I'm sorry about all this, Benni. I wanted this party to be perfect for you and Gabe."

"Don't worry about it. I'm having a wonderful time," I said. "Anyway, what's a party without a little prehistoric male head-banging?"

"I suppose so," she said, still sounding miserable.

The door to the living room swung open, and four or five chattering women poured into the kitchen, each of them clasping something in her hand. Five seconds later, Gabe followed them.

"Here," he said to Becky and me, reaching into his pocket. He handed each of us a white poker chip.

"You've got to be kidding! Whose idea was this?" Becky said.

"Your husband's," Gabe answered. "He thought it

might help get everyone away from the bar and get a little exercise, burn off some of this tension. It was either this or croquet.''

"Please, not croquet," she moaned. "Stan gets vicious when someone hits his ball."

"What's this for?" I held up the poker chip.

Gabe glanced at his watch. "I have to join the guys back down in the basement. We're giving you ladies twenty minutes." He turned to me. "Becky will explain it to you. I'll catch you later." He leaned over and gave me a swift kiss.

"What's going on?" I asked. Angel and Cordie June rushed past us, laughing on their way out the back door.

"It's poker chip tag," Becky said, linking her arm in mine and pulling me out after them. "We used to play it when we were teenagers. The guys give us time to hide. The object of the game is to find people and get their chips. If you're caught, you have two choices: give up your poker chip or, if you can, persuade the person to let you keep it."

"And the one with the most chips at the end is the winner?" We stood in the open doorway and watched the giggling women spread out through the field behind the house.

Becky grinned. "Well, not exactly. The best-looking guys never seemed to get anyone's chips." She grabbed my arm and led me around to the front of the house. "Follow me. The Christmas tree farm is always a good place to hide. I just hope Stan called Otis. He knows we're having this party and that we get a little crazy sometimes, but he also keeps a loaded shotgun under his bed." We wove our way through the cars and ran down her driveway.

"Who's Otis?" I asked, following Becky across the dirt road and up the long driveway bisecting the farm. We were surrounded by six- and seven-foot pine trees which, in the pale scattered light of the quarter moon, looked like huge men in dark overcoats. The sharp, wintry scent of pine seemed incongruous with the hot summer air and the electrical buzz of locusts. At the end of the driveway the old two-story farmhouse I'd seen at a distance earlier that afternoon loomed as dark and spooky as Dracula's castle. A flickering yellow light illuminated a second-floor window.

"Otis Spears. He owns this place. My dad and he were best friends. They owned the garage together." Her sentences came out in short gasps. "Heavens, I need to start aerobics again. I'm exhausted already. Anyway, he's like a member of our family. In fact, my girls call him Grandpa Otis."

A figure appeared in the lighted window. Becky waved, and the person waved back. "Good, he knows." She pushed me gently between the shoulder blades. "Okay, you're on your own now, sister-in-law. It'll be harder to catch us if we split up." She disappeared into the forest of pines. "Oh, shoot," I heard her say, her voice growing fainter. "I should have sprayed my socks for chiggers."

Chiggers? Memories from my childhood visits in Arkansas caused me to scratch at my thighs prematurely. This was a Midwesterner's idea of a fun Saturday night? I started into the Christmas trees and had threaded my way to a thick bunch of overgrown, untrimmed pines when the sound of angry voices stopped me. I hid behind a wide pine, eavesdropping on yet another argument. This time both voices were vaguely familiar, but I'd met so many new people in such a short time and the gummy air and dense trees made their words almost indecipherable. The wind shifted, and I heard a low voice say, "How could you!" The other voice, frantic and high, said something I couldn't make out. Then the low voice returned. ". . . heartless . . ."

In the distance, muffled by the trees, men's voices, then rowdy laughter, moved up the driveway of the farm. I dashed through the trees and found a fence. Working my way by touch, I followed the fence until I reached the barn. I slid the door open. The scent of horse was strong and fresh, telling me it was a working barn. In the darkness a horse whinnied and pawed the ground. Not wanting to scare any animals, I decided against the barn. I came back out and edged my way around to the back of the building, trying to avoid the old cars and ancient farm implements only faintly illuminated by the silvery light. Something metal rang when I stepped on it. A cat screeched and darted in front of me, its yellow eyes glowing with fear. I jumped back and stumbled, then laughed at my overreaction.

"By the barn!" a male voice yelled. I looked around frantically for somewhere to hide, then decided speed was my best bet at this point and headed through a field of cropped wheat. In the distance, a grove of dark trees looked like a good hiding place. A thought flashed through my mind as my feet crunched through the hard wheat tufts. Just what kinds of snakes were indigenous to Kansas, and where exactly did they go at night? I reached the grove of elm and cottonwood trees and found a metal shed. Crickets fell silent as I inched around to the back of the shed and rested against its cool metal side. I unbuttoned my shirt one button and fanned at the sweat trickling down my breastbone. These people were crazy. We were too old, and it was too darn hot for this. I closed my eyes and pretended the sultry air was a cool, Pacific Ocean breeze blowing through the canyons into San Celina. In a few minutes, the crickets took up their symphony again, and the locusts continued their high-pitched sawing. I stuck my fingers in my ears and wondered how anyone could get used to that sound. Far off, I could still hear men's voices with an occasional shriek of laughter from a woman. Somebody was apparently losing a poker chip.

For what seemed like hours, I leaned against the wall of the shed. No one had said exactly how we'd know when the game was over. This was beginning to take on the suspiciously familiar aura of a snipe hunt, and I wondered if maybe it was some weird Midwestern initiation ritual. If so, Gabe was going to be one very sorry cop when I got him alone. I worried the chip in my hand, trying to decide if I should just show myself, give up my chip, and go snag one of the chocolate eclairs I'd spied in Becky's refrigerator. But the competitive side of me refused to give in. I wasn't about to let these Jayhawkers think Californians couldn't cut the mustard.

The low humming of crickets stopped. I froze, cautiously peeking around the corner of the shed. Something skittered around the dark trunk of a twisted cottonwood tree. I narrowed my eyes, trying to make out what it was. From behind, a strong arm grabbed me around the waist and lifted me up. A huge, rough hand clamped over my mouth.

Adrenaline shot through my veins. I kicked out and flung my arms backward trying to get loose. My fist smashed into skin and bone. I heard a surprised yelp; then my attacker dropped me. Pain shot through my tailbone when I landed hard on my butt. I scrambled up and faced my moaning assailant, furious when I saw it was Gabe.

"What are you trying to do?" I screamed. "Scare me to death?"

"I told you to leave the brass knuckles at home," he said, rubbing his cheek.

"Geeze Louise, Gabe, what did you expect, sneaking up and grabbing me like that?" I pushed his hand away and ran my fingers over his cheek where a small knot was already beginning to form. "Are you okay?"

"I'm fine, but sneaking up is the whole point of the game." He took my hand and kissed the knuckle. "Now, where's your poker chip?"

I looked around in the dark weeds. "It's here somewhere. I dropped it when you grabbed me. Besides, I'm not about to give it to you."

"That means you've got to persuade me that I don't

want it.'' He laced his hands in mine and pinned me against the wall of the shed.

I struggled against him, laughing. ''How am I supposed to do that?''

''That's your problem.''

''I'm beginning to see the point of this juvenile game now.''

''That's why I made sure I found you before anyone else did.'' He bent and kissed me.

After a minute or so, we came up for air. He groaned softly. ''This makes me feel like a teenager again.''

''In more ways than one.'' I bumped my pelvis against his.

A low rumble came from the back of his throat, and he bent to kiss me again. I turned my head and laughed. ''One kiss per poker chip, Friday. Those are the rules.''

He released my hands and grabbed my face, turning it back toward him. ''Who told you that? There are no rules in this—''

Before he could finish, a woman's scream echoed through the warm night air. Gabe's face went rigid, listening, still holding my face in his hands. The scream was long and steady, with an edge of hysteria that told us it wasn't the pretend shriek of a woman playing a game.

''It's coming from the tree farm,'' he said.

THREE

"LET'S GO," GABE said, grabbing my hand. We ran across the field toward the screaming. As we passed the farmhouse, an elderly man in dark overalls and a stained yellow John Deere feed cap was coming down the front porch steps. He held a shotgun in one hand, a long black flashlight in the other. "Called the police," he said. He tossed the flashlight to Gabe.

"Thanks," Gabe said, catching it with one hand. "Where?"

"Sounds like the northeast corner. I'm guessin' three, four rows up from the fence."

"Stay here with Otis," Gabe commanded and disappeared into the rows of trees.

"You the new missus?" the man asked. Close-set dark eyes studied me from under the yellow cap. He pulled absently at one large ear.

"Yes, sir. Benni Harper."

"Good meetin' you. Otis Spears." He pulled a palm-sized flashlight out of his pocket. "Let's go after the boy."

I followed him into the Christmas tree lot, where the dense rows of pines had the spooky sameness of a house of mirrors at the county fair. Otis obviously knew this property well because he didn't hesitate once as we crisscrossed through the trees. Fine spider webs swept across my face, and I scrubbed frantically at my cheeks, trying to wipe away the shivery, repulsive feel. The steamy smell of pine became overpowering as we moved deeper into the trees toward the murmuring voices. I bit back a gasp when someone burst out of the trees to the left of us.

"What's going on?" Dewey asked, breathing heavily.

"We don't know." I pointed into the trees. "Gabe went that way." Dewey disappeared down a row. "How big is this place?" I asked Otis.

"Fifty acres," he said, switching the shotgun from one arm to the other without breaking his stride. "Twenty of it's Christmas trees."

I could make out Gabe's flashlight now and could hear his straining-to-be-polite but autocratic chief-of-police voice through the pines. "Everyone move away from the area. Now."

Otis and I elbowed our way through the gathered crowd. Gabe and Dewey were stooped over someone lying between two perfectly trimmed Christmas trees. The party guests craned to view the area lit by Gabe's flashlight. "I said move back," he snapped harshly over his shoulder, his genial civil servant persona gone now. They obeyed silently, moving back a foot or two. I edged around the crowd and came up behind Gabe. When he stood up, I touched his elbow. His angry expression turned troubled.

"I don't think you should see this," he said, slipping his arm around my shoulders. His strained voice made me hesitate before glancing at the body.

Tyler lay face down on a blanket of pine needles, the back of her blond head smashed in and thick with blood. I inhaled sharply at the brutal savagery of her wounds and turned my head into Gabe's shoulder.

"Are you going to be all right?" He tightened his arm.

"Yes," I said, swallowing hard.

Lawrence walked up, his round eyes unblinking and dilated behind his glasses. "What do you want us to do, Gabe?"

"One last time, everyone needs to move back," Gabe repeated in a loud voice. "Get over by the fence. Don't move and don't touch anything. It shouldn't be long until the authorities arrive."

"Is there something I can do?" I asked.

He pulled me aside and said in a low voice, "There's not much anyone can do at this point. Dewey and I need to secure the area. With this many people walking around, a lot of evidence has probably already been destroyed." He scanned the group and swore softly in Spanish. "I'm glad this isn't my case. I can't imagine a bunch of people I'd less like to question."

An undertone of sound came from the nervous crowd. Otis pushed his way through, carrying an old quilt he'd apparently fetched from his house. He laid it gently over Tyler's ravaged body.

"Otis," Gabe protested. "This is a murder scene. You can't . . ."

"She deserves some dignity," Otis said, pulling the yellow and white basket quilt over her head. One pale square soaked up blood like a paper towel.

"What are you going to do?" I whispered to Gabe.

He pulled at his mustache irritably. "Leave it. The damage is already done. I'll explain it to the detectives when they get here."

"All right, you heard Gabe. Move over near the fence," Dewey said. We all turned to look at him, surprised to hear him speak. Gabe's authoritative presence had made us forget this was actually Dewey's jurisdiction. I joined the crowd over by the split-rail fence and leaned against a post.

"Rob," Lawrence suddenly said next to me. "Where's Rob?"

As if on cue, he appeared out of the trees. "What's

all the commotion?'' he asked, his voice light. ''I was
down near the pond when I heard someone scream.
Scared the crap out of me.'' He froze when he saw the
quilt-covered body lying on the ground with Tyler's tiny
black boots sticking out from under it.

He looked at Gabe, confused. ''What's going on?''

Gabe took his arm and started to lead him away.
''Rob, I'm sorry. It's Tyler.''

''Tyler?'' he repeated, his voice catching. He shook
off Gabe's restraining hand and tore the quilt off her
body.

''No!'' His wail seemed smothered in the heavy damp
air. He reached down to touch her.

''Rob, don't,'' Dewey said, catching his hand.

''Call an ambulance!'' Rob yelled frantically at us.

''Rob,'' Gabe said quietly. ''We've called the police.''

''But we need the paramedics. We need an ambulance. Did someone call an ambulance?'' No one answered. Our silence was explanation enough. He turned
to Gabe, the skin around his eyes white with anger. ''Are
you saying she's dead? Is that what you're saying?''

Gabe put a hand on Rob's shoulder. ''I'm sorry,
Rob.''

''Who would do this? Why?''

Gabe answered him in a careful voice. ''We don't
know, Rob. But we'll find out.''

''Yes,'' Dewey said, scrutinizing Rob's ravaged face.
''We will.''

In the next hour, the dirt road in front of the tree farm
was jammed with a variety of official vehicles—the
white and blue squad cars of the Derby and Wichita
police, a couple of Sedgwick County Sheriff cars, a navy
blue crime-scene investigation van, a paramedic's truck,
and a couple of obviously official cars of the unmarked
variety. From what I could pick up, they were having
trouble deciding just whose jurisdiction this was. That
became an especially sticky problem when the re-

porters from the local television stations and newspapers arrived and demanded information.

The Sheriff's Department took control until jurisdiction could be established. Becky and Stan's house would be used as a place to question everyone. A tall, distinguished man smoking a cigar, apparently Derby's chief of police, sternly informed us to please refrain from talking among ourselves and to ignore the reporters shouting questions at us. Gabe and Dewey were still talking to the investigating officers when two Derby patrol officers escorted us like schoolchildren across the road. The flashing lights of the police cars glowed red, blue, and amber across our faces, making everyone appear as if they were wearing some grotesque Halloween makeup. At the house, they divided us into two groups—men and women. The men were relegated to the basement with a young Sheriff's Department detective; the women were taken to the living room accompanied by a Wichita detective with a reddish nose and an incessant smoker's cough. He pulled out a package of cigarettes, then hastily slipped them back in the pocket of his blue suit when Becky frowned at him.

"Could I make some coffee?" Becky asked the detective after we'd sat quietly for twenty minutes with nothing happening.

"We'll question you first, and then you can," he answered tiredly. Five minutes later he took Becky outside to the front porch and questioned her. He chose me next, and without hesitation I told him about overhearing the argument between Tyler and the Amish man on the porch, as well as the argument I heard on the tree farm. "Would you be able to identify this Amish man?" the detective asked, drawing deeply on his cigarette.

"No," I said firmly. "All I saw was an outline."

"What about his voice?"

"I don't know. Maybe. I only heard a few words, and some of them were German, I think."

The detective perked up. "Do you remember any of them?"

I thought for a moment. "*Gott*." It was the only German word I knew, and I wasn't even sure where I'd learned it.

"Got?" He dropped his cigarette and ground it out on Becky's clean porch. "What's that mean?"

"God."

"Oh." He looked disappointed. "Tell me again what you heard on the tree farm," he said, lighting another cigarette. I fanned the air in front of me.

"Sorry." He held the cigarette behind his back, but didn't offer to put it out.

"All I heard were voices. They were arguing. One voice said, 'How could you,' and then I heard 'heartless.' "

"That's it?"

"Yes."

He turned around and took a drag on his cigarette. "A male and female voice. You're sure."

"I wouldn't bet my life on it, but it was a low voice and a somewhat higher one. I guess I just assumed it was a male and female."

"Could it have been two men?"

I shrugged. "I suppose."

"What about two women?"

That made me stop and think. "Maybe. If one of the women had a low voice or if she was angry and trying to keep her voice low. I guess it could have been."

After my interview, I went to the kitchen to help Becky with the coffee. She'd already brewed one pot for the women and was up on the counter searching one of her top cupboards for a carafe to send some down to the men. Gabe came in a few moments later, his questioning obviously finished.

"What's going on?" I asked, pouring milk into a small glass pitcher.

"It's a real mess out there. This is unincorporated

county land. That means that technically the Sheriff's Department has jurisdiction, but the land is in the middle of being annexed into Derby, so the Derby police will be involved, not to mention that it's a Wichita mailing address, so they'll want to put in their two cents worth. Then we're talking the problem of a Kansas law enforcement officer being involved, which the media will turn into tabloid heaven.'' He closed his eyes and rolled his neck to relieve the tension. ''I pity Dewey. I wouldn't touch this one with a fifty-foot pole.''

''So how do you fit in?'' Becky asked, climbing down off the counter holding a tall silver Coleman thermos.

Gabe opened his eyes and gave her a serious look. ''As an innocent bystander, period. I'll give Dewey a hand if he needs it, but with all the fingers that are going to be in this pie, he won't need one more.'' He turned to me. ''What's this about you hearing some arguments?''

I gave him a quick explanation of what I'd heard.

''Wow,'' Becky said. ''You might have heard the killer's voice.''

''I don't like this,'' Gabe said, frowning.

''Don't worry,'' I assured him. ''What I heard is virtually worthless. I doubt that I'd ever recognize the voices. It's hard to believe that someone at the party would kill Tyler. Everyone seemed so normal.''

''Unfortunately,'' Gabe said grimly, ''most murders are committed by people who look perfectly normal.''

''I know.'' I leaned my head against his solid chest, relaxing when he put his arms around me. ''We'd better call your mom before she hears it on the news. Aren't we allowed to make one phone call?''

He hugged me. ''Such a thoughtful daughter-in-law. We're not under arrest, so we can use the phone as long as it doesn't interfere with the questioning. I'll call her. We'll probably be here the rest of the night.''

He was right. It was almost dawn before the detectives finished questioning everyone. The guests left one by one, appearing shell-shocked and disbelieving. They kept saying, How could it be? Derby was a nice town, people didn't get murdered here. I couldn't help searching the expressions of each person, wondering if one of them hid the face of a killer. By the time the purple darkness turned to the pale mauve of early morning, only Gabe, Stan, Becky, Rob, and I sat in the living room. Rob stared down into his empty coffee cup. Every line in his face seemed etched deeper, adding years to his age. He didn't seem to know what to do next.

Stan walked over and rested a hand on his shoulder. "Let me drive you home. We'll bring your car over later."

Rob stared straight ahead, his eyes focused on Tyler's quilt across the room. "No." He shrugged off Stan's hand. "I'm fine." He stood up and ran his fingers through his rumpled hair. "I have to get a message to her family. I'll call the lady who owns the fabric store in Miller. She'll let Tyler's sister know."

"Call us if we can do anything," Stan said, walking him to the door. "Anything at all." Rob nodded mutely and left.

"What happens now, Gabe?" Becky asked, tucking her legs up under her on the sofa.

Gabe leaned forward and rested his elbows on his knees. "With so many agencies involved in the investigation, my guess is confusion."

I turned to Becky. "What will her family do?"

She traced her finger over the quilted pillow in her lap. "I don't know. They're Old Order Amish. When she left them to pursue her singing, they shunned her, which means no contact unless the congregation reinstates her. That only happens if she asks for forgiveness and for permission to return. But I can't imagine them just ignoring her death, though they do have some awfully strict beliefs. She hadn't seen her sister or her father since she left."

After saying goodbye, Gabe and I pulled out around

Dewey's brown GMC pickup, the only other car left in the driveway, and started for home. The sun was a bright half-ball on the horizon when we got back to his mother's house. Kathryn was in the kitchen cooking breakfast. The air crackled with the spicy scent of cooking sausage. The moment I smelled it, I became ravenous.

"Hope oatmeal is all right for you, dear," she said to Gabe, flipping sausage patties in a large iron skillet. "The peaches and blackberries are fresh." She turned to me. "I know my health-conscious son won't want any, but the sausage is from my sister Beulah's farm down in Coffeyville."

"It smells great," I said. Gabe picked up a slice of whole wheat toast and smeared it with orange marmalade. We ate without speaking. Even Daphne lying in her bed in the corner of the breakfast nook had picked up the mood and was strangely silent. I almost missed her growl. Almost.

After breakfast, with Kathryn's encouragement, we went upstairs to get some sleep. The air had never cooled off completely, so I slipped into a pink Jockey tank top and turned the window air conditioner on high, certain I would never be able to turn my brain off long enough to fall asleep. But the minute my head hit the pillow, I was out. When I woke up, the clock radio next to the bed said twelve-thirty. The fan sitting on the dresser weakly circulated the cold air from the air conditioner. Gabe was leaning against the headboard, reading. With his round wire-rimmed glasses and wearing nothing but black cotton running shorts, he looked like a very sexy college professor.

"Did you sleep?" I yawned and propped myself up on an elbow.

"I caught a few hours," he said, leaning over and kissing my forehead. "You slept enough for both of us."

"What are you reading?"

He looked back down at the book. "One of my thesis books."

"What's it about?"

"The point of suffering. The definition of evil." His thesis had something to do with the reason we suffer, whether suffering is just evil or a necessary experience for growth, or something like that. I think I understood the theory of what he was talking about, what he believed about suffering. I just wasn't sure I agreed. I'd seen too many people suffer who weren't one bit better for the experience. On the other hand, thinking of Jack's death and how it had changed me, I *was* more compassionate now toward others who had lost someone. Would I be as understanding if I hadn't experienced so much grief this last year? I guess in some ways Gabe and I did agree. I just didn't like to brood on it as much as he. Then again, I suspected my past didn't harbor as many ghosts as his.

I put my hand over the page. "Gabe, you're supposed to be on vacation. Considering the circumstances, maybe you should forget your thesis for a couple of weeks."

He looked down at me, his left eye twitching underneath his glasses. I reached up and touched the spot with my fingertip. It jumped under my touch. Taking hold of my hand, he brought it to his chest. I felt his heart beating beneath his cool damp skin. My hand rose as he sighed deeply.

"What?" I encouraged softly.

For a moment, his face held a look of utter despair. He brought my hand to his lips and kissed it gently, his thick mustache tickling the back of my hand.

"Gabe, tell me what's wrong."

He let go of my hand and looked at me, his face blank. "Wrong? Nothing's wrong. I'm just tired. You thirsty? I'll get us a Coke."

While he was gone, I picked up his book and glanced over the pages he'd been reading. It was a habit I'd started before we'd even married, this unabashed snooping for clues to his thoughts in underlined passages in his philosophy books.

"Human beings," the writer asserted, "are ultimately more frightened of killing than being killed. Because if *we* are the killer, there is no chance of escape. *Ever.*"

Did his underlining mean he agreed with this philosopher's beliefs? The thought troubled me. I knew that as a Marine he'd spent most of his time in Vietnam as a grunt. I also knew he'd probably killed people, though he never spoke of it. I'd assumed he'd worked all that out years ago. A cold, terrible feeling ran through me, the same feeling I'd had as a child playing at the beach. I'd turn to see a distant wave coming, and at first it would appear to be predictable, manageable, and I'd watch it, waist-deep in the cool salty water, fascinated by its rolling grace. But as it approached, it would gain momentum until it was too late and I was captured by its foamy power, tossed and turned uncontrollably, clawing to get away, certain I would never make it to the surface alive.

I put the book down before he returned with an icy glass of Coke. I wanted to ask him about the passage, but suppressed my urge and moved to safer ground.

"Who does Dewey really suspect?" I asked, sipping my drink before setting it on the nightstand. "And what about the murder weapon? Have they found it yet or even decided what it was?"

He leaned his head back and groaned. "Benni, leave it alone."

"You know something, don't you? I can tell by the look on your face you're not telling me everything." I straddled his thighs and put my hands around his neck. "Spill the beans, Friday, or I'll be forced to choke it out of you."

He laughed, grabbed my wrists, and we playfully wrestled for control. "*Querida,*" he said, "this is not my investigation. I have no jurisdiction. I want no jurisdiction. I'm on vacation."

"Don't you care who killed her? Aren't you curious? Do you think it was that Amish man?"

"Of course I care, but I repeat, this is not my investigation. I'll give Dewey any assistance he asks for, but I'm going to stay out of it except as a witness." He let go of my wrists, grabbed my hips, and pulled me to him, his big hands cradling me firmly in his lap. "And so are you."

I wrapped my legs around his waist and contemplated him silently, my face inches from his.

"Benni . . ." he warned. "You've given your statement, and that's as far as it goes."

"Okay, okay," I said. "You're right. It's just that . . ."

"It's just that nothing. The only police procedure I'd like to practice in the next few hours, providing we can get rid of my mother, is a little California Penal Code Section 4030d3."

"What's that?"

"Physical body search."

"Old joke, Chief. Get some new material." A sharp rap on the bedroom door interrupted my giggle.

"Yes?" Gabe called out.

"I'm sorry to disturb you," his mother called, "but Dewey's on the phone. He says he needs to speak with you immediately."

We untangled ourselves and pulled on jeans and T-shirts before running down the stairs.

I watched Gabe's face grow increasingly sober as he listened to Dewey. He motioned for a pencil and paper and wrote some information down in his neat, boxy handwriting. "That's assuming they let me talk to him," he said. He hung up, then slammed his fist down on the tiled counter.

"Gabe, dear, what is it?" his mother asked.

"Rob's being taken to Wichita. He tried to kill himself."

FOUR

WE LEFT KATHRYN in the kitchen trying to call Rob's
mother, and walked out to the car.

"What do you think it means?" I asked.

"I wish I knew," Gabe said, his face taut with worry.
"Look, you don't need to come with me. I'm going to
go with Dewey to Wichita. He asked me to talk to Rob.
Though I don't know how he thinks it will help, I
couldn't say no." He didn't voice what both of us were
wondering—had Rob tried to kill himself out of de-
spondency or remorse?

"Are you sure you don't want me to come along?"
I asked hopefully, squinting up in the bright sunlight.
He knew what I was trying to avoid.

He looked at me pointedly. "It wouldn't hurt for you
and Mom to spend some time getting to know each
other. She's going to be your mother-in-law for a long
time." He gave a half smile. "At least I hope so."

"We'll see," I grumbled.

"I'll be home when I can. Let Mom know where I'm
going, okay? Be a good *muchacha*."

"*Sí, papacito*," I answered irritably. He knew I hated
it when he went all paternal on me.

He smoothed the top of my hair with his hand. "I

think I've proven enough times that fatherly is the last thing I feel about you.''

I swatted at his hand, but smiled anyway. Kathryn walked out with her navy purse over her arm.

''Mattie's on her way to the hospital right now. I think I'll go be with her.'' She turned to me. ''Will you be all right, Benni? You'll have to fend for yourself for meals today.'' Her expression seemed to say there was some doubt about whether I could manage that difficult task.

''You can come with us if you want,'' Gabe said.

''No,'' I said. ''They don't even know me. I'll just be in the way. I'll be fine. There's always McDonald's if I'm on the verge of starvation.''

Kathryn nodded, though her expression was still doubtful. ''Leave Daphne inside if you decide to go any-where.''

Gabe gave me a quick kiss. ''We'll call when we know something.''

The mutt was waiting for me when I walked back into the house. ''Well, flatface, looks like it's you and me today. Want to go play fetch out on the highway?'' Growling deep in her throat, Daphne retreated to her pink cushion in front of the plaid Early American sofa. She curled up, resting her nose on her rump, keeping a wary eye on me. I growled back and claimed the brown vinyl recliner across the room.

I picked up Kathryn's July *Ladies Home Journal* and was in the middle of a particularly vicious ''Can This Marriage Be Saved?'' when the phone rang.

''Ortiz residence,'' I said.

''I'm going to kill myself.''

I paused for a moment, thinking the irony of this was entirely too . . . well, ironic. And a bit ghoulish. But then, Dove had no idea what had happened here in Derby in the last twenty-four hours.

Her dramatics didn't faze me. I'd learned early not to

add fuel to her capricious fires. "Dove, where are you *now*?"

I heard the rustling of what I assumed was a map. "Capitan," she finally said. "Capitan, New Mexico."

"Why are you calling me from Capitan . . . where?"

"New Mexico. We're visiting Smokey the Bear's grave. He was born here, you know. And it's his fiftieth anniversary. They got the prettiest little stained glass window with his picture on it. The museum's real interesting."

"Sounds like you're having fun."

"Well, I'm certainly trying, not that *some people* will let me. That father and uncle of yours are real close to joining Smokey in that eternal campsite in the sky if they don't straighten up and fly right."

"I thought you were going to kill yourself."

"Changed my mind. They're the ones driving *me* batty. I swear, I'm going to drop them two off by the side of the road one of these days."

"Now, Dove, they're your kids. You've got no one but yourself to blame for the way they act."

Before she could answer, my dad got on the phone. "Benni, that you?"

"Yes, Daddy. How's it going?"

"Slower than molasses in Alaska, that's how it's going. Your gramma has us stopping at every gole-durn side-of-the-road money-stealing sideshow a con man could think up. At this rate, it'll take us four weeks to get to Kansas." I heard him hack, then spit. "This Yogi Bear grave just beats all. Don't these people have better things to do with their time and money? You got the average rancher gettin' farther behind every year, and they spend money on a dead bear's grave. Between her yapping at me to stop here and yonder and Arnie nagging at me to drive my new truck, which will happen over my dead carcass, I'm about ready to put them both on the Greyhound and head on back home."

"Smokey the Bear," I corrected, trying not to laugh.

"Try and be patient, Daddy. Dove hasn't had a vacation in a long time. Humor her."

"He's a bear, dang it. A *bear*. And a fake one at that."

"Is not!" Dove squawked in the background. I heard the receiver clunk against something; then her voice bellowed over the line again. "This pea-brained son of mine doesn't know the difference between a cartoon bear and a real one. What do you think of that?"

"I think since *I'm* paying for the call we'd better get off. You all try and get along, or at least get it out of your system before you get to Kansas. You'd better behave while you're here and not embarrass me."

"Well, isn't that the mouse calling the cat a queen."

"I mean it. If you do, I'll . . ."

"You'll what?" Dove sounded smug.

Doggone it, she knew there wasn't a thing I could do. "Quit fighting," I said and hung up, for once before she did.

I had no sooner settled back down with my on-the-verge-of-divorce couple when the phone rang again.

"I don't want to hear it," I said, before she could speak. "You're all just going to have to try and get along or—"

"Oh," Becky said, her voice dropping an octave in surprise. "Is that you, Benni? Is my mom there?"

"Becky! I'm sorry. I thought you were— Oh, never mind. She went with Gabe to Wichita to be with Rob's mother. Did you hear about Rob?"

"Are you kidding? My phone started ringing before the paramedics pulled out of his driveway. Derby hasn't had this much excitement in years. Oh, my, not that Rob trying to commit suicide is exciting. I mean . . ."

"It's okay, I know what you mean. I'll tell her you called, but she didn't say exactly when they'd be home."

"No, don't bother. I was just going to ask her if she wanted to come with me to Miller to visit Hannah. I'm taking her some food and some flowers from my garden."

"Tyler's sister?"

"You know about Hannah?"

"Tyler told me a little. She said she's a marvelous quilter."

"Better than anyone I've ever seen, and I've seen plenty, believe me." She paused for a moment. "So, you're all alone?"

I looked down at a snoring Daphne and the magazine in my lap. "To all intents and purposes."

"Why don't you come with me, then? I'd love the company. We could get to know each other better."

"I'm game, but do you think Hannah would mind? I mean, she knows you, but I'm a stranger, and what with Tyler and all . . ."

"I don't think she'll mind. She's very gracious," Becky said. "I'll get her to show you some of her quilts if she's up to it. Who knows, getting her mind off Tyler's murder for a few minutes might help. I'll drop the girls off at their friends, then be there in about half an hour."

A disregard for speed limits was apparently a genetic trait in the Ortiz family, because Becky's forest-green Jeep Cherokee and heavy foot maneuvered us through Wichita in record time. On Highway 96, heading northwest toward the tiny Amish town of Miller, the landscape finally turned into the Kansas of my imagination: vast golden fields, cut short and spiky now; rows of lush and shadowy green milo, their bushy heads moving softly in the sweltering breeze; and acres of rich brown soil being tilled for the next planting. The shimmering blue sky faded into a starched white where it touched the dark silhouette of trees along the horizon. Becky and I shied away from talk of Tyler's death, discussing instead the quilt show this weekend, her quilt collection, her studies to become a professional quilt appraiser, and her plans, when her children were older, to conduct workshops and maybe write a book on her specialty—Midwestern Amish quilts. Her method of storing her quilt collection surprised me, layered flat on her guest bed, the top one turned backside up to avoid sun fading.

"I've found it's the best way," she said. "Folding is too tedious. You're always having to refold them so they don't get creases. And rolling them takes up too much room. I didn't think up the method. A lot of collectors do it that way." She laughed. "The only problem is when we have guests." After we exhausted all our quilt talk she asked, "How's my mother treating you?"

"Fine," I said, giving her a small smile. What did she expect me to say? That getting to know Greta Garbo would have been easier?

She turned the air conditioner on high and gave me an amused glance. "Hey, you don't have to pretend with me. I was raised by that woman. Between her and Angel, you might get enough conversation to last five minutes. That's after a couple of pots of coffee, *if* you've lived in Kansas all your life and if you hadn't stolen away their precious Gabe."

I laughed. "So it's not just me?"

She shook her head and smiled. "Now, my dad—you would have liked him. He really loved to talk. I was only nine when he died, but I do remember that about him. I guess I'm the only one who took after him."

We were silent for a moment. I glanced into the back seat. "What are you bringing to Hannah?"

"Some banana bread, a casserole, a ham. She doesn't really need it—the Amish community will probably inundate her with food—but it's the most acceptable way to express sympathy."

"So even though Hannah wasn't allowed to see or talk to her sister, they will still acknowledge that she has had a loss?"

Becky gave me a considering look and tapped her nails on the steering wheel. They were long and white under the clear polish. "How much do you know about Tyler?"

"I only talked with her for a short time last night. She told me a little about why she left the Amish to be a singer. And that a good friend helped her pick out her new name. Then we mostly talked about quilting. She said sometimes it was a prison to her. She told me about the stitching in your Amish Shoofly quilt.'' I shrugged. ''That's basically it.''

''Well, that's certainly the condensed version. Like most things with the Amish, it's more complicated than it appears. They're called the plain people, but their religion has a pretty complex set of unspoken rules and regulations. In some ways, their life is easy. In other ways, it's incredibly hard.''

''Too hard for Tyler, I guess.''

''The Amish are very strict in their beliefs about conformity, but they can also be the most compassionate people in the world. Physically and mentally disabled people are treated with the same respect and valued just as much as everyone else in the community. Actually, families consider themselves blessed when they have a 'special' child. They believe it helps teach the family patience and compassion. To them, there's no shame in having a handicap.''

''So why did Tyler leave?''

Becky sighed, signaled a turn, and pulled off the highway onto a smaller road. We passed a green sign so small it would have been easy to miss. Miller—2 miles. ''Tyler was special, too. You heard her sing. She had incredible talent. But that kind of special is not encouraged among the Old Order Amish. In fact, it's discouraged. Teamwork is the most important thing to them. Everyone has the same amount of education and is expected to live their lives exactly like the generations before. Any personal recognition for a special skill or talent is considered prideful. I guess Tyler just didn't feel that she could deny her talent.''

I considered her words for a moment before answering. ''Think about it, though—to pursue that talent she had to give up her whole family, her whole *life*. Seems like a pretty steep price.''

Becky nervously tapped the steering wheel again. "It really is so sad. When Tyler left about a year and a half ago—oh, and I forgot to mention, Hannah will call her Ruth, which was her original name before she changed it legally—anyway, after Tyler left, it was understood that the community would shun her. You see, she left the church after she joined it, which is one of the worst things you can do. It was very shameful for her family. But Hannah loved Tyler too much to never hear of her again, so that's where I came in."

"You?"

"Well, we don't know if it's quite legal according to Amish law, but it appeased Hannah's conscience, and also relieved her worry."

"What?"

"Right after I met Tyler, she told me about her sister's quilting. I went to Hannah's farm and introduced myself. In the conversation I let her know that a woman named Tyler who'd once been a plain person herself named Ruth, told me about her. Since then I've been a go-between for Hannah and her quilts. Some of them are consigned at Janet's store, Sunflower Quilts and Crafts in Derby, and I have them placed at three other stores in Kansas. It brings in a good side income for Hannah. If on my visits to Hannah my friend Tyler's life just happens to come up in the conversation, then . . ." Becky let her voice trail off.

"That's pretty amazing," I said, impressed with their clever skirting of the rules. "This must be devastating for Hannah. Have you talked with her since it happened?"

"No, that's why Rob called Fannie at the fabric store. The Amish don't have phones in their homes, though they will use public phones or the phones of their non-Amish neighbors if it's absolutely necessary. If Hannah had to hear news like that, Fannie would be the best person to hear it from. At least Rob wasn't the one to break it to her. I would have driven out and told her myself before I'd let that happen.'' Becky shook her head in disgust.

The difference between Miller and the other small towns in Kansas was apparent the minute you drove down Main Street. The first street sign we saw was a black and yellow ''Caution—Slow Vehicle'' sign depicting a silhouette of an Amish buggy pulled by a high-stepping horse. For such a small town, it had a surprising number of businesses, many with old-fashioned buggies parked outside. Becky slowed the Cherokee down to a crawl as we passed Johnson's Hardware, Fannie's Fabrics and Notions, Miller's Market, Hershberger Blacksmith, The Plain People Antiques, Miller Feed and Grain, The Old Prairie Buggy Shop. Hulking silver grain elevators—a staple in most small Kansas towns, I was rapidly discovering—towered over the town.

Becky parked in front of the Millstone Bakery, a slope-roofed building with brown shingles and a bright blue door.

''Miller seems to be a popular name,'' I commented, looking at the owner's name, Joshua Miller, under the bakery's hand-carved sign.

''They're one of the original settling families,'' Becky said. ''It's Tyler's maiden name. Her father is a minister, a very respected member of the community. That made her leaving even more scandalous.'' She hitched her purse over her shoulder. ''Stan and the girls will skin me alive if I don't buy some of Mrs. Bontranger's cinnamon pulaparts while I'm here.'' Next to us, tied to the hitching post running the length of the bakery, was a square black Amish buggy with a bright orange triangular slow vehicle warning sign underneath the back window. A dark brown gelding with one white sock waited patiently, his tail flicking at flies. ''Good boy,'' I murmured, running my hand down the horse's silky neck.

''You like horses?'' Becky asked.

''Yes,'' I said, following her into the cool, spicy-smelling bakery. "I used to ride every day on the ranch. I miss it now that I'm a townie."

"You and Gabe have both had to make big adjustments this last year, haven't you? We haven't talked yet about just how you and he got together." Becky opened the door to the bakery, standing aside to let me enter first. The smell of cinnamon and ginger immediately set my tastebuds to watering. "I've heard his version, but as much as I love my brother, I take a lot of what he says with a huge grain of salt. I have to admit, he surprised us all back here. We never expected him to get married again, much less to a cowgirl."

"Rancher," I said good-naturedly.

She gave an apologetic laugh. "Sorry."

"It's okay."

She looked at me curiously. "Maybe I shouldn't bring this up, but since we're talking about my brother, Mom says you aren't taking Gabe's name and that he's not exactly thrilled about it."

So he'd told them. I shrugged, not really wanting to go into it with my new sister-in-law, especially since we'd been getting along so well. Apparently this was going to be a stitch in more than one person's side. "It's not a big deal. I just want to keep my name."

"You mean your first husband's name."

"*My* name for the last fifteen years," I said, trying to keep the irritation out of my voice. "It really has nothing to do with how I feel about Gabe."

She gave me a crooked, appeasing smile. "I'm sorry, I didn't mean to upset you. I think it's rather funny actually. Gabe's always been too macho for his own good. It won't hurt him to be brought down a peg or two."

"This is not a political statement I'm making," I protested, irritated now. "I just don't want to change my name."

She wisely dropped the subject and stepped up to the bakery counter.

The woman behind the glass case was as round and

soft-looking as the fat dinner rolls she was packing eight
to a bag. While she wrapped up Becky's order, they
discussed Tyler's death in low tones. I sat at a small
plastic table drinking a cup of fresh coffee and eating a
hot, just-iced caramel roll. The Pennsylvania Dutch heritage of the owners was apparent in the selection of
baked goods in the sparkling clean display cases—flaky
gooseberry turnovers, dill bread, huge apple butter cookies, strawberry-rhubarb pie, cherry angel rounds, lemon
crunch coffee cake. Unable to resist, I bought a loaf of
pilgrim bread and some oatmeal-coconut cookies to take
back to Gabe and Kathryn.

Inside the Cherokee, the early afternoon sun had
turned the air as hot and steamy as a sauna. We packed
our baked goods into a cooler Becky had brought along,
and drove through the tree-shaded streets onto a small
country road, passing acres of bare wheat fields and four
or five neat white houses with deep front porches and
wildly colorful flower gardens. At the beginning of Hannah's long dirt driveway stood a hand-painted sign:
"Eggs, tomatoes, fresh cream, milk—No Sunday
sales." Driving toward the farm, Becky had to brake
quickly twice to avoid the flocks of chickens skittering
across our path. Hannah's house, like the others we'd
seen, was a two-story white wood structure with four
rectangular windows upstairs and three windows and a
new screen door below. The well-scrubbed front porch
held only three Shaker-style chairs. The flower garden
in front of the house exploded with ruby-red pansies,
lavender zinnias, and enormous sunflowers. The pine
and cottonwood trees shading the driveway were full of
scolding blue jays and a small gray bird whose call
sounded like a cat mewing. Two little girls burst out of
the house, screaming Becky's name. Wisps of hair the
color and texture of dandelion fluff escaped from the
sides of their miniature white caps. Above us, the blue
jays screeched in unison.

"Are Paige and Whitney with you?" the smaller of

the two girls asked. She looked about six and wore a
plain blue short-sleeve dress that swung around legs as
plump and smooth as summer zucchinis. Her sister,
wearing a similar dress, was older by a year or so. She
hopped up and down on one tanned bare foot. In her
serious gray eyes and delicate nose, I could see her
aunt's face as it must have looked twenty years ago.

"No, honey, I'm sorry," Becky said. "They're with
their daddy today. They had a swimming lesson they
couldn't miss."

"Oh." The girls' faces wrinkled in disappointment.
The screen door opened again, and their mother walked
out. I inhaled sharply when I saw her. The one thing
Becky forgot to tell me was that Hannah and Tyler were
identical twins.

Becky glanced at me, taking my surprised look to
heart. "Oh, my, I forgot to tell you, didn't I?"

I nodded mutely.

"Twins are genetically very common among the
Amish. I'm so used to it that it didn't even occur to me
to mention it."

"Becky, I'm so glad you came." Hannah held out a
hand. She wore a simple, dark brown dress closed at the
neck with straight pins, and a full white apron over it.
Her golden blond hair was pulled back in a bun and
tucked into a fitted white cap identical to her daughters'.
Her face—Tyler's face—was free of any makeup, making her appear younger than her twenty-seven years.

"Oh, Hannah, I'm so sorry." Becky's eyes filled with
tears. She took Hannah's hand, and they looked at each
other for a long, silent moment. Behind them, the girls
shuffled their bare feet and played with the loose strands
of hair feathering their faces. A small red hen broke the
emotional moment by jumping up on the porch and
pecking at the clean wood.

Hannah stepped away from Becky and briskly clapped
her hands. "Ruthie, Emma, I told you to round up those
chickens and put them in their pen. Get along with you

and do it now." Her voice was firm but loving.

"Can we show Becky the new chickies?" the younger girl asked, scurrying across the porch to catch the protesting hen and tuck it under her arm.

"Later, Emma. We have grown-up things to discuss right now." Hannah turned back to us. "Please come and eat with me."

Her house was as neat and plain inside as out. Hand-woven rugs softened our steps on the shiny hardwood floors. The long windows had white gossamer curtains pulled to the side, letting the slight breeze blow through a living room that with its simple sofa and straight-backed chairs appeared almost empty, so accustomed was I to the abundance of furniture in the average American home. A natural pine rocker sat next to the front window; a delicate spindle-legged table next to it held a twig basket full of fabric scraps and a frayed leather Bible. On the pale walls there was only a pegged rack, a handmade shelf displaying a curved mantel clock, and a shiny calendar showing a clear mountain lake reflecting a snow-capped mountain. Carrying the food we brought, we followed Hannah into the kitchen, where dishes covered with embroidered tea towels or aluminum foil crowded the countertops.

"There's plenty," she said, pulling plates from a cherry-wood hutch that dominated a corner of the kitchen. In the hutch, colorful crystal glassware and fancy teacups fought for space on shelves edged with an eyelet lace border. "Try some of Lavina Yoder's corn pie."

She filled our plates with the sweet-smelling pie, a helping of chow-chow that reminded me of my aunt Garnet's pickled spring vegetables, slices of ham crusted with a brown sugar glaze, and thick pieces of homemade white bread spread with cool, salty butter. While eating, we talked about quilting and Hannah's flower garden, how bad the tomato worms were this year and how hot it was. She asked me if I was enjoying Kansas and told me she'd always been curious about California. She blushed when she confessed that Disneyland, as worldly as it was, was someplace she'd always wanted to see. Finally the conversation turned to Tyler. Becky asked Hannah if the police had talked with her yet.

Before answering, Hannah cut each of us a slice of a four-layer coconut cake. She sat down and stared at her plate. "Yes, but I didn't have anything to tell them. You know I haven't seen her in over a year. I don't know what her life was like except for what you have told me." She picked up her fork, then laid it back down. A shininess appeared in her gray eyes.

Becky touched her friend's hand. "They'll find whoever did this."

Hannah pushed her cake away, and put a hand to her temple tentatively. "I know, Becky. In my heart I know that God allowed this to happen for a reason and that justice will be done, if not now, then in eternity." Becky and I finished our cake silently. Hannah picked at hers, then abruptly stood up, straightened her back, and walked over to the sink. With sharp, quick strokes, she scraped what remained of her cake into a large aluminum pan.

The back door flew open, and Ruthie and Emma tumbled into the kitchen. "Mama, can Becky come see the chickies now?"

Her face grew tender with affection. "Yes, if she wants."

"I most certainly do," Becky said, grabbing each girl's hand. "Hannah, Benni would love to see your quilts. Would you mind showing them to her?"

"If she likes," Hannah said.

She took me into an airy bedroom upstairs and opened a blue-painted highboy. Silently I named the patterns as she laid them across the narrow bed—Sawtooth Diamond, Sunshine and Shadow, Double Nine-Patch, Tree of Life, Fence Row, Wild Goose Chase, Grandmother's Flower Garden. All traditional Amish patterns using no printed fabric, their brilliantly colored symmetry and complex quilting exemplified the reasons that these quilts were so prized by collectors and lovers of folk art. Each seemed more impressive than the last, and finally I ceased exclaiming over them and just enjoyed their beauty. The last one she pulled out was a traditional Star of Bethlehem, that arresting pattern of hundreds of tiny diamond-shaped pieces, in this case ranging in color from bright purple to sky-blue to Turkey-red to the dark green of a summer pine. Only one thing marred its adherence to Amish tradition. The final diamond on each tip of the eight-pointed star was made with a dark green material with the tiniest print of flowers. A small cry of defiance in a stifling world of conformity.

"This is the only quilt I have left of Ruth's," Hannah said sadly, smoothing it as if it were a beloved child's unruly hair. "It was a birthday gift. She took all the others with her when she left, and sold them. I'm just thankful Becky bought some and that I have this one left."

"It's incredible," I said, studying the intricate stitching. I looked up at Hannah. A faint sheen of perspiration gave her face a rosy glow. Her brow furrowed. "This must be very hard for you."

"Yes," she said, the troubled expression on her face deepening. "Becky's brother . . ." she began, then cleared her throat delicately. "Your husband. He's a police officer, isn't he?"

"Yes," I said, mystified. "Why?"

She looked down and started folding up the quilts quickly. I helped her silently, sensing that she'd finish her thought when she was ready. She carefully laid Ruth's quilt on top of the others in the chest, giving it a sorrowful look before closing the doors. Then she turned to me, her neat, pointed jaw set determinedly. For a moment, with that look of stubborn resolve, the similarity between her and Tyler was eerie.

"I have something I must show you," she said.

FIVE

HANNAH AND I walked across the backyard to the paint-peeled barn, the strong, tangy odor of pigs surrounding us. The clouds had moved south, and through the shimmering heat of the clear afternoon air we could hear Becky's teasing voice in the distance and the high, excited squeals of Hannah's daughters. Inside the cool barn, she led me to a small room in the back. Tack of all sizes hung on the rough walls. Wood shavings decorated the floor around four straight-backed wooden chairs. Two men were in the room; both had the traditional untrimmed beard and bare upper lip of the Old Order Amish male. One had pale thinning hair, ice-blue eyes and a penny-sized mole on his left cheek. He sat behind a scarred desk cleaning a bridle worn dark brown from use. The buttery-sweet smell of saddle soap filled the room. The other man, leaning against the wall across from him, was about six feet tall, with dark eyes, a weathered complexion, and long legs. They stopped talking when we entered.

"This is my husband, Eli," Hannah said, pointing to the blue-eyed man cleaning tack. "And our friend, John Stoltzfus. This is Becky's sister-in-law, Benni. The one who's married to the policeman. I'm giving it to her."

"Nice to meet you," I said.

Eli frowned at me, then slowly dipped his head in acknowledgment. The other man, John, stared at me silently. Hannah opened the top drawer of an old wood cabinet and pulled out a legal-sized envelope. She gestured at me to follow her back outside.

In the backyard, under the cool shade of a massive walnut tree, she handed me the envelope. "Please excuse my husband's unfriendliness," she said. "Since the police came to question us this morning, he and John have not been in the best of moods."

"Why would it bother John?"

She looked surprised, then flushed with emotion. "Becky has not told you about John?"

"No," I said carefully. "I guess she didn't."

"John and Ruth are married. When she left, he was very upset. It has been hard for him."

Married? I thought. Tyler is—was—married? I was speechless for a moment. "What—" I started, not certain what I wanted to ask. "How—"

"We do not believe in divorce," Hannah said quietly. "For us, marriage is until death."

"So what is he supposed to do?" I realized after I said it that it wasn't a problem for him now. "I mean, before— What did he do?"

"Lived his life according to the Scriptures, prayed for her return. The bishop told him he must look upon it as a test of faith."

"But no remarriage. No children." I knew enough about the Amish to understand how that would be the ultimate sacrifice, the supreme test of faith.

"No. No children."

I looked into her sad eyes, and the unspoken truth hung between us heavy as pollen in the air. Now he could remarry and have a family within the bounds of the community. Had anyone told the police that Tyler was married? Was he the Amish man who argued with Tyler on the porch last night? And could a man raised

Amish actually kill someone?

I contemplated the envelope she'd handed me. It had been opened and resealed with Scotch tape. "What is this?"

"Ruth's bank book," she said. "I looked, though perhaps I shouldn't have. There's a lot of money in it."

Taking that as a cue, I opened the envelope. The account, on deposit in a downtown branch of the First Bank of Wichita, was opened on January twelfth of this year with a starting balance of ten thousand dollars. It showed a balance of $6258.67 as of last Friday, when five hundred dollars had been withdrawn. Five withdrawals had been made during the last six months. I guessed Tyler had been using this money to supplement her unpredictable earnings as a singer.

"Why do you have this?" I asked, slipping the bank book back in the envelope. "I thought you and Ty—Ruth didn't communicate. Oh, I forgot. Becky." Had Becky failed to tell the police about this money, as she'd failed to tell them about Tyler's husband? I wondered what else she knew that she hadn't told.

"Oh, no," Hannah said, shaking her head in protest. "Becky doesn't know about this. For some reason, Ruth did not confide in her about this money. A couple of days ago Ruth came out and gave the bank book to Fannie Fisher, the woman who owns the fabric store in town. She is an old school friend of ours. Ruth told Fannie to give it to me if anything should happen to her, that she wanted the money to be mine and Eli's. She told her to tell me to sign her name and draw the money out. But I can't do that. I don't know where Ruth got this kind of money. She had nothing when she left, and I know she didn't make that much singing . . ." Hannah's voice trailed off. Above us, in the thick foliage of the tree, a squirrel chattered at a crow holding something red and raw in its beak. "It's as if she knew she was in danger. Doesn't it seem so? Oh, how I wish she'd never left us."

I ran my fingers up and down the edge of the envelope, trying to figure this out. "Why didn't you give this to the police officer this morning?"

"I don't know. He was so cold and uncaring. He seemed so certain that Ruth did something to cause her own death." She blinked rapidly.

"I don't understand. What do you want me to do?"

"Your husband. He's a policeman. Becky has told me he is a man of great honesty. I thought perhaps . . ."

"Hannah, he's a police officer in California. He doesn't have any jurisdiction here. He'll just have to turn it over to the local police himself."

Pressing two fingers to the space between her eyes, she said, "I know. I just want it out of here." Her eyes pleaded with me. "I realize you don't know me and that none of this is your concern, but I don't know who else to turn to. I don't want Becky involved, because she lives here and I don't know where my sister got this money, but I suspect it came from something that wasn't good. Ruth wasn't always the easiest person to love, but I did love her." She said the last sentence passionately. "But to keep this money would be wrong. Please, could you just give it to your husband?"

I folded the envelope in half and stuck it in the back pocket of my jeans. "Yes, but the police will eventually want to question you about it."

"I know, but it gives me some time. To think . . . and to pray. Eli is very upset about this. John is like a brother to him." She touched my forearm. "Please, don't tell Becky about this. She has been so kind to me and Ruth. I'm so afraid to involve her in something bad."

"All right," I said, not feeling entirely good about the whole situation. But a part of me was intrigued. Considering the amount of money in the account and knowing the poverty in which most aspiring musicians lived, Hannah was probably right in guessing that Tyler hadn't gotten this money legitimately. The question remained, Where did she get it and did it involve her murder? We returned to the house and sat on the front porch waiting for Becky and the girls. ''I'd love to purchase one of your quilts,'' I told Hannah, trying to steer the conversation toward a pleasanter subject than her sister's murder. ''Or perhaps commission you to make one for me.''

''That would probably be best,'' she said. ''You could meet me at Fannie's store in Miller and pick out fabric. Just call Fannie and tell her what day you're coming, and I'll meet you there. Anytime is fine with me.''

''Hey, you two,'' Becky called from across the yard. She was carrying a round melon basket over her arm. Ruthie and Emma tumbled around her legs like two golden retriever puppies. ''Your hens are really going to town this summer. I'd like to buy two dozen eggs if you can spare them.''

''Of course I can,'' Hannah said, smiling. We talked about her hens and the quilt she would make me as she packed up the eggs. She insisted we take three jars of raspberry preserves and an apple strudel she'd made that morning. As we drove slowly down the soft dirt driveway, Ruthie and Emma ran alongside the Cherokee, tripping over their own legs like gawky colts.

On the highway, Becky turned on the cruise control and the radio. Tanya Tucker was having some kind of trouble and her preacher was tellin' her that all God's children got their own kind of trouble. Amen, I thought.

''I met Hannah's husband while you and the girls were looking at the chickens,'' I said. ''And Tyler's husband, John.''

''She told you, then,'' Becky said, her voice relieved. ''So, what do you think?''

''What do you mean?''

''About John. You know, that doesn't look real good, you seeing him at the house last night right before she was killed. . . .''

''I didn't see *him* exactly,'' I reminded her. ''I saw an Amish man. It could have been anyone.''

She shook her head and made a disbelieving noise in her throat.

"Why didn't you tell me Tyler was married?" I asked, slightly irritated. Along with a taste for speeding, this habit of suppressing information seemed to be an Ortiz family trait.

"I didn't even tell the police. I figured they'd find out soon enough when they questioned Hannah and Eli. And if I told you, you'd have felt obligated to tell Gabe, who would then have felt obligated to tell Dewey."

I followed her logic, but was still irritated.

"Well," she said, "they apparently know now. So, what do you think?"

I thought for a moment, then answered her with a question. "Do you really think John could have killed her? Isn't that kind of violence way out of character for someone who's Amish?"

"Absolutely," she said. "And if the police have any brains at all, they'll realize that, too."

Thinking about Gabe and the other cops I'd become acquainted with and their often justifiable cynicism about human behavior, I had a strong hunch that John being Amish wasn't going to impress any branch of Kansas law enforcement.

When we arrived back at Kathryn's house, the empty driveway told us that she and Gabe had not returned from the hospital. During the trip, the envelope in my back pocket felt as if it had doubled in size. I was anxious to tell Gabe what I learned, but that apparently was going to have to wait.

"It's past six o'clock," Becky said. "Why don't you leave them a note on the door and have dinner with us? Gabe can pick you up when he gets home. No point in you sitting here alone. Besides, you haven't met my girls yet."

Stan, Paige, and Whitney were just climbing out of a dark blue Grand Marquis sedan when Becky and I drove up. Paige, the twelve-year-old, had a thin, serious face and a freckled, sun-peeled nose. She politely held out a water-wrinkled hand when Becky introduced us. Whitney, four years younger, with two missing front teeth and hair tinted pale green from chlorine, giggled and waved.

Becky threw together a magazine-perfect summer supper of cold garlic and rosemary chicken breasts, Caesar salads, and fresh sourdough bread. Afterwards, we sat out on the front porch on her white wicker furniture, sipped lemonade, and watched the sun dip toward the horizon. I glanced at my watch. It was almost eight o'clock now, and I wondered if I was ever going to hear from my husband again. Paige and Whitney dressed and undressed Whitney's Barbie dolls until Paige became bored and started bugging her mom to go across the street.

"I want to see Grandpa," she whined. "And Cinnamon."

Becky glanced at Stan. "I don't know. It's going to be dark soon . . ." I could see the fear in her eyes, and it hit me suddenly how frightening Tyler's murder must be for this small town.

"Who's Cinnamon?" I asked.

"Grandpa Otis' new horse," Whitney piped up. "He's training Cinnamon so he can sell him. He won him in a poker game."

"Had a choice between the horse and the guy's '85 Buick Skyhawk," Stan commented in his lazy voice. "He chose the horse."

I smiled. "Good choice. I've never seen a horse that was won in a poker match. How about if I go with them?"

"That would be fine," Becky said, her voice relieved. "I'll make some chocolate ice cream while you're gone."

Whitney, who had accepted me as her Aunt Benni with the unquestioning blitheness of an eight-year-old, grabbed my hand and swung it as we walked down the long driveway and across the road to the Christmas tree farm. Paige bounded ahead of us, brandishing a stick as if it were a sword. Neither girl could resist stopping and staring past the yellow police tape into the thick clump of trees. The actual murder spot couldn't be seen from the gravel driveway, so Whitney peppered me with questions.

"Was it scary?" she asked, her eyes bright. "Was there blood everywhere? Did you throw up?"

"Whitney!" Paige scolded. "Don't be so gross." She shot her younger sister an impatient look. Her serious face was apologetic when she turned to me. "Please ignore her. She's very immature." Her clipped words sounded so much like Kathryn's, I had to smile.

"Am not," Whitney said, pushing her sister.

"Are, too," Paige retorted. They continued to pick on each other as we walked around to the side of the house where the corral was located. When they spotted the old man I'd met last night, they stopped their fighting and dashed over to him.

"Grandpa Otis," they cried, climbing up on the corral's metal railing. "Make Cinnamon gallop!"

In the center of the arena, Otis, still wearing his yellow feed cap, held a nylon lunge line and exercised a narrow-necked, elegant-legged red roan gelding that appeared to have more than a little thoroughbred in it. He cracked his long lunge whip, and the horse went into an extended trot.

I joined the girls on the railing and watched Otis put the gelding through its paces. The horse had a smooth, graceful gait, and responded with energy and just the slightest show of rebellion to the snap of Otis's whip. We watched Cinnamon walk, jog, go into an extended trot, lope, and full gallop. The girls squealed with delight when the horse raced around Otis, its white-streaked red mane flying in the warm breeze.

Otis brought the roan back to a walk and called out to the girls, "Hey there, my little chickadees. What do you think of your Grandpa's horse now?''

"Let us ride him,'' they begged. "We won't tell Mom.''

He ignored their pleading, looked over at me, and touched the edge of the whip to his hat. "How do, Mrs. Ortiz.''

"Just Benni,'' I called back.

He reeled in the lunge line and walked Cinnamon over to us. Paige pulled out a sugar cube from the pocket of her shorts and fed it to the horse. I jumped off the railing and reached up to stroke its velvety cheek.

"So where's your new husband, Just Benni?'' Otis gave me a slow, teasing grin.

I grinned back. "Still in Wichita, I guess. You heard about Rob?''

"Yep.'' Otis's smile faded. He clipped a lead rope onto the halter and undid the lunge line and stud chain. "Bad thing.''

"Yes.'' I continued stroking the horse. "Have the police been back out here?''

His bristly gray eyebrows contracted. "Want to ride the old boy?''

"Sure,'' I said enthusiastically.

He turned to Paige and Whitney. "You girls want to go get Old Sinful's bridle for me?''

They giggled at the horse's nickname and scrambled across the driveway, racing toward the barn. Otis turned back to me.

"Sinful?'' I asked.

"It fits,'' he said. "You'll see.'' He pointed with the whip to a pile of used bricks next to the barn. "Didn't want to talk about it in front of the young'uns, but all sorts of official types were out here most of the day going through that bunch of bricks I use to prop up some of the trees. Appears that was what she was killed with, and they're trying to find it.''

"Did they?'' Otis handed me the lunge line, and I started rolling it up, trying not to think what it would feel like to have the back of my head bashed in with a brick. Someone must have been angry, really angry.

"Didn't tell me if they did. They took a few with 'em. Won't do much good, I imagine. Bricks is something we got plenty of here in Kansas." He shrugged and adjusted the strap of his faded overalls. "It's a sorry thing, pretty young girl like that. Who could have wanted to do that to her?"

"I have no idea, but I'm sure they'll find out soon. A lot of people are working on it."

He just grunted, and I knew he saw through my polite assurances. Otis had lived long enough to know that finding the killer wouldn't be as easy as it looked on a one-hour TV show.

We bridled Sinful, and because he was such a big horse, about sixteen hands, and because I was riding bareback, Otis gave me a leg up. Sinful danced around, making me work for control. I pulled back firmly on the reins, not giving in, and he eventually settled down when he realized I wasn't kidding and would fight him for the position of power.

"We're taking riding lessons at Dewey and Belinda's, but Mom won't let us ride Cinnamon," Paige said, looking up at me longingly.

"He's a bit feisty for a chickadee your size," Otis said. "Someday, maybe. When I've calmed him down a bit and you get a little more meat on those chicken bones."

"Dewey and Belinda's?" I asked.

"They own a stable about five miles out of town," Otis said. "She's his first wife. Bore his young'uns."

"Oh," I said thoughtfully. They still owned a stable together. That was an interesting fact that Gabe forgot to mention.

The girls yelled encouragement while I rode Sinful around the ring, then gradually lost interest and disappeared into the barn, where Otis had told them there were some new kittens. Otis leaned against the gate, chewing on a pipe he'd pulled from his overalls' deep front pocket, and watched me wrangle his horse for control. Sinful (Otis was right, the name was more appropriate than Cinnamon) was a good horse with a lot of potential, but it was obvious he hadn't been ridden regularly. He loved to run and was responsive to the slightest voice commands, but he definitely needed work on his braking system. I totally lost track of time and my surroundings as I moved Sinful through his paces and got him accustomed to holding a rider again.

The sun had dropped past the horizon when I trotted up in front of Otis. I was showing him an abrasion under Sinful's mane when Gabe walked around the corner of the barn. Whitney was perched on his shoulders, and Paige ran along beside him, jabbering a mile a minute.

"I knew you'd eventually end up here," Gabe said, depositing Whitney on the corral's top railing. He opened the gate and came in. "Hey, Otis, this your poker horse?"

Otis grinned around his pipe. "Don't you go telling your mother now. She'd have to put in extra hours at church a-prayin' for me, and we both know she don't have time for that."

"Your secret's safe with me." Gabe reached over and stroked the horse's muzzle. "Nice-looking piece of horseflesh. Make a lot of cans of dog chow out of him."

"Uncle Gabe, that's not funny," Paige said, smacking the side of his leg.

He ruffled her hair and winked up at me. "I'm just teasing you, *m'hija.* Becky says the ice cream's done, and we better get back before Stan eats it all. You too, Otis."

"Gotta put up the hay burner first," Otis said.

"I'll clean him up," I offered. "I'm the one that got him all sweaty. Just don't eat my share."

"I'll stay and help her," Gabe put in.

"Good idea," I said, watching Otis and the girls head down the driveway. It would give me time to tell him quickly about the contents of the envelope and about Tyler being married.

"Let me walk him around the ring a few times to cool him off," I said.

"Okay," Gabe agreed and before I realized it, he'd swung himself up behind me.

"What are you doing?" I exclaimed.

Sinful started slightly, surprised by the extra weight, though he was plenty capable of carrying it. Gabe scooted close, grabbed the reins from my hand, and pulled back until the horse adjusted himself to the additional load. He clucked, and Sinful started at an easy walk.

"What are you doing?" I repeated.

"Going for an intimate ride with my wife," he whispered in my ear, bringing his right arm around my waist and pulling me back tightly against him. "Tell me the truth, doesn't a good ride just make you want to . . ."

"I thought you didn't ride," I said, trying to push his arm away.

He tightened his arm and pressed his leg against Sinful's side, signaling the horse to move toward the railing. "I told you when we first met, I'd ridden once. Not that hard."

"You've ridden more than once," I accused after we'd circled the arena three times and I noted that he cued Sinful properly for every change of gait.

He stopped at the gate and handed me the reins, then swung off and unhooked the latch. "Well, maybe it was once or twice."

"You said you didn't ride," I insisted, sliding down and leading Sinful toward the barn.

"I *never* said that." Once in the barn, he took the reins from me. "Here, let me. I know where everything is." He slipped the halter around Sinful's neck, undid his bridle, pulled the halter back over his nose, and secured him with the crossties. From a square wooden crib with a hinged cover he took out brushes and a hoof pick and proceeded to groom the gelding with the ease and familiarity of someone who'd done it more than once or twice.

"You dirty dog," I said. "All these months you've come out to the ranch with me you never once let on you knew anything about horses. You said you didn't ride."

"I repeat, I never said that."

"You implied it." I crossed my arms and glared at him as he adroitly lifted up each hoof and cleaned the debris out.

"Benni, I'm just not all that crazy about horses or riding. I didn't intentionally lead you to believe I didn't know anything about them. I just don't share your enthusiasm."

I clamped my lips shut in anger. He wasn't even getting what I was saying—that it was another instance in which he kept something secret I should have known about him.

"Just how long were you going to keep it a secret?" I asked.

"It's not a secret, sweetheart. You're making a big deal out of nothing." He finished with the hooves and started brushing Sinful.

"Watch what you're doing. There's a cut under his mane on the left side," I snapped.

Gabe inspected it, then dug through the wood crib for a bottle of Betadine scrub and a can of Furall. He cleaned the wound, washed it with water, then sprayed it with the yellow-tinted Furall. The fact that he knew exactly what to do made my anger bubble as furiously as the disinfectant on Sinful's wound.

I leaned against the stall and angrily watched him finish the grooming. When he'd closed the horse in his stall and put the equipment away, he turned to me.

"Are we going to fight over this?" he asked. "Because if we are, I'd like to get something to eat first. I haven't eaten since early this afternoon."

"Just tell me who taught you to ride."

He sighed. "Initially, Otis. He's always owned horses. He tried breeding Arabians for a couple of years when I was a teenager. Then for six months, right after I got out of the Marines, before I became a cop, I cleaned stalls and exercised horses at the Santa Anita Racetrack for a friend of Otis's. Believe me, after that I never had the desire to ride a horse again. That's the extent of my equine experience. Can we drop it now?"

"For the time being." I didn't want to go back to Becky's house in the middle of a fight any more than he did, but if he thought the matter was settled, he obviously didn't know me very well. "How's Rob?"

He closed the barn door behind us and slipped his arm around my shoulders. "He's fine. I don't think this was a serious attempt. He took about half a bottle of Valium, then immediately called 911. When a man's serious about killing himself, he'll usually just eat his gun."

"Do you think he did it just to make it look like he didn't kill her?"

"If he did, it won't work. If anything, it makes him look more suspicious. Believe me, the sheriff's detectives are looking at him real close."

"Why would he do it, then?"

"Who knows? Rob always liked being the center of attention. Then again, it might be an attempt to get people's sympathy just in case he does have something to hide."

"Like what?"

"Sweetheart, I have no idea. I haven't seen these people for seven years. And to tell you the truth, I don't want to know."

"Did you find out anything from him?"

He shook his head. "No, I think Dewey just wanted me along for the company."

"Did you hear about the bricks?"

"Yes, but I doubt that any they took was the murder

weapon. I don't think this person was that stupid. We were all running around like crazy that night. That brick could be anywhere.''

I stopped at the end of Becky's driveway. ''There's something I found out today about Tyler.'' I told him quickly about the bank book.

''What do you think it means?'' I asked.

''Who knows? Tyler might have had a very legitimate reason for having that money. Unless they can prove it comes from something illegal, it doesn't make much of a motive except maybe for her sister, who is the next-of-kin.''

''News flash. Hannah isn't her next-of-kin. Tyler was married.''

''What?''

''His name's John Stoltzfus. I met him today. He has a great motive for murder. He couldn't remarry and have children as long as she was alive.''

He rested his hands on my shoulders, stroking my neck with his thumbs. ''Benni, was he the man you saw on the porch last night?''

I grimaced. ''I don't know. If you're asking if I can absolutely identify him, the answer is no. I did see an Amish man, and it certainly makes sense it would be him. But I also saw him leave.''

''He could have come back. That's the whole problem with this investigation. The area was so open, and people were coming and going all night. In all honesty, it could have been anyone.''

''But that makes it virtually impossible to find who did it!''

''Exactly.''

''So what will they do?''

''Tedious questioning and digging and more questioning. Not everyone at the party knew her. That eliminates people right there. But that's all Dewey's worry. I'll take the bank book to the police department tomorrow. The Sheriff's Department has set up shop in a spare office next to Dewey's. Unfortunately, there's a new problem they're having to deal with."

"What?"

"About three weeks ago, the city voted to annex this parcel of land into the Derby city limits. So technically this is Dewey's territory. Of course, since he was on the premises when it happened, it compromises his authority. Just his luck, he said. First homicide in Derby, and he can't officially work on it."

"So who's in charge?"

"For the time being, Derby's chief of police. But Dewey's their most experienced detective. They're using him, but trying to keep that from the press, who would scream cover-up just to sell papers."

"Who are the chief suspects?"

"Let's quit talking about this, okay? I've had to hear about it all day, and I'm exhausted. This is not my idea of a fun vacation." He looked down at me seriously. "And one more thing. I *don't* want you involved in this."

"One last question. Is Dewey being investigated? Are you?"

He kissed the top of my head and laughed. "That's two questions. We are all suspects, *querida*, but unless there's something you're not telling me, you and I don't have to worry. Now, let's get some of that chocolate ice cream before it's history. Maybe I can even sweet-talk my baby sister into making me a sandwich."

We stayed until almost eleven o'clock eating ice cream and Becky's homemade oatmeal cookies. She and Otis and Gabe laughed over old childhood escapades while Stan and I listened and smiled and the girls fell asleep in a gangly puddle of arms and legs on the living-room carpet.

Otis turned to me before he left. "You come out now anytime you want and ride Sinful. He needs some of that wildness worked out of him."

"Thanks, I'll take you up on that," I said.

"Benni, don't forget the quilt guild meeting tomorrow afternoon at three," Becky said, walking us to the door. "I'd like you to meet some of our guild members. It's in the new Presbyterian church's recreation hall on Madison. Gabe can tell you where it is. Afterwards we're going to practice setup of the quilt frames for Friday."

"Becky," Stan said, "this is supposed to be Benni's vacation."

She brought a hand up to her mouth. "Oh, I'm sorry. I forgot this is what you do for a living. You don't have to come. Well, come, but we won't make you work."

"It's okay," I said. "I'll be glad to help as long as you handle all incoming quilt emergencies."

"Deal," she said.

I was silent on the short drive back to Kathryn's house, thinking about Hannah and what it must feel like to have violence touch a life that was as sheltered as hers. What would she tell her daughters about their aunt when they grew older and faced similar temptations? Was Tyler's husband really capable of murder? And where in the world did Tyler get all that money?

"Why so quiet?" Gabe asked. "If you're thinking about the horse thing . . ."

"Actually I wasn't, but now that you've brought it up, I wouldn't mind discussing it."

"We're here." He was out of the car and heading up the steps before I could say more. I followed him, peeved but also determined. Determined to find out more—about both Tyler and this man I'd married. One to appease my curiosity, the other to appease my heart.

SIX

GABE'S SIDE OF the bed was empty the next morning. I dressed in anticipation of another muggy day, putting on white cotton shorts, a pink T-shirt that said "Mahi's Fish Taco," and a new pair of leather Nikes. Gabe sat alone at the breakfast table reading the *Wichita Eagle*. He was dressed in cotton shorts and a tank top, his hair damp and unruly from his run.

"How far did you run this morning?" I asked.

"Only two miles. The radio this morning said the humidity is already eighty-nine percent. I remember now why I left Kansas. Mom's gone to Wichita for some kind of ex-teacher's meeting. She left biscuits in the oven."

I tried to make myself look disappointed. The big smile on my face must have given me away.

"You could try a little harder to get to know her," Gabe said wryly, looking over the newspaper at me. "Try giving her a chance."

Somehow it seemed to have flown right over his head that she didn't seem real anxious to get to know me. "Maybe we should talk about what other things in your life you've kept hidden from me," I answered, pouring myself a cup of coffee. I slathered a biscuit with butter and blackberry jam, giving him time to digest my point.

He gave an irritated grunt and retreated behind the paper.

"So, what are we going to do today?" I said after my third biscuit.

He folded up the paper and set it on the table. "I thought I'd go look up some old high-school friends. Then I'll probably go see Rob. Otherwise, I'm just going to goof off. You want to come?"

"No, thanks. How about giving me an idea about what fun things there are to do in the Derby metropolitan area?"

"Don't you have some quilt thing with Becky?"

"That's not until three o'clock." I glanced at the plastic sunflower clock on the wall behind him. "It's only ten-thirty."

"I could drop you off at the mall in Wichita."

I contemplated that. "I'm not in the mood to shop. Why don't you just drop me off downtown? I'll find the feed store. I'll need some gloves to work with Sinful. Maybe I'll walk over to Otis's. It's not that far, is it?"

"About three miles. I don't want you walking that far in this heat. Let me grab a quick shower, and you can take me to the police station. I'll bum Dewey's truck off him, and you can have the car. By the way, we're having dinner with him and Cordie June tonight."

"Oh, boy," I said, rolling my eyes. "Maybe she and I can play jacks while you two men discuss grown-up stuff."

"Brat," he said, laughing.

After dropping him off, I drove down Madison, Derby's main street, and pulled into the dusty parking lot of Harlow's Feed and Grain. I wondered if Janet and Lawrence's troublemaking daughter, Megan, was working today. Two vehicles were parked in front—an old Jeep Wrangler with ripped front seats and a faded red Suburban. The usual Purina checkerboard sign proclaimed that Harlow's was the place to shop for dog, rabbit, cat, and chicken chow. A rusty cowbell on the wooden screen door announced my entrance. I inhaled the familiar feed store smell of sweet hay and sharp, tangy ointments.

"Howdy," a female voice called from the back. "I'll be out in two shakes."

I smiled when Janet walked out from behind a row of veterinary supplies carrying a bundle of bills.

"You work here?" I asked. "I thought you ran a craft store."

"Run it and own it, fool that I am. Sunflower Quilts and Crafts, four blocks up the street. My sister's watching it today. I'm just helping out until . . ." Her voice trailed off.

"Have you heard anything?" I asked.

"No." She walked around the counter and opened the cash register, slipping the bills in. "Lawrence is going back into Wichita to see Rob this morning. He feels real bad about fighting with him last night. Megan, my daughter, is going with him. That's why I'm taking her shift today."

"Janet, where do you keep your Corona ointment?" a hoarse, good-natured female voice called across the store. "Darn, you're not out, are you? I haven't got time for a trip to Wichita today. I've got four horses to exercise and six lessons booked. And on such a pisser of a hot day, too." The woman abruptly stopped talking when she reached the counter and saw that Janet wasn't alone. "Oh, sorry. Didn't realize you had a customer." She was lean and freckled with gray-blond hair pulled back in a thick braid. I guessed her to be somewhere in her early forties; she wore bright blue Rocky Mountain jeans, a tight, cropped tank top, and tan manure-caked lace-up Ropers.

"This is Benni," Janet said. "Gabe's new wife."

Her pale green eyes flicked over me in a quick, condescending once-over. "Benni, huh? Where'd you get a name like that?"

"My given name is Albenia. My father's name is

Ben. My mother's was Alice."

She gave a curt nod. "Cute. So, how'd you meet our Gabe?"

"I was a suspect in one of his murder investigations."

She snorted and laughed, revealing a gold crown on one of her molars. "Leave it to Gabe. At least he didn't stoop to using the personal ads."

"Excuse me," I said, gritting my teeth. "I didn't catch your name."

"Where are my manners?" Janet said. "This is Belinda Champagne."

Dewey's ex-wife. I studied the woman with more interest now.

"Didn't you and Gabe even date at one time?" Janet asked Belinda.

"Once or twice," she said. "He never much cared for horsey women."

Involuntarily, my lips tightened. Was that meant to be a barb? I was at a disadvantage here because I didn't know how much she knew about me and my background. I was familiar with the superior attitude some horse people took with those not completely enamored of all things equine. Taking in my white cotton shorts, Nikes, and surfer-type T-shirt, she probably figured I was some kind of California beach bunny. I hated being judged by the clothes I wore or by whether I happened to have learned how to make a horse behave. And loving animals was no guarantee you were a decent human being. I've known some pretty rotten individuals who were great with horses, dogs, and cattle.

"That's certainly changed now, I'd imagine," Janet said diplomatically. "Benni grew up on a cattle ranch."

"That right?" Belinda looked at me with a bit more respect, but her voice was still tinged with sarcasm. "Well, gee willikers, a real-life cowgirl. So I guess you ride, then."

"Since I was two years old," I said stiffly.

"Well, if you get bored, come on out to the stables.

We've got some real solid little ponies, and they always need exercising.''

I thanked her and stood quietly while Janet found the ointment and walked Belinda out the door to the parking lot. I watched them through the rusty screen, suspecting their low conversation concerned Tyler's murder and Rob's attempted suicide. There was no way I could eavesdrop without being seen, so I tried on leather gloves until Janet came back into the store. I selected a pair of buttery-soft Berlin deerskins.

"I'm going to help Otis work his new horse," I said, explaining my purchase. "It'll give me something to do while Gabe is gallivanting around."

"You should take Belinda up on her offer, then," Janet suggested. "I know she seems a little gruff, but she's really a sweet person once you get to know her. I'm sure you two would get along famously."

"Maybe," I said, thinking, Not in this lifetime, honey. I had no intention of seeing that woman again. I slipped the gloves into my purse.

Janet gave a small embarrassed smile. "Well, I'm sure you'll be going out to the stable sometime during your visit. Dewey's so proud of his horses, he shows them off any chance he can get. He breeds quarter horses."

"I'm looking forward to it. He and Belinda both own the stable, right?"

"Yes, and it's worked out well for them even if their marriage didn't. They board a lot of horses for people in Wichita, and that helps pay for their breeding operation. He and his son, Chet, used to team-rope before Chet got bit by the bull-riding bug. Chet's going to compete this weekend at the Pretty Prairie Rodeo. Are you and Gabe going?"

"I don't know, but I imagine so if Dewey's son is going to ride in it."

"Well, come by Sunflower Quilts sometime before

you leave. We've got some wonderful Amish quilts and rugs you might like.''

"Sounds great. I will.''

I climbed back in the Camaro and pulled out of the parking lot trying to decide what I should do. It was getting close to noon and was already too hot and muggy to give Sinful or myself a workout. I drove through town and thought about the rest of the vacation looming ahead of me. When I reached the end of town and passed Derby Bowl, Angel happened to be climbing out of her white Toyota truck and spotted the Camaro. She gestured enthusiastically, so reluctantly I turned around and pulled into the parking lot. I had a feeling that from the street she couldn't tell who was driving. As I suspected, her face fell when she saw me step out of the car. She recovered quickly and tried to look friendly.

"Ran out of lowfat milk for the coffee,'' she said, pulling a Food 4 Less sack out of the truck's cab. "Senior citizen leagues,'' she explained.

I followed her into the twelve-lane bowling alley. All the lanes were full with laughing seniors wearing square-hemmed bowling shirts in a rainbow of colors. Their team names made me smile. Dial-A-Prayer, Retha's Raiders, Gutter Tramps, Bea's Bombers, Dusty's Tomatoes. The one thing I've always liked about bowlers is their wacky sense of humor.

"Let me put this away and I'll show you around the place,'' Angel said.

She filled the plastic cow-shaped milk servers on the snack bar counter and put the rest of the milk in the refrigerator. I studied the small bowling alley as she worked. Though they'd acquired modern computerized score-keeping equipment, the alley itself, with its orange, beige, and green plastic chairs and slow-moving ceiling fans circulating the cool air reminded me of the one I bowled at in San Celina before it closed down in the seventies.

"Let's go in my office,'' Angel said, pointing to a

white door behind the snack counter.

I declined the coffee she offered, and sat in the chair next to her desk. The office walls were bare except for a tarnished gold-framed picture of Kathryn, Gabe, Angel, and Becky that must have been taken in the early sixties. The girls looked to be about five or so, Gabe about eleven. In gold stick-on letters across the bottom were the words *Mi Vida*—My Life.

She noticed me studying it. "That hung in my father's office down at the garage until the day he died."

I didn't answer. I didn't know what to say to Angel. She and I hadn't hit it off all that well at the party, and so now, figuring the only other thing we had in common besides her brother was the murder, I asked, "Did you hear that they decided it was a brick that killed Tyler?"

"Yeah, Becky told me. That just means it could have been anyone."

"Yes, I suppose so." There was a minute of uncomfortable silence.

"Where's Gabe?" she asked.

"Meeting some old friends. And he's going to visit Rob again."

"Rob's an ass." Angel's intense brown eyes watched for my reaction.

"Do you think he killed her?" I asked. In the background, bowling pins rumbled across the wooden lanes. The bowlers gave thin, high cheers.

"He's too much of a wimp. This suicide thing is just for attention."

Since she seemed to be fairly open about it, I decided to push the conversation a little further. "So who do you think did it?"

"I imagine there were a lot of people who might want to kill her."

Her comment surprised me. "Why?" And who? I added silently.

She shrugged. "I've worked as a bartender for more

years than I care to admit. People like Tyler are a whole separate species."

"What do you mean?"

She propped her foot on the desk and fiddled with the laces on her sneakers. "Ambitious, competitive, willing to do anything to succeed."

"She didn't seem that way when I met her," I said. And I couldn't help remembering how she moved the audience when she sang. Perhaps I was naive, but I wanted to believe there was some depth to a talent like hers.

"Plenty of these creative types have got that 'public face' down pat. And some really *are* good people. It's difficult sometimes to figure out who's real and who's just playing you like a fiddle."

"You're saying Tyler was a fiddle player?"

"I'm just saying don't be fooled by her innocent demeanor. It took someone incredibly determined and one-track-minded to walk away from her family like she did." Angel took a big swallow of coffee. "And in my experience, people with one-track minds sometimes have a tendency to derail."

"Then who do you think did it?"

Her voice was low but penetrating, with a hint of laughter in it. "Could have been any of us, don't you think?"

"I don't think so," I asserted. "I, for one, had no reason to kill her. Neither did Gabe."

"That eliminates two out of what—thirty or forty?"

"So," I repeated, "who do you think might have done it?"

"You're as persistent as a yellow jacket, aren't you? Okay, Gabe says you like playing detective. Who do you think are likely suspects?"

"What about that fight that Rob and Lawrence had? Did it have any connection with Tyler?"

"I think they're both suspects, but that fight had to

do with Rob dating Lawrence's daughter. Now if Rob had been killed . . ."

"Okay, so it probably wasn't Lawrence, unless he was trying to hurt Rob through Tyler. What about the daughter? Was Megan there?"

"I don't recall her being there, but I'm sure she knew the party was going on. Not to mention she has one heck of a crush on Rob."

"So, who else?"

"Well, there's Cordie June."

"Yes, I can see that." I thought about the look on her face when Tyler captured the audience with her last song. "Jealousy is always a good motive for murder. But how would killing Tyler further Cordie June's career?"

"I don't know, but I know who would."

"Who?"

"One of their band members. When I worked as a bartender, I used to hang out with the guys in the band. Believe me, they know all the gossip and, for a few beers, are willing to dish it."

I thought of T.K., Tyler's friend and the lead guitarist in the band. How was he taking her death? And how much did he know?

"If Lawrence's daughter could have done it, so could Janet," I blurted, then immediately clamped my mouth shut, feeling my face turn warm. I'd forgotten for a moment that these people were Angel's friends, people she'd grown up with, and here I was dispassionately accusing them of murder.

"Janet . . ." Angel mused, apparently not insulted. "Could be."

Her nonchalance surprised me. "Doesn't this bother you? I mean, thinking of your friends as suspects in a murder?"

"Acquaintances," Angel said, giving me a jaded look. "I may have known them all my life, but that doesn't make them my friends."

"Say, Angel, have you seen . . . ?" Dewey stuck his head around the corner of the door and smiled when he saw me. "You're just the lady I'm hunting. I promised your husband I'd keep an eye on you, so I'm here to take you to one of Derby's finer dining establishments for lunch."

The idea that I needed checking on irritated me, but I tried to give Gabe the benefit of the doubt and assume he just didn't want me to have to eat lunch alone. "How'd you know I was here?"

"Not too many cherry-red Camaros in a town this size."

He leaned up against the wall of Angel's office, hands stuck in his pants pockets, jingling change. He looked entirely different today in a conservative navy sport coat, dark gray slacks, white shirt, and conservative tie. I'm always amazed at how dress clothes instantly give a man more perceived authority, and how often we make snap judgments about people, based solely on their attire. It made me think of Belinda this morning. There was no doubt in my mind she would have treated me differently had I been dressed in my everyday Wranglers and worn Justin boots. I thought of Cordie June and her flashy clothes worn with the sole purpose of attracting attention, and Tyler's sister, Hannah, and how her clothes were chosen for the exact opposite effect. It was inevitable, this immediate judging of people by outward appearances, but foolish.

"Looks like you're grinding some brain gears there," Dewey said. "What're you thinking about?"

"Nothing," I said, shaking my head and laughing. "Where are we going for lunch?"

"Gabe says you love foods of the cheap fried variety. Have I got a place for you!"

"You'll have to drive," he said, walking out to the parking lot. "I had a patrol officer drop me off. Your husband smooth-talked me out of my truck."

We drove five blocks to a cafe named Cricket's Coffee Hutch. It was twenty degrees cooler inside, and lunch started to sound actually appealing. The small restaurant had red gingham curtains and matching tablecloths. At the counter, a row of old men in stained overalls and Dickie workpants held up by elastic suspenders drank white mugs of coffee and vigorously debated some farm bill. Behind the front counter, rearranging an assortment of gum, candy bars, and chewing tobacco, was a tall middle-aged woman with thickly painted coral lips and a red hairdo that reminded me of a football helmet.

"Why, Detective Champagne," she said. "You sweet thing. Where have you been? It's been a dog's age since I've had the pleasure of serving a member of Derby's fine law enforcement." Her accent was deep South, though I couldn't tell from exactly where. "And who is this you got here? You're robbing the cradle again, you wicked boy. What have you done with little ole Cordie June?"

Dewey laughed. "Unfortunately, this one's not mine, Norma. This is Benni, Gabe Ortiz's new wife. They're here from California, visiting Kathryn."

"That right?" Her Joan Crawford eyebrows flew up with interest. "You know any movie stars? You know David Hasselhoff? From *Baywatch?* Honey, that man sends more than my heart aflutter, if you get my drift."

"No, I'm sorry," I said. "I live quite a bit north of Hollywood and Malibu. No movie stars in my neck of the woods."

"Shame," she said. "So, you're Kathryn's new daughter-in-law. You know she meets here once a week with the Friends of the Library. She was showing around a picture of her son a couple of weeks ago. He is one sexy-looking devil, I tell you what. I was real sorry to hear he'd been snatched up. And me not even getting a crack at him. Now, the special is roast beef and mashed potatoes. It's a good piece of meat—I picked it out myself—and it comes with salad and a big ole hunk of pecan pie. How's that sound?''

Dewey gave me an amused wink. ''Sound okay, Benni?''

''Fine,'' I said, smiling back at him. I wasn't about to nix anything this woman said.

Our food arrived quickly, and for fifteen minutes we ate and talked about Dewey's stable and horses and his successes and failures with breeding. I told him about meeting Belinda and her offer to ride some of their horses.

''Absolutely,'' he said, sipping his iced tea. ''I'll give you a tour tonight, and then you come on out whenever you want. We'll probably be having a barbecue this weekend, too, since Chet's in town and he just turned twenty-one last week. You going to come to see him ride in Pretty Prairie?''

''I wouldn't miss it,'' I said.

The mention of Chet got him started on what was, I could tell, a favorite subject. Chet was doing extremely well on the rodeo circuit this year, but had been on the road for three months solid. Dewey pulled out his wallet and unfolded a newspaper picture of his son stumbling away from a wild, slobbering bull, a painful grimace on his young face. ''Chet Champagne scores an astounding 91 riding Bobby's Axeman,'' the headline read.

''Here's what he looks like when he's not running from a crazy bull.'' Dewey handed me a picture of Chet flanked by his parents. The picture showed a good-looking young man with Belinda's lean frame and Dewey's dark hair and lazy smile.

''I bet you're real proud of him,'' I commented, handing back the clipping.

''He started rodeoing when he was just four years old,'' Dewey said, folding the article up carefully. ''Rode in the Li'l Britches Rodeo. You should have seen him bouncing off that old lamb, picking himself back up like a pro, not shedding a tear. I thought Belinda was going to break the fence down running out there to help him up. He pushed her away and told her he didn't need no help, thank you very much. He's going to be World Champion All Around soon, mark my words." He rubbed the back of his fingers across his jaw. "That boy is the best thing that Belinda and I ever did together."

I noticed that he didn't mention his daughter, and I wondered just what the circumstances surrounding her death were. By the time Norma served us our pecan pie and refilled our iced teas for the third time, we were talking as if we'd known each other forever. I could understand how Dewey and Gabe were attracted to each other as friends. Dewey, for all his joking, had an easy air about him—a way of cocking his head and really listening to your words that made him enjoyable to talk to. He was the perfect complement to Gabe's often reticent and distrusting personality.

"How's the investigation going?" I asked casually.

He opened a packet of sugar, dumped it in his iced tea, and gave me an indulgent smile. "Gabe said you'd eventually get around to asking that."

"I'm not asking you to reveal any department secrets," I said crisply. "I'm just interested."

"Gabe said you'd say that, too."

I looked back down at my half-eaten pie, really irritated now.

He reached over and took my hand, shaking it gently. "Now, don't go getting mad at Gabe. He's just concerned about your safety."

"If I had a quarter for every time I heard that one . . ."

He laughed and pushed his empty pie plate aside. "Actually, I don't have any problem talking to you about the case. There's still not much to go on. You saw how many people were at the party. Technically, any of them had the opportunity. On the other hand, we haven't found anyone who has an overt motive to want her dead. Yet."

"What about the money in the bank book Hannah gave me?"

"Gabe gave it to me this morning. I passed it on to the Sheriff's investigator. It's interesting, but she could have just been an excellent saver." He ran his fingers up and down the side of his sweating glass.

"Somehow in her line of work, I find that hard to believe. You don't save that kind of money singing in cheap bars here and there or by picking up buck-and-a-half tips waitressing in coffee shops."

"There is certainly some truth to that, Benni Harper. But, as my mom used to say, it'll all come out in the wash eventually. She had four sons, so that little piece of wisdom had real meaning in our household."

There was silence between us for a few minutes. I wanted to ask more, but I restrained myself. I wasn't sure how much they were telling Dewey, since he was technically a suspect, and how much that bothered him. Eventually our conversation started up again and turned to the one thing we had in common besides horses and Tyler's murder.

"What was Gabe like as a kid?" I asked.

Dewey sat back and rested his arm across the back of the booth. "Not much different than he is now. Quiet, kinda moody, absolutely fearless. He was always willing to try anything once. But stubborn. As my mom would say, he was so obstinate he wouldn't move camp for a prairie fire. We all used to get into some hairy situations as kids, but there was one thing about Gabe. If he didn't want to do something, no amount of teasing or pushing could change his mind. He was the same way in 'Nam. Most of the time he went along with the program, but when he didn't, that was it. He was a stone. Of course, how people viewed him never seemed to bother Gabe. I always wondered if it was because he felt so different anyway, being part Mexican and all."

"I've wondered that myself," I said. "He's never

mentioned feeling different from everyone else, but I imagine it must have affected him and Angel and Becky as children.''

Dewey motioned at the busboy to refill our water glasses. ''Well, it didn't seem like it. They were all real popular in school. Becky was a cheerleader. Angel couldn't have possibly gone on all the dates she was asked on in high school, from what I hear. And Gabe . . . he was our star quarterback until Kathryn sent him to California during his junior year. And, I don't mean to make you nervous, but ever since he was a kid the girls have sashayed around him like mares in heat.''

I played with the remains of my pie and smiled. ''He said that was how the girls acted with Rob.''

''Well, it's true, but he gave Rob a good run for his money. Lawrence and I were lucky enough to get their leftovers sometimes.'' He gave me a wry smile. Remembering that Belinda said she and Gabe had dated briefly, I wondered if that was what he meant.

''Gabe doesn't talk much about Vietnam,'' I said. ''But he did say one time that you were as nervy as a badger.''

''A stupid-ass kid is more like it. I had this thing about walking point. You know, the guy that's in the front of everyone, checking everything out? Wanted to set the record for the most times, like some kind of Pete Rose of the jungle or something. I kept track by scratching marks inside my helmet. I don't know where my brain was. All the times I charged ahead without thinking about what was up ahead. I could have got my friggin' brains blown out.'' His eyes darkened in memory.

''You weren't thinking. That's part of being young. So, was that why your nickname was Cowboy?''

He grinned. ''Where'd you hear that?''

''I saw an old picture of you and Gabe and some other guy. It was on your helmet.'' I paused, trying to decide whether I should ask any more questions. I wanted to hear about Gabe's experiences in Vietnam, but I would have preferred hearing about them from him.

"Yeah, well, being smaller than the other guys probably had something to do with it, too."

"What do you mean?"

His grin widened. "As if you don't know. You're a tiny little thing, and I'll bet you a week's wages that if I took you out to my stables right now, you'd want to ride the biggest, wildest, meanest old stallion I got on the place just to prove you can."

I grinned back at him. "Well, I don't think I'm going to answer that on the grounds it might incriminate me."

He laughed and drained his glass. "You've been hanging out with cops too long." He glanced at his watch. "I've got to get back to work. You want to drop me off at the station, or am I going to have to hoof it in this heat?"

"I guess I'll give you a lift, since you were kind enough to buy me lunch."

"I'm buying?" he asked, feigning surprise.

"You bet."

When we reached the police department, I asked him how Rob was doing.

"From what I hear, he's going home today."

"You don't think he did it, do you?"

He shook his finger at me in mock admonishment and climbed out of the car. "See you tonight" was all he said.

Dense heat shimmered over the hood of the car as I watched him walk through the brilliant sunlight into the brick building. I turned the air conditioner on high and headed for the Presbyterian church. The disc jockey on KYQQ joked about the steamy weather. "Folks, this is going to be one of your woman-stabs-fiancé-with-steak-knife kind of nights, so head on out to Prairie City Nights where the beer is cold and the music is hot. Tonight, Snake Poison Posse featuring Cordie June Rodell. Don't miss it!"

It certainly didn't take her long to get over her grief, I thought, then chided myself. What did I expect Cordie June and the band to do, give up their careers? I tried to ignore the little twitch in the back of my mind that said a week off in consideration of Tyler's death wouldn't have been too much to ask. But, the other side of me argued, most musicians and singers lived on the edge and needed every penny they could make. Some of them had families to support. Which started me thinking about Tyler's bank book again, and how Dewey hadn't really told me anything about the case and how he'd avoided the subject in such a pleasant, unassuming way. He was probably an excellent interrogator. He'd just talk so sweet and friendly that before you knew it, you were confessing to whatever it was he wanted, just so you could make his day a little easier.

I found Becky standing behind a wooden podium in the church's recreation hall going through her notes. The room was blessedly cool.

"Oh, good, you made it," she said. She shuffled the papers in front of her. "Usually our meetings are in the evening, but the choir has something going on tonight so we had to make it earlier. Most of the ladies who work outside the home are probably coming here on their lunch hour, so we'll make it a fast meeting." People started arriving at this point, and I left Becky to the myriad discussions that many of the thirty-odd members needed to have with her. After getting my guest name tag, I perused the flyer table and was talked into purchasing five raffle tickets for the opportunity quilt the guild made for the show—an Amish-style Double Pinwheel in aqua, black, gold, bright pink, and green copied from an 1875 Amish pattern.

Never having been involved in a quilt guild, I settled down with a glass of lemonade and a large raisin-studded oatmeal cookie and watched the proceedings with interest, thinking some of the procedures might be adapted to our co-op meetings. Becky moved rapidly through the business part of the meeting—approval of last month's minutes, various announcements, the librarian's report and good-natured scolding for overdue books, a progress report on the guild's latest philanthropy program, making child-size quilts for Derby and Wichita police officers to give to youngsters taken out of abusive home situations. She moved on to Block-of-the-Month, Secret Pals, and the "Elvis Lives" Quilt Challenge. The Elvis quilts would be unveiled and displayed at the opening of the quilt show this Friday night. Finally, there was a vote on donating a hundred dollars to a reward fund that had been started for Tyler by the members of her band and employees of Prairie City Nights. Apparently Tyler had been a not-very-active member of the quilt guild.

Becky announced the official meeting adjourned and told the women to break up into their separate committees to discuss final plans for the show. I sat on the edge of Becky's committee, half-listening to her discuss set-up and take-down procedures as I scanned the guild's July newsletter. The lemonade finally seeped down to my bladder, and I slipped away, hunting a restroom. I spotted one down a long corridor and opened the door. Hearing someone inside mention Tyler's name caused me to stop with the door half open and blatantly eavesdrop.

"I just don't agree with it," a woman's voice said from one of the two stalls. "I love Becky to pieces, but donating the guild's money to a reward fund. I mean, really. Tyler may have paid her twenty-five-dollar yearly dues and come to a few meetings, but that doesn't make her one of us."

"I guess it's the thought," the woman in the other stall answered. "She wasn't my kind of person, but she did make beautiful quilts."

"I still find it hard to believe she was ever Amish."

"From what I hear, she did seem to take to the worldly life awfully easy. Buck says that innocent act of hers got them more bookings. Men just couldn't say no to her."

"That's right, your brother-in-law's in her band. I'd forgotten all about that. How are they all taking it?"

"Hard, of course. The guys in the band liked her real well. Buck says she always treated them real respectful, which is more than you can say for Cordie June."

"Really?"

"I guess Cordie June's practicing her temperamental artist act, 'cause Buck says sometimes they want to wring her skinny neck she gets so high on her horse. Her and Tyler used to fight about that all the time. Tyler was smarter than Cordie June, that way. She knew which side to butter her bread. Buck says the backup band can do a lot to make a singer look good or bad. You know, my money is on Cordie June. According to Buck, she has a real hot temper. He said one time he worked with her in a bar in Kansas City, and she tried to stab another woman with a fingernail file for insulting her outfit."

"No kidding! Do you think . . . ?"

I heard the toilet flush and started to back out.

"Now, Marsha, it's a long way from stabbing someone with a fingernail file and outright killing somebody. Besides, you know about Lawrence and Tyler. Maybe *he* did it. I'm just glad that Janet wasn't here today. That hundred dollars would have been the very last straw on that camel's back. Sometimes Becky's just *too* nice, you know? Anyway, Buck says Lawrence . . ."

The stall door opened, and I never heard what Buck said about Lawrence and Tyler. To avoid getting caught, I ducked in the men's room next door and, since I was there, decided to make use of it. I heard Marsha and her friend chattering past the door, and I waited a few minutes before cautiously peeking my head out to see if the coast was clear. What they had to say started

me really wondering about Cordie June. And about
Lawrence. Maybe that fight between him and Rob at
Becky's party didn't actually have anything to do with
Lawrence's daughter, Megan. With a little voice that
sounded an awful lot like Gabe's telling me none of this
was my business, I wondered just how competitive Tyler
and Cordie June had really been, and where Lawrence
fit into Tyler's life besides being her boss. As the owner-
manager of the club, maybe he had ultimate say in who
was the headliner. What would Tyler do to get that spot?
What would Cordie June do to snatch it away? Even
though I knew I'd get a lecture, I couldn't wait to tell
Gabe all this. Then again, why should he get mad? I
hadn't gone looking for this information. It just dropped
in my lap. Serendipity.

The committees had broken up by the time I came
back into the recreation hall, and most of the guild members were gathering up their purses and leaving. I
scanned the crowd of women and wondered which ones
were Marsha and her gossipy friend.

"Where have you been?" Becky said, coming over
to me. "When's Gabe supposed to be home and what
are you two doing for dinner tonight?"

"In the bathroom," I said. "And we're having dinner
with Dewey."

"Well, drop by if you get away early, though knowing Dewey, you probably won't. He'll show you his stables, and we'll never see you again."

I laughed. "I'm not that bad. Besides, I'm going to
help Otis with Sinful, so you'll be seeing plenty of me,
I'm sure."

She glanced at her watch. "Oh, dear, it's five o'clock
already. Stan's going to be home soon. I still have to
pick up the girls at the community center. I guess it's a
Charlie's Chicken and Barbecue night."

Kathryn's beige Plymouth was in the driveway when
I drove up. I walked into the living room and was
greeted by my friend Daphne. She shot a halfhearted

snap in my direction, not bothering to get up because of the heat.

"You know, there are certain groups of people in this world who would gladly put you in a stewpot," I told her.

"Oh, you're back." Kathryn walked into the living room with a startled look on her face. She held an embroidered tea towel in her hands. I felt myself flush and wondered if she'd heard my comment. "Where's Gabe?" she asked, her face becoming bland again. Maybe her hearing is going, I thought optimistically.

"Still with his friends, I guess."

We contemplated each other silently for a moment. Gabe's coming and goings seemed to be the only topic of conversation we'd been able to manage so far. I stood there awkwardly searching my mind for something to keep the conversation going.

"Well," she said finally, "are you finding enough to do around our little town? There are some museums in Wichita, and we do have two malls. I'm sure they're not what you're accustomed to, but they're quite nice."

"I'm keeping busy," I said politely, wondering where she thought I lived in California—Beverly Hills? "If Gabe doesn't have anything planned, I think I'll go out to Otis's tomorrow and work with his horse."

"Yes, well, that's good," she said, folding the tea towel carefully. Luckily, before either of us was forced into thinking up any more painfully polite small talk, Gabe walked in.

After promising his mother that tomorrow night for sure we'd have dinner with her, he started up the stairs to change. I dogged his heels, listening to him reminisce about his old friends, waiting for him to finish so I could bring up what I'd heard at the quilt guild meeting.

"So, did Dewey take you out to lunch?" he asked.

"Yes, sir, Chief Ortiz," I answered. "He kept a *real* good eye on me. And he even took off the handcuffs to let me eat."

"That's not how I meant it," he protested. I poked him in the stomach when his T-shirt was only halfway off. "Hey, offsides. Ten-yard penalty."

"I'll penalize you, Friday," I said, poking him again.

"You'll what?" He laughed and, using his shirt as a lasso, slipped it around my neck and pulled me to him. "Now, tell me again what you're going to do to me?" We kissed deeply; he dropped the shirt and moved his hands down to hold me firmly in the small of my back. His chest was hot and damp, and a deliciously familiar desire rose up in me.

"*Querida*," he whispered. "You're driving me crazy."

I broke away. "Put an ice pack on it, pal. We've got a dinner date with Dewey and Cordie June. Did you find out what time?"

He glanced at the nightstand clock. "We're supposed to meet him in thirty minutes. We're going to a steak place in Wichita." He reached into the closet where he'd neatly hung all his shirts and pulled out a white polo shirt.

"Steak? You? Isn't he aware you are no longer a bovine flesh eater?"

He pulled the shirt over his head. "They have fish, too, Miss Smart Mouth. Just don't come crying to me when they're having to ream out your veins so your blood can find a path to your heart."

I clasped my hands to my chest dramatically and fell backward on the bed. "Oh, baby, I get so turned on when you talk healthy. Please, tell me about protein supplements again and I'll tear my clothes off right now."

He balled up his damp T-shirt and threw it at me. "You're asking for trouble big time, *niña*."

I slipped on clean denim Wranglers, a pink sleeveless shirt, and boots. I was looking forward to seeing Dewey again and to touring his stables. On the twenty-minute drive to the restaurant, I filled Gabe in on what I'd heard at the guild meeting.

"You shouldn't be involved in this," he said predictably.

"Look, I'm telling you everything I hear just so you can't say I don't trust you."

That had been a bone of contention between us from the first time we met—my tendency to, as he puts it, run off half-cocked. "I'd fire you in two minutes if you worked for me," he'd told me more than once. "Hot-doggers only get themselves or other people hurt or killed."

"I still don't like you snooping around," he said now.

"I *wasn't* snooping around," I argued. "I happened to overhear an interesting conversation while seeking a place to answer nature's call. And let's not forget I *am* telling you about it."

"That's true," he reluctantly conceded.

"So, what do you think? I mean, about Cordie June? And about Lawrence? What do you think the thing between him and Tyler was?"

He was quiet for a moment, then slowly pulled the car over to the side of the road and stopped. He flexed his fingers on the steering wheel for a few seconds before facing me. The muscle under his eye twitched again. "Benni, these people are my friends. I grew up with Lawrence. When I was six years old he gave me my first bloody nose. He was quite a fighter."

"Lawrence?" I exclaimed, astonished. Remembering the fight at the party, it appeared my theory was once again proven true; you really can't judge people by outward appearances.

Gabe's mustache tilted in a glimmer of a smile. "He hit me with his Superman lunchbox because I smashed his Twinkie. I deserved it." His smile disappeared. "The point is, I grew up with these guys, and you want me to speculate whether one of them is a cold-blooded killer. Would you want to consider Elvia or Miguel or Mac in that light?"

His naming of my best friend, one of her younger brothers, and the local minister who had been a child-hood buddy brought me up short. He was right. I wasn't considering his feelings in this. These people were strangers to me; it didn't matter to me who the killer was. But to him they were his personal history, a part of who he was and is.

"I'm sorry," I said, laying my hand lightly on his forearm. "I wasn't even thinking. Honestly, I didn't go looking for that information. I just overheard it. Should I just ignore it next time?"

He ran his fingers through his black hair. "No, that wouldn't be right. Tell me if you hear anything else, and I'll pass it on to Dewey. As for the thing between Lawrence and Tyler, if those two ladies from the guild knew about it, I'm certain Dewey knows, too."

I didn't answer because I didn't agree with him. In my experience, there'd been more times when the women I knew sensed a conflict or fluctuation in a relationship long before the men did. I don't know if most females communicate better or just flat out pay more attention to the people around them, but I suspect Randy Travis sang the answer best when he sagely pointed out that old men sit around and talk about the weather and old women sit around and talk about old men.

Gabe restarted the car. "I'm glad *that's* settled," he said in a tone that implied he was crossing something off a list. I wasn't quite sure what it was we got settled, but I wasn't about to debate it right before meeting Dewey and Cordie June.

The decor at the restaurant, Buffalo Barney's Hoof and Fin, was strictly Hollywood Western, but the Midwestern steaks were cornfed, thick, and juicy, and even Gabe had to compliment the cook's broiled Alaska salmon. In her heehaw accent, Cordie June, dressed in a minuscule red suede skirt and chest-hugging matching vest, kept us laughing with tales of one-night gigs at county fairs and redneck bars back in Oklahoma. When she turned on the charm, Cordie June was an original, no doubt about it.

"I swear," she said, holding up a long-nailed hand.

''There was chicken-wire fence in front of the stage so we wouldn't get hit by flying beer bottles. Out near Hooker, Oklahoma. They got some rowdy bars out there on the panhandle. You gotta really want it to keep going through that kind of crap.'' She grimaced. ''But my daddy was a mean old Okie dirt farmer who raised me not to take no shit from no one. 'Cordelia June,' he'd say to me, 'don't you never take no shit from no one, girl, or I'll whip your butt.' '' She gave a throaty laugh. ''He always told me there wasn't nobody gonna give me a free ride in this ole world, and that old fart was right as rain.''

No one mentioned Tyler or her murder until we were sipping iced tea and picking at the remains of our strawberry shortcake. Cordie June wasn't going with us to the stables because, as I'd heard on the radio, she and the band were playing at Prairie City Nights that evening.

''We're making an announcement about Tyler's reward fund before each set,'' she said, licking her skinny straw. ''Are y'all coming by later?''

''Not tonight, babe,'' Dewey said. ''How about tomorrow?'' He looked at Gabe and me. ''That okay with you two?''

Gabe looked at me, and I nodded. ''Count us in,'' he said.

''Okay,'' Cordie June said. ''I'll tell Lawrence to reserve y'all a table.'' She slipped her fringed leather purse over her shoulder and nudged Dewey with her hip. ''I need to hit the little cowgirls room before I drive to the club.'' She stood up and tugged at the bottom of her short skirt, causing the Western-clad waiter behind her to almost drop his tray of dessert samples.

''I'll join you,'' I said.

''Why do women always go in pairs?'' Dewey said, giving Gabe a mystified look. ''Is it some kind of herd instinct, this desire to pee in unison?''

I turned to Gabe and said sweetly, ''Slap him around a little while we're gone, okay?''

''My pleasure, ma'am,'' he said.

Dewey groaned. "Gabe, Gabe, old buddy, only five months married and already—"

"Your comment better not have any feline references in it," I warned over my shoulder.

"Henpecked," Dewey finished. Their hearty laughter followed us.

The women's restroom was huge and designed to look like a Western brothel with red-flocked wallpaper and fancy gold-plated faucets. In front of the gilded mirror, picking at her lion's mane of hair, Cordie June rambled on about the songs she was singing that night and how her greatest dream was to sing in the Grand Ole Opry before her daddy died. I inspected my thirty-five-year-old complexion, trying not to compare it to hers, only half-listening until I heard the word "producer."

"I'm sorry," I said. "What did you say?" I pulled a comb out of my purse and, trying not to look directly at her, poked at my own curls.

"I said a real famous producer from Nashville is passin' through here for a Randy Travis concert, and he's dropping by to see the band perform tomorrow night. It could be my . . . our big break. All you need these days is the right management." She pulled a miniature can of hair spray out of her purse and misted her glossy hair and everyone in the general vicinity. "I heard he was the one who made Trisha Yearwood famous." In the mirror, her shiny lips tightened around the edges. "You know, sometimes you only get one shot in life. I intend to take advantage of it."

"Cordie June, you're what—twenty-two, twenty-three? You have lots of time."

She gave her hair one last look and turned to me, her expression uncompromising. "You don't know what it's like. They're grooming people younger and younger to be stars now. It's not just talent, it's looks and age, too. I saw the video of a girl the other day who just turned seventeen. She's landed a million-dollar contract promoting her music *and* a line of Western clothes for J.C.

Penney's. She's got a killer first single, she looks like dynamite, and she's almost six years younger'n me. Believe me, every minute counts.''

"Amazing," I said, trying to ignore the questions racing through my mind. How long had everyone known about this producer's visit? Was it Tyler he was expecting to see? And most of all, just how far would Cordie June go to eliminate her competition?

SEVEN

When we rejoined the men, Dewey walked Cordie June to her car, and Gabe and I waited while they said an affectionate goodbye. Under his cream-colored Stetson, Dewey's face was flushed when he came over to our car.

"I'd be careful if I were you, Dewey," Gabe said. "Looks like she's causing that old blood pressure to rise a little too high. Men your age . . ."

Dewey grinned and ignored Gabe's teasing. "The stable's about ten miles from here. Just follow me. And try to obey the speed limits this time, Chief Ortiz." He winked at me.

We followed Dewey over back country roads, eventually turning down a long gravel driveway through a field of freshly-turned-over soil. The air had a sweet grassy smell, like cooking hops. A faded green tractor sat in the middle of the field like a toy abandoned by a child. In the distance, about a half mile from the road, I could see the stables surrounded by a grove of huge cottonwood trees. We passed under a metal archway that spelled out "Champagne Quarter Horses" in fancy black wrought iron. The sharp, hot wind that always seemed to be cropping up swung the varnished wood sign under it: "Horses boarded and trained—Dewey Champagne—Belinda Champagne."

"They must have had an amicable divorce to be able to work together," I commented.

"I think she's still hoping he'll come back," Gabe said. I looked over at him, my mouth wide open in surprise.

"*You* know a piece of gossip? I don't believe it. Where did you hear that?"

"Angel or Becky, I can't remember who told me." He reached over and gave my chin a gentle shake. "Close your mouth. The flies in Kansas have been known to choke people. I know a lot more than you think. I just don't go around announcing it every chance I get."

I swiped his hand away. "Telling your wife is not announcing it. It's called communication. Want me to spell it for you?"

"Brat," he said good-naturedly, pulling the car to a stop.

"Despot," I retorted.

"Very good. Dove will be thrilled to hear you are utilizing the college education she paid for."

"What are you two arguing about?" Dewey said, coming around and opening my door.

"She's begging to move to Kansas, and I said no," Gabe replied. Leave it to him to find the one thing that could make me laugh.

"Quit making fun of your roots," Dewey told him. "You might be able to fool other people, but I know the real you. You're a flatlander at heart."

"Shut up and show us around," Gabe said.

Behind the long ranch-style house were four breeze-way barns containing, I guessed from their size, thirty enclosed stalls. Most of them sounded full, which meant Dewey probably boarded about a hundred horses, give or take a few. It was an impressive operation for a mostly rural area where many people kept their horses on their own property.

"Either of you want something to drink?" Dewey asked. We both declined, but he got himself a bottle of Samuel Adams and drank it as he gave us a quick tour. His pride in the stables was apparent in his quiet enthusiasm. He and Belinda had built a first-class stable that included a large, spotless training arena with a set of redwood bleachers, two hot walkers, two bullpens, an indoor wash rack with hot and cold water, and a tack room so organized it resembled a store. Bridles, halters, whips, saddles—everything was in its place, clean and labeled. Champagne Stables was the most immaculate stable I'd ever seen. As he was showing us a rose-and-maple-leaf-carved Charles Hape saddle he'd just had custom made, a young girl wearing tan English breeches, shiny black boots, and a pink Beauty and the Beast T-shirt walked in and threw a bridle haphazardly up on an empty hook.

"Hey, Sarah," Dewey said sharply. "You know better than that. Hang it right." He tossed his empty beer bottle in a plastic-lined trash can.

She rolled her eyes dramatically, but walked back and rehung the bridle properly.

I laughed. "You're as bad as Gabe. For Pete's sake, you've both been out of the Marines for twenty years. Are you ever going to relax?"

"Relax and you're dead," they said simultaneously, then looked at each other and laughed.

"Sergeant Cochran's first rule of thumb," Gabe said.

"Sergeant Cochran?" I asked.

"Our drill instructor," said Dewey. "Meanest man who ever lived, but his training probably saved our *huevos* more than once."

"Well, as irritating as compulsively neat people can be to live with . . ." I dodged the back of Gabe's hand swatting at my butt. "Just like Gabe, you're probably a great investigator."

"Watch it," Gabe said. "She's buttering you up for use later on."

"Well, whatever this little lady wants, I'd probably do it." Dewey gave me a friendly smile. "I have to admit, I've acquired quite a soft spot for your wife already."

I smirked at Gabe and unfortunately wasn't quick enough to miss his hand this time. "Hey, cut it out," I said. "That's police brutality."

"Settle down, you two," Dewey said, "or I'll have to put you both to work." As we followed him back through the stalls toward the house, he explained the way he and Belinda ran the stable. "Belinda supervises most of the day-to-day stuff—lessons and exercising and the shows we put on for the kids a couple of times a year. I see to the breeding and the paperwork and working with some of the rougher horses. We just bought a new stud—Apache's Red Power. He's a Thoroughbred just off the track."

We stopped at Apache's stall, where he was pawing at the fresh wood shavings. He was black as a night sky, with an almost blue sheen to his coat. He had the lean head and the lanky, matchstick legs of a quality Thoroughbred. Hearing Dewey's voice, the horse's small, neat ears pricked and turned like little radar dishes. Dewey reached over the stall door and stroked the stallion's neck. "Never intended on owning a Thoroughbred. Too temperamental for me. But the price was right. And he was kind of a challenge. He might make a good riding horse yet."

"He's beautiful," I said, reaching over and fondling his soft muzzle. Apache blew an excited, watery breath. I stroked his dark face. "No treats today, Apache," I said. "Maybe next time I come, after we get better acquainted." I looked up at Dewey and smiled winningly.

"No way," he said, shaking his head firmly. "I won't even let Belinda or any of the stablehands ride him."

"Just around the arena. Just once," I coaxed.

"I told you she was buttering you up for something," Gabe said, laughing.

"Please," I begged.

"There are plenty of other good horses around here for you to ride," Dewey answered.

"But I want to ride Apache."

"Nope, sorry."

"Why not?"

"Because I said so."

"But . . ."

He pulled his hat off and gently smacked the top of my head. "But nothing." He grinned at me, teasing, and I knew that was the best answer I was going to get.

"Well, I think that stinks."

He turned to Gabe. "Is she always this persistent?"

"You haven't seen anything yet," Gabe assured him.

"You know," I said, "I can probably handle that stud better than either of you. You don't need a . . . more weight to let a horse know who's boss."

They were teasing me about my comment when two preteen girls walked a mare past us and cross-tied her a few feet away from Apache's stall. The mare let all of us know she was in season as she sprayed the ground with urine, releasing her scent into the stable. Apache, reacting as nature compelled him, started kicking at his stall and letting out loud whinnies. The girls giggled and started brushing the mare. Apache blew air loudly and kicked at the door with his front leg.

"Get that mare outta here," Dewey snapped at the two girls. "Go groom her somewhere else." Apache tossed his head and kicked a dent in the back of his stall. The girls led the mare out, giggling again as they passed Apache. "Oh, be quiet," one of the girls called to the agitated stallion.

"Dang stable rats," Dewey muttered at the girls. He went over to Apache and started murmuring under his breath. "Calm down, fella. There you go. That old mare's not worth breaking a leg over." He looked over at us. "Let's go in the house and have a drink." As we followed him out of the stable, Gabe reached over and patted the horse's forehead.

"I know how you feel, old boy."

"Very funny," I said, bumping him with my hip.

Dewey's large brick house was set off from the stables about a football field's distance away. I was curious about where Belinda lived, though that was a question I knew I'd be better off asking Becky. Once inside, he poured me a Coke, Gabe a mineral water, and grabbed a couple of bottles of Samuel Adams for himself. We settled down in the spacious, distinctly western-style living room decorated in rusts, browns, and tans with rawhide lamp shades, end tables with tiny wagon-wheel carvings, and striped Pendleton blanket-type fabric on the sofa and loveseat. The subject of Apache came up again.

"I'm going to talk you into letting me ride him," I announced.

"Not a chance," Dewey said.

"Did you hear about Otis's poker horse?" Gabe asked.

"Heard about it?" Dewey said, giving a loud chortle. "I was at the game. The guy who lost was royally pissed, but he's one of those old boys who just doesn't know when to pack it in. How's Old Sinful doing?"

"I'm going to go out and work with him tomorrow," I said.

"He's a nice-looking gelding. Kind of green, but nothing you can't handle. He's a good horse for you." I frowned at him, annoyed at his macho I-know-what's-best-for-you tone. He ignored my look and went over to a liquor cabinet where he filled an old-fashioned glass from a half-empty fifth of Jim Beam bourbon. "Sure you don't want something stronger than that fizzy water, Gabe?" He held up the bottle of bourbon.

"No, this is fine," Gabe said evenly.

Dewey downed his drink and poured another. "Suit yourself."

While he and Gabe reminisced about an old high-school escapade that involved a dead frog, bread crumbs, and a squeamish home economics teacher, I wandered around the living room looking at the pictures on the walls. Photographs of Chet from babyhood to his latest rodeo covered almost every inch of the rough paneling. Working my way around the room, I followed the life of Dewey's son. One recent picture showed Chet and a smiling young girl of about sixteen or seventeen. This must have been DeeDee, the daughter who died. I reached back into my memory for what Gabe had said. Thrown off a horse and killed. Flashing the unknown photographer a dazzling smile, DeeDee looked so young and happy, it was hard to believe she was dead. She wore tight red jeans, a ruffled white cowboy shirt, and a tall, pale cowboy hat with a fancy feather band. A white sash across her chest announced in gold glitter: Miss Rodeo Sedgwick County.

"That's my little girl." Dewey's voice rumbled behind me. I turned and looked up at him. His face held a dark expression, and his breath was sharp from the bourbon. "I shot the mare that killed her."

"I'm sorry," I said.

He shrugged and turned back to Gabe. While the two of them talked about some truck that Gabe's dad bought the year he was born, I wandered over to a built-in bookcase that flanked the liquor cabinet. Dewey's choice of reading matter was predictable for someone who raised horses—various veterinary books, books on equine lineage and breeding, back issues of *Western Horseman* magazine. He also owned a large collection of books on Vietnam. I pulled out books randomly, leafing through them. He seemed to prefer oral histories; something he and I had in common. As biased as they sometimes are, I've always felt that in the long run they give us a more accurate representation of an era than any accounts found in a history book. I pulled out a paperback that, judging by the softness of its cover, had obviously been read or thumbed through many times. I opened it to the middle to look at the pictures, and found an old war photograph stuck there.

The photograph showed the weathered back of a man's neck and a young, sober-faced Gabe facing the camera. Gabe's eyes were shaded by his helmet, but even minus his thick mustache, the proud, stubborn set of his jaw was as familiar to me now as Dove's nagging. His worn camouflage fatigues were rumpled but clean, and it appeared as if he'd just shaved. The man facing him was pinning something on Gabe's shirt; his beefy hand concealed the shape of it. "Oh," I exclaimed.

The men stopped talking and looked over at me. "What is it?" Gabe asked. Dewey came over and took the picture out of my hand.

"Well, I'll be dipped. I wondered what had happened to this picture. I was talking to Chet about it the other day when I told him you were coming out from California. I was telling him how he would have never been here to ride bulls or anything else if it hadn't been for my good brave buddy, Gabe Ortiz." Dewey's words slurred slightly, and I couldn't tell if it was just the liquor or if there was a tinge of sarcasm in his voice.

I glanced over at Gabe's frozen face. His eyes had turned steel-gray. "Shut up, Dewey," he said, his voice low and controlled.

Dewey said to me, "Did your hubby ever tell you he saved my life?"

I shook my head slowly and looked back at Gabe, questioning.

"Dewey, let it go," Gabe said.

Dewey looked at Gabe with a surprised expression. "You never told her? Shit, Gabe, that was your finest hour." He turned to me. A sheen of perspiration had formed on his upper lip. "Saved me. Saved a full bird colonel, too. Big ole fat rich sucker by the name of Johnston. Tilton Lee Johnston. Leave it to Gabe to do it right. If you're gonna risk your balls saving someone, make it an officer with friends in high places. Tell her the story, Gabe. Benni, honey, it's a regular John Wayne movie." He held up the picture. "A two-star general pinned the Silver Star on Gabe himself. Got it right here with my trusty little Kodak. I say we need a toast. Here's to Gabriel Ortiz. Bravest son of a . . . ."

"Dewey, I said shut up." Gabe strode across the room, ripped the picture out of his hand and crumpled it. "You're out of line. It's time for us to go. Benni." He grabbed my hand and pulled me toward the door.

"Ah, Gabe," Dewey said. "I didn't mean anything by it. Don't leave, buddy. Benni, tell him I was just kiddin'." He pleaded with glassy eyes.

I gave a futile shrug and followed Gabe, having no choice with the tight grip he had on my hand.

He drove fast and silently down the long driveway. I listened to the ping, ping of scattered gravel and chewed the side of my lip, trying to decide how to bring up what just happened. When we reached the wide smooth asphalt of the highway, I decided that blunt had served me well for thirty-five years, so I'd just stick with it.

"What was that all about?" I asked.

"I don't want to talk about it." He reached down and turned on the radio. The disc jockey was laughing at some guy who was requesting a song to be dedicated to a girl who'd dumped him. He'd asked for the Travis Tritt song "Here's A Quarter, Call Someone Who Cares."

"Gabe," I said.

"I said I didn't want to talk about it."

I punched the radio off. "Well, I don't much care what you want—we *are* going to talk about this."

He didn't answer.

"Gabe." I softened my voice and squeezed his upper arm gently. "Talk to me. Please."

He stared straight ahead, his hands rigid on the wheel as he concentrated on the empty country road. It was as if I wasn't even there.

"Gabe."

Silence.

I felt my temper bubbling. His behavior reminded me too much of my uncle Arnie and his teenage friends when I was a girl. We'd be sitting out back of the barn on the large corral fences watching one of them practice for a coming rodeo, and I'd ask some question about roping or riding. They'd just squint at each other, spit forbidden tobacco juice, and ignore me. When I persisted, they'd smirk, wave their dirt-stained hands about and drawl, "Horseflies sure are bad this year, don'tcha think?" They would continue this tactic until they'd achieved their purpose—a frustrated me slinking away so they could turn their conversation back to the cruder topics that Dove wouldn't let them discuss when I was around. It worked until I discovered a way to get them to, if not answer my questions, at least acknowledge I was there. It was extremely childish and incredibly effective, and I did it now. I sat back in my seat, took a deep breath, and screamed as loud as I could.

Gabe jumped, let out a string of Spanish words, and slammed on the brakes so hard I would have hit the dashboard except for my seat belt. We stopped in front of a dense field of ripe corn.

"What in the—" He turned to me, his face bloodless.

I smiled serenely. "Now that I have your attention . . ."

Anger turned his cheeks a reddish nutmeg. "Are you out of your mind? You could have gotten us killed."

"I checked. There were no cars near us. We're all alone out here. Are you ready to talk to me now?"

"This is by far the most childish thing I've ever seen you do."

"Actually, I don't think so. I've done much more childish things."

He gave me a stony look that instantly stopped my smart remarks. I knew his temper. I knew I was playing with fire. I also knew that he would never hurt me except with his excluding silence.

"Gabe," I said softly, "I hate it when you shut me out."

His expression still hard and unyielding, he started the car and pulled slowly out onto the road. A hot wind had come up, fluttering the wide leaves of the corn. They moved back and forth, dark green, light green, and they appeared in the blur filming my eyes, like hands waving goodbye. When we arrived home, he walked ahead of me into the house, not looking back. I turned and headed the opposite way, down the driveway to the dirt road. It was dark now, and the locusts had resumed their unbearable sawing. Helicopter blades, I thought. They sound like helicopter blades. I followed the dirt road to the paved street that I knew, after a half mile or so, led to town. Trying to ignore the emotions churning inside me, I concentrated on putting one foot in front of the other. On the bridge over the Arkansas River, the air felt damper, though not one degree cooler. I yearned for just five minutes of San Celina's cool ocean breezes. Momentarily turning my thoughts away from Gabe and Kansas and that sizzling, insistent sound of the locusts, I imagined instead the sweet smell of burning oakwood, the teasing camaraderie with longtime friends in Blind Harry's Bookstore after one of Elvia's literary events, the comforting rhythmic coo of the mourning doves outside my Spanish bungalow's bedroom window.

Derby was fairly busy for nine-thirty on a Tuesday evening. I didn't feel frightened walking down Madison peering into the windows of stores that had closed hours before. Set off by itself on a small lot was the Sunflower Quilts and Crafts store. It was a bright yellow clapboard building with china-blue shutters decorated with tiny, smiling sunflowers. I cupped my hands against the glass and peered into the storefront window crowded with quilts, handmade dolls, and bears. I made a note to come back the next day, when the store was open. I sighed and started back up the street. Maybe tomorrow would be a good day to go out and see Hannah about making that quilt for me. If nothing else, it would keep me away from Gabe the better part of the day. I passed Cricket's Coffee Hutch, hoping it was open so I'd have somewhere to sit down, have a Coke, and think, but I wasn't surprised to see it had closed hours ago. I knew at the far end of town all the fast-food joints would be open, but the thought of then walking all the way back to Kathryn's house wasn't especially appealing.

In front of the empty VFW building on the corner of Washington and Madison, out of the corner of my eye I noticed a truck slow down beside me. I crossed the street quickly, thinking it wanted to turn left off Madison. I felt my heart start pounding when it continued to follow me, shifting into a lower gear. I moved my purse to my other arm, stopped abruptly, and turned around, thinking that I could slip behind the truck and get across Madison to the crowded parking lot of an open gas station. The driver caught my maneuver, suddenly backed up, and blocked my way. The door flew open, and I turned and started to run.

"Benni! Wait!"

The sound of my name surprised me into stopping. A figure emerged from the cab of the truck, cursing under his breath. His familiar cream-colored cowboy hat caused me to exhale the breath I'd been holding.

"It's Dewey," he said. "I couldn't get the doggone window down before you hot-footed it outta here like a deer in hunting season."

"You scared me," I said, walking up to him. He didn't appear drunk now, though it had only been an hour or so since we'd left his house, and I wondered how much of that volatile scene could be attributed to alcohol.

"Sorry," he said. "What are you doing out this late?"

I shrugged. "I felt like taking a walk."

His eyes flashed perceptively. "He's royally pissed, isn't he?" He gave me an apologetic half-smile.

"Yes, he is."

He rubbed his knuckles against his jaw. I could hear the scritch scritch of their roughness against his whiskers. "Hey, want a cup of coffee?"

"Sure."

"Actually, I was heading up to the station to pick up some work. I can make us some there." He held open the driver's door, and I climbed into the cab, sliding across to the passenger side.

At the station Dewey unlocked the back door and let the dispatcher know we were in his office. I sat in his one vinyl office chair and watched him fiddle with the drip coffee machine on the credenza behind his desk. His office was square, impersonal, and messy. Its single window was covered with white miniblinds. The pale walls held only one framed picture of Dewey and Chet in front of the livestock pens at some rodeo. Chet had a deep, fresh-looking scratch on the side of his smooth cheek.

Dewey sank into his high-backed chair, and we both silently watched the glass pot fill to the halfway point. He handed me my coffee in a black plastic D.A.R.E. To Stay Off Drugs mug and leaned back in his chair.

"I blew it big time tonight," he said, taking a large swallow of coffee.

I sipped my coffee and didn't answer, not wanting to tell him I was in no position to point a finger.

For a minute or so, the only sound was the buzzing fluorescent lights overhead and an occasional gurgle from the coffee machine. I stared down into my cup and decided to steer the conversation away from Gabe. "How's the investigation going? Are they letting you work much on it?"

His face grew irritated. "Not as much as I'd like."

"What have they got so far?"

"Not much. There was hardly any physical evidence.

We never did find the brick that killed her. At this point all they're doing is interviewing and reinterviewing people. Then the fun part begins.''

''What's that?''

''Reading the interviews over and over until you come up with something that doesn't look right.'' He smiled at me, his skin grayish under the harsh light. He picked up a pencil and tapped the green desk blotter in front of him. ''You're married to a cop. You know how the routine goes.''

''So they're letting you read the interviews.''

He patted a stack of manila folders. ''That's what I came back to get. Bill, he's the sheriff's detective in charge of the investigation, said if he reads these one more time he'll go cross-eyed. I'm going through them to see if he missed anything. If the media found out he's letting me go through this stuff, they'd have a conniption fit screaming collusion and cover-up and who knows what else, but me and Bill go way back to our rookie days. We spent some quality time at Miller U together.''

''Miller U?'' I asked. ''Is that some kind of beer joke among cops?''

He picked up a blue plastic squirt gun that was resting on one of the file folders and scratched his cheek with it. ''Nah, Miller U is the Kansas Law Enforcement Training Center out near the town of Miller. A lot of Kansas police agencies train there. We just nicknamed it Miller U. Though with some of the extracurricular activities those guys get involved with, it's more appropriate than you think.''

''So, who do you think did it?'' I asked.

''Now, Benni, don't go asking me to make a bet when all the cards aren't dealt yet.''

I laughed. ''That sounds like something my Gramma Dove would say.''

''Is she a poker player?''

''Her third greatest talent.''

"After?" He waited, his dark eyes red-rimmed and tired.

"Her fluffy buttermilk biscuits and her nosiness."

"Hmm," he said, laying the plastic gun down. "Sounds like granddaughter takes a little after grandmother."

"Oh, no," I said solemnly. "My biscuits are as hard as rocks."

He threw back his head and laughed. "Sugar, you are a real piece of business—you ever been told that?"

"Once or twice," I said wryly. I picked up the squirt gun, and suddenly an idea popped in my head. "Is this yours? Can I borrow it?"

He gave me a mystified look. "You can have it. Somebody's kid left it a while back, and we've just been screwing around with it."

I stuck it in my purse. "So, there are no real leads, then?"

"Nope." He stood up and started stacking file folders. "Not even when they searched her place. I was there. Nothing. I've never seen anything like this homicide." He turned off the coffeemaker and tucked the files under his arm. "Ready to go? I'll drop you off at Kathryn's."

"What happens to all Tyler's stuff now that you've searched her place?"

"Someone needs to claim it. And they better do it soon. The lady she was renting a room from called late this afternoon. Wants it gone. Says she needs to rent the room out real bad." He settled his hat square on his head.

"I guess everything she owns would belong to her husband, John."

"Yep, he's the next of kin. But those Amish are heck to get a hold of, not having phones. We'll send someone out tomorrow to tell him."

"I was thinking about going out to see Tyler's sister tomorrow. I could tell her to tell Tyler's husband."

He cocked his head. "You know the victim's sister?"

"I met her yesterday when Becky and I went out to take her some food. She's agreed to make a quilt for me. That's why I thought maybe I'd go see her tomorrow." I set my empty coffee cup on the desk. "I feel bad for them. Violent crime is hard enough to cope with when you're basically exposed to it all the time the way that we are. What must it be like for the Amish? They don't even have television."

"Well, TV or not, all I can say is, if I were Bill, I'd be paying real close attention to that husband of hers."

"But he's Amish. It would be completely out of character."

"When it comes to affairs of the heart, Benni, all bets are off, including the religious ones." He held my elbow lightly, directing me through the maze of hallways.

"I don't know," I said doubtfully.

"Trust me," Dewey said, his voice weary. "I've been in this business a long time. Gabe will back me up on this. Domestic violence crosses *all* boundaries—money, class, race, and religion."

Dewey turned his headlights off when we pulled into Kathryn's driveway so he wouldn't disturb anyone in the dark house. For all his effort, the loud rumble of the truck's engine announced our arrival as surely as the trumpet of my husband's namesake. I felt irrationally guilty, like a teenager trying to sneak in past curfew. He cut the engine.

"Benni," he said, his voice low. "I just want to apologize . . ."

"Don't," I interrupted, embarrassed. "This is between you and Gabe."

"No." He reached over and grabbed my hand. "I am sorry for acting like such a jackass. I'd blame it on the booze, but that's no excuse. The thing of it is . . ." His voice cracked, and he started over. "The thing of it is, Gabe really did save my life, and I wasn't trying to make fun of him or piss him off. I just wanted him to know that I know, *I know* I wouldn't even be here if it wasn't for him and how . . .'' His voice faltered again, and he let go of my hand. "Just tell him I'm sorry, will you? I'll call him tomorrow and tell him myself, but for tonight, let him know I'm sorry. Please?''

"Okay, I will. Now go home and get some sleep.''

He gave a tired smile and patted the files.

"No," I said firmly. "You can do that tomorrow. Get some sleep.''

"I will if you will,'' he said, touching two fingers to his hat.

"You got a deal.''

I walked up the steps, turning to wave at Dewey, though I wasn't sure if he could see me. I opened the screen door slowly, hoping they'd left the door unlocked so I wouldn't be forced to either wake someone or sleep on the redwood chaise longue. A voice from a dark corner of the porch caused me to practically jump out of my boots.

"Where have you been?'' Gabe asked.

EIGHT

THE WORDS ON the tip of my tongue were, What's it to you? but having acquired a small measure of sense in the last thirty-five years, I just grumbled an unintelligible reply.

He moved out of the darkness and leaned against the railing, studying me with unblinking eyes. "I was worried about you."

"No reason to. Most of the time I was at the police station."

He didn't answer, waiting for me to elaborate. The crickets next to the porch stopped, then started again. "Look, Dewey saw me walking down the street and took me to the station while he picked up some work. We had some coffee, and he dropped me off here. That satisfy you? It's certainly more information than you usually give me."

He didn't answer.

"Oh, and by the way, he's sorry for acting like such a jerk tonight." There, I'd done it. Not in the sweet, cajoling way Dewey was probably hoping would grease his path, but I'd done as he asked. Now all I wanted to do was go to bed. I reached for the screen door.

"We have a problem," Gabe said.

The dense night air did little to soften the sharpness of my laugh. "Always right on top of things, aren't you, Chief Ortiz?"

"Benni, how can I make you understand that certain events during that time of my life aren't things I like to remember? That some things are just better left in the past?" He turned away and stared into the dark front yard. Against the sky, the trees were all black-green silhouettes. The stars pulsed white-cold and seemed close enough to touch.

I walked over and stood next to him, following his gaze, wondered what he was seeing. "I'm not asking you to give me a blow-by-blow account of your time in Vietnam, but, Gabe, it's all the little things you keep hidden from me that make me wonder if I even know who you are."

"Like what?"

"Like your background with horses."

"That's not a big deal."

"To *me* it is. And it's not only that. It's why you don't drink, it's—"

"Seems like you, of all people, would appreciate that."

"I do, but *why* don't you drink?"

"I just don't."

"But why?"

"I . . . just . . . don't." His hand slowly curled up in a tight fist.

"See what I mean? It's like reading someone's personnel file and never meeting them in person. I have the surface information on you but never anything deeper. How long do we have to be married before you let me through that concrete shell of yours?"

He took a deep breath and relaxed his fist. "Okay, since we're asking soul-searching questions here, I have one. Just how long are there going to be three people in this marriage?"

I swung around and faced him. "What did you say?"

His face was all black angles in the porch's shadows. "You heard me. You think because you don't say anything that I don't know that everything I do, every word coming out of my mouth, is measured and judged against a dead man's?"

"I don't—" I started, then stopped. Because he was right. Though it happened less and less as time went on, whatever Gabe did or said I unconsciously, and often consciously, compared to Jack.

"Do you have any idea what it's like to live like that?" The skin around his eyes and mouth pulled taut. "I'd always heard that marrying someone who'd had a bad marriage was asking for trouble. Believe me, it's got nothing on following a happy one."

I tried to think of some way to defend myself, but couldn't. I'd been so busy concentrating on what he wasn't giving me in this relationship, it never occurred to me that I was doing something wrong. My voice seemed trapped in the thick night air. "I don't know what to say," I finally managed.

"Benni, there's nothing more to say." His voice had a final sound, like falling timber. "Right now it's late, and we're not going to solve this tonight, so I think we'd better get some sleep and deal with it later."

Upstairs, we undressed silently and settled under the clammy sheets, being very careful not to touch each other. I turned my back to him and mentally replayed his words at least a dozen times, trying to figure out where things went wrong, what I could have done differently, what would happen now, until eventually I fell asleep, not one bit closer to a solution than when I started.

I was an emotional porcupine the next morning, too prickly to fake a pleasant conversation with Gabe and Kathryn. I excused myself and took an English muffin and a cup of coffee out to the front porch. Kathryn gave me an odd look but didn't say anything. Daphne growled irritably, and I almost kissed her ugly little muzzle. Ironically, I was beginning to look forward to her cranky moods, simply because it was the only completely predictable thing in my life right now. She followed me out to the porch, where I lay on the chaise longue and shot her with Dewey's squirt gun as the mood struck me. Her agitated snapping at the air was comical enough to elicit a few chuckles from me. I was in the midst of driving her to a frenzy when a Federal Express truck pulled into Kathryn's driveway. A trim young woman jogged up to the porch with a large, square box in her hands.

"Benni Harper?" Her voice was hopeful.

"Yes." I stuck the gun in my pocket and stood up to meet her.

"Sign here, please." She held out a clipboard.

I sat on the bottom step and looked at the sender's name. Dove Ramsey—Amarillo, Texas. What in the world would she be Federal Expressing me from Amarillo, Texas? I tore open the box and pulled out the contents.

A cowboy hat. One with a braided horsehair band that I'd recognize anywhere, seeing as I made the band myself. My father's hat. His good tan 20X dress hat that cost him two hundred dollars. My father's good dress Stetson with the crown smashed in and a suspicious-looking stain resembling a woman's size six footprint. This was not a good sign.

I looked back into the box and pulled out a short note written beneath the letterhead, "Wagon Train Motel— Pull Up Your Buckboard and Rest a Spell." I could almost hear Dove's grating voice as I read her spidery handwriting. "Next time, I'm sending an ear. P.S. We're on our way to Corsicana, Texas, Fruitcake Capital of the World. They'd better give free samples, or heads will roll. I'll send you a postcard."

Fruitcake, I thought—how appropriate for my family. Then, looking back at the crushed hat, I groaned so loudly that Daphne came over and nipped at my bare toes. I pulled out my plastic pistol and shot her a long, wet one, accidentally sending the stream right up her left nostril. She screeched and took off around the house, sneezing water as she ran.

"What's going on out here?" Gabe walked out onto the porch holding a mug of coffee.

I pocketed the gun quickly and handed him the hat and note. "This just came from Amarillo."

He scanned the note, his tired face managing a half-smile. "Well, the whole world seems to be at odds, doesn't it?"

I wanted to reach up and smooth out the tight lines around his eyes, but instead I took the hat back and tried to unsuccessfully re-form the crown.

"What are you planning to do today?" His voice was subdued.

I gave up on the hat. "I think I'd better drive into Wichita and drop this off at Shepler's and see if someone can clean and block it. Daddy's probably ready to hogtie and brand Dove. Maybe I'll go to the mall. Don't forget, we're supposed to go see Cordie June and the band perform tonight."

"I know. I'll call Dewey later and find out what time."

I was glad he'd decided not to let his argument with Dewey spoil his visit or their friendship. They had too much history to let one stupid remark come between them. I only wished that Gabe and I had that kind of history to fall back on. But the reality was, most of our lives had been spent without the other, and we'd probably do fine if we parted right now. Just fine. I felt tears prick at the corners of my eyes and I abruptly turned my head.

"So, is there any problem with me using the car today?" I asked, keeping my voice light.

"No, I'll be sticking around the house with Mom most of the day. She has some gutters that need repair and a bunch of shingles that blew off in the bad storm they had a couple of weeks ago."

"Okay." We looked at each other a moment, each of us waiting for the other to speak. "Well," I finally said. "Guess I'll see you later."

Driving through Derby, I passed Sunflower Quilts and Crafts just as Janet was opening the front door. I pulled in, remembering the Amish quilts I'd seen through the storefront window the night before. I wondered if any were Hannah's. Thinking of Hannah, I remembered promising Dewey that I would ask her to find out from John what to do about Tyler's belongings. Going to Miller would fill most of my day and keep my mind occupied, something I desperately needed right now. She had said I could come at any time.

"Hi!" Janet said brightly when I opened the screen door. "I was hoping you'd drop by some time during your visit."

"I peeked in the window last night when you were closed and saw some things I couldn't resist." She gave me a quick tour of the shop. They sold a lot of quilts made by guild members as well as some Amish and Mennonite women in the area, and native Midwestern crafts like the complex and delicate weavings made from wheat. I bought a book on the Amish that told about their customs as well as their quilts, and an elaborate wheat-weaving called Heart of Kansas, with plaited interlocked hearts and tiny wheat roses.

"Looks like you're going to do a little research," Janet said, glancing at the Amish book while adding it to my sales ticket. "So, are you enjoying Kansas so far? I mean, besides the murder."

"Yes." I looked at her curiously. "Have you heard anything more?"

"No, but then I'm always the last one to find out anything, anyway." Her voice carried a tart edge. I remembered what I'd overheard at the quilt guild meeting about Lawrence and Tyler, and wondered if Janet's tone had anything to do with that.

"Did you know Tyler well?" I asked casually, handing her my money.

"So, so. She'd been singing at Prairie City for about two months, but with the shop and the quilt guild and doing things for Megan, I didn't get down there much. Lawrence seemed to think the sun rose and set by her. I guess she was pretty popular with the regulars."

"What was she like?"

Janet shrugged and handed me my change. "Just another singer in my book. I've seen them come and go dozens of times in the ten years Lawrence has owned the club. What else can you say? A few make it, go on to Nashville or Las Vegas or Branson. Most don't, and end up singing in places like Prairie City until they're old and lose their looks or voices, or both."

"She was an incredible singer," I said.

"Talent doesn't give people the right to do whatever they please, to hurt innocent people." Janet's dark eyes flashed; then she abruptly looked down and concentrated on bagging my purchases.

"I guess it doesn't," I said carefully. "I've heard some interesting things about Tyler. I guess she wasn't all she appeared to be."

"That's the understatement of the year." She handed me my bag.

I wondered if she'd been this open with the police. Whether Gabe liked it or not, though, I was going to tell Dewey about Tyler and Lawrence. The only problem was how. Lawrence was his friend, and I was sure that a rumor about his involvement with Tyler would not be entirely welcome.

"I just hope that whoever killed her doesn't get away with it," I said.

Her answer was a minuscule tightening of her lower lip.

"Well, I'm going out to Miller and talk to her sister, Hannah," I said. "Dewey says Tyler's belongings need to be picked up. I was going out there to talk to Hannah about making a quilt, so I'm delivering the message.''

"Have the police searched Tyler's room?"

"Of course. They wouldn't be giving permission for it to be cleaned out if they hadn't. Why?"

"Just wondered."

"Are you coming to see Cordie June sing tonight?" I asked.

"I'm going to try. Lawrence is hosting a party for the old gang at the nightclub."

"Is your daughter going to be there?" I was curious to meet this Megan who would sleep with her father's old high-school friend. The romantic entanglements and double-dealing in this small town certainly rivaled any soap opera I'd ever watched.

"Probably."

"Well, I'd better get going." We said our goodbyes, and I stopped briefly at McDonald's to use the phone to call Fannie, the owner of the fabric store in Miller. She said she'd send her daughter down to Hannah's farm to let her know I'd be there in the next couple of hours. I drove into Wichita and dropped Daddy's hat off at Shepler's, promising the young man in the hat department my everlasting gratitude and a twenty-dollar tip if he could manage to clean, steam, and shape it into a semblance of its former glory. Then, pulling out my map, I decided to take backroads to Miller and enjoy some rural Kansas scenery.

To keep my mind from wandering back to last night's scene between Gabe and me, which I definitely wasn't ready to deal with yet, I turned my thoughts to Tyler and the strange group of people who surrounded her. Who was she? Gentle, torn ex-Amish woman who just wanted to use her musical gift? Or cold, ambitious artist who would do anything, including sleeping with someone else's husband, to make it to the top? Both? Neither? Somewhere in between? As miles of fields full of stubby wheat stalks rolled by, I listed in my mind the people who could possibly want Tyler dead and why.

Lawrence and their mysterious relationship; his daughter, Megan, and their rivalry for Rob; Rob himself, though I couldn't imagine why. Then there was Tyler's husband, John, who couldn't remarry and have children while she was alive, and Hannah's husband, Eli, for who knows what reason—maybe for putting Hannah at risk of being shunned, too? The Amish were longshots because of their passive beliefs, but deep down I had to agree with Dewey; being human made them as capable of murder as anyone else. Then there was Cordie June, who I could very easily see murdering anyone who got in her way on the road to stardom. And of course Janet, because of jealousy. More crimes are committed because of that complex emotion than for any other reason, Gabe once told me. I thought about myself and what I'd do if I caught some woman with Gabe. Then, though I fought it, my thoughts turned to what Gabe had said about my always comparing him to Jack. To be truthful, I didn't really understand it on an emotional level, though intellectually I could see his point. He'd been divorced so long, I never even thought about his ex-wife, Lydia, who lived in L.A. and was some kind of high-powered corporate attorney. Maybe I'd understand his feelings a little better if I were faced with seeing her or being reminded of her every day. Driving past the neat Amish farms outside Miller, I wondered if the life of these plain people, so structured but also so predictable, might be an easier, less stressful way to live.

In Miller, Fannie's Fabrics and Notions was a separate, wooden clapboard building in front of what appeared to be a private home. As with most of the buildings in Miller, there was a long rail in front for her Amish customers' buggies. A set of cheerful sleigh bells attached to the front door announced my arrival. The room was empty, so I wandered around, looking at the bolts of colorful fabric and at the products that told me this wasn't your ordinary chain fabric store. Hats of yellowish straw and black felt with flat crowns and wide brims, lined the high shelves in sizes to fit every Amish gentleman from age two to ninety-two. In the back, there were plastic bins containing packages of women's white cotton underwear, men's plain cotton handkerchiefs, books of stories for children that could have been written in the nineteenth century, and thin blue books titled *Favorite Songs and Hymns.* I picked up a hymn book and leafed through it. Many of them were old hymns I'd grown up singing at First Baptist in San Celina—"The Lily of the Valley," "When We All Get to Heaven," "Up From the Grave He Arose."

"That's the wilder music used for Sunday night singing," a voice said behind me. I turned and faced a heavyset woman in a pink calico dress. Her gray hair hung in a long thick braid down her back, reminding me of Dove. "That's when the Amish young people do their courting. They sing the songs in German first, then in English. You must be Benni. I'm Fannie."

"That's me," I said, smiling. "So what do they do after they sing?"

She gave a high little laugh, her shiny round cheeks bringing to mind one of the munchkins in the *Wizard of Oz.* "What all red-blooded teenagers do everywhere. They pair up, and the boys take the girls home in their buggies, racing each other, showing off and hoping to sneak in a little kissing before they reach the girl's farm."

"That's hard to picture," I said. "They all look so innocent."

"Oh, the Amish aren't any different from anyone else in that respect," she said. "There's been more than one *Hochzüt* that's been *wenn's pressiert*, believe you me." She spoke the German-sounding words with ease.

"What?"

She lowered her voice. "*Wenn's pressiert.* When the wedding is urgent because a little one is expected."

"Hanky-panky among the Amish?" I said, surprised.

"Well, you have to say this for them. They never have

any illegitimate children. If an Amish boy gets an Amish girl pregnant, there is no argument about what he has to do. We English should be so responsible.''

"English?" I asked.

"It's what the Amish call anyone not of their faith," she replied.

"You know a lot about the Amish."

"My grandmother was plain. She married outside the church, though, and that's why I'm Mennonite today. You'll find many of the old families around here have Amish in their background. I sent Esther, my granddaughter, to let Hannah know you were coming, and Hannah said she'd be by about twelve-thirty, right after she prepared Eli's dinner. Is that okay?"

I glanced at my watch. It was eleven-thirty now, and I was beginning to feel hungry. "That's great. Is there somewhere I can get some lunch?"

"Miller Cafe up on the highway is good and cheap." She gave her jolly little laugh again. "And the only place in town to eat."

"Sounds perfect," I said and started to walk out. Then I remembered something. "Excuse me, but may I ask you a question?"

Her eyes widened with curiosity. "Certainly."

"Did Hannah tell you she gave me her sister's bank book?"

Fannie's face grew serious. "Yes, she did. What did you do with it?"

"I gave it to my husband, like she asked. But he had to give it to the police in charge of the investigation."

"We assumed that is what would happen. But Hannah didn't want the money, so maybe it is best."

"Well, I just have a question about it—about her sister. When exactly did she give it to you?"

Fannie sighed. "Two days before she was killed."

"How was she acting?"

"What do you mean?"

"Did she act like she was, for example, afraid or

maybe anxious about something?''

Fannie rested her chubby elbows on the wooden counter. "I didn't talk with her long. I was very busy that day. My grandchildren were visiting, and it was crowded here in the store. She just pulled me aside and asked me to hold onto the envelope until she came back for it, and to give it to Hannah if anything happened to her. She seemed fine. A little tired maybe. A little sad. But she seemed that way every time I saw her, as seldom as that was, and I just assumed it was because of the type of life she led. I'm sorry, I don't know what you're looking for.''

"It's all right. I don't really know either."

At the busy cafe, I sat in a back booth and watched the young Amish waitresses serve customers who appeared to be mostly truckdrivers whose route passed Miller, or local farmers. The girls were all dressed identically in below-the-knee pastel dresses with oversized puffed sleeves. They looked so fresh and untouched, I could well imagine the appeal they must hold for men. I assumed this was the cafe where Tyler once worked. In the background Sammy Kershaw eulogized in song the queen of his doublewide trailer with her cheating black heart and pretty red neck. The laughing, innocent faces of the Amish girls didn't seem to comprehend what he was singing about. But then again, who knows what dwells in the heart of another person?

I dug enthusiastically into the special of the day— chicken and dumplings. The meat was white and tender, the gravy smooth and buttery-tasting, the dumplings light with just a hint of doughiness inside. It was the first completely relaxed meal I'd had since leaving California. I lingered over my blackberry cobbler and flipped through the book I'd just purchased about the Amish, reading paragraphs here and there and studying the pictures. Then I got serious and looked up "shunning" in the index. Apparently there were many behaviors that could bring on the community's complete rejection of one of their members: adultery, being a drunkard, blasphemy of the Holy Spirit, disobeying some prescript of the *Ordnung*, the unspoken rules of the local congregation. But the most deplorable of all, as Becky told me, was leaving the church after being baptized into it. Maybe it wasn't as predictable and easy a way to live as it appeared. Not if you were at all different.

A black buggy I assumed to be Hannah's was parked in front of Fannie's Fabrics when I came back. Inside the store bolts of fabric were already laid out on the cutting table.

"Benni!" Hannah said, her voice warm and delighted. "I was so happy when Fannie told me you were coming. Come and see what I've picked out."

We settled finally on a Hole in the Barn Door pattern, one that had been a favorite of mine since I was a little girl. I chose navy blue and maroon with a pine-green border, leaving the quilting pattern to Hannah's discretion. I insisted on paying for the fabric and giving her a hundred-dollar cash deposit.

We stood outside discussing stitching patterns while I petted her horse, a brown Standardbred with a mischievous glint in its eyes. She told me about a unique pattern her great-grandmother designed when she first came to Kansas at the turn of the century. In response to her new surroundings, she'd incorporated tiny sunflowers into a traditional feather-spray stitching.

"It doesn't sound like anything I've ever seen," I said.

"Would you like to come out to the farm and trace it?" she asked. "And you are more than welcome to share it with your friends."

"That would be wonderful. The quilters at the co-op are always looking for new patterns."

"Then you must come." She turned to Fannie. "Perhaps to save time, Esther could drive the buggy back, and I could go with Benni in her car."

Fannie nodded. "Esther loves driving your buggy."

"Are you allowed to ride in my car?" I asked, a bit taken back, though I remembered the Amish man, whom I was assuming was John at this point, leaving in a car the night he argued with Tyler.

Hannah and Fannie exchanged amused looks. "We can ride in cars," Hannah said. "We just can't own them."

"Oh," I said, not saying what I thought and hoping it didn't show on my face. That seemed awfully convenient to me.

"We don't have anything against cars, Benni," she said in her soft voice. "We just feel that owning them would make it too easy to go out into the world and be influenced by other, more harmful things."

"I see," I said, embarrassed as always at my inability to hide my feelings. When I started the car, the radio blasted Dwight Yoakam wailing he was a thousand miles from nowhere. He'd obviously visited Miller. I switched the radio off quickly, afraid that listening to it was somehow against Hannah's beliefs or that it might remind her of Tyler.

She briefly touched a thin, work-roughened hand to my arm. "It's your car, Benni. You can play whatever you please on the radio."

"Oh, okay," I said, but kept the radio off anyway.

In front of the house, Emma and Ruthie were having a tea party under the solid shade of a small willow tree. Inside, Hannah directed me to the living room while she went upstairs to find the pattern. Next to a large rectangular window she had set up a small quilting frame where she was working on a mulberry, tobacco-brown, and cream Tree of Life baby quilt, a pattern I knew from my reading was not common among traditional Amish except where they'd been influenced by outside sources, as the Midwestern Amish were. On the table next to her chair sat a twig basket full of pieced quilt squares. I picked them up and saw some picture postcards at the bottom of the basket. Their edges were soft, as if they had been handled often. I took one out and immediately recognized the white marble Arkansas state capitol. I hadn't seen it since I was a child and traveled on Amtrak cross country with Dove to visit her only sister in Sugartree, Arkansas, about fifty miles north of Little Rock. There were three other cards—one of Little Rock's famous rose gardens, one of Murray Dam, and one of the Old State House. Being human (and Dove's granddaughter) I turned them over to read the message and see who they were from. They were addressed to H.S. in care of Fannie's Fabrics, Miller, Kansas. No message. I peered closely at the blurry postmarks. Little Rock, Arkansas. The dates ranged from July 2 to December 17 of last year. I had a good hunch that the cards were probably from Tyler communicating with her sister in a way that wouldn't get Hannah in trouble. What in the world was Tyler doing in Little Rock for six months? Did it have anything to do with all that money? I struggled to remember the date the account was opened, but it hadn't been important enough at the time for me to make a note of it.

Behind me, a gruff voice said, "Is Hannah home?"

I guiltily shoved the postcards under the quilt squares in my lap and faced the unfriendly voice. John Stoltzfus stared at me from the doorway to the kitchen, his long face creased and somber.

"She's upstairs getting some quilt patterns for me to trace," I said as I set the quilt squares and postcards back in the basket. "We met before. I'm Benni Harper."

He nodded and held up a paper bag. "My sister sends some plums. Tell Hannah I will put them in the kitchen and be out in the barn with Eli."

"Okay," I said. He turned abruptly, and a moment later I heard the back door slam.

"I heard talking," Hannah said, coming down the stairs carrying a pasteboard box. "Has someone come?"

"Tyler's . . . uh, Ruth's husband, John," I said. "His

sister sent you some plums, and he said he would be in the barn with Eli.''

She set the box down on the floor in front of the sofa. Her face grew pensive. "He is a good man. He appears unfriendly, but underneath he is kindhearted.''

I looked at her and wondered if she was aware that he might have been at Becky's house the night Tyler was killed and if I should tell her.

"It has been very hard on him," she said.

"And you, too," I replied softly.

She sat on the floor and flipped through the patterns. "Yes," she said, her voice a whisper. "It has been like losing half of my own heart.''

I sat crosslegged next to her on the floor. "Hannah, I talked to Detective Champagne yesterday, and he says the place where Ruth was staying . . . Well, they want her things to be picked up. They need to rent the room out. John is officially her next of kin . . .''

"Oh, I didn't even think about that." She touched her cheek with her fingertips, her face stricken. "I'm not sure about what to do with her things. I'm sure John would not want anything. And I . . ." Her voice trailed off. "I think it is something we must ask our bishop." She looked away from me. "Now, where did I file that pattern?" I heard the catch in her voice and I knew she was fighting to keep from breaking down. "Here it is." She held up a thin piece of paper. I traced the unusual quilting pattern and wrote down the information about her grandmother to tell the quilters back at the co-op. I traced a few more uncommon ones from her collection, then stood up to leave.

"Thank you," I said. "For letting me trace these and for making the quilt. Let me know the postage costs as well as the final amount.''

"It is my pleasure," she said. When we went out into the front yard, I saw that her buggy had made it back from Fannie's.

"How will Fannie's daughter get home?" I asked.

She gave me a surprised look. "Walk. It is only a few miles."

I smiled, thinking about the teenagers I knew in San Celina who'd rather cut off their big toe than walk anywhere. Hannah walked me to my car, and as I opened the door, she blurted out, "Could you do it for us?"

"Do what?" I answered automatically. Then it occurred to me what she meant. Tyler's possessions. My stomach churned with dread, but I also felt a guilty excitement. "Are you sure?"

"Perhaps Becky will help. Oh, forgive me for being so forward. You hardly know me."

"I don't mind, really. And I'm sure Becky will be glad she can help you, too. But I wouldn't be surprised if we'll need some kind of written permission. Would John give us that?"

"Let me go ask." She ran back to the barn and returned a few minutes later holding a folded sheet of notebook paper. "Will this do?"

I scanned the neatly written note. "I'm no expert, but I can't imagine anyone disputing this. I'll show it to Detective Champagne."

"Thank you, Benni. This is very kind of you."

"It's the least I can do," I said, feeling embarrassed because she thought I was only helping her out of altruism. I certainly would have done it whether I was curious or not, but the prospect of poking through Tyler's stuff intrigued me more than I cared to admit. "What would you like me to do with her things?"

She tentatively fingered the hanging string of her white cap. "John said we should just give it all to charity but . . . could you just ask Becky if she would mind keeping it until I . . ." She let her sentence taper off. I wondered what she was thinking—until she asked her bishop? or until she could bear to look at the remnants of her sister's worldly life?

"I'm sure she'll be glad to."

A look of intense grief suddenly washed over Hannah's pale face. "You know, when our mother died, Ruth and I were only three years old. We did not remember her, so we did not grieve. It is difficult to grieve for a person one never knew. When Ruth left, I thought it was the deepest hurt I could ever feel. Somehow I could bear it because I knew she was out there. I haven't heard her voice in a year and a half, but in my mind it is as clear as Emma's or Ruthie's. I cannot imagine a world without her in it. I do not understand why this has happened. We are taught by our bishop that suffering is a blessing. That it can make our faith grow. I don't know. I feel so confused. How true is my faith when I am filled with so many doubts?"

I didn't have any answers for her. I did know that all the theology you've ever been taught doesn't mean anything when you are in the midst of such fresh grief. I could only offer her what I myself had discovered. That God was still there. That her faith would sustain her. Maybe not in some hallelujah-angels-singing-from-on-high kind of way, but just by making it day to day until what seemed impossible to endure became possible.

"Give it time," I said. "I don't know how long it will take, but I do know it will get easier. That much I do know."

She gave an almost imperceptible nod and didn't answer.

I watched her slender figure as I backed out of the driveway. Standing motionless in front of her colorful flower bed in her dark dress and white cap, she looked like a painting from another era. I wondered what she thought about as she watched this English woman drive back to the world that had stolen her sister. Did she envy me? Pity me? Did my inadequate words of comfort only cause her more sorrow? I thought about the complexity of love and why it was we humans so desperately sought something that caused us as much pain as it did joy. I thought of my relationship with Gabe, how confusing it was, how I wished there were some simple answers to make it work, like a course in school—learn these rules, take the test, get an A, and live happily ever after.

Thinking of Hannah and Tyler and John and Eli, whose lives were governed by their vast set of unspoken rules, it came to me that the quandary of life was a common human predicament, that even within their ordered lives, they were filled with as much confusion and doubt as I was, especially when those lives were touched so closely by violent death, something that seemed so unnatural simply because it was. And that even though I believed in the same God they did, He was still so much a mystery to me, but that was somehow okay because who, after all, could possibly want to believe in a God small enough to be comprehended?

NINE

IT WAS FIVE o'clock when I dropped by the Derby police station. I knew I'd better hustle because Kathryn would probably be cooking supper tonight, and since I'd not done much to endear myself to her so far, I didn't want to make matters worse by being tardy. Dewey leaned back in his chair, boots propped up on his desk, a beeping Game Boy in his hand.

I flopped down on the vinyl office chair. "Boy, *I* certainly feel safer knowing Derby's Chief of Detectives Dewey Champagne is on the job."

He gave a good-natured raspberry. A chorus of miniature cheers erupted from the electronic game.

"Are you going to Lawrence's club tonight?" I asked.

He swung his legs down. "As if I have a choice. I've been to so many of Cordie June's performances, I could sing backup."

I laughed. "That's something I'd pay at least a nickel to see."

"That'd be about what it's worth. Now, what can I do for you?"

"I've got something that'll make your life easier." I handed him the note that John had written.

"I'm always up for that." He scanned the notebook paper.

"Do you think it'll be okay?"

"Looks all right to me. Just show it to the landlady. I'll let the sheriff's detectives know."

"So, just how much of a mess did you guys make?" I teased.

"Now, watch what you say. I was there when they very neatly searched it. It didn't take long. She didn't have much."

"Did you find anything useful?"

He shook a finger at me. "That's privileged information. Don't you worry your pretty little head about it."

"Well, oink, oink to you, Officer Porky."

He laughed and handed John's note back to me. "Just let us know if you find anything we missed."

"Aren't you all going to feel really stupid when we do?" I threw over my shoulder as I walked out the door. He snorted in reply.

The scent of roasting chicken told me I was right about dinner. After a quick supper and an even quicker shower, I changed into black Wranglers, my black Tony Lama boots, and a forest-green tank top with a lacy V-neck. I stood in front of the mirror and frowned critically at my curly reddish-blond hair. It had been waist-length until last December, when, in an emotionally over-wrought moment, I'd cut it to the middle of my neck. It was now just touching the top of my shoulders and was still too short to braid, so most of the time I just let it hang there. I picked up a brush and attempted to tame it.

"You look great," Gabe said, coming up behind me and taking the brush out of my hand. He brushed my hair for a few seconds, then lifted it and softly kissed the nape of my neck. "I wanted to do that the very first time I brushed your hair. Remember?"

A lump lodged in my throat. How could we care so

much about each other and still have this huge gulf between us? Then I got annoyed. Men. Instead of really trying to solve a problem, they trot out old memories to distract us. And invariably we fall for it. I moved away from his seductive lips and changed the conversation. "Did you and Dewey talk?"

"Yes, I called him this afternoon. Don't worry. He and I have been growling and snapping at each other since we were kids." He rested his hands on my shoulders and gave me his most devastating smile. "How was the mall?"

"I didn't go to the mall. I went out to Miller to visit Hannah."

His genial look dissolved. "You said you were going to the mall."

"I changed my mind."

"What business do you have with Tyler's sister?"

"When I visited her with Becky, she agreed to make a quilt for me, so I met her at the fabric store in Miller to pick out fabric. Then I went to her house to copy some quilting patterns her grandmother designed. She asked me and Becky to pack up Tyler's things and store them at Becky's until she could decide what to do with them. Tyler's husband didn't want them." I still found that incredibly sad. I thought about the first six months after Jack died and how being surrounded by his possessions was the only thing that kept me sane. I remember picking up the last T-shirt he'd worn before he was killed. I folded it and set it on his side of the bed. Eventually I threw it out because I couldn't bear to wash his scent away.

Gabe tucked his burgundy polo shirt into his Levi's, his jaw muscles tight, hard knots. "I assume the police have searched her place already."

"Yes, I stopped by the station on the way here and asked Dewey. He said it was okay."

"I'm glad he feels so free about giving my wife permission to get involved in his murder investigation."

"For cryin' out loud, I'm not involved in the investigation. I'm just helping Hannah. What could you possibly find wrong with that?"

He ran a hand over his face. "I just don't like you being involved in this, even peripherally. I'm not crazy about the fact that you might be the only one who heard the person who murdered Tyler."

"The trees muffled the voices. I can't really identify anyone."

"That person doesn't know that."

"Gabe, we've only got a little more than a week left here. You know as well as I do they probably won't solve her murder that quickly. Then we'll fly back to San Celina, and this will just be a bad memory. I'm going to be okay." I dug through my leather backpack and pulled out the essentials—keys, comb, wallet, lip gloss—to put into a compact leather-tooled purse that would be easier to carry at a club. I stuck John's note in to show to Becky. "Really, Gabe, I'm going to be fine," I repeated when he didn't answer.

He just gave me a skeptical look.

Prairie City Nights was a square, monstrous building sandwiched between a Dollar-Rent-A-Car repair lot and a Wichita Holiday Inn that had seen better times. A little after eight o'clock, the parking lot was already teeming with trucks of all ages and colors with the brand names leaning toward Dodge, Ford, and Chevy. The barrel-chested bouncers, dressed in black Wranglers, black cowboy shirts, and red bandannas were already guarding the double width doors taking tickets and checking ID's. Gabe and I picked up the passes Lawrence had left for us at the ticket booth and squeezed our way into the gymnasium-style building. Lawrence and his silent business partner, one of the biggest cattle ranchers in eastern Kansas, had turned Prairie City Nights into Wichita's most popular country-western nightclub. An oval bar dominated the center of the room with a dance floor circling it like a running track. At one end of the rectangular room, two big-screen televisions hung over a "pickup" bar made of an old red and white Chevy pickup truck cut in half horizontally; opposite the bar was the elevated stage where the band performed. Compared to the outside temperature, the air was icy cold and already pungent with the heady smell of beer, cigarettes, and the sweet cornucopia of women's perfumes. Across the packed dance floor couples two-stepped and twirled to Vince Gill begging his lady to not let their love go slippin' away.

"Over there." Gabe pointed to a roped-off group of tables next to the bandstand. Janet stood up and waved to us. Becky and Stan were already there, talking to an attractive young woman with wavy brown hair and thick eye makeup, who I assumed was Janet and Lawrence's troublemaking daughter, Megan. Cordie June was on stage fiddling with some equipment while the band set up. She wore shiny black leggings with silver, black, and electric-blue cowboy boots and a spangly blue Western jacket. I scanned the five guys in Snake Poison Posse and wondered which one was Tyler's friend T.K.

After we ordered drinks—Coke for me and club soda for Gabe—Lawrence joined us, entering the club from a side door that was almost hidden in the wood paneling. "Everyone set up okay? Remember, everything's on the house."

Within the next hour Dewey and Rob both arrived. Rob was pale, and I noticed his hand tremble slightly when the waitress handed him a bottle of Coors. Initially everyone was overly solicitous of him, especially when Cordie June requested donations for Tyler's reward fund, but when the band started playing, attention was diverted from Rob, and I could see him start to relax. I watched him out of the corner of my eye as he watched Cordie June sing the lead vocals on songs that only last week had been Tyler's.

"Has anybody out there ever been in love?" Cordie June cooed into the microphone. The red spotlight turned her hair to fire. A lusty cheer rose from the crowd. "Has anybody out there ever been in love and out in one night?" The crowd screamed their affirmation. "Then this one's for you." The band rolled into Highway 101's "Love Walks." She strutted across the stage, throwing everything she had into the performance, whining the words into the microphone, cradling it in her hands and sassing back to the electric guitars as if they were renegade lovers. Tonight she was getting what she'd always wanted—center stage. I scanned the crowd, wondering if the producer she'd mentioned last night was out there making a decision that could change her life forever. One little decision and her life takes another road, I thought. Just like the decision Tyler made leaving the Amish. Just like the decision the killer made when he or she took Tyler's life.

"Hey, sugar." Dewey came up to me and held out his hand. "Think the old man there would care if I twirled you around the track a time or two?"

I glanced over at Gabe, deep in conversation with Stan about the President's latest crime bill. "Who cares what he thinks? Besides, he probably wouldn't even notice."

"Oh, he'll notice," Dewey said, pulling me up and leading me to the dance floor. "But we'll do it, anyway." We caught the last minute of the Highway 101 song. The band started a slow dance, and the couples moved closer together while Cordie June and one of the band members harmonized on a Patsy Cline song—"I'll Be Loving You Always."

"Hope Cordie June doesn't get jealous," I said as we danced in front of the stage. "I'm too old to get in a cat fight over a man."

Dewey's soft laugh sounded double-edged. "Don't worry about that. When the queen of country is on stage, she isn't thinking of anything but herself."

"Well, cowboy," I said, after we'd circled the dance floor twice. "You may not be able to sing, but you're a darn good dancer."

"Thank my mother for that," he said. "She always told me that women would flock to a guy who knew how to dance."

"Was she right?"

"No."

"C'mon, women love men who can take them dancing."

"Let me ask you something. Did Gabe ever take you dancing?"

"Gabe? Dance?" I laughed. "No way."

"And he's never had trouble getting women."

"Are you trying to make me jealous?" I asked. "It won't work."

"Just stating facts. You want to know what really attracts women?"

"Wait, let me get my tape recorder. Can I quote you on this, Mr. Hugh Hefner of the High Plains?"

"Don't smart-mouth me. This here is the inside scoop on the male psyche."

"Hey, don't stop. I'm making mental notes. Maybe I'll write a book."

"What really attracts women is silence."

"What?"

"You heard me." The song ended, and he took my hand and led me over to the center bar. "One Coke and one Chivas Regal, straight," he told the bartender. He leaned against the bar and gave me his lazy grin.

"You're wrong. Women *hate* that. We want men who will talk to us."

"Hah! That's what you all *say*, but you all love those quiet, brooding types who won't open up to you. Drives you crazy, but you can't get enough."

"You're full of baloney."

"Am I? What about you and Gabe? I bet he has you running in circles trying to figure out his innermost secret thoughts."

I grabbed my Coke and started back toward the tables. What had started out as a casual joking conversation about men and women in general had turned way too personal. And it hit way too close to home.

"Don't get your feathers all ruffled," he said, following me. "Men are just as bad. We love the unattainable, too. Can't resist the challenge."

I ignored him and kept walking.

"Now, sugar, don't be mad. I was just rattling on," he wheedled.

"What's he rattling on about now?" Belinda asked when we reached the group. She and Chet had arrived while Dewey and I were on the dance floor. Everyone was making a fuss over their son, teasing him about past bull and bronc rides and making jokes about what would likely happen to certain parts of his anatomy tomorrow night at the Pretty Prairie Rodeo. He endured everyone's kidding with a shy, good-natured grin.

I sat next to Becky. "I went out to see Hannah today."

"You did?" She looked surprised. "Why?"

I told her about the quilt pattern and material we picked out, then quickly told her about Tyler's belongings and John's not wanting them.

"Poor Hannah," Becky said, stirring her drink absently. "This is so hard for her."

"She wants us to clean out Tyler's place and asked if you would store her stuff until she can decide what to do with it." I pulled the note out of my purse and handed it to her.

She read it, then looked up at me. "It's okay with the police?"

"Yes, I checked with Dewey."

"Let me think," she said. "Tomorrow's Thursday. The quilt show doesn't open until Friday at four. We're hanging the quilts Friday morning . . . going to the rodeo tomorrow night. How about tomorrow morning? I've got a bunch of empty boxes in my garage."

"Sounds fine to me," I said. "As far as I know, my day is free."

Belinda and Janet walked up and set a couple of platters of nachos on our table. "What are you two cooking up over here?" Belinda asked.

"We're going to clean out Tyler's room tomorrow," Becky said, showing her the note. Janet and Belinda glanced over it quickly. For some reason, I wished no one knew we were doing this except Dewey, but since it didn't seem to bother Becky, I shrugged off my uneasy feeling.

"Glad it's you and not me," Janet said. "What a way to spend a day."

"I don't know," Belinda said, dipping her head back and drinking from her bottle of Coors. "Might be kind of interesting, playing detective. Maybe Becky and Benni will find something the cops have missed."

I looked at her curiously, wondering why she'd be thinking the exact same thing that had crossed my mind. She arched one eyebrow and gave me a small half-smile. I took the note back and slipped it into my purse. The conversation moved away from Tyler and focused on the upcoming rodeo. In the course of the conversation, I learned that Cordie June was taking Tyler's place in yet one more thing—she would sing the national anthem on opening night. Belinda gave a disgusted snort when Janet brought it up.

"Now, girls," Becky said, trying to keep peace. I picked at the guacamole-and-sour-cream-covered nachos and listened without joining in.

Gabe sat down next to me, snatching the tortilla chip en route to my mouth and popping it into his. "What's the deal between you and Dewey?"

I shrugged and reached for another chip. "What do you mean?"

"Over at the bar. What was he saying that you didn't like?"

I looked at him coolly, still smarting from Dewey's casual but accurate assessment of our relationship. "It wasn't anything important."

"The look on your face said it was."

"Well, it wasn't." I flashed a big, phony smile. I could play the secrets game myself.

"Are you all right?" he asked, his voice concerned and a bit confused.

"Just fine." I turned back to Becky. "By the way, which guy in the band is T.K.?"

She pointed to the man holding a bright red electric guitar. He was as lanky as a eucalyptus tree, with black waist-length hair pulled back in a braid. The scowling Yosemite Sam picture on his T-shirt matched the expression on his rangy face. Becky leaned over and whispered to me, "Lawrence said he's taking Tyler's death real hard. He's thinking about leaving the band. Apparently he and Cordie June don't get along that well."

When the set ended and the disc jockey took over for the band's half-hour break, Cordie June and the rest of the band wandered over to our tables. After a quick round of introductions, I noticed T.K. go through the same door in the paneling that Lawrence had disappeared through earlier. I assumed it led to the club's offices. I glanced at Gabe, now talking to Chet and Dewey, then got up and followed T.K. The door opened onto a long hallway that led to a couple of storage rooms and a door with a small metal sign that said "Office." It opened, and Lawrence walked out.

"Benni," he said. "Is there something you need?" Up close, out of the softened amber lights of the bar, he looked harried and tired. Swollen purplish half-moons, enlarged by his glasses, framed the bottom of his eyes.

"No," I said quickly. "I'm just looking for a little fresh air."

He pointed down the long hallway. "Turn left at the end of this hall, the second door on your right is an exit. Be careful, though—that's the back parking lot. Sometimes it gets a little rough back there."

"I'll stick close by the door."

"Don't let it close on you," he cautioned. "It locks automatically."

"Thanks for the warning." I started to walk away.

"Hey." He grabbed my arm, his face twitching with nervous tension. "I heard you and Becky are cleaning out Tyler's room tomorrow."

Word does get around fast, I thought. "Yes, we are. Why?"

"No reason." His Adam's apple moved up and down convulsively, belying his casual tone. "What are you going to do with her things?"

I could have said, Why do you want to know? but I answered evenly, "Becky's going to store them until Tyler's sister decides what she wants to do with them. Apparently Tyler's husband has no interest in any of her personal stuff."

He looked disgusted. "And people wonder why she left."

"I think there's always two sides to every story," I said carefully. Lawrence would naturally be on Tyler's side, but he had no idea of the difficult position she'd left John in. I sympathized with Tyler but thought, after reading about the rules of the Amish, it would have been kinder if she'd made the decision to leave the community before she married John.

"So, the police have already searched her place," Lawrence went on. He pushed his sliding eyeglasses up with a long finger.

"Yes, that's why they're letting Becky and me pack up her stuff."

"Did they find anything that might point to who did it?" he asked casually. Too casually, it seemed to me.

"If they did, they aren't telling me. Why don't you ask Dewey?"

"Doesn't matter. I was just curious."

Taking a stab in the dark, I asked, "Is there something specific you're thinking about?"

He looked at me sharply. "No. Why do you ask?"

I shrugged. "I don't know—it just sounded as if you had something specific in mind. If there's something you want us to look for . . ."

"She sang in my club," he said, his voice stiff. "She was a friend as well as an employee. That's all there was to it, no matter what anyone says."

So far, except for some ambiguous remarks made by his wife, no one had said anything. Of course, he didn't know that. It confirmed Gabe's theory about interrogating people. The average, non-criminally-oriented person will tell you much more than he intended to if you simply lead him with a few well-chosen questions and then let him talk. Unfortunately Lawrence was not average, or had some experience at being interrogated. He abruptly changed the subject.

"Like I said, better be careful. It can get real rowdy out there sometimes." This time, his words came out almost harshly and sent a small shiver down my spine. Was there the tiniest hint of a threat in his words?

"I'll be okay," I said, telling myself I was imagining things. "Gabe knows where I am," I lied, just for good measure.

"Good," he said, his face mild again. He turned and went toward the door that led back to the nightclub.

Outside, I found the person I was looking for. T.K. was leaning against the back wall, smoking and watching a couple next to an El Camino argue about who was going to drive. "Hi," I said, reinserting the piece of cardboard T.K. had shoved in the doorjamb to keep from being locked out. He nodded to me. We silently watched the woman stomp her white-booted foot like a child. Her teased hair had some kind of glitter in it that sparkled under the parking lot lights. The man's voice was liquor-loud and carried easily across the big lot. I cheered to myself when it appeared she'd won the argument and climbed into the driver's seat. From the way her companion staggered around the car, I knew *he* wasn't in any shape to drive. I just hoped she was. The night sky was thick with jagged clouds and the air was warm and gluey; a storm seemed to be brewing in more than the couple's car. I rubbed my hands up and down my arms, not because I was cold, but because the electricity in the air made me feel tense and edgy.

I waited a moment for T.K. to speak, then blurted out, "I met Tyler the other night at Becky's party. She was very nice to me."

He kept staring straight ahead and took another drag on his cigarette. "That right?"

T.K. was not going to be an easy nut to crack. "I'm sorry about what happened. She talked about you to me. Said you were a really good friend to her. That maybe you were her only real friend."

He dropped his cigarette and ground it out with the scuffed tip of his sharp-toed boots. "She had to be able to depend on someone." His accent was soft and slurry, Alabama maybe, or Arkansas.

"Well, she was lucky to have you." I decided to push a little further. "The police are working hard on finding out who did it, I hear."

He grunted. "Those lazy jerks. They're never going to find out who did it, though I have my suspicions."

"Did you tell the detectives?"

His laugh was sarcastic. "As if it would do any good. They're not going to listen to some flaky musician."

"How do you know if you don't try?"

"Look, all they wanted to know was if I'd ever slept with her. When I tried to tell them that she wasn't like that, they just blew me off. They're determined to make her some kind of whore." He gave me a fierce look. "Tyler was good people. I'm not saying she wasn't ambitious. Shoot, we all are. We're all hoping for that one-in-a-million break. The chance to be that person up there on the stage. We all have dreamed about it ever since we can remember dreaming. Not many of us make it, but enough do that it gives the rest of us hope. Tyler was going to go all the way. She had the talent and the drive. She would have given anything to make it. Now that ain't worth shit.'' He kicked at the loose gravel under his boot.

''Maybe that was the problem,'' I couldn't help saying. ''Maybe she was willing to give up too much.''

He narrowed his eyes. ''You think you wouldn't if you'd been in her place? It's a high you can't even believe, being up there in front of a crowd, them shouting your name, screaming for more. And seeing your name in lights? It's like a shot of cocaine that goes straight to your brain. There are a lot of people willing to give up everything to get all that.''

Tyler did, I thought. She gave up her life. ''To be truthful, I can't understand giving up what she did. Giving up the people you love.''

''No, you got it wrong. *They* gave *her* up.''

I didn't answer, not quite sure how. He was right in a sense—they did give her up. But only after she left them. Who was right, who was wrong? The real trouble was, there was no compromise on either side. The inability to compromise had caused more than one war and broken up more than one marriage throughout the course of history. The irony in regard to my own marital situation was not lost on me. I decided to change the subject and do a little fishing at the same time. ''Where are you from?''

''Arkansas. Why?''

''I thought I recognized your accent. A lot of my family is from there.'' My mind flashed to the postcards at Hannah's house. Was T.K. connected with them in some way? ''Do you still have family in Arkansas?''

He hitched up his loose jeans. ''Some. Around Little Rock mostly.''

''When did you last visit them?''

''Why?''

I shrugged. ''Just making conversation.''

He kept his eyes pinned on my face, his expression suspicious. There was a long silence. Finally he spoke.

"Look, I know what they're saying about her. That she played around. That she used people to get what she wanted. That maybe she deserved what she got. I ain't sayin' she was perfect. All I know is when my sister, Amilee, was dying of bone cancer up in Kansas City and she was crazy scared, Tyler went in and talked with her for five hours straight. I don't know what she said to her, but my baby sister changed after that. She told me that Tyler helped her more than anyone else who'd talked to her. All I know is Amilee died two days later as peaceful as you please. People don't know *that* Tyler." He swallowed hard and fumbled for another cigarette. He stuck it unlit into his mouth.

"Then you should tell them," I said quietly. Before I could say more, the back door opened. Rob stepped out.

"Guess I'm not the only one who needs a break from the honky-tonk lights," he said. Even underneath the unforgiving bluish-white fluorescent security light, Rob was handsome, but there was also a haggard look to him, as if he needed a good solid week of sleep.

T.K. shot Rob a savage look and shoved past him. I caught the door before it slammed shut and wedged the cardboard back in the jamb.

"What's his problem?" Rob asked.

I shrugged and looked at my watch. "I'm not much for the honky-tonk scene anymore myself," I said, answering his earlier comment. "Getting too old, I guess. It's almost past my bedtime." Far off, a bolt of lightning lit up the clouds, the zigzag edge showing from the bottom as in a child's simplistic drawing. Thunder sizzled in the distance.

"That's funny, Gabe was just saying the same thing. Of course, if I had such a sweet little thing like you to come home to, I'd sure as heck consider an early bedtime myself. Every night and twice on Sundays."

I looked at the ground, embarrassed by his hokey flirting. That sort of joking so soon after his girlfriend's death struck me as rather cold-blooded, and it really made me wonder about his so-called suicide attempt. Another blaze of electricity brightened the sky, followed by rumbling thunder.

"Becky and I are cleaning out Tyler's room tomorrow," I blurted out, changing the subject. "I'm sure she has some stuff of yours. Do you want us to set it aside for you to look through?" I had to admit I was fishing again, though I wasn't sure what for. I thought I was safe in assuming that Hannah would have no interest in whatever things Rob had given her sister.

"You're what?" His eyes widened in disbelief.

"We have permission," I said quickly. "Her . . . husband gave it to us."

"Why wasn't I told?" he demanded. He raised a trembling hand to his jaw. Could he fake a reaction like that? I thought about his emotional outburst the night that Tyler's body was found. His display of grief hadn't looked fake to me. Then again, I'd read enough about sociopaths to know that their own feelings were abnormally important to them. His emotional devastation could just as well have been caused by the realization that she was no longer around for *his* pleasure. Could he have killed her? I felt my stomach flip-flop as the thought zipped through my mind. If there was the remotest possibility that Rob was a killer, what in the world was I doing standing out here in a deserted parking lot with him?

"I should have been informed," he repeated.

"Why?" I asked.

"Dewey's going to hear about this." He swung around and barreled through the back door.

"Wait . . ." I grabbed for the door, but I was too slow. It slammed shut. The piece of cardboard lay uselessly on the stained concrete step.

"Well, this is just great," I said out loud. The long back wall of the club loomed in front of me. I'd have to walk along it, around the corner, and down the length of the club to get to the front entrance. I started inching that way, trying not to think about how deserted the parking lot was. Of course, deserted could be a lot less dangerous than occupied, depending on who did the occupying. I thought about the three men I'd just talked to, how Tyler was a different person to each of them. Who was Tyler/Ruth? Had she herself even known? I reached the corner of the building and looked down the long expanse of wall I'd have to follow to the entrance.

A sharp crack of lightning caused me to jump. Then everything went black. My heart moved into my throat. Stop? Keep going? My mind swung back and forth between the two. In the distance, I could hear screaming and the loud rumble of male voices. I stood back against the rough wall of the club and watched the light-show in the sky. Every time the sky lit up, I inched a little farther down the building. Then a flood of bright lights temporarily blinded me. I felt like an animal caught in the cross hairs of a giant rifle.

"Are you okay, honey?" a male voice yelled out. The array of lights on his four-wheel-drive pickup would have put a Broadway stage to shame.

"Yes," I called back, using his lights to make my way quickly around to the front of the building. "Thanks." His horn honked a "Wish I was in the land of Dixie" reply. At the front of the club, bouncers with huge police-sized flashlights were trying to maintain calm among the people pouring out of the crowded building. Then, as quickly as they'd gone out, the lights flickered back on. A huge cheer went up from the people still inside.

"What happened?" I asked one of the bouncers.

"Lightning probably hit a generator," he said. "We're using backup now." From behind the corner I'd just come around, Gabe appeared, his face stiff and scared.

"Are you okay?" He pulled me to him.

"Fine," I mumbled into his chest.

He held me at arm's length and looked into my eyes.
"Are you sure?"

"Yes," I said. "Was that exciting or what? You Kansans sure know how to put on a party." Then I yawned. It really was getting past my bedtime.

"You should have seen the chaos inside," Gabe said, pulling me back to his side, his arm tight around me. "I couldn't find you. I saw you go out back. I— Look, this about makes it a night for me. What about you?"

I answered him with another yawn. "I have to go back and get my purse. It was hanging on my chair."

Inside, people were still laughing and comparing stories about what they were doing during the three- or four-minute blackout. Over where we'd been sitting, Becky and Janet were wiping up a beer that had spilled across the round table.

"Good, you found her," Becky said to Gabe. She pushed a wad of soggy napkins to the middle of the table and with another wad blotted at a large wet stain on the left leg of her jeans. "When the lights went out, all I heard was Gabe yelling your name, and then someone spilled this beer on me."

"I was out back getting some fresh air," I said.

She threw the wet napkins down with the rest and looked with disgust at her leg. "Well, this ends the party for me. It's after eleven anyway, and we have a busy day tomorrow."

I grabbed my purse from the back of the chair next to her while Gabe went over to see how the rest of the group had fared in the blackout. "I'm with you. I just came back to get this." I opened it and quickly checked the contents. Keys, lip gloss, comb, and most important, wallet . . . and something else, though I couldn't remember what. Then it hit me. John's note.

I turned to Becky. "Did you give me back that note from John?"

"Yes, you stuck it in your purse."

"Are you sure?"

She looked at me oddly. "Of course. I watched you do it. Why?"

"It's gone. Somebody must have taken it when the lights were out."

"Why would someone do that?"

"Do what?" Gabe asked, walking back up to our table.

"Someone took the note Tyler's husband wrote giving us permission to pack up her things," I said.

His lips tightened visibly under his mustache. "I didn't like the idea of you doing it anyway."

"We're still going to do it, Gabe," his sister said, exasperated. "Except now I'm going to have to drive out to Miller tomorrow morning and get another note. That will make me late to the quilt setup."

"I could go to Hannah's," I volunteered.

Gabe started to open his mouth, but his sister jumped in before he could protest. "No, I'll go. I'd like to see how she's doing. You've spent enough of your vacation running errands. Do something fun tomorrow."

We made plans to meet at one o'clock at Becky's house and then drive to the house in Northeast Wichita where Tyler had rented a room.

Gabe and I didn't talk on the twenty-minute drive back to Derby. I was thinking about who would steal John's note. The culprit had to realize it would only delay us looking through her things. I thought about who had the opportunity, and came to the conclusion that everyone at our table did and a good many of them could have something to hide about their connection to Tyler. I considered Lawrence and his possible relationship with her, pondered my funny feelings about Rob, Janet's cryptic words that afternoon, and T.K.'s revelation about the kind and giving side of Tyler. He probably saw more of the side of Tyler who was Ruth, the person Hannah grew up with and loved. Tyler had been much more complex than any of us could imagine. I wondered if the police knew any of this about her and if it would do them any good. Then, though I fought it, I turned my mind to Dewey's words about men and women and how he'd hit the nail on the head when he said Gabe had me running in circles. I felt myself becoming increasingly irritated as I thought about it. Feeling like an idiot, I swore to myself I'd never ask my husband again what he was feeling. Ever.

"What were you doing out in the parking lot?" Gabe asked suddenly as we pulled into his mother's driveway.

I shrugged. "Talking."

"To who?"

"A guy in the band. And to Rob. He came on to me." I don't know why I threw that out. Maybe to keep Gabe from asking what T.K. and I talked about. Maybe just because I was tired. Maybe, as Dove would probably say, I wanted to rub the cat's fur the wrong way just to see the sparks.

"Who, the guy in the band?" Gabe said.

"No, Rob."

"Are you sure?"

"Geeze, Gabe, I'm certainly not as experienced as you, but I think I know when a guy is flirting with me."

"What are you mad about?" he said evenly. I recognized the tone, his I'm-acting-like-a-grown-up-even-if-you-aren't voice.

"I'm not mad," I snapped. "I'm tired."

"What did Rob say to you?" he asked patiently.

"Nothing I couldn't handle." I opened the door and climbed out. "I just think it's pathetic that a guy can act like that so soon after his girlfriend is murdered, but then I guess I'm expecting men to have the same sensitivity as women, and we all know *that's* asking the impossible."

He didn't answer, even though I'd thrown down that tempting gauntlet. We didn't speak even after we'd both settled under the sheets, the fan blowing air that seemed to be filled with tiny arrows of electricity. The storm had started again, and lightning lit up the room as bright as daylight, over and over until it seemed to me that there couldn't possibly be any electricity left in the world. Why couldn't someone harness all that power and do something useful with it? Then finally the rain came, and I listened to the clop-clop of the heavy drops on the wooden roof—the same roof, the same sound that Gabe grew up hearing. I tried to imagine being inside his mind, being a young boy lying in this room, listening to the rain, dreaming his little boy dreams.

I felt him stir next to me.

"I know this probably doesn't mean much to you now," he said. With his back to me, his voice sounded far away, as if he were calling over a great canyon. "But I love you."

Feeling as mean as I ever have in my life and hating myself for doing it, I bit my trembling lip and didn't answer.

TEN

"COULD YOU DROP me off over at Otis's?" I asked Gabe the next day as I stood at the kitchen sink washing the breakfast dishes.

"There's no need for you to do those," Kathryn said.

"I want to," I insisted, thinking, You may not think I'm the perfect mate for your son, and for all I know you might be right, but I sure as heck am not going to give you a reason to call me lazy.

"I thought you were going to help Becky with Tyler's things," Gabe said, not even trying to keep the sarcasm out of his voice.

"Not until this afternoon."

His feelings were written all over his face. He opened his mouth to say something. Before he could get the words out, I said, "I'm going to help her. No discussion." He and his mother glanced at each other. I turned back to the sink and scrubbed furiously at the coffee-stained mug in my hand. Fine, I thought, the two of you can just sit and exchange disapproving looks all day. "So, what time is the rodeo tonight?"

"Eight o'clock," Gabe said, his voice as tart as a green apple. "We need to leave by six. Pretty Prairie's about sixty-five miles away."

I turned around and gave him and Kathryn a big smile. "Well, if I'm not back in time, go ahead without me. I'll catch a ride with Becky."

"Fine," Gabe said, retreating behind his morning *Wichita Eagle*.

"Will you be home in time for supper?" Kathryn asked. Her stern face looked worried. For a moment, I felt a small stab of sympathy. She loved Gabe and was probably just not sure if I was the right person for him. Well, Mrs. Ortiz, take a number.

"I don't know," I said, rinsing off the last plate and wedging it in the white plastic dish drainer. "But don't worry about me. You know rodeos. They always have lots of junk food. I'll be fine."

I was drying my hands with a white flour-sack tea towel when the phone rang. Kathryn answered it, then held it out to me.

"A gentleman is asking for you," she said. Gabe lowered the paper and watched me with that irritatingly blank look on his face.

I took the phone, wondering what man would be calling me at Kathryn's and why. When I heard the voice at the other end, I almost hung up.

"It's not my fault," my uncle Arnie whined. "I swear, Benni, it's not my—" I heard someone grappling for the phone, and then my father's deep baritone bellowed through the line.

"I swear this time I'm going to strangle her," he said. "I'm going to have her committed. I'm going to send her to live with Garnet. This takes the cake. This is the last nail in the keg. This is the straw that—"

"Broke the camel's back," I finished. "I know, I know. Enough of the hysterical homilies. What in the heck is going on?"

"She's *your* grandmother."

"Your grandmother," Arnie echoed in the background.

Somewhere in the miles between California and Kansas, it had slipped their minds that she was *their* mother before she was my grandmother.

I sighed and leaned against the wall, giving Gabe and his mother a perfunctory smile. What did it matter now what Kathryn thought about me or my family? There was no avoiding the inevitable, no whitewashing the truth. She would find out sooner or later that her son had married into a certifiably, Looney-Tunes-has-nothing-on-us nutso Southern family—Lord have mercy on his poor, bland Midwestern soul.

"What's she done now?" I asked. Hearing his voice reminded me that I needed to call Shepler's and check on the progress of his hat.

"Done? She's done gone, is what she is!"

"Gone? As in gone to the bathroom, gone to lunch, gone to—"

"As in gone for good," Daddy said.

I straightened up and yelled into the phone. "What? She's not—" My head started to get light, and stars sparkled in front of my eyes. Was this my father's awkward way of telling me . . . ?

"Oh, for cryin' out loud," Daddy said. "She's not dead. She up and left us. Left nothing but a note with the motel clerk. Said she'd meet us in Derby Saturday after."

I took a deep breath. By now Gabe had gotten up and was standing next to me, his face furrowed with worry. I held up one finger and mouthed, Just a minute.

"Daddy," I said patiently, "calm down and tell me what happened. Slowly. From the beginning. First, where are you?"

"At the Yellow Rose of Texas Motel and Truckateria."

"Where's that?"

" 'Bout a mile outside the town of Old Dime Box."

"Where in the heck is Old Dime Box?"

"Near the town of Dime Box." He chuckled. In the background, I heard Arnie chuckling too. If there were a way to reach through these phone wires and knock their two heads together . . .

"And where's Dime Box?" I asked through gritted teeth.

"Texas. Anyway, we woke up and knocked on her door. When she didn't answer, we figured she was at the coffee shop that's attached to the motel. But she wasn't, and so we went back to the room and knocked again. 'Course, by this time we was gettin' a little bit worried, so we walked around the grounds a little bit, and then Arnie almost stepped on a rattler, ignorant fool that he is—"

"Daddy." I broke into his monologue before it turned into one of the long, convoluted tales our family is known for. "Just tell me where she is."

"According to the motel clerk, she took off with Brother Dwaine."

"Who?"

"Brother Dwaine Porter Wilburn. Apparently he's some kind of travelin' preacher to truckers or something. He's got himself one of them big rigs, a brand new Peterbilt, and goes all around the country preachin' in a church he has in the back. Even has the Lord's Supper back there. He was once a trucker himself; then he decided that God was calling him to minister out on the road. His truck is painted white with a big blue dove on it."

"You seem to know an awful lot about this guy," I said suspiciously.

"Oh, we met him last night when we were having supper in the cafe. He and your gramma hit it off like a ball of fire. He seemed like a nice enough fella." In the course of our conversation, Daddy had managed to talk himself into thinking everything was peachy-keen.

"Daddy, he's a perfect stranger and he has Dove!"

"Now, pumpkin, he's not a perfect stranger." My father's voice took on the cajoling tone he used whenever he knew he'd really blown it. "We did meet him, and Amos Bob says he's on the up and up. Has himself a regular route. Amos Bob says he's been through here dozens of times.''

"Who's Amos Bob?" This was beginning to sound like a bad episode of *The Dukes of Hazzard*.

"Amos Bob Carter. Owns the Yellow Rose Cafe here. No relation to Jimmy, but get a load of his initials— ABC. Ain't that somethin'?''

"Oh, yes," I said. "Really something. Now, about Dove—"

"It'll be all right, Benni. I've already got that figured out. Amos Bob says all we got to do is listen to the CB, that the Reverend Dwaine's always trying to convert someone on it. We'll find her.''

"You'd better," I snapped. "Do you realize what could happen? You know, if you and Arnie would just quit squabbling like teenagers . . .''

"She stomped on my good hat and then she threw it away," Daddy said. "And just for the record, young lady, this is your daddy you're talking to. I'll be asking for a little more respect than you're giving.''

"Don't even think about showing up without her," I said and hung up.

"What's going on?" Gabe asked, his face sober, but his eyes twinkling, having caught the gist of the conversation. He'd tangled with Dove himself, and he was no doubt thanking his lucky stars this skirmish didn't involve him.

"You heard," I snapped. "My grandmother is running amuck with a truck-driving evangelist she's known for two hours, and Daddy and Arnie, doing their Three-Stooges-minus-one act, are trying to find her via the truckers' CB network. Just another uneventful day with the Ramsey clan. Excuse me." I turned and left, tears burning my eyes. I was in the bedroom pulling on my boots when Gabe appeared in the doorway.

"Is there anything you want me to do about Dove?" he asked gently. He knew me well enough to know I was really afraid for her safety.

"Unless you can put out an all-points bulletin, I guess not."

"She's an adult, and though you doubt it sometimes, completely sane and rational," he said. "Unless there's some reason to believe she's being held against her will, we really can't do anything."

"I know." I leaned over and rested my head on my knees. His large hand stroked my hair, and I almost gave in to the sob swelling like a balloon in my chest. I sat up and moved out of his reach. No matter what was going on with Dove, that didn't change things between Gabe and me. "Can you take me to Otis's now?"

"Sure," he said, pulling his hand back abruptly, his voice cool. As was becoming our habit these days, we didn't speak during the ten-minute drive. "See you tonight" was all he said when I climbed out in the farmhouse driveway. He waved to Otis, who watched our grim faces from his front porch.

Otis greeted me with an easy smile, not commenting on my troubled expression. He took me into the barn, pointed out where he kept the tack, and with great kindness and wisdom left me alone. I stood for a moment inhaling the comforting smell of horse, straw, and leather, then gradually lost myself in the familiar routine of grooming. I cleaned each of Sinful's hooves with the thoroughness of a new horse-lover and brushed his coat until it gleamed. The extra attention seemed to agree with him. If he'd been a cat, he would have probably purred. For the next two hours, I completely avoided thoughts of Gabe, Dove, murder, and Kansas, and just worked with Sinful. He was a lively, strong horse with excellent timing and a real desire to please once he realized you were the boss. By the time the sun was directly overhead and the humidity was at the point where I knew it was dangerous to keep working, Sinful and I were both sweaty and tired and ready for a break. I spent another hour giving him a bath and cleaning him up. I was a happy mess when I walked out of the barn.

Otis got up from his rocking chair on the front porch and called to me. "Got lunch ready if you're hungry."

"Absolutely," I said enthusiastically, bounding up the steps. I followed him into the old farmhouse kitchen where he had set two places for lunch. The faded calico-patterned wallpaper and gingham curtains made me feel as though I'd stepped back in time and was seeing the kitchen as it was in the thirties.

"You know," he said, setting a platter of tuna on white bread sandwiches on the round claw-foot table, "you're a lot prettier when you're smiling."

"You know," I said, taking a sandwich and grinning, "you're only getting away with such a chauvinistic remark because you're so much older than me."

He gave a deep belly laugh and set a carton of store-bought macaroni salad and a big bag of barbecue potato chips in front of me. "You're right."

We talked easily about Sinful and what I'd done with the horse that morning, and then somehow Otis steered the conversation around to Gabe and his dad.

"Rogelio was my best friend," he said, sitting back in his chair. "But he was a hardheaded son of a gun. He and Gabe used to get in some hair-raising fights. Especially after Gabe became a teenager. I'm here to tell you, I stood between those two many times. That's because Gabe was as stubborn as his pa. Loyal, though. Those Ortiz men are loyal as the day is long."

I murmured a vague reply, attempting to discourage his reminiscing. Before, I would have tried to add these pieces to the puzzle that was my husband, but I was tired of hearing his life through other people's words. I wanted to hear about Gabe and his dad, but I wanted to hear it from Gabe.

"Have the police been back out here?" I asked, pushing around the remains of the macaroni salad on my plate.

"They were in and out about a dozen times those first

few days, but I think they're done now.''

''Who do you think did it?''

''To tell you the truth, I never much liked that Rob Harlow. Spoiled brat since he was a young'un.''

''So you think he did it?''

''I didn't say that. Just said I never liked him.'' Otis grinned at me and stuck his pipe between his teeth.

In other words, he didn't want to speculate. Well, I couldn't blame him. He'd known these people since they were kids. ''Are you ever going to light that thing?'' I asked, laughing.

He took the pipe out of his mouth and looked at it as if surprised to see it was there. ''This old thing? Land sake's, no. Doc Bradley made me quit smoking ten years ago. This here's just for looks. The ladies down at the senior citizen center say it gives me a certain air.'' He brushed the air around him as if something smelled bad. ''Reckon that's a compliment or you think they're trying to tell me something?''

A few minutes later Becky called. ''Said she'll meet you out front in ten minutes,'' Otis told me. He walked me out to the yard. ''You make sure and come back now. Old Sinful's gotten used to being rode, and we don't want to disappoint him.''

''I'll come again soon as I can.''

As we walked past the barn, he touched my elbow. ''I want to show you something. See what you think.'' I followed him around the back of the barn to a small garage-like building with dusty windows. He slid the door open and beckoned me to follow him. It was an auto mechanic's dream. Obviously this was where he kept all the tools from the garage he and Gabe's dad had owned. A vehicle was parked inside, a stiff new tarp thrown over it.

''I've been working on this old thing for a while now.'' He pulled the tarp off the vehicle and stood back. For a moment I was speechless.

"It looks like the old Chevy pickup in the picture of Gabe and his dad!"

"It *is* the one in the picture," he said proudly, stroking a fender with one knotty, oil-stained hand. "A 1950 Chevrolet three-speed three-quarter ton. I was with Rogelio when he bought it. First new truck he ever owned. Bought it in honor of his son being born."

"You did a wonderful job restoring it." I walked around the shiny blue truck, opened the driver's side door, and peered in at the restored upholstery. "Have you had it all these years?"

"Nah, Kathryn asked me to get rid of it after Rogelio died. I sold it to a fella down in Winfield. About a year later I got a bug in my ear about it. I knew one thing about that old Winfield boy, he never threw nothing out. Sure enough, it was sitting there out back of his barn. I've been tinkering with it, waiting for the right time to give it to Gabe. Him getting married again and living there in the country, such as it is in California, seemed like a good time. Think it'll be a fitting wedding present for you two?"

"It's incredible. I love it. He's going to love it."

He chewed on the stem of his pipe, his cheeks rosy with pleasure. "Well, now, I thought you two being a bit long in the tooth and both married before, you probably already had a toaster oven."

Out front, Becky's horn honked, and I hurriedly helped Otis pull the tarp back over the truck.

"No one knows about this but you and me," he said, locking the door behind us. "Keep it under your hat."

"Cowboy's honor," I said, crossing my heart.

"What were you and Otis doing back in his garage?" Becky asked, pulling out on the highway.

"He was just showing me some of his tools."

"Heaven knows, he has enough of them." She took a backroad that eventually brought us to the entrance of the Kansas turnpike. "This'll get us into Wichita faster. So, are you all ready to do a little sleuthing, Sherlock?"

"You know as well as I do that the cops have already taken anything remotely suspicious," I said. "I am curious, though, about how Tyler lived. After hearing how she grew up, I can't help wondering what our world must have initially seemed like to her. Talk about culture shock."

"No kidding." Becky took the ticket from the toll attendant, and seconds later we were barreling down the turnpike at eighty miles an hour. "I've got about ten boxes in the back there. Hope it's enough."

"I assume you know where we're going," I said.

"I called Dewey this morning and got the address as well as the phone number of her landlady, Mrs. Parker. She sounded relieved that someone was picking up Tyler's stuff. I guess there's some kind of family crisis, and she needs the room cleaned out right away."

The Wichita neighborhood where Tyler had lived was an older one of moderately maintained two- and three-story wood-frame houses built in that utilitarian farmhouse style that seemed so popular everywhere in the Midwest. Children, both black and white, rode their bicycles along cracked sidewalks under trees lush and ancient enough to shade the whole width of the street. It was a neighborhood of fifteen-year-old cars, wraparound porches filled with vinyl-webbed aluminum patio furniture, and patchy front lawns. Mrs. Parker's three-story house was painted a deep blue with white trim. Someone obviously liked zinnias, because they filled the front-yard flower bed in a riotous blast of yellow and red.

We pulled into the driveway, walked up the front steps, and knocked at the door. Mrs. Parker let us in. She was a tall, full-bodied black woman with fluffy hair the color of an oyster shell and a silky contralto voice that was probably the pride and joy of her church's choir.

"I'm sure sorry I got to put you through this so soon after that poor child's misfortune, but my sister's done kicked her son out the house, and he's stayin' on my

living room sofa. His snoring's about to drive me crazy.
I got to get him in his own room.'' We followed her
lumbering form up steep wooden stairs. ''You relatives
of Tyler's?''

''No, just friends,'' I said. ''But we have permission
from her husband to get her things.'' I held out the note
for her to read.

She flipped it away. ''Oh, I believe you, honey. I can't
imagine anyone wanting to steal any of her stuff. Sweet
little thing, she was, but she didn't have much. She'd
come down to the parlor sometimes, and her and me,
we'd sing like two of the Lord's sweetest birds. Musta
been raised in the church 'cause she knew all the old
hymns by heart.'' When we reached the third floor, she
stopped and looked at us. ''Husband, huh? Well, she
never said nothin' about him, but I had my suspicions
she was running from something. Seen it before and will
more'n likely see it again. She was a good tenant,
though. Always paid her rent right on time. What was
he, one of them abusive types?''

''Oh, I don't think so,'' I said. ''He's, uh, Amish.''

''Amish? You mean those people who dress like the
pilgrims and do all that pretty quilting? Well, bless my
soul. I always thought she was kinda odd. If that just
don't beat all.'' She shook her head and opened a door
with one of the keys from a huge ring on her patent
leather belt. ''Well, if you ladies need any help, just give
me a holler. I'll be downstairs in the kitchen.'' She
shook her head. ''Like I said, she was a real sweet young
girl. Too sweet to be in the business she was in. I knew
that the first time I met her. Me bein' up till all hours
waiting for my no-good son to be gettin' in, I'd watch
her come in all wrung out and tired, big ole black circles
under her eyes, and I'd say, 'Honey, what are you doin'
killing yourself for this fool thing that may never happen? Nothin's worth this much pain. Why don't you go
on home?' And she say, 'Louella, I can't. I just can't.'
Oh, she wanted that fame and fortune, all right. She just

wanted it so bad. I reckon I just don't understand wantin' something that bad.'' She gave us a perplexed look and headed down the stairs.

I stepped across the threshold into Tyler's room. It was small with only a single bed, mirrored dresser, rocking chair, bookcase, nightstand, and a small student desk in that cheap Early American maple style popular in the fifties. The room was warm and stuffy, since the one screenless window was closed. With a few hard shoves, I managed to get it open.

Becky wrinkled her nose and frowned. ''All that trouble to get her husband's permission, and Mrs. Parker didn't even glance at the note.''

''But if we hadn't, maybe we'd be breaking some kind of law.''

''I suppose. Why do you think that first note got stolen?''

I shrugged and opened the middle drawer of the desk. ''Who knows? Maybe it wasn't stolen. Maybe it just fell out of my purse in all that craziness.'' Or, I thought, maybe there's something here someone doesn't want us to find.

Becky placed her hands on her hips. ''Mrs. Parker said the furniture came with the room, so I guess everything else must be Tyler's.''

''The police were pretty neat,'' I said. ''You can't even tell anyone's been through her stuff.'' A paperback rhyming dictionary lying on the nightstand caught my eye. Its pages were flimsy and slightly oily from use. It sat on top of a two-week-old issue of *Billboard* and a copy of *Country Weekly* magazine with a picture of Rick Trevino, an up-and-coming young singer, on the cover. The sight of those trade publications and all the dreams they represented to Tyler, dampened my interest in looking for clues among her belongings.

''I'll get the boxes,'' Becky said. ''Guess you may as well start.''

I went back to the desk and peered into all the drawers. They were full of the usual paraphernalia that most people shove into a desk. I started taking out the pencils, papers, rubber bands, and other junk and piling it on the bed.

Becky and I were a good team. I started at one end of the room, she at the opposite end, and we worked toward each other, filling the cartons, occasionally making a comment about some little thing we picked up. We both became increasingly quiet and sober as we folded and packed. I stood up after pulling out bags of winter clothes she had stored under the bed and wiped at the sweat trickling down my face.

"Here," Becky said, reaching into a box she'd just brought up and tossing me an icy cold bottle of Evian water. "I knew we'd get thirsty."

"Bless the foresight of experienced mothers." I sat cross-legged on the hardwood floor and leaned against a wall. "All we have left is the closet."

She sat on the bed and gave me a tired look. "This is harder than I thought it would be. And creepier."

"Yeah." I picked at the Evian label and thought of the day Dove and I cleaned out Jack's things and packed them in boxes that were still sitting in the back of the barn. What should I do with them now? I had wondered. What will Hannah do with Tyler's possessions? Boxes of books and cards and letters and the different little mementos we pick up here and there as we live life, never thinking that someday someone will have to find a place for these things. That's why there were antique stores, I supposed. I'd always wondered where those stained pictures of sober-faced people and ashtrays bought at the Chicago World's Fair came from. Now I knew.

"Well, let's get it done," I said, draining the bottle of water and standing up. We opened the closet and started pulling clothes off hangers and folding them up. Becky pulled out a white cardboard box and set it on the bed.

I dug through a box that contained a slew of rejection letters from music publishing companies, sheets of notebook paper with what appeared to be half-finished song lyrics scribbled on them, old phone bills, and still more rejection letters. I sighed, wondering what I expected. Any personal letters would have certainly been taken by the detectives.

"Benni, look at this." Becky's voice was excited.

I backed out of the closet and faced her.

She held up a small rectangular wall quilt made of navy blue, bright pink, forest-green, and black. "Can you believe it? I thought Tyler had sold all her quilts."

I walked over to her and stared down at the pattern, searching my store of knowledge for its name. The single-star pattern made from triangles seemed familiar, as if I'd seen it recently. The name tickled the tip of my tongue, but wouldn't come to mind.

"Just look at these stitches," Becky said. "I've seen a lot of Tyler's work, but this is the best quilting of hers I've ever seen. I'm taking this right out to Hannah. I'm sure she'll want it. Maybe it'll make her feel better. Do you recognize the pattern? You did pretty good that first night at my house."

"It looks familiar, but I can't think of it."

"Oh, well, we'll look it up in one of my reference books when we get home. It's not important. I'm sure that Hannah will be thrilled to have it."

We finished packing up the rest of Tyler's clothes and carried the boxes down to the car. As Becky turned on the ignition, I made an excuse to go see Mrs. Parker again.

"I'm going to tell her we're all through," I said.

"Okay," Becky replied, leaning her face close to the air conditioning vent. "I'll cool off the car."

Mrs. Parker was in her large red and yellow kitchen stirring a pot of dark green vegetables.

"We're finished," I said from the doorway. She gestured me in. I walked over and peered into the simmering pot. Tiny pieces of ham floated in the bubbling liquid. "Turnip greens?" I asked.

"Why, that's right!" she exclaimed. "Where'd you say you was from?"

"California," I said, smiling. "But my family's from Arkansas."

"Why, so's mine!" She put the lid back on the pot and faced me, wiping her hands on her flowered apron. "My mama's side anyway. Papa's side hails from Alabama." She looked at me curiously. "How'd you come to be involved with that crazy business up there?" She gestured above us.

"Becky—that's the lady who's with me—was friends with Tyler. Becky's my sister-in-law. I married her brother about five months ago."

"Umm . . ." She nodded her head. "Meetin' the new family, huh?"

I smiled and shrugged. "Yeah, something like that."

"Well, I just hope that poor girl Tyler's family gives her a proper buryin'. She deserves at least that. We all deserve at least that."

"I'm sure they will," I said, even though I wasn't.

"And I hope they catch whoever did that terrible thing to her. I told those policemen that, too."

"I guess they questioned you right away," I said.

"Next day. Three of them. If *that* ain't just the craziest thing. I told them I couldn't tell three of them any more than I could tell one. No wonder our taxes is so high. Too many people doin' the same thing."

I nodded and made an agreeing sound. "What did you tell them?"

"Not much to tell. She didn't bring men home, which is what they really wanted to know. She was a nice girl, ain't nobody gonna convince me of nothin' different. She didn't have a phone, you know. Had to use mine. But she always left money on the table, even if it was a local call. There's others around here that ain't that considerate." She sniffed irritably and turned around to pull a bag of cornmeal from the shelf over the stove.

"Did she get many phone calls?"

"The police asked me that, and my answer hasn't changed. Not many, although this last coupla weeks she got more than usual. Always the same man. Always late at night. Always said, is Tyler there. That's it." She ripped open the paper sack and poured some cornmeal into a bowl without using a measuring cup, just like Dove.

"Would you recognize the voice?" It was a remote possibility, but I had to ask.

"Police asked me that, too. Tell you what I told them. All Midwestern white folks sound the same to me." She chuckled and shook her head.

I laughed in agreement. It was true; like native Californians, Kansans really had no discernible accent. Of course, that didn't help me, seeing as all the people who were suspects had been born and raised here.

"Well, it was nice talking to you." I started for the door.

"He made her cry the last time," Mrs. Parker said.

I swung around and faced her. "He did?"

"Most of the time she wasn't here to take his calls, and far as I know, she didn't return them. Anyways, she didn't use *my* phone to return them. But the last time he called he was real mad. Told me to tell her to call or else. After she did, she started bawlin' her eyes out right here in my kitchen."

"About what?"

"She wouldn't say. Just said that men are the same everywhere. That they think they own you, can take your life and twist it around however they want. I told her that's why I never remarried after Lyle died. I like being my own boss. Ain't no man never going to be telling me what to do anymore." Her jovial face grew hard. I wondered about her late husband and what he'd done to cause her dark eyes to flash so angrily.

"That's all she told you?"

"That's it."

"Did you tell the police that?"

"I sure did. I want them to catch that lowlife who killed her. 'Course, they took it about as serious as you'd expect a bunch of white men to take the ramblings of an old black woman. With a pinch of nothing.'' She rubbed her thumb and forefinger together and tossed imaginary salt over her shoulder.

"Did she ever get any calls from women?"

"Not that I ever took."

"Thanks."

"What took you so long?" Becky asked when I returned. The Jeep had cooled off to a wonderful winter-like chill.

"Sorry, I just got to talking with Mrs. Parker about Southern cooking.'' We listened to the news as we sped down the turnpike toward Derby. This time I was thankful for Becky's heavy foot. I wanted to get back in time to take a quick shower before the rodeo that night. She started talking about the quilt show on Friday and what she had to do to get ready and who was a help in the guild and who was just a big pain in the butt. I nodded and murmured an appropriate response occasionally, but my mind drifted, thinking about the man who kept calling Tyler, the boxes of Tyler's things in the back of the Cherokee, and especially about the quilt. There was something about the quilt that bothered me, but I couldn't put my finger on it. It wasn't just that I couldn't think of the name of the pattern; something else had set off a warning buzz in me.

"Earth to Benni," Becky said, reaching over and tapping my thigh.

"I'm sorry. What did you say?"

"I was saying that my mother told me that your aunt Garnet in Arkansas is an award-winning quilter. Too bad she can't see our show."

"She is," I said automatically. Then it dawned on me. "That's it!"

"What's it?"

"The pattern. I've seen it before because Aunt Garnet pieced one for my grandmother the last time she visited her. It was right around the time I met Gabe." I knew it wouldn't mean anything to anyone but me. Not to Becky. And certainly not to the police. The question was, what was the connection, and what should I do with the information?

"So, is this twenty questions or what?" Becky asked.

"Arkansas Traveler," I said.

ELEVEN

"I WONDER WHY she picked that pattern?" Becky said, pulling into her mother's driveway. "It's not exactly traditional Amish."

"Maybe that's what attracted her."

Becky shrugged. "Guess I'll see you at the rodeo. Tyler was supposed to sing the national anthem there tonight. I heard Cordie June's taking her place, just like at the club."

"An odd run of luck for Cordie June."

Becky rolled her eyes. "This sounds terrible, but I can't stand Cordie June. She's so set on becoming rich and famous that if I didn't know any better I'd guess she . . . well . . . never mind. It's just too unbelievable to contemplate."

"I suppose," I murmured, wondering what Becky would think if she knew there was supposed to be a producer in the audience last night, that Tyler's death was more than just convenient for Cordie June, it was her golden opportunity. I wondered if Dewey knew about it. If so, would he slack off on the investigation because of his relationship with Cordie June? Then again, he wasn't even supposed to be officially working on the case. I decided that I would tell Gabe about the producer and let him decide who should be advised. That would ease my conscience on one thing. The quilt we found in Tyler's room . . . that was another story. I suspected Tyler made it to remember something about Arkansas. I didn't know how to tell anyone what I knew without admitting I'd snooped in Hannah's house and dragging her deeper into it. Tyler was down in Arkansas for six months and apparently made a commemorative quilt while she was there. What did she want to remember about Arkansas? Was T.K. involved somehow, since he came from there?

"See you in a couple of hours," Becky said. "Tell my mom I've got all the quilts moved off the guest bed so she can sleep there tonight."

"Why is she sleeping at your house?"

"She's staying with the girls tonight because Stan and I want to go to the dance after the rodeo. We'll take the kids and Mom to tomorrow night's performance. We'll probably get in late, so Mom may as well spend the night. Gotta run." She threw the Cherokee in reverse and whipped out of the driveway, gravel clattering over her tires like rain on a tin roof.

I relayed the message to Kathryn before going upstairs to take a quick shower and change. A note from Gabe and a highlighted map lay on the pillow next to the Camaro's keys. "Caught a ride with Dewey and Chet. See you at the rodeo. Gabe."

I sighed and carried my clothes into the bathroom. With the tension between us, there was only one thing I was absolutely certain about tonight—it was going to be long. I took my time dressing so that by the time I emerged from the bathroom, Kathryn and, thankfully, Daphne, had already left.

I drove leisurely through Wichita until eventually city and semirural suburb became open prairie. The turnoff to Pretty Prairie, Highway 17, was a small, lonely road that bisected endless rows of green corn and dark plowed-under wheat fields. For twenty minutes at a time

I was the only vehicle on the road, but the isolation soothed me as did the emerald and black fields with their neatness and purpose. I wondered which fields were round like the ones I saw from the plane, and thought of what Gabe had said—how from this point of view no one would ever know their shape; that to see the truth of the fields you had to look at them from another per-spective. Was it like that with Tyler's murder? Was there something right in front of all our eyes that we were overlooking because our perspective was wrong?

I passed a huge white Mennonite church set in the mid-dle of nowhere, and a few fields and passing trucks later, I entered the town of Pretty Prairie—population six hun-dred. To my right were the grain elevators I was getting used to seeing in any Kansas town boasting a population of fifty or more, and a huge white banner announcing "Welcome Rodeo Fans! Kansas' Largest Night Rodeo—Free Chuckwagon Barbecue w/Friday Night Rodeo Ticket." My stomach growled at the thought, and I was sorry it was Thursday instead of Friday. You could stand at one end of Main Street and take in the entire town in one glance—the red brick high school, the bar with a faded Budweiser sign above the door, the post office, the Wagon Wheel Cafe, The Country Cafe (Mexican Food on Saturday Eve), D & J Grocery (Where Pleasant People Shop), The Country Parlor (Homemade Gifts, Crafts and Baked Goods). The street was already half filled with every color and make of pickup truck.

I parked the Camaro in front of the Pretty Prairie Civic Theater, an old movie house that appeared to be in the middle of renovation. The pink flyer taped to the box-office window said that the theater had originally opened in June of 1936 with movies and live stage pro-ductions, but was closed in 1955 due to the outbreak of a disease we're still trying to find a vaccine for—tele-vision. Apparently some brave souls were trying to keep the old girl alive, however, as they were advertising an upcoming Fall Classic Film Series—all of them from the forties and fifties. Each feature was to be accompanied by an *Our Gang* short because the actor who played Alfalfa apparently lived in Pretty Prairie during the fifties. *Spencer's Mountain*, one of my favorite movies, was playing November 5th.

"Tickets are only three dollars," a low, pleasant voice called out. A smiling man in a plaid shirt and white apron was sweeping the sidewalk in front of D & J Grocery. "And we make the best popcorn in town."

"I'd come if I could," I said, smiling back. "Unfortunately, by that time I'll be back home in California."

"I'm sorry to hear that," he said with a teasing grin. "But I guess someone has to live there."

I followed the crowds walking toward what I assumed were the rodeo grounds, behind the grain elevators. An American flag proudly fluttered on top of one silver column that seemed to stretch a mile into the hard blue sky. I inhaled the familiar aroma of rodeos—the same in Kansas as it was in California and Nevada and Montana and everywhere else cowboys gather to strut their stuff—that pungent mixture of damp earth and manure, frying beef, lemonade, the acidic leathery scent of the cowboys, and a sweetness in the air from that rodeo staple, cotton candy. I'd been to hundreds of rodeos in my life, but I never grew tired of the high-pitched excitement that always hovered over everyone like an electrified cloud. I paid my admission and stood staring up at the huge packed arena, wondering what would be the best way to find Gabe and Becky and the rest of the gang. Around me, people were already flocking to the concession stands behind the white metal bleachers, stocking up before the rodeo action started, on Cokes, popcorn, beer, hamburgers, hot dogs, crispy funnel cakes, and fresh corn on the cob. My stomach reminded me again that I hadn't eaten since this morning.

I walked past the bullpen, the fenced-off area where the cowboy contestants spread out their gear, helped each other pin on their numbers, rosined their ropes and gloves, and generally shot the breeze until their event came up. In the middle of the sea of cowboy hats, I spotted Gabe's bare head. He was pinning Chet's paper number on the back of his fuchsia and black cowboy shirt while Dewey, an intense look on his face, gave his son some last-minute advice. As if a small voice had whispered in his ear, Gabe looked up at that moment, searched the crowd, and found me. His face relaxed, and I felt my heart soften, relieved he was still concerned enough to worry, even though it drove me crazy. His face hardened again, as if remembering we weren't speaking, and he gave a curt nod before turning back to Dewey and Chet.

I melted into the crowd, watching with amusement the buckle bunnies with their ruffled shorts and fringed boots giggle over the cowboys who subtly preened by performing elaborate leg stretches and joking crudely in booming, feverish voices. The cowboys' peacock-bright shirts and chaps—items of clothing I'd watched over the years become as gaudy as a Las Vegas showgirl's—made them seem like a flock of gruff-voiced tropical birds. The color combinations were spectacular—royal purple and fire-engine red, hot pink and black, the glowing orange and yellow of Monarch butterflies. The long metallic fringe on their stained chaps sparkled like fool's gold under the stadium lights. The one thing that never changed were the Wranglers, seats ground dark with dirt, sporting the faint Skoal ring on the back pocket from a tobacco-chewing habit that was as much a part of rodeo as being thrown.

Then there were the cowboys themselves—the bareback riders with their temperamental personalities and almost flat-brimmed hats; the hefty but light-footed steer wrestlers, who needed the weight to wrestle a thousand-pound steer to the ground; the ropers with their intelligent faces and missing fingers; the saddle bronc riders, the traditionalists of rodeo, who can often dismount a bucking horse with the finesse of an Olympic gymnast, landing on their feet and strutting away with the confidence of a banty rooster; the barrel racers, the only female event now, where woman and horse seem to meld into one creature as they spur for those precious hundredths of a second, riding the cloverleaf pattern around the three sponsor barrels with an intensity you can almost taste. And always the bull-riders, last in the lineup, but first in the hearts of many rodeo fans. They were the macho men of rodeo, with their flamboyant grins, deep chests, and stiff horseshoe walks; they personified all that is romantic and exciting about rodeo—man against beast in a singular contest that left you breathless wondering which one you should root for.

I glanced around again, looking for our group, thinking I might be forced into going to Gabe to ask where everyone was sitting, when, as if on cue, Janet and Lawrence appeared next to me. "Everyone was wondering when you'd get here," Janet said. "Gabe was starting to pace. We're over there." She pointed to the bleachers on our right.

About halfway up the crowded bleachers, I saw Becky stand and rearrange her padded stadium seat.

"I see them," I said.

"We're going on a beer run," Lawrence said. "Want one?"

"No, thanks. I'll check out the food later," I said.

Up in the bleachers, Becky, Stan, Belinda, and Rob had saved enough seats for everyone. In the distance, the sun dipped toward the hazy gray-blue horizon causing the sky to turn as pink as the cotton candy they were selling below us. From our high perch we could see in the distance an irrigation sprayer watering a field, the stream of water a long arch with a rainbow forming in its mist. In the slowly deepening sky, the faint edge of a half-moon appeared, promising at least some illumination for the trip back to our cars when the rodeo ended.

"Did Gabe find you?" Becky asked me. "He was starting to worry."

"He saw me. He's with Dewey, helping Chet get ready for his ride."

Belinda snorted and took a long drink of her cup of beer. "Dewey just can't resist giving Chet some last-minute advice."

"So, he's riding bareback as well as bulls tonight," I said, looking at the program Becky handed me.

"Yep." Belinda grinned proudly. "No saddle broncs tonight, though. He didn't like the pick, so he didn't enter. I'm telling you, he's going to snatch that World Champion All Around title right from under Ty Murray's nose. Maybe not this year, but he'll make the National Finals in Las Vegas for sure. He's number nineteen in bulls and seventeen in bareback." She pointed to his name in the *ProRodeo News*, the bi-weekly newspaper that followed rodeo standings throughout the year.

I couldn't help smiling at her motherly enthusiasm. "Well, we're certainly pulling for him. Ty's hogged it long enough."

"My feelings exactly." She held out a box of popcorn. "Want some?"

"No, thanks. I haven't had dinner yet. I think I'll go down and get a hamburger after the opening ceremonies and Chet rides."

"Well, he's first up," she said. "Then he doesn't ride again until the bulls at the end."

A few minutes later, the announcer's liquid voice crooned over the crowd, attempting to get their attention. "Testing, one, two, one, two." He tapped the microphone. The thump echoed over the buzzing voices.

The rodeo clown in his baggy denim overalls, red-and-white face makeup, and tennis shoes advertising Bud Lite, joked into his hidden microphone. "Ladies and gents, that there's Hadley Barrett, rodeo announcer extraordinaire, counting his teeth." The audience tittered, the laughter rippling around the stadium like a vocal version of the "wave."

"Now, Swingler, you behave yourself," the announcer good-naturedly countered. "We got ourselves a long night ahead of us. You'd best not antagonize me right off."

"Hey, Hadley," the clown said. "Did you hear that Kansas now has the world's largest zoo?"

The announcer chuckled, knowing he was being set up. "No, I didn't."

"Yep," the clown said, leaning on the padded barrel he'd be spending half the night tucked into, avoiding the dangerous hooves and horns of the irritated bulls. "They done put a fence around Nebraska."

The audience, made up mostly of Kansans, roared and stomped their feet, causing the bleachers to rumble like thunder. Gabe had told me about the traditional rivalry between Nebraska and Kansas, but this was the first time I'd seen it for myself.

"How can the two states make fun of each other?" I'd asked Gabe. "They look just alike."

He'd given me a pained look. "Spoken like a true Californian."

"I was technically born in Arkansas," I retorted.

"Enough said," he replied.

Once the announcer gained control of the audience again, the rodeo began with a tribute to the event's sponsors. One of the contract acts, Vickie Tyer and the All American Trick Riders in their shiny white spandex outfits assisted by the young kids of the Pretty Prairie Saddle Club, circled the arena on adrenaline-charged horses carrying sponsor flags that snapped in the wind like gunshots. They ended their ride facing us in the traditional lineup featuring Debra Jean Jackson, Miss Rodeo Kansas, in the middle on a nervous appaloosa. The sponsors were as American as rodeo itself—Justin Boots, Bud Lite, *American Cowboy* magazine, Dodge Trucks, Coca-Cola, John Deere Tractors, and Copenhagen Skoal, whose name was also emblazoned on the brand-new bright green computerized scoreboard. "Howdy, folks, from Kansas' Largest Night Rodeo" it flashed, then showed a moving picture of a long-horned bull with its back legs in the air. We stood for the singing of the national anthem. The sun was almost down now, and the stadium lights cast a hazy glow over the dirt in the arena, giving it a reddish-brown sheen like old leather. Black clouds cut the dim lavender sky into jagged pieces.

"And now," the announcer said. " 'The Star-Spangled Banner' sung by Cordie June Rodell of Kermit, Oklahoma."

Rob abruptly pushed his way past us and stomped down the bleacher steps, an intense look of disgust on his face.

"This must be hard for him," Becky whispered to me. "I don't understand why he even came tonight."

We watched Cordie June strut to the middle of the arena. Her costume tonight was bright but conservative—a red satin cowboy shirt with black sequined trim, matching calf-length skirt, and sharp-toed crimson cowboy boots. She performed a slow, seductive rendition of our national anthem, giving the audience considerable second thoughts about the meaning of the "rockets' red glare, the bombs bursting in air."

"I'll just bet that wasn't *exactly* what old Francis Scott Key had in mind when he wrote it," Becky said out of the side of her mouth.

Overhearing, Belinda snapped, "Somebody ought to throw a bucket of ice water on that woman."

Becky raised her eyebrows slightly.

We'd only been seated a few seconds when the announcer gave the traditional call to the crowd, "Are you ready to rodeo?" The audience answered with a noisy cheer.

"First up," he said when the noise died down, "we got us a cowboy who's been on a hot streak lately. Bulls or broncs, he doesn't care, he'll just ride 'em. It's rumored that this young man might just might make it to Las Vegas and give ole Ty a run for his money. Hailing from Derby, Kansas, and riding Bad Buffalo Bill—Chet Champagne!''

The chute burst open, and a stout buckskin with a long black mane did his best to get rid of the flailing human attached to his back. Chet's spurring action was good— smooth and rhythmic—and his style was loose, but there was no doubt in that first crucial second of his ride, when the rider has to judge just what kind of ride he's in for, that Chet was in control of this horse. The eight-second horn blared, and the Dodge pickup men in their red-and-white chaps rode alongside Chet, one releasing the bucking horse's flank strap, the other wrapping his arm around Chet's upper torso and pulling him to safety.

''What a way to start a show!'' the announcer told the audience. ''If that's an indication of how the evening's going to go, we're going to see some championship riding tonight. This is going to be hard to beat.'' He paused as the judges passed him Chet's score. ''Derby is gonna be proud of their hometown boy tonight. This fine young cowboy gets a whopping eighty-eight!''

Belinda threw her box of popcorn in the air, showering us with the salty kernels. We all laughed and screamed and hugged each other. An eighty-eight would be a hard score to beat, so it was definite that Chet would finish ''in the money'' tonight as well as adding to his overall score for the year.

''Now I can breathe again until the bulls,'' Belinda said. We settled back down in our seats to watch the rest of the rodeo, talking casually and not paying much attention now that the person we'd come to see had made his ride. In the next few minutes we were joined by Gabe, Dewey, and Cordie June. Gabe sat down beside me, and Becky and Dewey sat behind us with Belinda on one side, Cordie June on the other.

''Did you see that boy ride?'' Dewey kept repeating

until Belinda playfully shoved some popcorn in his mouth to shut him up. They exchanged an intimate glance that clearly annoyed Cordie June.

"What'd y'all think of my singing?" she unabashedly fished.

Dewey turned to her, his face apologetic. "Sorry, babe. You were great, just great. Best this ole arena has ever heard."

Belinda frowned and stepped down to our row and sat next to me.

"How did it go today?" Gabe asked me, his voice casual.

I looked around to see if Rob had returned. I didn't want to bring up our afternoon's activity in front of him. "Fine," I said, shrugging. "Definitely sobering. Made me consider going home and cleaning out all my drawers and closets just in case."

His face grew sad. "Next to informing the victim's next-of-kin, that was the part of homicide investigation I really hated. I can't imagine anything more humiliating than having strangers go through your personal possessions."

I looked at him in surprise. The first time I visited the house he'd rented in San Celina before we were married, I'd been struck by how empty it was. I assumed that since he had planned on being in San Celina temporarily, most of his belongings were in storage somewhere. But after we married, I discovered that what was in the house was literally everything he owned. Was this the reason why? Had he seen so many people's belongings being poked through that he decided no one would ever do that with his things?

"Are you talking about Tyler's stuff?" Belinda asked loudly. At the mention of Tyler's name, everyone stopped talking and looked at us.

Becky moved to our row and said, "It was sad, packing up someone's life like that. Everything's in my garage until her sister decides what to do."

"So, did the Snoop Sisters find any clues we missed?" Dewey joked. I glanced back at him and Cordie June. Her face held an odd, furtive look. Next to her, Janet intently studied her rodeo program, and Lawrence's face was a frozen mask. I thought about the comment Lawrence had made last night, how interested he'd been in the fact that Becky and I were going to clean out Tyler's room. Was there something there he was afraid would point a finger at him? *Did* he and Tyler have something going? Janet looked up and caught me staring at her husband. Her eyes darkened, and I looked back to Becky, who was replaying our afternoon's activities in detail.

"It was kind of creepy," she said, giving a small shudder and tucking her arm through Gabe's. "But we did find something. A quilt."

"A quilt?" Janet's face brightened with interest.

"Actually, a wall hanging. The stitching is exquisite. Tyler must have spent a long time making it. Let me tell you, Benni's a whiz. It didn't take her long to figure out the pattern."

"What was it?" Janet asked.

"A star pattern called Arkansas Traveler," Becky answered before I could. "It's absolutely gorgeous. I wish I could buy it, but I'm sure her sister will want it. We were trying to figure out why in the world she'd make that pattern. Maybe there's a clue in that." She gave a merry laugh.

"The clue in the quilt," Belinda said sarcastically. "Shades of Jessica Fletcher."

"If it were only that easy," Dewey said, shaking his head.

I worked on keeping my expression bland, hoping my face didn't reveal my feeling that the quilt might actually be a clue.

"Well, I just hope they find out who did it soon," Becky said with a sigh. "I'll certainly rest easier at night."

I stood up and stretched. "Well, steer wrestling isn't my favorite event. I'm going to hit the concession stands. Anybody want anything?"

There was a general murmur of dissent.

"I'll go with you," Gabe said, taking my elbow. I felt my face warm up. Darn, I should have known he'd see through me. Faces like mine should come equipped with a ski mask.

"You want anything?" I asked, walking up to the hamburger line. He gave me a rueful look. "A Coke?" I persisted.

He pulled at his mustache irritably. "Sure. I'll wait for you over there." He pointed to a picnic bench next to the fence, slightly apart from the milling crowd and the bright arena lights. Night had fallen, but the air remained as warm and clammy as it had been in the afternoon.

It took me ten minutes to reach the front of the line. Gabe watched me the whole time, working his familiar interrogation technique without saying a word. He assumed by the time I sat down across from him I'd be confessing to every remotely illegal thought and deed of my life. Ha, I thought. Guess again, pal.

"Hello again, Miss California," the plaid-shirted man with the salt-and-pepper hair said. His horse-shaped name tag said "Darrell." "Be prepared to enjoy the best hamburger you've ever eaten."

"He's not kidding," said a short-haired woman with a perky voice and a sparkling smile. Her name tag, shaped like a cowboy's hat, informed me her name was Joyce.

"Great, I'm starved," I said, ordering one with the works and two Cokes.

"Rodeos sure can work up an awful big thirst," Darrell said, handing me a wrapped hamburger and the two Cokes.

"One's for my husband."

"You aren't going to feed him?"

"He doesn't eat beef." I slid my money across the counter.

"Another Californian?" Darrell grinned at me and made change.

"Actually, he isn't. He's from Kansas."

"Well, what's that boy's problem that he doesn't like beef?"

"You got me."

"Sounds like you might need to straighten him out a little."

Joyce smacked his shoulder with the back of her hand in an affectionate way that told me this couple had loved each other for a long time. "Now, Darrell, quit teasing the girl."

I walked over to the picnic bench and slid the paper cup of Coke across to Gabe. "Aren't you going to eat anything?" I asked.

"I ate with Mom."

"She's spending the night at Becky's."

"So I heard."

Having run the gamut of polite conversation, I ate and he watched me. I debated with myself while chewing— should I tell him about the postcards and the connection with the quilt or keep it to myself until I found out more? What about the producer and Cordie June? Say nothing and reduce myself to his negligible level of communication? Tell him what I'd found out and endure yet another lecture?

He broke into my reverie, forcing a showdown. "Okay, let's quit playing games," he said.

"Fine with me." I looked at him in challenge.

"What are you hiding *this* time?"

I bristled at the words "this time." Except, of course, that he was right. "Okay, I'll tell you what I know. Then will you kindly let me finish my hamburger in peace?" I took an angry bite.

He didn't answer. There was one thing you had to say

about Gabriel Ortiz. He never made promises he couldn't keep.

I sipped my Coke and took another bite, deliberately taking my time chewing and swallowing. He sat patiently waiting, his face never deviating from its chilly expression.

I looked him straight in his cold blue eyes. "Cordie June told me the other night at the restaurant that there was going to be a Nashville producer in the audience at the club last night. He's here for the Randy Travis concert."

He kept his eyes on my face. "So?"

"She *didn't* say how long ago his visit was planned. She also said that sometimes people only get one chance in life, and they have to grab it."

"And from this you've deduced that Cordie June killed Tyler just so the producer wouldn't see her."

"Well, if you were a Nashville producer and you saw Cordie June and Tyler perform, which one would you pick to invest your time and money in?"

I watched him process the information, and could tell he didn't like having to concede I was right.

"Let me guess," he finally said. "You think I should tell Dewey."

I looked down at my hamburger, avoiding his scrutiny. "What you do with it is your business."

He let out a weary sigh. "I hate this."

"I didn't pry the information out of Cordie June," I said, defending myself. "She volunteered it."

"Look, I'll bring it up to Dewey in a casual way, but I'm sure he already knows about it. They *are* dating."

I hesitated, then blurted out, "Do you think that he'd cover up evidence if he thought she did it?" I knew I was skating on thin ice, but I felt compelled to say it.

"I've thought of that."

"You have?"

"Benni, when are you going to realize that this is what I do for a living? That I've been doing it for over twenty years. Believe me, any suspicion you have, I've thought of long before.''

What he didn't say, because maybe he didn't realize it, was that he wasn't thinking rationally this time because everyone involved except for Cordie June were his friends.

''They've got experienced investigators working on this,'' he continued. ''Let them do their job.'' His last sentence came out in his macho I'm-the-chief tone of voice.

I tightened my lips and didn't answer.

He took a deep breath, then slowly exhaled. ''So, what's the rest of the story?''

I set my half-eaten hamburger down and gave an intelligent ''Huh?''

''Let me rephrase that to make it more personal. Are you telling me everything you know?''

''Yes.'' Then I hesitated, doubt causing a miniature tornado in my chest. I hadn't lied or hidden anything from him since we'd been married. I knew that if I started now, our relationship would take a turn down a road that just might eventually lead to a dead end. I knew what Dove would say, what she'd said to me so many other times when doubt about something made me hesitate. ''Honeybun, if your heart's feeling doubt, you'd best be taking another look at what you're doing.''

''No,'' I quickly amended.

He leaned back and folded his arms. In a rush of words, I told him about the postcards, the quilt, and my connection with the pattern name.

He waited a long moment before commenting. ''Is that it?''

''Yes.'' I bit the word off angrily.

He drained the rest of his soft drink and stood up. ''I'll tell Dewey.'' He started walking away.

''That's *all* you're going to say?'' I called after his retreating back.

He whipped around and came back. He grabbed my elbows, pulling me up from the bench, bringing his face close until it was inches from mine. "What is it you want me to say, Benni? You want me to praise you for being such a great detective? You want some kind of medal for the most audacious snooping I've ever seen? Why can't you understand that if I'd wanted to marry a cop, I would have?"

"I didn't do any of this on purpose," I snapped, struggling to free myself from his iron grip.

"Except the snooping at the Amish lady's house."

"I wasn't snooping! I was looking at her quilt squares."

"You know what really bothers me about this? That you look like you're enjoying it."

"I am not!" His words felt like a slap across the cheek. Was he right? I had to admit I liked figuring things out, putting the pieces together like quilt squares until the whole pattern was discernible and sense was made of all the separate parts. I was curious about who Tyler Brown/Ruth Stoltzfus really was, why she chose the life she did, what she was willing to do for her dreams, what circumstances led someone to kill her. But enjoy it? The way he put it, it sounded sick.

"I am not," I repeated, with somewhat less conviction this time.

"We could fight about this all night, but I'm sick and tired of arguing."

"Finally, something we agree on."

He let go of me and started walking away again. I picked up my half-eaten hamburger and threw it at him. It hit the back of his left leg. A large splash of ketchup trailed down his faded jeans.

"Good shot, hon," called a bouffant-haired woman in tight apple-green Wranglers.

He turned slowly around and walked back toward me. Anger caused a stain of red to start at his neck and spread to his high cheekbones. When he reached me, he said in a voice so low I strained to hear it over the boisterous crowd, "Has it ever occurred to you that we made a big mistake when we got married?"

I swallowed hard and answered, "More than once, Ortiz. *More than once.*"

He turned away, and this time kept going. Through the blur in my eyes, the red streak on his pant leg looked like an open wound.

I picked up my purse and started through the crowd toward the exit. This rodeo was over for me. I'd give my apologies to Dewey and everyone else tomorrow, make up some excuse about feeling sick. I shook my head at a gap-toothed concessionaire's attempt to sell me a glow-in-the-dark lariat and started back toward Main Street where the Camaro was parked.

"Benni, wait!" I stopped and turned around. Rob strode toward me, his face blazing with agitation. "I want to talk to you."

He moved close, deliberately invading my personal space. I folded my arms across my chest and backed up slightly.

"What did you find in Tyler's room?" he demanded.

I met his angry gaze. "Did I miss something? Were we supposed to give you a checklist of her possessions?"

"She *was* my fiancée."

"Funny," I said coolly. "I thought she already had a husband."

"We'd talked about marriage, when she . . . got things straightened out."

"Well, if you want to look through her things, you'll have to get permission from her husband."

He spat at the ground. "You're kidding, right?"

"Nope."

He thrust his jaw out belligerently. "I have my rights. She had some things of mine."

I shrugged. "Rob, I don't know what your rights are and frankly I don't care. I only know one thing. Tyler's belongings are legally her husband's, and he gave permission for Becky and me to pack them up and store them. If you want to look through them, you need to talk to him. Or the police. Maybe *they* have what you're looking for.'' I smiled innocently.

He pointed a finger at me. "You better just watch it. This isn't any of your business.''

"Why, Rob,'' I said, keeping my voice amazingly calm, considering I felt like burying my boot tip in his crotch, "if I didn't know any better I'd take that as a threat. But it isn't, is it? Because if it was, I just might have to tell Gabe and Dewey, and they just might have to look a little closer into your part in Tyler's murder.''

Calling me a five-letter word that would have been socially acceptable had I been a female member of the canine persuasion, he whipped around and pushed his way back through the crowd.

I headed through the gates toward Main Street and my car, boiling at his remark, wishing at that moment that I was a man, one big enough to beat the crap out of him. As I moved away from the arena, the sounds of the rodeo grew fainter. In the humid night air, I could still hear the blare of the eight-second horn, the chipper voice of the announcer, and the wail of the spectators, a monolithic ocean sound that rose and fell with the start and end of each cowboy's ride.

Main Street was almost empty of people. I opened the door of the Camaro and threw my purse on the seat, still so mad I could hardly see. I closed the door and pocketed the keys. There was no doubt that it would be better to walk off my anger before getting behind the wheel. I headed down Main Street and just kept going. My mind was churning with questions—who killed Tyler, which of Gabe's friends was really a murderer, was I really enjoying this like Gabe said, and did he mean it when he said our marriage might be a mistake? And did I really think it was, too? I didn't notice until my side started to ache that I'd followed the street clear out of

town and into the dark prairie. I stopped along the side
of the road and stared up into the night sky. If possible,
it seemed even bigger at night than during the day. The
words of an old song came to me—something about
deep purple nights. That was the sky's exact shade at
that moment—a deep, heavy purple. A color that
matched my mood perfectly. I closed my eyes and took
a deep breath of the turbid air, recalling something I
once read by Willa Cather about the prairie, about how
between the earth and sky she felt erased, blotted out.

My eyes flew open when the quiet night was pierced
by the shrieks from a truck full of teenagers speeding
past. An aluminum can ricocheted off the pavement and
hit my leg. I jumped into the small ditch along the road
to avoid another one. It was definitely time to head back
toward town. Now that my anger had subsided, it occurred to me that meandering along a dark highway at
night was not one of my smarter moves. I turned and
started walking briskly toward the town's flickering
lights.

More headlights approached. I moved closer to the
side of the road even though the vehicle was traveling
on the opposite side. The bright lights blinded me for a
second before the truck rumbled past. I let out the breath
I'd unconsciously been holding and continued walking
toward town. Behind me I heard another truck engine. I
stepped off the pavement to give it more room. It down-
shifted with a rumbling growl. In the next second a puls-
ing roar enveloped me. Metal hit the side of my thigh.
My arm flew up and smashed against the protruding side
mirror.

"No!" I screamed as my feet lost touch with the
ground. An animal shriek—my own voice—pierced the
thick air, sounding high and thin and desperate. I tumbled into damp, scratchy weeds, hitting the ground with
a sickening thump. A muscle in my back popped. Bone-
rattling pain seemed to meld me into one mind-numbing
ball of sparkling nerves. I rolled to a stop at the bottom

of the shallow ditch. Instinctively I curled up in a fetal position, swallowing my whimper. Get up, some deep part of me commanded. Get away. But another part of me registered the sound of the truck driving away. Its menacing engine grew fainter and fainter until the only sound I heard was the whispery whirr of night insects and the faint drone of the rodeo announcer's voice.

I don't know how long I lay there in the darkness. I remember the stab of the wheat stalks poking through my shirt, the hiss of corn leaves rustling in the wind, the rattle of an old car driving past. The air was hot and fuzzy and tasted sharp like metal, then sweet like pollen. My brain flickered from one irrelevant subject to another while it tried to figure out what to do. Wheat grows along the side of the road in Kansas. Volunteer wheat, Gabe said his Grandfather Smith called it, 'cause it grew anywhere it darn well pleased. Dark purple sky. So dark and deep I could drown in it. Like the ocean. Like sleep. Like death. Sleep sounded so good. A chuckling, bass voice from my past roused me. "Cowboy up now." The favorite expression of my uncle Luke in Nevada. He had been a part-time rodeo clown in his younger days. "Bullfighter," he'd correct everyone in his dignified voice. One time at a Lions' Club Rodeo in San Celina, Luke jumped off his barrel and ran straight down the back of a snot-spraying Brahma named Terrible Tootsie. The crowd gave him a standing ovation. "Luke, you stupid fool," Daddy had said. "You always did have more balls than brains." Uncle Luke just spit and grinned. "Cowboy up" he'd tell us kids when we fell off our horses or smashed our thumbs or came crying to him after a bully pushed us around. Don't let the bad guys get you down, he was trying to teach us. Fight back, play through the pain. Real cowboys and cowgirls don't ever give up.

Cowboy up, Benni.

I lifted my head, slowly unrolled myself, and struggled to my knees. Stars sparkled in front of my eyes, and I knelt for a moment, gasping in pain as my injuries became separate entities. My tingling arm, the throbbing in my thigh, the ache in my back, each screamed for my brain's pain center to *pay attention, take care of us*. But my shoulder and side had taken the brunt of the fall, and though I ached all over, I hadn't hit my head. I'd been thrown off horses enough times to know nothing was broken. Still, the walk back to town wouldn't be fun. I stood up slowly, my arms flailing for support that wasn't there, and forced myself to put one foot in front of the other. Concentrate, I told myself, counting out each step. Think of how good it will feel to sit on that soft Camaro seat.

A few minutes later, a small white compact slowed down beside me. Had it been a truck, I would have tried to run. Since it wasn't, I just kept my snail-like pace toward the town's lights.

The car stopped, and the passenger window rolled down. "Sweetie, are you all right?" a woman's voice called out. She leaned across from the driver's side. "I know it's not far, but do you need a ride to town?"

I glanced quickly in the car. There was a plaid baby seat in the back, a small box of Pampers on the passenger seat. Other than that, the car was empty.

I sent up a prayer. Thank you, Lord. "Yes," I said, my voice shaky. "I could use a ride back to my car."

She opened the door and tossed the box of Pampers in back. "My daughter ran out of diapers, but she didn't want to miss her husband's ride," she explained. "And one of our mares is about to foal. I wanted to check on her." She regarded me curiously with kind toffee-colored eyes framed by a fluffy cloud of matching curls. "Are you all right?"

"Fine, thank you," I said, holding my hand up and attempting to cover the throbbing left side of my face.

"Why, you're bleeding," she exclaimed. She pulled out a couple of tissues from the box on the dashboard and passed them to me.

"Thank you." I dabbed the side of my face tentatively. Nerves screamed when the tissues touched my raw skin.

The lady clucked under her breath. "Sweetie, I don't know you, but I feel like I just got to say something. No cowboy is worth this no matter how good he looks in a pair of Wranglers. You don't have to take this kind of crap."

"It's not what you think." My voice sounded thick and wet, as if I had a head cold. I clenched my teeth. Don't cry, I commanded myself, *don't cry*. "I'm parked in front of the Civic Theater."

She just shook her head and slowed down near the center of town.

"There." I pointed to the Camaro. She stopped the car, and I gingerly stepped out. "Thank you," I said, closing the door. "I'll be okay, really."

She shook her head again, a resigned look on her motherly face. "I'll be praying for you, sweetie."

"Thank you." I sank into the buttery leather seat of the Camaro and sat for minute, trying to will the pain away. I dug through my purse for some aspirin, then realized after I found them that I didn't have any water. The Wagon Wheel Cafe's sign was still turned to Open, so I inched my way back out of the car and bought a Coke to go. Limping back toward the car, I swallowed four aspirin and drank half the Coke. I was concentrating so hard on making it back to the car, Cordie June had to shout to get my attention.

She was leaning against the side of a Ford pickup, smoking a cigarette.

"Where've you been?" she asked, pursing her lips and forming a perfect smoke ring.

"I didn't know you smoked," I said, ducking my head and letting my hair fall over my scraped face.

"Only when I'm nervous." She smiled lazily through the smoke, then dropped the cigarette on the ground, mashing it with the tip of her boot. "Becky was wondering where you'd gotten to. I told her with all these cute cowboys wandering around, you probably got distracted.''

''I'm not feeling too good.'' I started moving toward my car. ''Let the others know I went home, okay?''

''Sure.'' She gave a thin smile, then peered closer at me, her eyes widening. ''Shoot howdy, what happened to your face?''

I touched it carefully with my fingertips. ''I slipped and fell. I'm okay, but I think I'll go on back to Derby anyway.'' I opened the car door.

''You want me to tell Gabe?''

''No!'' I said sharply. ''I'll tell him about it when he gets home. I'm *all right*.'' To prove my point, I forced myself to slide into the seat easily. Every muscle in my body protested the masquerade.

''Whatever,'' she said, shrugging. ''See you later.'' She started to walk away, then turned abruptly and tapped on the car window.

I rolled it down. ''What is it?''

''I didn't do it,'' she blurted. I could swear I smelled fear mixed in with the vanilla scent of her perfume.

''Do what?'' I bit my lip and willed the aspirin to work faster.

''I'm not saying I'm not taking advantage of it. I am. And let me tell you something. If the places were reversed, she would have, too.''

''You really think so?'' I asked in a noncommittal tone.

''I know so. And I wouldn't have blamed her one bit. I didn't like Tyler, but I learned a lot from her about not letting anything or anyone stand in the way of what you want.'' She ran her tongue nervously over her teeth.

''I'm sorry,'' I said, a bit sickened by her callousness. ''But I can't say I understand.''

''Maybe it's because you never wanted anything that bad. Maybe it's because your life has always been easy. Maybe . . .''

"Maybe you'd just better stop right there," I snapped. My mind flashed on my father handing me a rose to place on my mother's coffin when I was barely six years old, going to the police station to claim the plastic bag filled with the contents of Jack's pockets, signing the bankruptcy papers on the Harper Ranch, the ranch I poured my heart and soul into for fifteen years. "You don't know anything about me or my life."

She hesitated for a moment. "Okay, maybe I don't. But I do know one thing. You're snooping around in places that are none of your business. I'm warning you, things aren't always what they look like." She scowled and strode back toward the rodeo grounds, her hair glistening like spun sugar under the street lights.

The sixty-five-mile drive back to Wichita seemed to take an eternity. Every time headlights came toward me on the lonely country road, my body tensed in apprehension until the red tail lights disappeared into the ink-colored night. Every vehicle appeared sinister, and more than once I regretted not sending Cordie June for Gabe. But I would have had to face his anger—at the person who attacked me and at me for putting myself in a vulnerable position. Tired down to my toes, I wanted to delay that confrontation as long as possible. I pushed the car to eighty miles an hour, wanting to go faster but afraid to with my reflexes as shaky as they were. I gripped the steering wheel when a spasm of shuddering overcame me and forced me to slow down to sixty-five. On the radio, sad country songs crackled through the black prairie night. A farm report came on—"Sows holding steady. Eighty-five dollars top price paid for some steers in Sioux City." I concentrated on the prices, trying to forget what had just happened to me and what could have happened.

Within a half hour, the aspirin finally started taking effect, and my pain began subsiding. Unable to help myself, I compulsively replayed the accident over in my mind. Though it was possible that the driver was just a drunk weaving down the road, I knew it was more likely he deliberately swerved to hit me and that it probably was connected with Tyler's murder. Was it a co-incidence that Cordie June happened to be in front of the Civic Theater next to the Camaro just as the lady in the small white car dropped me off? And her veiled warnings were something I knew I should tell Gabe or Dewey or someone. She said she didn't kill Tyler, and though I thought she was a self-centered opportunist, something inside me believed her.

Once I hit Highway 54, the road into Wichita, the muscles in my arms slowly started to unknot. Small stores that were still open and lit-up houses became more frequent as I neared the city limits. I lowered my speed and drove carefully through the outskirts of Wichita and into Derby. Tears started down my face when I pulled into Kathryn's driveway, and the sobs that had narrowed my throat all the way home started bubbling out of me in choking, convulsive weeping. I fumbled with the house key Gabe had attached to the rental car key chain and finally unlocked the door.

I dropped my purse and limped up the stairs, tearing off my shirt. All I wanted was a hot shower and to crawl into bed. Halfway up the stairs, I turned and lurched back down to the front door and locked it. I wanted a hot shower, but I'd also seen the movie *Psycho*.

I stood under the hot stream for a long time, washing away the dirt, blood, and tears. My crying slowed to an occasional soft hiccup. The hot water soothed my aching muscles, but my upper left thigh and hip, where the truck's fender had struck full force, felt like it had been burned with a hot brand. The whole left side of me was already a mass of pale blue and purple bruises that would no doubt darken to an angry plum color by morning. I tried to think—Would ice help? Did I want to try making it up and down those stairs again? I pulled on a clean T-shirt, then took two more aspirin, dipping my head and drinking from the bathroom faucet. My stomach started burning seconds later, and I knew I'd have to go downstairs and get some milk. I was at the top of the stairs, contemplating the distance with despair, when I heard the front door fly open and Gabe's deep voice bellow my name. I hesitated, torn between stumbling down the stairs and throwing myself in his arms or staggering back to the bathroom and locking the door. My mind, still partly in shock, decided for me by freezing every muscle in my body.

He yelled my name again.

"Up here," I called back, my voice faltering.

He appeared at the bottom of the stairs, his eyes looking as if someone had lit a bright blue fire behind them. His breath came in short, hard gasps as he took the stairs two at a time.

"Cordie June said you fell," he said, tilting his head to inspect my face. "Are you okay? Why didn't you come get me?"

"How did you get in?" I twisted my head, avoiding his determined gaze. "How did you get back?"

"Mom keeps a key hidden." He turned my chin toward him, sucking his breath in sharply when he saw my face. "And I borrowed Dewey's truck. You're going to the hospital."

"No!" I pulled away from him. "I just want to lie down." I went into the bedroom and crawled into bed. As I did, my T-shirt rode up, and he spotted the bruises on my legs and thigh.

"Benni, what happened? How did you get these?" He sat on the bed and pushed my T-shirt higher, exposing all the bruises up to my underarm. He ran his fingers gently over them.

"Stop it," I said, tugging down my shirt. "Leave me alone." Swallowing a sob, I turned away from him and pulled the edge of the thin chenille bedspread over me, trying to hide my shaking.

He tugged the bedspread off me and gathered me in his arms, whispering softly against the top of my head,

"*Está bien, querida. Todo va á estar bien. No dejaré que nadie te haga daño.* It's okay, I won't let anyone hurt you. *Está bien*, it's okay, *está bien*." He rocked me back and forth, murmuring in a mixture of English and Spanish until my trembling slowly subsided. His voice was so soothing and I felt so safe that I didn't want him to ever stop. But eventually he did, and, when he did, he had questions. Loving husband with a touch of Sergeant Friday.

"Tell me how this happened," he said, his voice firm, though his hand still stroked my hair.

"I need some milk," I said. "I took six aspirin. My stomach hurts."

He started to say something, then stopped. He went downstairs, brought me back a glass of warm milk, and silently watched me drink it. The air between us was thick and sultry with tension. When I finished, he sat the glass on the nightstand and said, "Now, talk."

My voice still raspy from crying, I told him everything, from my heated conversation with Rob to my encounter with the truck to Cordie June's veiled warning. "That's all," I concluded with a shuddering breath and watched his grave face, waiting for him to get mad, start lecturing me, *something*.

He stared blankly at the wall behind me, his face somber, his thoughts and feelings a secret. Was his reticence partly my fault? I couldn't help but wonder, thinking back to all the times I'd withheld the truth from him, not lying exactly, but not trusting him either. Why didn't I go straight to him when I was attacked tonight? Had he been Jack, I would have. I knew it and I suspected he did, too. It was like a tug of war between us—neither one of us willing to let go, be the first to be completely vulnerable, completely trusting. I wanted to ask what he was thinking, but instead closed my eyes and rested my head against the headboard.

"Did you hit your head?" he finally asked. "I think we should get you checked out."

"No. I don't have a concussion and I'm sure nothing's broken. The truck just sort of pushed me. I rolled when I hit, and the ground was padded with weeds." I brought my knees up to my chest. "Please, Gabe, I don't want to go to the hospital. I just want to stay here with you."

"Okay," he said. "It's against my better judgment, but—" His face grew hard. Apprehension seized my heart. The attack on me put things on a whole other level for him now.

"What are you going to do?" I asked uneasily.

"Shhh." He gently brushed his lips across my forehead. "Not tonight. We'll talk about it tomorrow. Right now, you need to sleep. Are you hungry? Do you want me to fix you something to eat?"

"No. I'm tired. I do want to sleep." I could barely get the words out. His tenderness was almost harder to take than anger because it was so unexpected. Downstairs, the phone rang.

"It's probably Becky," he said. "She was worried when she heard you fell. I'll set her mind at ease and then come to bed after I take a shower."

Feeling absolutely safe now, I fell asleep immediately and never heard him get into bed. But during the night, something woke me, the faint touch of lips on my neck, a warm breath in my ear.

"*Querida*," he whispered, his hands under my shirt, avoiding my bruises, softly caressing me in places he knew I couldn't resist. "I want to make love to you." Emotion roughened his voice. Though I couldn't see them in the dark I knew the exact shade of his eyes—a dark, cloudy blue. "You can say no . . . if it hurts . . ."

"Yes." My answer came out as a sigh, and in my mind I tasted him already. I traced his jawline, rough as sandpaper under my fingertips.

So, in his childhood room we made slow, gentle love. As I held him close, my head tucked into his shoulder, smothered in his musky scent, I wondered what it was that drew me to this man, why I so desperately wanted to crack his granite shell and what I would do if this was all we ever had. Afterwards, when we lay wrapped around each other and his measured breathing told me he was asleep, I thought of Jack, as I did at odd times, and how quickly and irrevocably my life changed when he died, in the blink of an eye, it seemed. I thought about how different love was with Gabe. And that someday, when the time seemed right, I would tell him how the passion I felt to connect with him overwhelmed me at times, how this desire was not like anything I'd ever experienced, even with Jack; how the feel of his hands, his husky, foreign words, the distant, troubled light in his eyes, haunted me.

I ran my palm lightly down his forearm as it curled around me, possessive and protective even in his sleep. Someday I would tell him. But not tonight.

TWELVE

"Thanks, but we'll have to take a raincheck," Gabe said into the phone as I hobbled into the kitchen the next morning. I wasn't as sore as I expected, but I certainly wasn't going to be dancing the ten-step tonight. He hung up the phone and turned to me, his face somber. "How do you feel?"

"I'll heal." I poured myself a cup of coffee. "Who was that?"

"Becky. She wanted to know how you were feeling and if we wanted to come over for blueberry pancakes."

I sat at the kitchen table. "What did you tell her?"

"That we were going out to eat. She said to come over whenever you want, but that she'd be leaving for the church at eleven o'clock for the quilt show." He poured himself another cup of coffee and sat across from me. "We need to talk about what happened last night, Benni."

I looked at him and smiled. "I was half asleep, but if I remember correctly, it was pretty wonderful."

He smiled back. "It was, but that's not what I'm referring to."

I sighed. "I know."

"I've been up since dawn thinking, and though I hate

it, we're going to have to work together on this."

"You hate having to work with me? Thanks a lot."

He reached over and took my hand, his thumb stroking the top of it. "What I hate is you being in danger."

"So, what do we do?"

"First, have you told me absolutely everything you know? We can't work together if you're holding back any information."

I said without hesitation, "Yes."

He contemplated me for a minute, then nodded, apparently satisfied. For some reason, in this small exchange I felt like a great milestone had been reached in our relationship.

"Okay," he said, releasing my hand. "The first rule is, don't tell anyone anything."

"Even Dewey?"

He sipped his coffee, looking over the rim of his mug with troubled eyes. "Even Dewey."

"Do you suspect him?"

"I don't suspect him—we just can't trust anyone at this point."

"It's because of Cordie June, isn't it? Gabe, I don't think she did it."

"And why is that?"

I took a moment to answer. Why did I think she'd been telling the truth last night? Because she was the most obvious one? Or because I related to her being an outsider with Gabe's friends? I touched my scraped face gingerly. The skin had already formed a thin scab. "It just doesn't feel right."

"That's the first thing a good cop learns."

"What's that?"

"Most of the time, feelings can't be trusted."

"But sometimes they can."

He picked up our empty coffee cups and took them over to the sink. "Trust me, Benni, feelings very rarely catch a criminal. More often than not, it's just slow, tedious footwork. Putting the tiny pieces together until you complete the puzzle. And lots of times, the puzzle is never finished.''

''Do you think that's going to happen this time?''

He leaned back against the sink and didn't answer. Instead, his eyes tapered at the corners and became hard. The dark shadow of his unshaven face gave him a ruthless look that had its beginning I suspect in the time he spent in Vietnam and later in the drug-infested streets of East L.A. I teased him about it once, telling him that he looked like one of those sociopathic Mafia hitmen you see in the movies. The hurt in his eyes when he smiled at my comment caused me never to say it again.

''I don't care,'' he said grimly. ''All I care about is getting you home safe. My instincts tell me to make an airline reservation for today.''

''We can't leave.'' I went over and slipped my arms around his waist, hugging him hard. ''How would we explain it to your mom? Besides, Becky and Angel have our wedding reception planned for next Saturday, and Dove and Daddy and Arnie are on their way.'' I rested the uninjured side of my face on his solid chest. His warm morning smell made me want to forget all this talk of murder and suspects and secrets and drag him back upstairs to bed. ''At least, Daddy and Arnie are. Heaven only knows where Dove is.''

''That reminds me,'' Gabe said. ''Dove called while you were asleep.''

I jerked out of his arms. ''Why didn't you wake me up? What did she say? Where is she? Is she all right?''

''She said she'd hang up if I went for you. She promised she'd be here in time for the reception, and is apparently having a ball with Brother Dwaine. They had two conversions and a baptism last night and they're delivering a load of donated cheese to an AIDS food bank in Muskogee.''

I growled in frustration. ''I could just strangle her. She knew she'd really get an earful if I talked to her.''

He looked at me mildly. "I imagine that's why she didn't want to."

"What about Daddy and Arnie?"

"Haven't heard a word." He pulled me back to him, rubbing his bristly chin on my hair. "Let's get dressed and have some breakfast. We've got plans to make."

Feeling almost normal after a hot shower, I pulled on my loosest jeans and one of Gabe's T-shirts, letting the long sleeves hang down to my elbows to hide the worst of my bruises. To make sure we didn't run into anyone we knew, we drove over to a restaurant on the outskirts of Haysville, a town west of Derby. Sally's Cafe was a flat-roofed concrete-colored building with a narrow, gravel parking lot.

"My dad and I used to eat here every Saturday morning," Gabe said. "He used to call it the Goat Roper Inn even though back then it was called Bernie's."

"Why did he call it that?" I asked, opening the stained front door. My question was answered when I peered around the crowded cafe. It was obviously a hangout for local farmers. Gabe and I were the only ones not wearing dirty overalls, Western shirts, and hats advertising Kansas Pipeline Safety. Across the room we could hear some farmer saying to another, "Now, this ain't no bullshit, he said he was an artist and he wanted to buy the bones. For a good price, too."

Gabe grinned at me over the black plastic menu. "Dad would have loved that," he said.

As we ate our breakfast, his voice moved into its no-argument chief-of-police tone. "Don't tell anyone about the truck running you down. That's a piece of information we need to keep to ourselves for the time being. I'm going over to the station and hang around, talk to Dewey and the deputy in charge of the investigation. Maybe somebody will say something."

"Then what?" I doused my buttered French toast with more maple syrup, or what appeared to be a reasonable facsimile.

"Then I'll work my way through the list—Lawrence, Rob, Janet, Belinda."

"I wonder who has a truck," I mused.

"Dewey, Rob, and Lawrence all own trucks. But last night Dewey was passing his keys around to everyone because he had a cooler of Sam Adams in the cab, so it really could have been anyone. Are you sure you can't remember the make or the color?"

"No. I told you, it was really dark. The headlights blinded me when it first passed, and then it hit me from behind. I fell before I could see anything." I thought for a moment. "You didn't have Cordie June on your list." I wanted to be fair, even though my instincts said she didn't do it.

"I don't know how I can manage a conversation with her without it looking suspicious. The rest of those people are my friends." He stuck a piece of cantaloupe in his mouth and chewed it thoughtfully. "But I'm not quite as certain of her innocence as you are. Dewey probably kept a pretty close eye on her whereabouts last night. I'll just have to figure out a way to ask him about it."

"What about Megan? And don't forget Tyler's husband, John. They're possibilities."

"Slight. I can't imagine Megan killing anyone. Especially over Rob."

"That's where *your* feelings are getting in the way, Friday. Just because you knew her as a little girl doesn't mean she didn't grow up to be capable of murder."

His swift frown told me I'd hit a nerve. "I know that."

"So, what do I do?"

His answer was immediate, with no hesitation. "Nothing."

"What!" I slammed my fork down on my plate. "You said we were working together on this. How is that possible if you're out questioning everyone and I'm doing nothing?"

"Don't you have a quilt show to help Becky with?" He gave me his most winning smile.

"That is such a chauvinistic remark that if we weren't in public I'd smack you upside the head."

His smile faded. "You were almost killed," he said. "I want you to keep a low profile."

"I was not. A truck knocked me into a ditch. If the person had wanted to kill me, they would have just run me down."

His expression darkened. "My point exactly."

"Gabe . . ."

"This is not up for discussion, sweetheart. I'm the one making the decisions here."

"Says who!"

"Says me by virtue of being the detective in charge."

"And who, pray tell, appointed you boss?"

"I'm boss because I have more experience. And I'm older. And I'm bigger." He sipped his coffee and smirked at me.

"Well, I'm . . . I'm . . ." I stammered, trying to come up with a retort. "I'm fresher."

"Truer words never spoken."

I bunched up my paper napkin and threw it at him. "I mean I'm not as jaded. I'm capable of looking at things in a *fresh* way."

"Are you implying I'm too set in my ways?" His voice held an edge of impatience.

"If the stiff neck fits . . ." I shrugged and finished my orange juice. Our waitress came back, cleared away the empty plates, and refilled our coffee cups. We sparred with our eyes until she walked away.

Gabe gave in first. "Benni, things are even more dangerous now, because this person has started to panic. Whoever attacked you knows I'll most likely be looking more closely into things now, and that puts you at an even greater risk."

"You're always trying to wrap me up in cotton. I'm

the one this person is after. I need to have some control over my situation.''

He considered my words, his face struggling with a kinetic mixture of frustration, anger, and fear. "Okay," he said. "Let me see what I come up with today, and we'll discuss it again tonight. How's that?"

I eyed him suspiciously. I wouldn't put it past him to keep dallying with me until we got back to San Celina. Not that home didn't sound awfully good right now. The thing was, I felt a strange commitment to Tyler and Hannah, a compulsion to see this through to the end. To the officers working on the murder, Tyler was just another statistic, another case to clear off the books. They'd never met her, heard her sing, touched the quilts she'd made. Did they even notice the pain in Hannah's eyes when she talked about her sister? And, I had to admit, I wanted to see if Gabe and I could really work together on something important for once. It was a big step for him to even consider me in the role of partner. Maybe this time a little compromise would elicit more trust than arguing.

"Okay, just until tonight," I agreed reluctantly. "The quilt show lasts until nine o'clock. Pick me up then."

"Great." He pushed his bowl of oatmeal back. "Just lay low today until I can get a feel for what everyone was doing when you were attacked."

"I'll probably see Janet at the quilt show and maybe Belinda, too. I'm not sure if Belinda's involved with the guild, but since I'll be there I could maybe casually mention . . ."

"No. Keep the conversation away from Tyler's murder."

"What if they bring it up?"

"Benni, I mean it. If we're going to work together, you're going to have to do what I say. Is that possible?"

"Yes," I said irritably. I held three fingers up. "I solemnly swear to my extremely *senior* partner that I will not make a move unless I check with him first. Is there a loyalty oath you want me to sign?''

"No need for you to be sarcastic.''

"No need for you to be arrogant or chauvinistic either, but you are.''

He picked up the check and handed it to me. "Well, consider this my first act of becoming liberated, then. I'll wait for you in the car. Don't forget the tip. Make it twenty percent. She was a good waitress. Did her job without any backtalk. Such a rare quality in people these days.''

"Smartass,'' I muttered, digging through my purse for my wallet.

Kathryn and Daphne were back home when Gabe and I returned. Gabe was greeted by a hug; I was greeted by a growl. From Daphne, not Kathryn.

"Benni, are you all right?'' Kathryn asked, her keen eyes zeroing in on my scraped face. "Becky said you fell.''

"Yeah, clumsy me. How's Becky doing with the quilt show?''

Kathryn gave me a doubtful look, but didn't press the subject. "As you can imagine, she's been in a tizzy this morning. The setup committee chairman called her at seven o'clock. Apparently some vendors are unhappy with their space assignments and are demanding something be done.''

"I can sympathize with Becky,'' I said, thinking of my own wrangling with the artists in the co-op. Whenever we had a joint booth at a festival or a chunk of money was donated to the co-op, there was a fight about whose crafts were displayed where and which group of artists received the contribution. "Maybe I'll go over there and give her some moral support.''

"Good idea,'' Gabe said. "Let me drop you off.''

"What are you going to do today, Gabe?'' his mother asked.

"Just hang out, visit some of the gang.'' His face had the affable innocence of a toddler's. Kathryn glanced at her son, then at me. She knew something was up, but tightened her lips and didn't say any more.

"Your mother's suspicious," I said on the ride over to Becky's house.

"The less she knows, the better," he said. "I have enough problems worrying about your safety."

I started to crack a smart remark, but stopped when I noticed the real apprehension tightening the muscles around his eyes. Someone he loved was being threatened, most likely by someone else he cared about. What a vacation this had turned out to be.

Stan was outside watering the flower beds when Gabe and I drove up. A bemused expression wrinkled his square face.

"I'm not crazy about leaving you alone today," Gabe said, his face tight with worry.

"I'm not going to be alone," I pointed out, "but if you're really nervous, I could come with you. I'll watch people while you question them, observe their body language."

He ruffled my hair and smiled. "No, thanks. With your ability to hide your feelings, we'd be found out in two minutes."

"That's not true! I can keep as straight a face as the next person."

"If the next person is a monkey."

I brandished my fist at him. "I swear, you are really going to get it someday."

He covered my fist with his hand and shook it gently. "*Querida*, it's not an insult. In fact, it's one of the things I especially enjoy about making love to you."

I felt my face grow warm. "Oh, geeze, close your eyes next time, Friday."

His delighted laugh momentarily erased the worried slant of his eyes. "It's amazing. I can still make you blush."

"I'm leaving," I said, pulling my hand away and

opening the car door, "before I choke on all this free-floating machismo."

Stan turned off the water and greeted us with a big smile. "The queen bee's inside, but I better warn you, we've all scattered to the wind trying to stay out of her way. I think that phone is permanently attached to her ear."

"Why aren't you working?" Gabe asked.

"One of the advantages of owning your own business," Stan said, wiping his hands on his khaki shorts. "I took today off to watch the girls so Becky could do her quilt thing." He looked at me curiously. "You okay? I heard you took a tumble last night."

"I'm fine," I said. "Just tripped over my own feet. I think I'll go in and see if Becky needs any help." I looked up at Gabe. "I'll see you tonight, unless we run into each other around town."

"I'll pick you up." He brushed a kiss across my cheek. "Be careful," he whispered in my ear.

I found Becky in the kitchen, shouldering the phone as she rinsed dishes and stacked them in the dishwasher. Her pink T-shirt said "A good mother is like a quilt— she keeps you warm but doesn't smother you." She raised her eyebrows at me and continued her conversation. "No," she said firmly. "I told you I don't care who she is, the vendor slots were set a month ago. Unless she can get someone to change with her, she's stuck by the restrooms." She paused and listened, then shoved the dishwasher door closed with a bang. "Tell her everyone has to use the restrooms at some time during the show. It's actually a very good spot." I could hear a tinny voice whine something back. "Okay, okay, I'll talk to her. I'll be there in about half an hour." She pushed the Off button on the phone and threw it on the counter with a clatter. "I hope it's broken," she said. It buzzed again. She groaned. "Let the machine get it. I need a cup of tea. Want one?"

"Sure. Anything I can do to help?"

Her face twisted ruefully. "Take over my presidency?"

I laughed. "How about I just take the easy way out and raise your two kids and finish your next five quilts?"

"Ah, the voice of experience."

She turned the teakettle on and gestured for me to have a seat at the kitchen table. "I'm about ready to run screaming into the nearest cornfield. I don't know what possessed me to add these evening hours to the quilt show. Saturday and Sunday would have been plenty, but no, I had to be different and suggest we open Friday evening for the extra exposure." She set two white china teacups on the table, depositing a tea bag in each one.

"It'll be fine," I assured her. "By Sunday night it'll all be over."

"And I'll be a raving lunatic."

After our quick cup of tea, when she took the time to inspect my facial wounds and hear my concocted story of falling with the concern of a seasoned mother, we loaded up her Cherokee with the last-minute raffle tickets, lists, and other sundry items for the show. Going downstairs to the family room to find the rolls of Scotch tape she said were there, I spotted Tyler's wall hanging spread across the back of a loveseat. I traced my fingers over the fine stitching again, then picked it up and turned it over. The backing was plain muslin—no date, no name. Nothing to indicate what this quilt was about. Nothing except the pattern. I set it down again and went back upstairs. The same questions darted around my mind like hungry goldfish. What *was* Tyler doing in Arkansas? Would I ever find out, or would it just be one of those questions I'd keep asking myself the rest of my life?

Becky talked nonstop on the ten-minute drive to the church. The adrenaline rush she was experiencing, a rush that was very familiar to me, was the only thing that would keep her going for the next three days. I did what I've found it best to do when someone is in one of those states—I listened, and murmured general sounds of agreement. The church parking lot was already teeming with cars and trucks, though it was only eleven o'clock and the show wouldn't open until four. We squeezed around vendors unloading boxes of merchandise, waving at Janet as she directed two husky teenage boys carrying rolled quilts to her vendor spot in the spacious recreation room.

"We're allowing the Panther Pep Squad to put on a bake sale at the show," Becky said, rescuing the tilting box of cupcakes a young girl in a cheerleader's outfit was struggling with. "You're in space twenty-three," she told her. "Over by the water fountain."

"Thanks, Mrs. Kolanowski," the girl said, giggling.

The quilts, hung and labeled the day before on specially made metal poles covered with white sheets, were already set in place, though the rest of the room didn't look as if it would be ready for weeks, much less in four hours. I followed Becky to the entrance, where the ticket and opportunity quilt committee were counting change, organizing raffle tickets, and setting out the red-and-white printed programs. In the corner behind them, a tall woman wearing a ruffled white apron was giving instructions to a group of "white glove ladies," the women who strolled up and down the aisles and lifted the quilts with their gloved hands so visitors could inspect the stitching more closely without touching the quilts themselves.

"What do you think of our president's quilt from last year?" Becky asked. The jointly made quilt, a traditional gift from the guild to the outgoing president, was a sampler quilt made of myriad gold and brown plaids and calicos with enough touches of green to give it spark. Each square had a Midwestern or farming motif—Ohio Star, Kansas Dugout, Prairie Queen, Road to Oklahoma, Hole in the Barn Door, Whirlwind, Turkey Tracks. "We named it Heartland Memories. It took a total of two hundred seventy-nine hours to quilt."

"It's beautiful," I said. "So, what can I do to help?"

"Actually, everything's under control, though it may not look that way. Why don't you check with Janet? She called me this morning hot as a chili pepper because Megan bought tickets to see Randy Travis in Kansas City tonight and can't—or rather, won't—help her tonight."

"I'd be glad to." What a break, I thought, ignoring Gabe's voice inside me telling me to keep a low profile. Maybe I could casually quiz her about the rodeo and her whereabouts last night.

Janet was sitting in the center of the carpeted floor of her booth, a disgruntled expression on her face. A smudge of dirt bisected her cheek, and her silver-streaked dark hair was pulled up in a crooked ponytail. Unpacked boxes of merchandise from the craft store surrounded her.

"Becky told me you might need some help," I said.

She gazed up at me, chewing the bottom of her lip. "I'm sitting here wondering why in the world I ever bore a child, ungrateful little brats that they are. And my sister, curses on her evil heart, is on a cruise in the Caribbean." Her eyebrows went up when she noticed my face. "What in the world happened to your face?"

"I fell last night at the rodeo. No big deal." I stooped down and started pulling quilt books out of a box. Was Janet faking it? Could she have been the one who tried to run me down? It was difficult for me to imagine her or any of Gabe's friends in that capacity. What must it be like for Gabe? "Who needs her, anyway?" I said blithely, changing the subject. "I have all day, and I'm not doing anything this evening. If you promise me an hour or so to see the show and a free hot dog, I'll sell my little heart out for you."

"Bless you, my child." She stood up and went over to a pile of black plastic trash bags filled with quilts. "I'll send out for steak sandwiches if you're serious."

"Pizza, with pepperoni and black olives," I countered. "And Coke. The real stuff, not some grocery store brand." My joking made her smile.

"You've got a deal," she declared.

In the next four hours we unpacked the boxes and arranged the quilts, hooked rugs, and various craft items in a way that hopefully would compel people to part with their hard-earned dollars. One hour before show time, we were sitting on the floor eating the promised pizza when Becky joined us.

"I can't believe it," she said, flopping down next to us. She grabbed a slice of pizza and a brown paper towel. "We're going to open on time. It's a miracle."

"I would have never made it without Benni," Janet said, toasting me with a slice of pizza. "Thanks."

"No problem." I drained my Coke and stood up. "I do want to take a quick look at the show before we start work, though."

"Don't miss the Elvis quilts," Becky said. "They're a hoot."

I made a quick trip around the perimeter of the large room, glancing quickly over the vendors' wares to see if there was anything I couldn't buy in San Celina. The vendors were the usual ones always seen at quilt shows: purveyors of thimbles, quilt pins and needles, templates and patterns; pattern search companies and sellers of hand-dyed fabric, batting (cotton or polyester—the controversy rages on), cards, calendars, and pictures featuring every type of quilt you could imagine. There were also quilt books galore and the always present canisters of Bag Balm. I picked up the tiny green and pink can, remembering the first time Gabe saw one sitting on an end table at home.

"What's this for?" he had asked. "Are you hiding a milk cow in the spare room?"

"It's for my fingers," I answered. "Quilting makes them sore, especially now that I don't quilt as much as I used to." He gave me a skeptical look. "Really, it's also good for calluses, even ones caused by working on cars. Let me show you." I took his hand and started rubbing some of the lanolin-based leathery-scented salve into his rough fingertips and down his fingers. We started out laughing and ended up making love on the living-room floor.

I cruised the rest of the vendors quickly, not seeing anything I didn't already have or could buy at home except for a book on Kansas quilters and a book for the co-op's library, an encyclopedia of four thousand quilt patterns. I glanced at my watch. Forty minutes before the doors opened. Plenty of time to see the show. Following the program's suggested route, I worked my way up and down the aisles.

The first set of quilts was the general competition between the guild members—no set theme or requirements. Becky had posted a Polaroid picture of each quilter next to the explanation of her work. It was a wonderful touch, making the stories behind the quilts even more personal. The reasons why women quilt were as varied as the quilts themselves.

"I bought some of the fabric for this quilt at a TG & Y in Bakersfield, California, twenty-five years ago when visiting my sister," one Wichita woman wrote about her Pinwheel Log Cabin quilt. "The rest is scraps because we Mennonites hate to waste anything." Her rosy, well-fed face attested to that fact.

"I made this quilt for my sister, Martha," another quilter wrote of her Robbing Peter to Pay Paul quilt made of primarily red, yellow, and brown calicos, "because she was always borrowing my clothes when we were girls." The Polaroid showed two smiling ladies in their sixties with Lucille Ball–red hair. One held two fingers in a V behind the head of the other.

"This was made for my best friend when she was getting over cancer. I hand-pieced a lot of it waiting for her during her chemotherapy treatments," wrote another lady pictured in a white Stetson with a long feather stuck in the brim. "She's from Texas, and she's doing great now." The quilt was a Lone Star pattern done in pinks, yellows, greens, and tan.

The "Elvis Lives" Quilt Challenge was next. The innovative ways that people rose to the challenge was fun—fancy jean jackets with quilted Elvis faces, and pictorial quilts based on his hit songs. One swirling, colorful interpretation called Elvis in a Blender was made by a quilter who wasn't especially fond of the singer but entered the competition anyway.

After the Elvis exhibit came the antique quilts. This section had a theme—A Century of Quilts. It displayed quilts from 1840 through 1940 with small cards giving a corresponding piece of quilt trivia. When the 1840 Chips and Whetstones quilt was made, quilters paid half a cent for a spool of thread; when the 1870 Ocean Waves quilt was being stitched, a whole quilt cost $3.00 to have quilted; and in 1920, when the pastel David and Goliath quilt was finished, Sears was selling American Standard Fancy Calico for ten cents a yard.

The last exhibit was fun and touching, and the quilters rose to the occasion as they usually do with both humor and warmth. Guild members were asked to show a baby quilt they'd made and tell the story behind its conception—a play on words, playfully intended.

The display of quilts ran the gamut from a green and blue split rail with tiny cowboys depicted in the background ("Grandpa is a semiprofessional rodeo announcer") to a red and white nine-patch with miniature baseball bats and gloves embroidered on every other square ("She never missed a Kansas City Chiefs game except the day I delivered her") to an elaborate appliquéd carousel quilt made with fabric as glittery as jewels ("Her father and I met on a carousel. He was the operator and he let me ride five times for free"). Both of Becky's daughters' quilts were Amish. Whitney's was a Tumbling Blocks design in cool blues, purples, and greens; Paige's a colorful Amish Baskets in yellow, orange, and browns.

Customers were already starting to line up when I got back to Janet's booth. We worked steadily for the next few hours, only speaking when I needed to ask her how to write something up or the price of some unmarked item. By a quarter to nine, the crowd had thinned considerably.

"Two more days of this," Janet moaned. She opened the cash box, and her face brightened. "On the other hand, we've sold more today than I probably have all week."

"Becky told me she advertised within a hundred-mile radius," I said, sipping on the Coke I had hidden behind some quilted tissue-box holders. "Looks like it did some good, and this is only the preshowing." I glanced toward the entrance just in time to see Gabe walk in. Relief washed over me. Though I'd never admit it to him, I was still apprehensive and a bit nervous about being run off the road by that truck. It had preyed on my mind the whole day.

Becky, working the front ticket table, saw Gabe seconds after he walked through the door and pulled him over to the Amish-style opportunity quilt to start her raffle-ticket pitch. He pulled out his wallet as she talked and handed her some bills, at the same time searching the crowded room. I waved when his eyes swept past Janet's booth, and his tense face relaxed. He smiled, his teeth vividly white against his dark skin. I watched him follow Becky to the raffle table, enjoying the view of him from the back as much as his smile.

"I remember when Lawrence used to look at me that way," Janet said.

I turned to her. "What?"

"The way Gabe looks when he sees you." Her voice held an edge of bitterness.

"Believe me," I said wryly, "he has his irritating moments. He can be very domineering at times. And stubborn as an old mule."

"And I bet he's not the only one."

"What do you mean by that?" Our conversation had taken an uncomfortable turn, and it happened so fast, I wasn't sure what caused it or exactly how to react.

"Lawrence called me today," she said, her eyes glued to the stacks of bills. Her neck flushed a pale shade of pink. "He said Gabe dropped by the club and was asking an awful lot of questions about Tyler. Do you know why he'd be doing that? Is he working with Dewey?" Her tone had a light but definite confrontational tone to it.

I played with the pop-top on my can of Coke. "I don't know, Janet. Maybe you should ask Gabe."

Tightening her lips, she pulled out a fistful of bills and started separating them into piles on the table. "You know, people who don't know all the details about things shouldn't be making hasty judgments. You know what they say about walking a mile in someone else's moccasins."

I tossed my empty can into the waste basket. "Do you need my help tomorrow?" I asked, trying to keep my voice neutral.

Her tone turned contrite. "No, Megan should be here. Thanks so much for helping me, Benni. I really owe you for today."

I studied her face, involuntarily reaching up to touch the side of mine, not wanting to think what I was thinking. Were her earlier words a subtle threat? Did her eyes shift guiltily when I touched my face? Or was I starting to see things where nothing existed?

"You're welcome," I said. "It was fun, really. I'd better go now before Becky talks Gabe into spending his police retirement on raffle tickets."

Janet gave a half smile and started stacking quarters. "Becky's a born saleswoman, no doubt about that."

I walked up behind Gabe, who was contemplating the table of flyers that advertised the various quilt shows and quilting products and services available in the Central Kansas area. I circled his waist with my arms and laid my head against his solid back. "Hey, good lookin'. Whatcha got cookin'?"

He laughed and pulled me around to the front of him, hugging me warmly. "Nothing I can show you in public, but it's definitely of gourmet quality."

"Brother," I said. "Give a guy an inch, and he thinks he owns the whole forest."

"Your metaphors are a bit convoluted, but I'll let it pass. You hungry?"

"Not really. I just had pizza. Are you?"

"Starved."

"Is your mom cooking dinner?"

"No, I told her you and I were going into Wichita to eat."

"So no one can eavesdrop?"

"Exactly."

"What did you find out?" I asked the minute we were in the car.

"Pull back on the reins there, Calamity Jane. Give me a chance to put the car in Drive." On the way to Wichita, he told me there'd been so much activity at the rodeo that he couldn't pinpoint anyone's movements for very long. "We're back to where we started with everyone being suspect."

"I found out something," I said. "I think."

A smoldering look started in his eyes. "I thought we agreed you were going to keep a low profile."

"I am." I reached over and stroked the back of his hair. "Calm your ruffled tail feathers, Friday. Janet volunteered this information. She said she talked to Lawrence, and he was suspicious about the questions you were asking about him and Tyler. I'm sure they had or were having an affair."

"Did she say they were?"

"No, but I could hear it in her voice."

"Well," he said, pulling into the parking lot of the Eastgate Mall. "This time I think your feelings are right on the mark. He didn't say it in so many words, but I think Lawrence and Tyler did have something going on.'' We stopped in front of a busy, yuppie-style cafe called Willie C's. The decor was fifties nostalgia and the food a nineties version of home-style cooking. Gabe ordered a chicken fajita salad, and I ordered cherry cobbler à la mode. Above us, a Hamm's Beer bear in red cowboy boots revolved on a pedestal while Elvis sang about being all shook up. The Friday night crowd was loud enough that no one could possibly overhear us.

"So," I said. "The question is, when did they have their affair, was it still going on, and why would he kill her.''

"Or why would Janet kill her.'' In an instant, amidst all the noise and music, Gabe's eyes drooped, and a sadness seemed to weight his features. I reached across the table and took his hand. Again, in my eagerness to solve the puzzle of Tyler's murder, I'd forgotten these people were his friends and that the consequences of this would probably haunt him the rest of his life.

"Let's forget it while we eat," I said. "That was all I got from Janet, and you can tell me the rest later.''

He nodded and picked up his fork. As we ate, I told him about the the various quilts in the show, which guild entry won my vote, the Elvis Challenge, the stories behind the baby quilts. His face started to relax, and by the time we were done, I'd almost managed to erase the sadness in his eyes.

He reached across the table and took my hand, interlocking our fingers. "It's good to hear your voice. I missed you today.''

"Me, too.'' I squeezed his hand and smiled. "I wish we were back home in San Celina. Alone.''

He lifted his dark eyebrows, a smile in his eyes. "There's a La Quinta Inn on the other side of the parking lot. I could get us a room.''

"Sixty-some dollars for just a couple of hours?''

"Right now I'd pay five hundred bucks for an hour with you."

I feigned hurt. "Just five hundred? I'm insulted. I figure I'm worth at least a thousand."

"Women. You can never satisfy them."

"Oh, I don't know. You've done all right by me."

He laughed. "Just all right?"

Before I could answer, the waitress brought our check. On the way out to the car, we resumed talking about the quilt show.

"Did Becky have any of her quilts there?" Gabe asked.

"Yes, and you'd better drop by tomorrow and see them so she doesn't get her feelings hurt. She's got a cute Elvis quilt based on his 'Clam Bake' song in *Blue Hawaii*—the clams' mouths actually move—and one in the general show—a Solomon's Puzzle quilt with a black background that shows a really interesting combination of positive and negative space, and there are also two baby quilts she made for Paige and Whitney."

"I can't believe how much those girls have grown," he said as he started driving out of the parking lot. "It seems like only yesterday that Becky was pregnant with Whitney. I remember visiting when she was eight months along. She sat in my mom's recliner sewing on that quilt. She was as big as a barn and cranky as a—"

"That's it!" I grabbed Gabe's arm, causing him to swerve and just miss sideswiping a Toyota full of teenagers.

"Benni, watch it!"

"I don't know why I didn't think of it before. It was right there in front of my face! Geeze, sometimes I can be such a dope."

He pulled the car to a stop in a vacant part of the dark parking lot. "What are you talking about?" he demanded.

"The wall hanging that Tyler made," I said, so excited I could barely contain myself. "It's not a wall hanging at all. Gabe, I think it's a baby quilt."

THIRTEEN

"BABY QUILT?" GABE sounded skeptical. "Why would you think that?"

"It makes sense. I'll bet my last healthy heifer that she went down to Arkansas to have a baby and made the quilt while she was waiting for it to be born. Think about it. Six months. She'd just start showing at three or four months, so the timing fits. I bet she stayed with T.K.'s family or somebody he knew. Maybe we can pry it out of him. Isn't there some way we can find out from the autopsy if she'd recently had a baby?"

He shook his head. "Slow down there, Calamity. I think you're reaching now. There's no way I can ask a question like that without having the sheriff's department climb all over me."

I sat back in the seat, frustrated. "This would have been a lot easier in San Celina. We'd have all the medical reports at our fingertips."

"We?" He gave a sardonic grunt and restarted the car. "First off, *we* wouldn't have anything. *I* would. Frankly I wish we were in San Celina because then I'd have some control. Right now, I feel like—"

"A civilian who can't get any information? Welcome to the club, Chief. Now you know what it feels like."

"You were attacked once. I don't intend for it to happen again."

"Look, we have to find out if that really is a baby blanket. If one of those men got her pregnant, maybe that's a motive. Maybe all that money in her bank account came from a blackmailing scheme. Maybe—"

"Maybe you'd better just slow down there. You're making more out of this so-called baby quilt than is really there. It's a common problem among *inexperienced* detectives. They tend to manufacture evidence out of the smallest, most insignificant details."

"It's not insignificant," I snapped, turning to gaze out my window. "I wish you'd just take me seriously for once."

We didn't speak again until we pulled up in his mother's driveway.

He turned off the ignition and turned to me. "Sweetheart, let's not argue about this. I'm sorry if you think I'm not taking you seriously. I just want you to be safe."

"Or maybe you're afraid I might solve this first and show you up."

"You're getting juvenile now. Your impetuousness has landed you in some tight spots that so far you have managed to squeeze out of without too much harm. This time you might not be as lucky."

"I'm trying to think this through before doing anything, but you won't let me. That's not impetuous." I crossed my arms over my chest.

He played with the turn signal, clicking it back and forth, his eyes straight ahead. Finally he gave a small growl and hit the steering wheel. "Woman, *tu me vuelves loco*!"

"Friday, you make me crazy, too. But at least *I'm* open-minded enough to listen to other people's ideas."

He pointed a finger at me. "I still think it's farfetched, but I'll listen. Just what do you plan on doing with this cockeyed theory of yours?"

"You know what they say, a cop is only as good as his sources."

"In all my years in law enforcement, I've never heard anyone say that."

"Okay, maybe I heard it on TV. Anyway, I have a great source who can find out whether Tyler did have a baby in Arkansas, providing she gave birth in a place where they keep records."

"What source?" he asked suspiciously.

"My cousin Emory in Sugartree."

He groaned and laid his head back against the headrest. "I'm afraid to ask. Just how are you related?"

"His father, Boone Littleton, is my third or fourth cousin. I think. His daddy and Dove's daddy were first cousins by marriage, but then Boone married my mom's third cousin, Ervalean, so I think I'm related to Emory on both sides. Emory's a year younger than me, and we used to play together when Dove and I visited Aunt Garnet in Sugartree."

"And just how is Cousin Emory going to help?"

"He's a newspaper reporter, sort of. And sort of a private detective."

Gabe's eyebrows went up. "And how is someone sort of a newspaper reporter, sort of a private detective?"

"Well, you know how the economy is in Arkansas these days. Emory made it all the way to his last year in law school, then had to drop out 'cause Boone's smoked chicken business took a downturn, and he couldn't pay Emory's tuition. The thing is, Emory's a real sweetheart, but he's not the brightest guy in the world by any means, so that let out any scholarships. But Boone has lots of contacts, being in the chicken business for so long, so he pulled some strings and got Emory a job at the *Bozwell Courier Tribune*. Bozwell's a town south of Sugartree, and Boone practically supports the newspaper with his chicken advertising. Anyway, it turned out that Emory was actually pretty good at reporting, being the type of guy you just can't help telling your whole life story to, and so he even did a little investigative reporting, such as it is in the Bozwell-Sugartree area. His claim to fame is finding the governor's mother's kidnapped poodle, though it was quite by accident during an afternoon tête-à-tête with the daughter of a man running a puppy mill. He collected quite a substantial reward, and of course the exposure got him more clients and— Why are you laughing?''

''Tell me, do any of these cousins have two thumbs?'' I scowled at him.

''Sorry.'' He held up his hands. ''Just run that last part by me again. I got lost somewhere between the kidnapped chickens and smoked poodles.''

''Very funny,'' I said. ''The point I was trying to make is that Emory has a lot of contacts both from his law school days in Little Rock and his newspaper job. Those postcards were postmarked Little Rock. Maybe he can use those contacts to find out if Tyler had a baby there. ''

''I still think you're going overboard on this baby quilt theory.''

''All it will cost us is a phone call.''

''I guess it can't hurt. Just let me know what he finds out. Immediately. Promise.'' He gave me a stern look.

''On my honor, Chief Ortiz. Honestly, you really need to learn to trust your investigators a little more.'' I climbed out and looked toward the house. ''All the lights are on. It looks like your mom waited up for us.''

''I guess some things never change.''

''She knows something's going on,'' I said, following him up the steps. ''Maybe we should go ahead and tell her.''

He grabbed my upper arm and stopped me before I could open the front door. ''No, Benni. It's not that I don't trust Mom, but she's taught a lot of these people, and some of their parents are her closest friends. I don't want to place that burden on her.''

''Okay,'' I said, sighing. ''I just hate her thinking that

we're arguing about something petty. She already thinks you made a big mistake when you married me.''

"No, she doesn't," he said evenly. "You're just overly sensitive."

"Easy for you to say. I'm going to call Emory right away."

He glanced at his watch. "It's past eleven."

"Emory's a real night owl. Always was, even as a kid. If I know him, he's just getting warmed up."

Kathryn was awake, but already in her bedroom. While Gabe went in to tell her good night, I dialed Arkansas. Just as I suspected, Emory was wide-awake and primed to chitchat the night away. After we went through the litany of family gossip with me pointedly leaving out Dove's latest adventure, he said in his smooth Arkansas drawl, "Okay, cuz, as much of a pleasure this has been talkin' to your sweet self, you're wantin' something. Am I right?''

"Well . . ." I hedged.

"Sweetcakes, don't be lyin' to me. I know everything. You know Aunt Damson always said I had the 'second sense.' ''

"What she said was you had *no sense*."

He chuckled. "Now let's not get feline here. So, what can I be doin' for you, and it better not involve anything of a monetary nature 'cause my wallet's as parched as Aunt Garnet's liquor cabinet."

"No money involved. I need you to find some information for me about someone who lived in Little Rock or the general area about seven or eight months ago. Or at least I think she lived there." After extracting a promise that this was entirely confidential, I told him the whole story. "What I'd like to know is who's listed as the father on the birth certificate."

"Do you think she'd tell the truth?" he asked.

"Maybe. Especially if she didn't use the name she sang under. I'm guessing she had the baby under her Amish name—Ruth Stoltzfus, or maybe her maiden name,

Ruth Miller. Who would ever connect either of them with Tyler Brown, aspiring country-western singer?''

I listened to him whistle softly through his teeth as he wrote down the information. ''Little Rock's a big city, cuz.''

''I know it's a lot of work, Emory, but she was murdered. And I'm afraid the person who killed her might get away with it.''

''That money really intrigues me. How much did you say it was?''

''Well, the opening balance was ten thousand dollars, but she'd apparently been living off it because it was almost half gone.''

''You know what that probably means?''

Just as his words came over the phone, the pieces clicked together. ''Emory, if she had a baby, she probably sold it to someone.''

''That's sure what it sounds like.''

''Well, that certainly explains the money, but it still doesn't give a clue as to why she was killed.'' I traced a finger over the pattern in the kitchen wallpaper.

''That, thank goodness, is your territory. I'll get my network started on it and let you know what I find out *tout suite*. Now.'' The timbre of his voice deepened. ''There's the business of my fee.''

''Your fee? I'm family, Emory Delano Littleton. If you don't do this for me, I'll tell Aunt Garnet that you were the one who spilled Hawaiian Punch on Great-gramma Littleton's Path in the Wilderness quilt.''

''That's blackmail, sweetcakes, and an incredibly pathetic attempt at it, too, I might add. I'm not asking you for money, just a teensy little favor.''

''What?'' I asked warily. Emory always had been a sneaky kid. More than once I'd been caught holding the bag when he'd talked me into some mischief, then disappeared like magic when Dove and Aunt Garnet showed up.

"Your friend Elvia." His molasses voice fondled her name.

"What about her?" Elvia Aragon was my best friend back in San Celina. A tiny, gorgeous firebrand of a woman, she ran Blind Harry's Bookstore and Coffee-house with the steel-nerved precision of a seasoned general and the obsessive love of a new mother. We'd been friends since the first day of school in Mrs. Lawndale's second-grade class when she informed me in her intense little soprano voice that the red bows in my braids didn't match the maroon in my dress. I responded to this bit of fashion advice by spitting on her. It was a friendship made in heaven. She is still trying to coordinate my wardrobe, but I don't spit on her anymore.

"I want a date with Elvia," he said.

"With Elvia?" I repeated, hoping I'd heard wrong.

"Hello, is anyone home? Yes, with Elvia. Can you arrange it?"

I stuttered for a moment, grasping for straws. "But you live in Arkansas."

"For a date with her, I'll fly to California. Is it a deal?"

She'll kill me, I thought. No, she'll torture me and then she'll kill me. And she's very creative. And smart. And well-read. The possibilities sent a chill down my spine. I hesitated exactly two seconds.

"Sure," I said.

"Okay, I'll get on it right away. If I come up with a birth certificate, you want me to fax it to you?"

"Call me first. Except for the police department, I'm not sure where there's a fax machine. I don't want any-one to know about this until I do."

"Not even *tu esposo el chota*?"

Great, Spanish with an Arkansas drawl. I pictured the contemptuous expression on Elvia's face when Emory tried to impress her with his language skills. I studied my hands. Just how painful was it to have your finger-nails yanked out one by one? "Except for Gabe, of course. If I'm not here, you can tell him, but don't worry, I'll be here.''

"Okay, I'll see what I can worm out of people. I'll try tomorrow, but I'll probably have to wait until Monday. I'll get back to you asap.''

"Thanks, Emory.''

"*Hasta la vista*, sweetcakes.''

Upstairs in bed with Gabe, I repeated my conversation with Emory.

"I still think you're reaching,'' he said, "but since it's free, we might as well see what he can find out.''

"Well, it's not exactly free.'' I told him the conditions of Emory's help. Gabe let out a war whoop of a laugh.

"You sold Elvia? I want to be there when you tell her,'' he said. "I'd skip the Superbowl to watch you try to wriggle out of *this* one.''

"He's just bluffing. He'll never come to California. He hates to fly.''

"Well, you are one dead little *gringa* if he does.''

"I know,'' I said, pulling a pillow over my face.

The next day Gabe, Kathryn, and I drove back downtown to the quilt show. Gabe and his mother walked through the exhibits while I helped Becky with raffle tickets. Around noon, Dewey dropped by and asked if Gabe and I would like to come out to the stable later for a barbecue he and Belinda were having for Chet to celebrate his winning first place in both bulls and bareback.

"He's on his way to the National Finals, no doubt about it,'' Dewey said. "And besides getting to sample some of my expert cooking, there's a new little quarter horse named Lucy you might like to try out.''

"I'm sure it'll be all right with Gabe,'' I said. "He's wandering around the show somewhere with his mom, but as soon as he gets back, I'll ask him.''

He bent his head and studied the side of my face. "Heard you took a tumble at the rodeo. How're you feeling?''

"Fine." I laughed and retold my fictional story. "Didn't have a drop to drink either. Just tripped over my own feet."

"Well, maybe we ought to saddle up old Grapenuts for you to ride. He's going on thirty and might be more your speed."

I showed him a fist. "Don't·you worry, Detective Champagne. I can take care of myself."

He pushed his hat back and grinned at me. "Okay, don't say I didn't offer. Tell Kathryn she's welcome, too. Chet'll be there with some of his rodeo buddies. How's a nice juicy, cornfed Kansas City steak sound? I even bought some range chicken for your picky husband."

"Great. We'll be there unless Gabe's made other plans."

When they returned, I told them about the invitation, but Kathryn declined, saying she'd already made plans to eat with friends. Gabe and I headed out to the stable alone.

We found Dewey in front of the house manning a steel barrel barbecue and surrounded by the tangy, smoky smell of cooking chicken and beef. "Chet's out back looking at my new mare," Dewey said. "Cordie June and Belinda are in the kitchen stirring up potato salad or dip or something."

"I'd bet on the something," Gabe said in a laconic voice.

Dewey grinned broadly, pointing toward the kitchen with his long-handled spatula. "I guess having the ex-squeeze and the current squeeze at the same meal isn't the smartest thing a man can do, but this barbecue's for Chet and his friends. Belinda's his mom, but I couldn't leave out Cordie June, now could I?"

"Cowboy," Gabe said, trying to hold back a smile and not succeeding, "you're playing chicken with a hand grenade pin."

"Always did love a good fireworks show."

"Excuse me," I said, irritated by his patronizing attitude toward his ex-wife and his girlfriend, and by Gabe's nonchalant acquiescence to it. "I think I'll go see if they need any help."

"Better put on a bulletproof vest," Dewey called after me.

Inside the kitchen, Belinda and Cordie June were silently working at opposite ends of the room. On the radio the lead singer of Sawyer Brown was telling us that some girls don't like boys like him, but some girls do. They both looked up when I walked in. Belinda wore tight, old jeans and a faded Western shirt with the tails hanging out. Cordie June wore a short, bright orange jean skirt and a thin tank top that showed off her tanned young arms.

"Hi," I said. "I thought maybe you could use an extra set of hands."

Belinda handed me a metal bowl of green apples. "I was going to make an apple brown Betty. You could peel these apples." She started opening up drawers, looking for a knife.

After letting Belinda search through four drawers, Cordie June said, "Oh, I moved them to a more convenient spot." She opened a drawer and pulled out a wood-handled paring knife. Offering it to Belinda, she flashed an impudent grin.

Belinda's freckled face flushed a deep, mottled red. Swallowing an angry sound deep in her throat, she stormed through the kitchen door, slamming it hard enough to rattle the glass.

Cordie June stared after her, her small hand still grasping the knife. She turned and stabbed it deep into a fat green apple. "Heavens," she said, her mouth twisting into a sly smile. "I reckon some people just don't take well to change."

I didn't answer, knowing her cocky self-confidence would be cured soon enough by the aging process.

Though it didn't seem possible to her right now, she wouldn't be twenty-two forever, and someday she could very well be the old being replaced by the new. I went out the back door and headed across the backyard to the breezeway barns where I suspected Belinda had retreated. She was in the tack room, swearing steadily as she struggled with a tangle of bridles someone had dropped in a spaghetti-like heap on the floor.

"Need help?" I asked.

She continued to wrestle with the twisted tack. "These stupid kids. Sometimes I think I'd be better off closing this place and getting a job managing a McDonald's in Wichita."

I laughed lightly. "So you can get away from kids?"

She looked up, her thin face chagrined. "I guess you're right." She hung one freed bridle on an open hook. "Sorry about what happened in the kitchen. It's just irritating to find out your kitchen has been rearranged by your ex-husband's latest bimbo."

"It must be." I picked up the other bridle and straightened it out.

Her wide mouth drew down sullenly. "I'm surprised you'd even be sympathetic to me." The abruptly hostile tone of her voice reminded me how she'd rubbed me the wrong way the first time we met.

"Why's that?" I asked, trying to keep my voice level.

"Seems to me that you, being the *younger* second wife, would be more on Cordie June's side." She picked up a red and black saddle blanket and held it to her chest.

I looked at her coldly. "Belinda, I don't know either of you well enough to take sides, and to be perfectly honest with you, I don't want to. And though it's really none of your business, Gabe was divorced for seven years before we got married. I've never even met his first wife, but from what I understand, she's been happily remarried for three years. You know, nothing pisses me off more than someone assuming something about me that isn't true. So you can take your habit of instantly judging people and shove it.'' I tossed the bridle at her. She dropped the saddle blanket and caught it, surprise causing her mouth to drop open.

I turned and started for the door.

''Benni, wait,'' she called, running after me. She caught my upper arm in a steel grip.

I jerked out of her grasp. ''Watch it.''

She held her hands up. ''Sorry. Hey, really, I'm sorry. I don't know why I get like this. It was just seeing Cordie June so . . . at home in my kitchen. The kitchen where I raised my kids—where me and Dewey . . .'' Her voice cracked; her eyes looked as miserable as a sick calf's.

I stubbornly fought the pity that started creeping into my heart. It couldn't be easy what she'd gone through these last couple of years, losing her daughter, her husband, and even the small comfort of everything being in the same place in the home that held so many memories. Who's to say I wouldn't be just as prickly and suspicious if I'd experienced what she had?

''Before you go to making up your mind about someone too fast, try to imagine yourself pullin' their boots on every morning,'' Dove had always told us kids. ''You'll understand them better, and maybe the pinches in your own boots won't hurt as much.''

''It's okay,'' I said to Belinda. ''Let's just forget it and go eat. That steak is beginning to smell awfully good.''

She hung her head and said in a low voice, ''I need to cool down more before I see . . . that woman again. I'm going to grain some of the horses. You want to come with me?'' Her face held a question, almost a plea, for acceptance.

I wanted to say no. Chances were she'd pop off again, but the alternative was going back and helping Cordie June. And, hearing Dove's voice in my head, it would be the forgiving thing to do.

"Do you mind me asking something personal?" I asked as we walked through one of the barns, giving grain to some horses who'd been sick recently and needed the extra nutrition.

"Depends," she said.

"Why does Dewey live in the house when you're out here more?"

She shrugged. "It was part of the divorce settlement. At the time, I didn't want to live in this place where all those memories were of him and me and Chet and especially DeeDee." Her voice sparked with bitterness. "He can forget things easier than me, I guess. The place didn't seem to make him feel bad. So he took out a second mortgage and paid me off. I bought a small house in Derby, close to my parents. But now that time has passed, I wish I'd fought for the house. Especially since he started bringing women here. I don't know why I let Cordie June rattle me. She's not the first cheap tramp in his life and certainly won't be the last." She tapped her nails against the bucket of grain she carried. A pale buckskin moved out of the shadowed corner of his stall and stuck his head over the door. "No grain for you, Coley, but here's a goodie." She pulled a carrot out of her pocket and fed it to him. Her eyes grew shiny. "Sometimes I just miss our old life so much. If DeeDee hadn't . . . if I'd just . . ." She dumped the remaining grain in the last stall. A sharp-ribbed bay moseyed over to the trough. "Like I said, I should have stayed in the house and made *him* leave."

"I'm sorry," I said.

She brushed off my sympathy with a harsh laugh. "Yeah, well, as they say, hindsight and all that."

We walked up to Apache's stall. He stuck his head over the metal door, and I patted the side of his neck while she fed him a carrot. "Ever ride him?" I asked.

"Sure. Dewey doesn't know it, though. He can be such a tightass sometimes." Her eyes shifted sideways and gave me a shrewd look. "Want to try him out?"

Instinctively, I looked behind me. "I don't know . . .
Dewey said . . ."

"Forget Dewey," she said. "But if you think you
can't handle him—"

"That's not it," I said sharply. "I just don't believe
in riding someone's horse without their permission."

She smirked at me. "Honey, I own half this stable,
and that includes all the critters in it. So *I'm* giving you
permission."

"Then let's go."

I followed her to a smaller tack room at the back of
the barn. She pulled a soft maroon-colored bareback pad
off a saddle rack and handed it to me. "He's not broke
to Western saddle yet. He can get a little frisky. That
okay with you?"

"No problem," I said.

Apache blew air and jerked his head high when Belinda
haltered him. She led him into the breezeway to cross-tie
him. I threw the pad over his back and buckled it.

"Better use this." Half smiling, she handed me a
shiny D-ring snaffle bit. He fought me as I tried to slip
it into his mouth, jerking his head away sharply, like a
child avoiding bitter-tasting medicine. Apparently he'd
decided he liked standing in his stall and doing nothing
but processing alfalfa.

Belinda stepped to the side, her hands stuck in her
back pockets. "Need any help?" she asked, her slightly
mocking tone back in place.

"Nope." Finally he took the bit. I pulled the reins
over his head, suddenly feeling uneasy. "You can see
the arena from the front yard. Dewey will come barreling out the minute we walk Apache in."

"We've got another arena out back of the old barn,"
she said. "He'll never see us out there."

Leading the skittish horse, I followed her out the back
of the breezeway toward an ancient, ramshackle barn.
Behind it was a split-wood corral that must have been
built around the same time as the barn. The gate hung

crookedly by one rusty hinge. I opened it carefully and led Apache to the center of the ring.

"He's pretty big." She laced her fingers. "I'll give you a leg up."

Apache balked at the pressure of me on his back, jumping around while I struggled for control. Irritably he whipped his long tail up and struck me on the shoulder. It was clear he was still not ready to become a co-operative working partner with a human being. I wondered just how long it had been since he was last ridden.

"Maybe you should tie the reins," she called, moving back behind the corral's fence away from us.

I shook my head and scowled. It was a deliberate barb meant to make me mad, and it worked. Only kids and beginners tied their reins as a precaution against losing them. Apache arched his head and pawed the ground angrily. I pulled back hard. He blew another angry breath. Unlike Sinful, who had eventually settled down after his initial fight for control, Apache, reminding me a lot of a certain police chief, wasn't about to let anyone tell him what to do. In the next few minutes, using everything I'd ever been taught about breaking horses, I managed to make him walk around the ring. Belinda's eyes were glued on me the whole time, waiting for me to make a mistake. More than once, Apache slammed me against the splintery boards of the corral, trying to push me off. After his first attempt to dislodge me, I switched directions so that my injured side wouldn't get bruises on top of bruises. After about fifteen minutes, he seemed controlled enough for me to try a jog. I clucked and he immediately responded, though I never got secure enough to loosen the reins. I was beginning to enjoy his strength and spirited personality and turned to say so to Belinda, when a brown-striped squirrel scampered down a crooked box elder next to the corral and ran across the ring in front of us. The sudden movement broke my precarious control, and Apache reared up slightly, trying to shy away from the chattering squirrel.

"Whoa," I crooned. "Easy now . . ."

"Watch it!" I heard Belinda yell. "Don't lose the—"

Just as she said it, he reared up on his back legs, and the reins flew out of my hands. Instinctively I grabbed his mane. I held on as he started darting back and forth across the arena, reins dragging on the ground, the squirrel forgotten, but his adrenaline pumping enough now that he couldn't stop. He rammed me against the fence. I felt the soft saddle start to slip, and I gripped hard with my thighs, trying to keep a seat.

"Grab him!" another, deeper voice yelled out over Belinda's. Out of the corner of my eye I saw in a blur Dewey's angry face, the cowboy hats of Chet and his friends, and the shocked face of my husband.

Then I hit the ground. Pain shot through my already battered body like a jolt of lightning. I bit down hard, my teeth slamming against each other. Like I'd been taught in childhood, I ignored the pain and rolled away, forcing myself to scramble under the fence to safety. Gabe was there before I could stand up, pulling me up and cursing vehemently in Spanish.

"I'm okay," I said, leaning my head against his chest, breathing deep and hard. "Just a little weak. I'm all right." I swallowed, and the salty taste of blood flowed down the back of my throat.

Across the arena, a commotion caused us both to turn and stare.

"Are you out of your mind?" Dewey screamed at Belinda. "She could have been killed. You know he's too dangerous to ride. How could you do something so absolutely stupid?" Her broad shoulders slumped, and she seemed to shrink inches under his harsh words. "You're so all-fire bent on screwing things up for me, aren't you? Aren't you?" He gripped both her shoulders.

"Gabe, do something," I whispered, digging my nails into his forearm.

"Wait," he answered in a low voice. "This is between them. I'll step in if it looks like he's losing control."

"What were you thinking?" Dewey demanded, shaking Belinda slightly. That did it for Gabe, but before he could step in, Chet ran over and grabbed his dad's forearm. Dewey shook it off and snapped at his son, "This is between your mother and me. Go get Apache and put him up." Chet's face flushed angrily, but he did what Dewey said without a word.

"Hey, y'all," Cordie June called out, walking around the barn. "What's going on out here? I turned around, and everyone was gone." She looked at Belinda and Dewey, at the horse that Chet and his friends were still trying to round up, and at Gabe and me. "Is everything okay?" She cocked her hip and gave a flirty smile.

"Fine, Cordie June," Dewey said. Belinda jerked away from his grasp. "You get on back to the house and check the barbecue. We'll all be there in a minute." He turned back to Belinda. "We'll talk about this later."

She sputtered, her face white with anger. "Who do you think you are, Dewey Champagne? I own half this stable. I have just as much right—" His savage look stopped her words. She swung around and headed for the horse barns, cursing loudly. Chet handed Apache's reins to one of his friends, and after shooting his dad a black look, ran after his mother.

Dewey walked over to Gabe and me. "You okay?" he asked, his face amiable again.

"Yes," I said, brushing the dirt off my pant leg. "Look, it was just as much my fault as Belinda's."

"No, it wasn't. She knows how Apache is and she let you ride him anyway."

"I chose to ride him," I insisted. "I think you're being too hard on her. I think—" Gabe squeezed my shoulder firmly.

"This is not up for discussion," Dewey said bluntly. "Why don't you go in and get washed up. The food's probably ready." He turned and walked toward the house, his boots kicking up a small dirt cloud behind him.

I shrugged Gabe's hand off. "What was that all about? I think he's being a real jerk. Did you see how he was yelling at Belinda?"

"He's right," Gabe said. "She knew exactly what to expect from that horse, so she shouldn't have allowed you to ride him. And you should have known better yourself. You could have broken your neck."

"I knew what I was doing," I said. "He's not the first horse who's bucked me off and he more than likely won't be the last. Belinda had nothing to do with that."

"Maybe, maybe not. What were you thinking, trying to ride a green horse like that? Dewey told you he didn't want you riding him."

"I had to."

"What?"

"You wouldn't understand."

"Try me."

I exhaled sharply. "She made me feel like I *couldn't* do it. Like I wasn't capable of handling a horse like Apache."

He gave me an astonished look. "Let me get this straight. You did it because she *dared* you? Am I talking to a mature woman here, or a teenager?"

"She didn't . . ." But he was right. She did dare me, and I took the dare. I looked away, chewing on the corner of my lip, feeling heat rise up the back of my neck. "How do you always manage to make me feel like I'm the kid and you're the parent?"

"*Niña*, it isn't as difficult as it sounds."

"Very funny." I smacked him in the stomach, which only made him laugh. Then his face turned sober again, and he rested his hands on my shoulders, massaging them gently.

"Benni, let's get serious here. I don't like the way this came down. I told you that you need to be careful with everyone involved. That means sometimes backing down when you don't want to. There's more honor in that than forging ahead and getting yourself hurt or killed.''

''I know,'' I said, tilting my head back and relaxing under his gentle hands. ''I'll think twice before I do anything from now on. I promise.''

He bent and kissed me. ''Good. Now, let's get you cleaned up and get something to eat.''

Belinda had taken one of the stable's trucks and left before Gabe and I returned. No one mentioned the incident with Apache during lunch, but an uneasiness swirled through the festivities. Chet kept shooting his father angry side looks, which Dewey ignored. Later that afternoon, when everyone had gone inside to watch Chet's rodeo videos again, I excused myself and retreated to a wooden lawn chair under a thick shady ash next to the house. I watched a red-tailed hawk ride the air currents over the grassy meadow next to Dewey's property. The air felt warm and heavy on my arms. In the distance, through the glistening heat, I could see grain silos, tall and silvery-white, and it occurred to me for the first time that they were probably the inspiration for Frank L. Baum's Emerald City. The screen door opened, and Dewey stepped out on the porch. He strode across the lawn to join me.

''You feeling okay, short stuff?'' he asked, his brown eyes concerned.

I smiled and lifted the damp hair off the back of my neck. ''Dewey, I grew up on a ranch. I've had wrecks before and I've made it thirty-five years without experiencing any major plaster yet. I'm fine.''

''Then you know it was real stupid of you to ride that stud,'' he said, perching on the handle of my chair and resting his arm behind me. ''I told you—''

''I apologize,'' I said sharply, cutting into his lecture. ''It won't happen again.''

''Good.'' He picked up a long strand of wild wheat

and stuck it in his mouth. "Belinda says she's sorry. She'll tell you herself next time she sees you. Sometimes she doesn't always think things out before she does them."

"You don't have to apologize for her," I said, irritated at his condescending attitude. "What happened was between me and her. It's not your responsibility."

He gave me his lazy grin and rolled the wheat strand to the other side of his mouth. "Belinda and me, we were together a long time. Since high school. Kind of like the way it was between you and your first husband—what was his name, Jake?"

"Jack."

"Right, Jack. That's a lot of time, a lot of history. So I do feel responsible. Family loyalty means something to me. Even though we're divorced, she's still family in a way, because we have Chet. And because of DeeDee. So I always take responsibility for my family and my friends when they need help . . . or do stupid things." He squinted at me, his brown eyes slits under his thick dark eyebrows. "I have a sneaking suspicion you feel the same way. Am I right?"

"Yes," I said slowly. "But even family loyalty and friendship has its limits."

"Does it?" He was silent for a moment, his eyes challenging me to go further.

I turned away from his gaze and looked to the house, where shouts of laughter filtered through the screen door. "But none of this has anything to do with the fact that no one forced me to ride Apache. I made that decision on my own. That's what we're talking about, isn't it?"

He spit the weed out, gave a sharp laugh and stood up, adjusting his pale hat. "Well, of course it is. What else would we be talking about?"

"He knows who did it," I insisted after repeating his cryptic comments to Gabe on the drive home. "Or at least he suspects."

"He's not stupid," Gabe said. "He certainly has the same suspicions we do." He frowned, his jaw setting in a familiar granite position. "What he said bothers me."

"I think he was fishing, but I didn't give anything away."

"I don't like his threatening tone."

"You didn't even hear his tone! How do you know it was threatening?" I sat back in my seat. "You know what I think? I think he suspects Belinda did it, though I can't imagine why. I could imagine her killing Cordie June—but Tyler?" Then something dawned on me. "What if Dewey was having an affair with Tyler?"

Gabe pulled the car over to the side of the road and stopped, letting the engine idle. He leaned his head against the steering wheel, one fist clutched against his leg. "I don't want to do this," he said. "Think of them this way. I wished we'd never come. If we'd never come—"

I touched his forearm gently. "It would have happened anyway. Our coming didn't cause this. You know that." Suddenly, all I wanted to do was go back to California. At that moment, I didn't care who killed Tyler, who had an affair with her, why any of this happened. I only cared about Gabe and how this was tearing him up and how he'd never be able to look into the faces of his friends again without wondering. I knew how that felt. For one incident to totally change your whole life, shake up the very foundations you thought would never be moved. But I also knew he'd never be completely satisfied unless he found out the truth. Truth, even when it was painful, was eventually always better than lies.

The next day, Sunday, we didn't see anyone except his mother. I knew I couldn't expect an answer from Emory until Monday morning when his sources were back at work, but I was antsy all day. Kathryn kept giving me odd looks, as if she were on the verge of saying something, then held back. We went to bed early that night simply because there was nothing else to do.

On Monday I woke early and tried not to hover around the phone. "Why don't you go over to Otis's and ride Sinful?" Gabe suggested when he grew weary of my pacing around the house. He'd started work on some electrical outlets that needed replacing.

"I want to be here when Emory calls."

"I'll be here."

"I don't feel like riding."

He shrugged and went back to work. Halfway through, he discovered he needed two more outlets.

"I'm going down to the hardware store," he said. I walked with him out to the car. "If your cousin calls, do not, I repeat, do not act on any information before I get back."

"Yes, sir, Chief," I said, saluting.

He took my chin in his hand and shook it gently. "I mean it, *niña*. This isn't a game."

I swatted at his hand. "Stick a needle in my eye, Friday. Geeze."

While he was gone, I sat on the front porch, wrote postcards to the people back home, and replayed Saturday's conversation with Dewey in my head. He and Tyler? Could they have carried on a relationship without anyone knowing about it? I thought of what her landlady told me—the arguments with some man over the phone. Could it have been Dewey she was fighting with over the phone? And if it was, who killed her? Cordie June because of jealousy? For that matter, jealousy could have driven any of them to do it—Belinda, Lawrence, Janet, Rob—even possibly her husband, John, though I still couldn't imagine *that* in a million years. Maybe Dewey himself? But why? I doodled on the postcard in front of me, which showed a horrified Dorothy staring at a farmhouse with sparkling red slippers sticking out from under the crooked foundation. "I'm bringing down the house in Kansas," it said in fancy script.

"Is Gabe back yet?" Kathryn called through the screen door.

"Not yet."

"Oh, dear." Her voice dropped in dismay.

"What's wrong?"

"I'm in the middle of baking lemon meringue pies and I've run out of eggs. I was hoping he could run to the store and get me a dozen."

"Oh." I cringed inside, knowing what she was expecting. I also knew that crucial phone call would probably come when I was at the store. She waited expectantly, and finally I caved in. "I can do it if you don't mind lending me your car."

"Not at all. As long as you're going, would you mind picking up a few other things? You'll probably have to go out to the big Dillon's on Rock Road. We're going to a potluck at Mrs. Cleveland's house tonight. She was Gabe's kindergarten teacher."

I sighed, knowing I was stuck. "No problem."

At Dillon's it appeared everyone was doing the grocery shopping they'd put off all weekend, because it took me almost an hour to maneuver my way through the crowds. I stood in the checkout line trying to keep my impatience from getting the better of me by glancing through the magazines that grocery stores always tempt you with along with Milky Way bars, purse-sized flashlights, and rolls of Scotch tape. I picked up a quilting magazine and flipped through the pages, my attention caught by an article on quilt patterns. Apparently some woman in California had developed a computer database of quilt patterns, their origins, a cross-reference of their many names, and where they could be found in various pattern and quilt history books. I studied the examples and wondered about setting up something similar on a smaller scale at the folk art museum, though we didn't have a computer yet. Our library had grown fairly extensive, especially in the quilting area. I tossed the magazine in with the rest of the groceries and filed it in my mind as something to look into when I got back home.

I was back at Kathryn's, lugging in two bulky bags

of groceries, when what I'd read in the article hit me. The answer had been there all along, but because I hadn't looked any farther than my own surface knowledge, I hadn't seen it. The baby quilt was possibly a commemorative quilt of Tyler's time in Arkansas, the birth of her baby, but could it also be a memory of the baby's father? I set the bags of groceries on the sofa and dashed upstairs to look through the quilt encyclopedia I'd bought at the quilt show.

"Benni, is that you?" Kathryn came upstairs and stood in the doorway of the bedroom as I feverishly searched for the page showing the Arkansas Traveler pattern.

"Yes?" I looked up from my place in the quilt book, my heart pounding. "Is Gabe back?" I asked before she could say anything further.

She touched a blue-veined hand to her chest. "That's what I was coming up to tell you. He came back from the hardware store, but left again. A man called asking for you, and Gabe took the call. Gabe said to tell you he had some personal business to take care of, that he'd tell you about it later."

"How long ago did he leave?" Not wanting to frighten her, I tried to keep the panic out of my voice.

"About half an hour. Benni, what's going on?"

"Did he say where he was going?"

"No, he didn't. But I'm worried. He seemed very upset. Do you know where he went?"

I found the page for Arkansas Traveler. The small notation read "This pattern dates from the late 1800's. At various times, it has been called Secret Drawer, Travel Star, and Teddy's Choice. During the early 1930's it was also called Cowboy Star."

"I'm pretty sure I do," I said.

FOURTEEN

"CAN I BORROW your car?" I asked Kathryn.

"What's wrong?" she immediately demanded.

I held her steady gaze. "Kathryn, there's no time to explain, but I have to go after Gabe. Can you just trust me on this?"

"Is he in danger?"

"I don't know."

"Should we call the police? Should we call Dewey?"

"No." My voice sharpened.

Her eyes darkened slightly, and in that instant I knew she knew. But this was her son we were talking about, and a woman who had only known him six months was asking her to trust his life to her judgment. She hesitated.

"There's no time to waste," I said softly.

Her lips tightened. "Go, then. Call me as soon as you can."

"I will." I touched her hand briefly.

Driving through Derby, I mentally kicked myself over and over for not looking for more than one name to that quilt pattern. Tyler had obviously wanted to remember Dewey as well as the baby she was about to have. Arkansas Traveler . . . Cowboy Star. What was she thinking about all the months she sat and stitched that quilt, growing bigger and bigger with Dewey's child? Then something hit me. Cowboy. Dewey wasn't the only cowboy involved in this. His son? Could the child have been Chet's? If Dewey would kill for anyone, it would be his son. But why? Even if she'd gotten pregnant with Chet's child, that wouldn't hurt his rodeo career. This was the nineties—children born out of wedlock didn't carry the stigma they once did.

I passed the police station, slowing down to check for Dewey's truck or the Camaro. Neither of them were in the parking lot, so there was only one other place they would likely be. I kept telling myself on the drive to Dewey's house that I'd probably walk in and find them laughing over cups of coffee, the whole thing a crazy mixup, that it wasn't his name on the birth certificate or Chet's. Neither of them had anything to do with her murder. Some stranger had killed her, but they had him in custody right this minute and everything would be back to the way it was and everyone could trust each other and be friends again.

Right, Benni.

The Camaro was parked behind Dewey's pickup truck. The truck that had most likely run me down last Saturday night. The skin on the back of my neck prickled. The question still remained . . . Who was driving? I turned off the ignition and waited, trying to decide what to do. Was I making things worse by coming? Was this something best left between Gabe and Dewey, friend to friend, cop to cop?

Well, you're here now, I told myself. You may as well go in.

In the distance, I could see Belinda gesturing with wide arm movements at a lone riding student. Other than that, it was quiet for a late Monday afternoon. Even through the heavy air the sound of Belinda's instructions rang clear. "Toes up, heels down," she coached in her gruff voice. "Quiet hands!" She saw me, and her gloved hand went up in a quick wave.

The front door opened when I reached the top step. Dewey appeared in the doorway. "Thought it might be you. You may as well join the party." His face was relaxed in a benevolent smile. I exhaled in relief. He seemed too calm for anything bad to be going on.

Inside, Gabe sat in an easy chair in the corner of the living room, both hands stiffly resting on the padded arms. The minute I saw his still face, I knew he'd confronted Dewey. I turned and faced Dewey, only then noticing the pistol in his hand. I looked into his eyes, so dark in the dim living room, they appeared black as charcoal.

Dewey gestured with the pistol. "Get on over there next to your husband while I try to figure out what to do here."

I moved across the room to Gabe, trying to catch his eye, but it was as if he hadn't even noticed I entered the room. He watched Dewey's face with the unblinking concentration of a snake.

"Not too close," Dewey said, his words slightly slurred. "Stand there." He pointed to a spot about five feet from Gabe. He picked up a bottle of Wild Turkey bourbon and tilted his head back, drinking straight from the bottle. His eyes never left Gabe. For a minute or so, no one said a word.

"What's going on?" I finally demanded.

Dewey set the bottle down and wiped the back of his mouth with his hand. "I sure wish you hadn't come. This makes things a lot more complicated. What am I supposed to do now?"

I looked to Gabe, hoping he'd give me some indication of what he was going to do. But he continued to watch Dewey, his eyes measuring, concentrating. I figured the best thing I could do was stall for time. I launched right in, verbal tap-dancing having always been a talent of mine. "Dewey, no one's going to blame you. Whoever it is you're protecting—Cordie June, Belinda, whoever—I'm sure the police will understand."

Dewey's eyes shone with an alcohol-induced brightness. "Protecting? You and Gabe, you two are priceless. Do you really think I'd risk my career, my life, for a cheap tramp like Cordie June? Or even for Lawrence or Belinda? Give me a break. There's only one person besides myself I'd do that for, and my son is, thankfully, a lot smarter about picking women than his old man."

"You killed her?" I said.

"Give the woman a kewpie doll."

"But why?"

"Why? She sold my child, that's why. She sold my daughter like a steer on the hoof. What kind of woman does that? What kind of *mother* does that?" He looked at us, his face truly perplexed, waiting for an answer.

"She didn't deserve to die for it," I couldn't help saying. "Why did you have to kill her?"

He picked up the bottle and drank again, his face sad. "I didn't want to, but I couldn't help it. It was *her* own fault. She wouldn't tell me where my daughter was. I'd been begging her for weeks. There was no way, she said, that I'd ever find her. If she'd just told me where my little girl was, everything would have been okay." The hand holding the pistol hung loosely at his side. Out of the corner of my eye, I saw an almost imperceptible tightening of Gabe's body. I attempted to keep Dewey talking.

"You met at the Miller Cafe, didn't you?"

He nodded. My stomach dropped when he tightened his grip on the pistol. His face grew liquid with memory.

"She was so pretty," he said. "And so innocent. I met her six years ago." He shook his head. "I can't believe it's been that long. She wasn't married then." He inhaled raggedly, and the skin around his eyes tightened. "She didn't want to marry that Amish guy, but she'd put him off, put her father off, as long as she could. I tried to get her to leave before, but she was too afraid. It killed me thinking he was with her."

"Did she continue working at the cafe after she was married?" I prompted.

"No, good little Amish women stay home and take care of their husbands and have babies. For a year the only time I saw her was when she dropped off the cherry and apple cobblers she and her sister baked for the cafe. I always knew the exact time she'd be there, and I waited for her. We planned her escape with snatches of conversation in the parking lot." He regarded me for a long moment. "I paid for her first pair of jeans. For her first guitar. And how does she repay me? She sells my daughter."

"Did she say why?" I asked softly.

His eyes turned hard. "She said she didn't have time for a baby. That it wasn't in her plans. That it would trap her." He mimicked her voice as he spoke the last sentence. A shudder ran down my spine. His voice dropped back to his own rough timbre. "I said I'd take our daughter. She wouldn't have to do a thing. She said it didn't work like that, that she wouldn't be able to stay away if she knew where she was. That it would be too much of a temptation." He shook his head. "Shit, I know how to pick 'em, don't I, Gabe?"

"How did you know the child was even yours?" I asked, taking a chance on angering him, but trying to buy Gabe and me some time.

He laughed bitterly. "I can add. When she first left her family, I was the only friend she had. We were to-gether a few months, and then she just up and disap-peared. I thought I'd go crazy. No calls, no letters. I looked everywhere. Then DeeDee was killed, and Be-linda and I broke up . . . it was a bad time."

"So you were with her when you were still with Be-linda. No one ever knew you and Tyler had a relation-ship." That explained why he was never a strong suspect.

He laughed. "She *is* a smart one, Gabe. A real asset

to your career, I'll just bet.'' He shook his head. ''Or a big pain in the ass.''

''What about the brick?'' I asked. ''Where did you hide it?''

''Oldest trick in the book. I simply put it in the trunk of my car. By the time they'd figured out that was what killed her, it was at the bottom of the Arkansas River. Besides, these guys were my buddies. They would never have even considered searching *my* car.''

''How did you find out about the baby? She hid it pretty well.''

''Well, now, that's the problem with having musicians for friends. They aren't always the most trustworthy people around. T.K. got drunk one night, and he and Cordie June got to talking. She was complaining that she was flat broke, and he said there was an easy way to make ten grand if she didn't mind being inconvenienced for about nine months. Said he'd be glad to be the 'donor' if she'd pay him a ten percent stud fee. Then he told her about this good friend of his who sold her baby to some desperate couple who wanted themselves a healthy white baby. She told me about it one night in bed, and I put two and two together. Gabe'll tell you, I'm a pretty good detective when I want to be.'' He pushed his hat back and grinned proudly. Then the grin faded, and he took another quick sip from the bottle. ''Now, enough of this crap.''

''Dewey, you can't do this,'' I said. ''Please.''

''I don't have any other choice. It was an accident, her dying like that, but I couldn't help it. She shouldn't have kept my little girl from me.''

I swallowed hard, so angry I wanted to scream. It was unbelievable. He actually thought what he did was justified. But I grabbed onto it. Keep him talking, a voice inside me said. Every minute is one Gabe can use to his advantage. I sent Gabe a mental message: You'd better do something quick, Friday, the soles of my tap shoes are getting paper-thin here.

"Then tell the detectives that," I said, lowering my voice to a soft, imploring tone. "They'll understand. You couldn't help it. Something can be worked out. I'm sure that if you'd just talk to the detectives, tell them your side of the story . . ."

His face darkened. "Shut up!" He swung the pistol up and pointed it at me. Gabe jumped up. Dewey grabbed me around the neck and stuck the pistol under my chin. "Don't even think about it, old friend." Gabe froze, his face drained of color.

The barrel of the gun was cold and hard against the soft flesh under my chin. My insides turned to water. I wondered briefly how long the pain would last. Please, Lord, I prayed. Don't let Gabe watch me die. Don't let his last minutes on earth be so agonizing.

Dewey loosened his grip on me, then turned the gun on Gabe. I could see Gabe visibly let out the breath he'd been holding. "Nice try, Benni, but I'm not stupid. We all know I'll get hung out to dry on this one. The media will just eat it up. Cop kills mother of child because she sold it to the highest bidder. I just hate what this will do to Chet. That's why it would be better if I leave. He's my family. I have to protect him."

"You can't," I whispered. "Dewey . . ."

"Like I said, I don't have a choice. You both know too much. I need to buy myself some time." He drank from the bottle again.

"No." Gabe's voice was deep, commanding. We both looked over at him in surprise. It was the first time he'd spoken since I walked in.

"What?" Dewey asked.

"You owe me," Gabe said, enunciating each word slowly, carefully. His eyes never left Dewey's face.

Dewey contemplated Gabe for a long moment. "I always wondered if you'd ever cash in on that. You're right, I do owe you. An eye for an eye, so to speak. One life. I owe you *one* life."

"Gabe, no . . ." I started.

"Let her go," Gabe answered.

Dewey smiled sadly. "I hate doing this. You know it. But they'll fry me." He turned and looked at me. "You do present a problem, young lady. Just how am I going to keep you from siccing the good guys on me before I reach Mexico?"

"Don't do this, Dewey," I said in one last desperate attempt to appeal to whatever good there was in him. "It's wrong. Think of Chet, what this'll do to him. Think of—"

"Shut up!" he snapped. "I've thought of that. That's why I'm leaving. It'll be better for him than a long, ugly trial. This is the only way."

"No, Dewey, it's not. We'll get you the best lawyer, we'll stick by you, we'll—"

He grabbed my upper arm, his fingers biting deep into my skin. "I said, shut up."

Gabe started toward us. Dewey's face twisted into a harsh, ugly expression. He pointed the gun at Gabe's chest and said one word: "Don't." In that instant I saw the man who had killed Tyler in raw anger simply because she wouldn't give him what he wanted. Little girl, I said, sending a mental message to his and Tyler's daughter, wherever you are, count your lucky stars he'll never be your daddy.

In those brief seconds, watching him aim the gun at my husband, knowing what he planned, I suddenly realized something about myself. That if I could, I would rip that gun from his hands and kill him. As simple as that. I would do it in a second, without regret. Maybe later, when I had a chance to think about it, the horror of my choice would tear at me and change me in ways I never thought possible. But I knew, in that moment, I could do it. To save Gabe, I not only could do it, but wanted to. And that thought chilled me to the deepest part of my soul. What Gabe's philosopher said was true—what we fear most isn't being killed, but killing, because only then do we understand the ugliness of our true natures. How each of us is, without God's grace, utterly and entirely capable of murder.

"Sit down," he commanded Gabe.

Gabe slowly backed up and sank down into the chair, his face for the first time showing just a shadow of tension. "Dewey, you need to quit drinking," he said in an amazingly calm voice. "If you're going to pull this off, you'll need all your wits about you. Remember Nam. If you get too stoned, they always get you. Remember."

Dewey scratched his cheek with the barrel of the gun, loosening his grip on my arm. "You're right, Gabe. Man, you're right. I really hate doin' this to you, buddy, but there isn't any other way. It's exactly like Nam, all right. It's a war, man. Life is a war. And us good guys are losing."

"I know," Gabe said, his voice smooth and soothing. He held out his hand, palm up. "Listen to me, and I'll help you. If you promise you won't hurt Benni, I'll help you."

He looked at Gabe, his face relaxing. "You always were better at getting us out of sticky situations." He gave him a beseeching look. "I don't want to hurt her, buddy, and I know I owe you, but what can I do?"

"Take her with you," Gabe said.

"Gabe!" I protested.

He looked directly at me for the first time since I came in. His eyes were hard and cold. His cop eyes. "Benni, stay out of this."

"After you kill me," Gabe continued, his voice as even and cool as if he were telling Dewey how to change a spark plug, "take the Camaro and drive to Mexico. Release Benni when you reach the border. Just make sure she has some money and you leave her in a place where she can safely call for someone to come get her. Then your debt's paid."

Dewey contemplated Gabe's plan. "How do I get her out to the car without her making a fuss?"

I looked over at Gabe, throwing him a furious look. What kind of plan was this? "I won't go," I said. "I'll scream. Belinda's out there, other people are out there. They'll hear me. I won't let him get away with this. I won't let him kill you."

"Benni, *shut up.*" Gabe's harsh words shocked me into silence.

Dewey frowned. "She's right, I'll never get her out there without her making a fuss unless I knock her out." He looked at the butt of his gun.

"No," Gabe said quickly. "She could get a concussion. I don't want her hurt." He nodded at the half empty bottle of bourbon. "Get her drunk, then tie her up and put her in the back seat. Cover her with a blanket. She never drinks, so I doubt that she can hold her liquor, and she's small. It won't take much."

"Gabe!" My voice was frantic now.

"It could work," Dewey mused, nodding his head. He picked up the bottle and handed it to me. "Drink."

I crossed my arms over my chest. "No."

He looked over at Gabe and shrugged. "Looks like we're stuck with plan B. I tried, old buddy."

"Benni, look at me." Gabe's voice was firm. I looked into his taut face, into his chameleon eyes, dark gray now from anxiety, and realized this might be the last time we ever saw each other. "Do what he says."

"I can't." My voice was thick; tears blurred my vision. "I can't lose you. Please, Gabe."

"You can," he said gently. "You can do it for me. Now drink."

Keeping my eyes on his face, I brought the bottle to my mouth and took a drink. It felt like a hot branding iron being shoved down my throat. I doubled over, coughing and gasping for breath.

"More," Dewey said, prodding me with his gun. I tilted the bottle back slightly. He pushed it higher and held it, forcing the bourbon to flow faster into me.

"Stop," I said, jerking my head away. A river of

whiskey ran down my cheek. "I can't breathe."

For the next ten minutes, with Gabe watching, his eyes full of pain, Dewey made me drink. I felt the effects of the liquor almost immediately. The edges around my eyes blurred, and everything sounded muted, like I was struggling through miles of a dense fog.

Dewey leaned against the wall next to me and talked as I drank, asking questions that, after a few drinks, I had trouble answering coherently.

"How did you figure out it was me?" he asked, screwing a silencer to the end of his pistol. My stomach felt heated and full from the bourbon. I knew what was going to happen and I wanted to do something, but I just couldn't get my arms and legs coordinated to do it.

"The quilt," I said, reaching for the arm of the chair. "I have to sit down or I'm going to fall."

"The quilt? How'd you tie me to that stupid quilt?"

"The pattern. Arkansas Traveler." A big heated wave crashed in my stomach. "It's also called Cowboy Star. She did it to remember you."

His head jerked up at my words. "Why would she do that?"

I looked at his confused face. Why *would* she want to remember him? Then I realized she made the quilt before all the bad feelings happened between them. He'd been the first friend in her new life, maybe the first man she ever loved. Would he have left Belinda to marry her? And would she have wanted him to? Tyler had apparently loved Dewey, but she loved her music more. Even more than she loved her own child. But with her background, abortion would have been unthinkable. So she went to her only other friend, T.K., and had the baby and gave it—sold it—to a couple who would give it the kind of home she obviously felt she couldn't. She probably still had feelings for Dewey while his child grew in her, and she wanted some tangible thing with which to remember both him and his child.

"She loved you," I said, my words slurring just

slightly, not knowing if it were true but hoping it would soften him. "Dewey, she really did."

"She didn't know the meaning of love," he spit out. He tapped the bottle with the pistol. "Now, shut up and keep drinking."

I gave Gabe a look, trying to send a message telling him, I'm sorry, I love you—somehow, somewhere we'll see each other again. He encouraged me with a nod, and in his eyes I saw his reply. I tilted the bottle back one last time and felt the warm liquid wash me toward a life without Gabe.

"How can you do this?" I suddenly blurted, the liquor making me brave . . . or foolish. "You're his friend."

Dewey took the bottle from me. "Friend? If Gabe were my friend, wouldn't he just forget all about this? Let justice be done?"

"Justice?" I sputtered, amazed at his total inability to comprehend any feelings but his own. "How is what you did justice?"

He ignored my comment and looked over at Gabe's calm face. The stoic, proud face I knew he would wear until his last breath. "But my old friend here has too much integrity for that. That was always his problem, you know. Even in Nam. Him and that other little Mexican dude—what was his name—Sal? Him and Gabe were always feeling guilty about the shit that went down. They went to confession every time some old priest wandered into our base. A lot of good confession did him, huh, Gabe? He got shafted anyway. Just forget it, I used to tell them. We kill Charlie, he kills us. That's war, man. That's *life*."

Behind him, the kitchen door swung open. "Put the gun down, Dewey," a strangled voice said behind us. We all stared at Belinda, standing there in her dusty boots, holding a small black pistol pointed at her ex-husband's head.

"Well, shit," Dewey said. "You know, my greatest

wish has always been that you'd stay in the barn where you belong. How much did you hear?''

''Enough,'' she said. ''Now put the gun down. It's over.''

For a moment it seemed as if everyone had stopped breathing. I looked over at Gabe. His eyes were moving back and forth between Belinda and Dewey. Dewey's hand trembled slightly. Gabe tensed. My eyes flew back to Belinda. Her face looked shadowed and old and deathly calm.

''I said put the gun down.'' She cocked the pistol. The sound was magnified in the quiet room, and my stomach roiled in another sick wave. Bourbon crept back up my throat, tasting sour.

Dewey sighed. ''I can't, honey. You know that.''

There was an airy pop. Gabe crumpled to the floor. I screamed. Another shot. An explosion this time. Though I don't remember how, I reached Gabe and pushed my hand down on the blood gushing somewhere out the front of him. It was slick and warm and stained my hand crimson.

''Oh, Jesus, no. Please, *please*, Jesus. Don't let him die. *Please*.'' I pressed down harder, watching his shirt become saturated. ''Don't you leave me,'' I commanded him, the words catching in my throat. ''Friday, don't you dare leave me. *Don't you dare*!'' I screamed at Belinda, ''Call 911!''

She just stood there, her face ashen, the pistol dangling at her side. I glanced down at Dewey's sprawled body. His head lay in a slowly spreading pool of blood. The gun slipped out of Belinda's hand and fell to the wooden floor with a hollow thump. Her hands came up and covered her face. A moan erupted from deep inside her.

I turned back to Gabe, looking around desperately for something to put over his wound while I called for help.

''*Querida*,'' Gabe said, his voice barely audible. He struggled up to a sitting position and leaned against the chair. "I'm okay. It's just a flesh wound. More messy than dangerous. Go call the police." He smiled at me, his features strained sharp with pain. "I'm not going to leave you. Who . . ." He laughed weakly, then coughed. "Who would fight with you if I died?" His eyes fluttered. Flesh wound or not, he was still losing blood, and I knew he needed the paramedics quickly.

I grabbed a crocheted afghan off the sofa and stuck it over the wound. He reached over and held it in place. "Go on now, do what I say," he said hoarsely.

I stumbled into the kitchen and dialed 911. Because of all the liquor in my system, everything I said and did seemed to be in slow motion. I repeated the address to the dispatcher twice, then screamed the magic words that I knew would get every officer in the area there in no time. "*Officer down.*"

I dropped the phone, leaving it to dangle, grabbed a couple of clean white dish towels, and staggered back into the living room.

Belinda sat next to Dewey, cradling his bloody head in her lap. As I rushed back to Gabe, she glanced up, an amazed expression on her pale face.

"He's dead," she said, her voice thin and high as a young girl's.

I sank down next to Gabe and replaced the afghan with the dish towels, relieved to see that the flow of blood seemed to have slowed. I pressed down hard, and he covered my hand with his. We watched Belinda rock Dewey's body back and forth as if she were rocking him to sleep, humming a soft lullaby under her breath. Soon, in the distance, sirens wailed, and she stopped humming and looked up. Her freckles stood out like tiny bright pennies.

"I didn't want to kill him," she said calmly. "He was my husband, but I didn't have a choice, did I?" When we didn't reply, she answered her own question. "I really didn't have a choice. I didn't." Then she started to cry.

FIFTEEN

"I'M GOING WITH him," I insisted when the paramedics loaded Gabe onto the gurney. "Don't anyone try and stop me." I hung on to the side of the gurney when the liquor still in my system made the earth start to rock under my feet. I found Gabe's hand and grasped it tightly.

"I'm sorry, Mrs. Ortiz," the sheriff's detective said. "But we need to question you right away. You'll be able to see your husband as soon as we're through."

"That's *Ms. Harper* to you," I snapped. Gabe laughed out loud. Tears welled up in my eyes. I felt as if someone had put all my emotions in a big blender and turned it on High. "Gabe, I want to come with you." I held his hand up to my cheek.

"Do what they say, *querida*," he said. "Don't forget, they're the good guys. I'll be there soon. I promise."

"Okay," I said in a cracked voice.

"Get some food in her," Gabe said to the detective standing next to me. "He made her drink an awful lot of . . ."

I didn't hear the rest of his words as my stomach suddenly reacted to all that bourbon. I turned away from Gabe and threw up on the driveway. The detective danced out of the spray, a dismayed and disgusted look on his round face.

"Never mind," Gabe said, laughing again.

They brought Gabe back to the station a couple of hours later. There was a thick bandage under his blood-stained shirt, and his arm was in a sling. I gave it a worried look.

"I told you it was just a flesh wound," he said. "How are you feeling? Did you eat anything?"

"I'm fine. They got me a hamburger and Coke from McDonald's."

We spent almost four more hours answering the questions of the Sedgwick County Sheriff's Department and the Derby police. They quizzed us over and over until I was almost sobbing with fatigue. Gabe finally insisted, in his most authoritative manner, that they'd heard it enough times and they could finish questioning us tomorrow. Derby's chief of police agreed and ordered a patrol officer to drive us home. We could see about Kathryn's car and the Camaro the next day.

"What's going to happen to Belinda?" I asked after the officer dropped us off at the house.

"Justifiable homicide, most likely," Gabe said, slowly walking up the front porch steps. "As far as they were concerned, Dewey was trying to kill me, and that made her action reasonable."

"He *was* trying to kill you," I said fiercely.

Gabe drew in a deep breath. "He was tops in his class in marksmanship, Benni, in both the Marines and the police department. And he had to qualify on a regular basis for his job. Even with all he'd had to drink, if he'd wanted to kill me, he would have."

"Oh, Gabe." It wasn't quite suicide, but it was close enough.

Word had spread fast, and Gabe's whole family was waiting inside. We repeated the story until finally I slumped against Gabe in exhaustion, and he insisted we needed to get some sleep. I woke late the next morning in a bed bathed in sunlight and still warm from Gabe's body. I jolted up, panicked until I saw him sitting across the room in a rocking chair, reading.

"Good morning," he said, setting his book on the floor. He came over and lay down next to me, groaning slightly as he pulled me to him.

"It doesn't seem real," I said, burrowing as close as possible without hurting his shoulder. His warm, gingery scent brought a lump to my throat when I thought about how close we came to losing each other.

"I know," he said, slipping his hand under my T-shirt and stroking my bare back.

"I'm so sorry," I said, tears springing up from nowhere.

"It's not your fault."

"I mean I'm sorry for you. Sorry this had to happen."

"Me, too," he said, his voice sadder than I'd ever heard it.

His mother wisely talked of other things as she made us breakfast. When the newspaper reporters finally made enough nuisance of themselves, Gabe went out and gave them an interview in his mother's front yard. He wouldn't allow them to talk to me, for which I was grateful. I was still so shaky that all they probably would have gotten was a blubbering mass of incoherent words. But I was worried about Gabe, too. He was taking all of this so calmly; his main concern was how it was affecting me. That first day we didn't venture farther than a few inches from each other. Every time the scene of Dewey firing the gun at Gabe flashed through my mind, I'd reach over and touch him, making sure he was really there.

That night, holding me before we went to sleep, he said, "It'll get better, *niña*. You won't be this afraid forever."

And he was right. By the next day, the horrifying scene in my mind had already started fading a little, and by the day after, even more.

On Thursday I told him there was one last thing I felt I had to do. I wanted to see Hannah.

"We'll go together," he said.

The farm was quiet when we walked up the dirt driveway. Eli saw us first and called for Hannah. After introductions were made, Eli offered Gabe a tour of the farm. Hannah and I strolled through her vegetable garden while we talked about Tyler and her baby.

"Thank you," she said. She stooped down to pull up a fat orange carrot, shook the dirt clods off, and placed it in her basket.

"For what?" I said.

"For finding out the truth. I feel that Ruth can rest now." She stood up and looked out over the black fields where Gabe and Eli were standing. The plowed earth shined in the bright sun as if flecks of metal were woven through it. Eli spread his arm out and gestured widely, explaining something to Gabe. Gabe tilted his head slightly, listening. "I'll never understand, though, how she could do that. How she could give away her own child." She turned to me, her face bewildered. A smattering of freckles dusted her translucent skin. "For the music? She always told me her music was from God. If it was, how could she sacrifice her child? What God would approve of that?"

I didn't answer, because I couldn't. And I don't think she really expected me to. I picked a ripe tomato off a thick vine and touched its smooth, warm skin to my cheek. "Will you try to find her baby?" I asked.

She shook her head. "No. Eli and I prayed about it and discussed it with our bishop. We will just let it be. I will always think of her, Ruth's little girl." Her gray eyes filled with tears. "And I will always pray for her. But I must have faith in this. Faith that God will take care of her since we cannot."

I nodded and placed the tomato in her basket. She would always wonder, though, as I would. Always wonder about the little girl who was growing up somewhere, hopefully with parents who loved her, who loved each other. A little girl with Tyler's blond hair and beautiful voice . . . and Dewey's wry smile. Twenty years from now, would I turn on the radio and hear Tyler's voice echo out of it? Would music be a blessing to this child or a curse? I said a quick prayer for the innocent little girl whose conception had started this whole chain of events that culminated in two senseless deaths, the deaths of her natural parents.

When we left, Hannah pressed two jars of elderberry jam into my hands. "I'll send you the quilt when it is finished."

"Thank you," I said, wanting to hug her, but holding back. I touched her forearm instead. "In spite of the circumstances, I'm very happy to have met you."

"And I you," she replied.

Later that afternoon, something happened that finally made me feel as if life would someday be normal again. Kathryn, knowing we needed to get back to some semblance of normality, sent us up to the Dillon's grocery store on Rock Road to buy some things she supposedly couldn't find at Food 4 Less downtown. We were walking out to the car, each of us carrying a grocery bag, when a pure white Peterbilt truck pulled into the parking lot. Painted across the wide expanse of the truck in shiny sky-blue was a Holy Spirit dove and the words "Jesus Is Coming Soon."

My mouth dropped open. "It . . . it couldn't be," I stammered. My last phone call from Daddy had been two days ago, and he'd said the best he could make out from the CB reports was that Dove was somewhere around Oklahoma City. Apparently she was going to make it to our reception in time, just as she promised. I don't know why I ever worried. Dove has never broken a promise to me in my life.

We shoved the grocery bags in the Camaro and ran over to the idling truck. Dove's white head poked out the open window, and she smiled a wide, bull-that-broke-out-of-the-pasture smile.

"You're right," she called over her shoulder to the driver of the truck. "All it took was prayer. That's my granddaughter and grandson right there."

"*Abuelita*!" Gabe said, laughing. "You made it!"

The passenger door opened, and she handed me her flowered suitcase. "I forgot Kathryn's address, but Brother Dwaine said all we'd have to do is ask the Lord and He'd lead us to the right place. And He did!"

A laughing, sonorous voice called after her. "Well, the Lord and Rand McNally."

I just stood there shaking my head as Gabe, with his good arm, helped her down from the truck's cab.

She waved to the man in the truck, who was wearing a silver-gray pompadour and face-splitting smile. "Thanks for the ride. Remember to drop by the ranch if you ever make it out West. I'll fry you up a rib-eye that'll make your taste buds sing 'Amazing Grace' backwards."

A thundering laugh reverberated from the cab. Brother Dwaine gave the truck's air horn a long, ear-shattering blow and pulled slowly out onto the highway.

She turned to me. "Come over here and hug my neck, honeybun. I'm starved. What's for supper? Are the boys here yet? And what kind of trouble have you two youngsters gotten into these last couple of weeks?"

We told her part of the story as we drove back to Kathryn's, where Arnie and Daddy had beat her by half an hour. They, apparently, hadn't lost Kathryn's address. We went through the story one more time, then declared it subject *non grata*.

Arnie, Daddy, and most of all, Dove, kept us amused the rest of the day, each telling their own particular "road story." Dove had just about decided that people were probably as tired of Charles Kuralt reruns as she was and were ready to see a more mature lady hit the road and give a report on America.

"Anyone in particular you think they should cast?" I teased. Gabe and I relaxed on the floor, he leaning against the wall, me with my head in his lap. Seeing the familiar faces of my family was just the medicine I needed. Even Daphne had gotten into the spirit of things and lay down about two inches from my thigh, her head on her paws. When I reached over to stroke her, a low growl vibrated from her throat. I snatched my hand back and joined Gabe in laughing. I guess like most of the Ortiz family, she just couldn't be rushed.

The next day, Friday, Becky came by and told us to come with her and Angel, that they had a surprise for us. Dove and Kathryn, who to my amazement had taken an instant liking to each other, came along. We ended up at Shepler's Western Wear in Wichita, where Becky said she and Angel were buying Gabe the proper clothes to wear to our wedding reception the next day. The party, in honor of me and my family, had a Western theme, and *no one* was getting out of dressing up for this one. According to his sisters, Gabe was getting his first pair of Wranglers and boots whether he liked it or not.

"We're going to make a cowboy out of you, if just for a day," Becky said firmly.

"Impossible," Gabe said just as firmly.

I laughed, and told Becky, "If you can get him into cowboy gear, you're a better woman than I am."

With a sister gripping each arm, he was dragged into Shepler's huge men's department. "Help," he called to me and Dove, a comical look of terror on his face. From across the store we watched with amusement as they threw shirts and jeans over the dressing room door to him and argued about boots and belts. I took possession of his American Express card and decided if he got a new outfit, then so would I. I settled on a gauzy white broomstick dress printed with tiny red horseshoes. It was short enough to make Dove *tsk* under her breath and mumble to Kathryn that sure wasn't how she'd raised me. I rounded out my outfit with a matching pair of handmade Lucchese boots in a bright crimson. Not ruby slippers, but they'd get me home, anyway.

"While I'm here," I said to the salesclerk, giving Dove the eye, "I have a hat I left to be cleaned and blocked. Could you see if it's ready yet?"

Dove had the grace to turn slightly pink. "I see a real nice-lookin' shirt over there that might near fit Ben. May as well pick it up for him."

"Good idea," I agreed.

While our purchases were being wrapped, I wandered over to see how Angel and Becky were faring.

"You're just in time," Becky said. "I think we've finally got the right look. Okay," she yelled into the dressing room. "You can come out now."

"I'm not coming out," I heard him grumble.

"If you don't, we're coming in to get you," Angel called.

I gasped when he walked out wearing the most sheepish look I'd ever seen on his face. Across the store, one of the female clerks let out a loud wolf whistle.

His faded, prewashed Wranglers fit him snugly in all the right places; a deep turquoise Western shirt with white pearl buttons made his blue eyes glow against his dark olive skin. With glossy Roper boots, a black cowboy hat, a silver belt buckle you could fry an egg on, and his thick sexy mustache, he looked like the star of a Western movie.

"Wow," I said, scanning him from boots to hat.

"George Strait," Becky said, "eat your heart out."

"Don't even think I will ever wear these clothes again after tomorrow," he warned me, his face flushing an attractive burnt sienna.

"Wow," I repeated.

"So what did you buy?" he asked on the drive back.

"Something she shouldn't be wearing in public," Dove carped. I almost fell out of my seat when Kathryn smiled and gave me an amused wink.

Gabe grinned. "Oh, yeah? Sounds interesting."

I complained in front of the mirror the next day as we got ready for the party. "I wish my legs were tanner, then maybe the bruises wouldn't show as much. But I refuse to wear pantyhose in this weather."

"Dove's right," he said, looking at my outfit with both a warm-blooded male appreciation and husbandly uncertainty. "That dress is pretty short."

"With the way you look in those skintight Wranglers, Friday, ain't nobody going to be looking at me."

"These things are embarrassing," he said, inspecting himself in the long mirror. "Becky and Angel made me buy a size too small."

"Nope," I said. "They're perfect. That's how cowboys wear them when they dress up. And today you've promised to be a real cowboy."

At that moment, a pained look swept over his face, and I knew he was thinking about Dewey. I also knew that if and when he was ready to talk about it . . . and anything else, it would have to come in his own time. I didn't have the right to push him to open up any faster than he felt comfortable doing. I had the right to ask—and I would keep on asking—but intimacy had to be freely given, just like love.

I slipped my arms around his neck, kissing him hard. "I'm so glad you're okay," I whispered.

He took my face in his hands and looked at me for a long moment. "I wouldn't want to live without you," he said.

At the party, for the first time since we'd been in Kansas, we relaxed and just had fun. Everyone got into the spirit of Becky's theme, and there was enough denim, leather, and pearl buttons to outfit an Alan Jackson road show. The highlight of the evening was the opening of our wedding presents. Some were practical, like the towels that Janet and Lawrence bought us; some were funny, like the matching T-shirts from Angel that said "There's No Place Like Home On the Range" along with a Victoria's Secret gift certificate made out to Gabe. Others were touching, like the antique Wedding Ring quilt from Becky and Stan. When all the presents appeared to have been opened, I looked over at Otis, who had been the last person to arrive at the party. He was holding a tiny gold box in his hands. The smile on my face was so big, I thought my face would splinter.

"What are you and Otis smirking at each other for?" Gabe asked.

"I think there's one more present," I said.

Otis passed the box to Gabe.

"You open it," Gabe said.

"No," I said. "This is one you have to open."

He untied the ribbon slowly, his face puzzled, until he lifted the lid of the shiny box and took out the worn truck key. For a minute, I thought I might see my new husband cry for the first time. Without a word, he stood up and walked out the front door. The old Chevy pickup was parked behind our rented Camaro.

The rest of us followed Gabe out, crowding behind him on the porch.

"Oh, Otis," Kathryn said, her hand on her chest. A tear slowly made its way down her cheek.

Otis cleared his throat and stuck his hands deep into his pockets, trying not to show the emotion he was feeling, too. When Gabe turned to thank him, he said, "Thought since you live out there in cattle country now, you'd be needin' yourself a truck."

During the next half hour, the men did what all men do when one of them gets a new vehicle—they walked around it, admired the paint job, kicked the tires, checked under the hood. Dove, Becky, Angel, and Janet wandered back into the house to get the steaks and chicken ready to barbecue. Eventually the only two people left on the porch were Kathryn and me.

"It's been a rough two weeks for you," she said, resting her hand on one of the posts.

"Yes," I said. "But there were good times, too." I turned and faced her. "We didn't get to know each other very well, but I'm glad we met. For Gabe's sake."

She studied me with her clear, no-nonsense eyes. "My son isn't an easy person to love."

I lifted my chin slightly and met her direct gaze, knowing she wouldn't fall for any feigned protestations. "No, he isn't."

She smiled slightly. "Neither was his father. And he *is* so much like his father. Gelio and I had some fights that would, as my father used to say, peel the paint off a barn door."

I felt my eyes widen, surprised by this woman for the second time in two days.

"Yes, he really upset the apple cart in this old school-marm's life, no doubt about it." For a moment, her eyes filmed over. "But for all the passion in our fighting, it didn't hold a candle to the making up."

"Yes," I said, smiling in agreement. "There's always that."

Her lips tightened, as if to say, Enough of this nonsense. "So, Benni Harper, do you love my son?" The question was put with the same tart inflection I could imagine her using when she demanded that one of her fifth graders name the first ten Presidents of the United States.

I answered without hesitation. "Yes, ma'am, I do."

She dropped her head in an approving nod. "Well, I guess a mother can't ask for any more than that." She started for the door, then turned around. "One more thing. About your name."

Involuntarily I stiffened. Just when we'd made some kind of bridge, here was a stick of dynamite all fused up and ready to blow it to smithereens. "What about it?" I asked, trying to keep my voice neutral.

"I want you to know I agree with you and I told Gabe so. I asked him how he would like it if I remarried and changed my name to Terkle or Lundquist or Perkins. He, of course, was horrified. He said that would be an insult to his father's memory. I said he was absolutely right. I told him that the only thing you have left to honor Jack with is his name and that he didn't have a right to take that away. Gabe, after all, has you.''

I looked up at her, my heart pounding as hard as if I'd sprinted a mile. She had said what I'd never been able to verbalize. In the last year and a half, each time I'd taken Jack's name off bank accounts, insurance policies, next-of-kin listings, it felt like he died over and over again. I guess I realized unconsciously that soon there would be nothing left of him except the engraving on his headstone. She was right—Jack's name was the last thing on earth that he had left. Unlike Gabe, who had a son to carry on his name, Jack had only me.

''Thank you,'' I said.

''You don't have to thank me, Benni,'' she said, touching my shoulder lightly. ''Just take good care of my son.''

After the men were done admiring the truck, Gabe came over to me. ''Let's go for a ride,'' he said.

''But we're going to eat in a minute.''

''They'll save us some. I want to show you something. Actually, there are two places I need to go.''

The first stop was someplace I'd been wondering about since we'd arrived in Kansas. He pulled into the El Paso Cemetery and drove slowly down the gravel paths, stopping when he came to the right spot.

''Come on,'' he said, opening the door and taking my hand.

It was an old-fashioned cemetery, the kind that looked just like what it was instead of trying to fool people into thinking it was a park or a golf course. We crisscrossed through rows of graves until we came to his father's. It was an upright black marble stone with a rounded top.

Rogelio Tomas Ortiz—January 30, 1923–June 12, 1966—Dearly loved and missed by his wife, children and friends—Vaya Con Dios.

Gabe stood for a long minute staring at the grave. Looking at the dates, I realized for the first time that

Gabe was now the same age his father had been when he died.

"When my father and I were alone, he would speak only Spanish to me," he said in a low voice. "He never told me about how important my Mexican heritage was . . . I mean, he never actually said the words. But he showed it to me. In that way and in lots of others. That's why I was raised Catholic. It must have been a deal he and Mom worked out early, because until the day he died, I would go to Mass with him every Sunday, and Mom and the girls would go to the Methodist church." He smiled to himself. "As a teenager, I used to complain about it because I thought the Methodist girls were prettier than the Catholic ones. Anyway, I heard they kissed better." He looked at me and winked. "Of course, if I'd only known then what I know now about Baptist girls . . ."

"Better not let Dove hear you say that," I said, laughing. I punched him on his good arm. He slipped it around me, pulling me close. In the white-oak trees surrounding us, a flock of birds rustled the leaves. We both looked up. He looked again at the headstone and started talking quietly, almost as if to himself.

"No one knows the whole story about my Silver Star. We were ambushed that day—me and Dewey and Sal and this fat old colonel from Maryland. The colonel was just along for, as he put it, the 'life experience.' He wanted to see what his boys were going through. Our lieutenant told us to take him out, hump him around for a few days until he got tired and dirty and couldn't take the leeches anymore, then bring him back. We walked him in circles for two days, telling him we were scouting for snipers. He had no idea we were just screwing with his head—letting him play soldier. Sal got word over the wire that some Vietcong had been spotted, and we'd better get our asses back to the main camp. We were ambushed trying to get the colonel back. We never did see them. It was crazy, like bushes and trees were trying to kill you. There must not have been that many, because after a couple of hours they stopped firing. We'd either capped them all or they ran off. But the colonel, Dewey, and Sal had all taken a hit and were out. I remember standing there, staring at them, thinking, What do I do now?

"Sal jabbed me with the butt of his M16. 'You gotta get 'em out, *mano*,' he said. 'I'm *todos para la chingada*.' All messed up. They'd got him in the legs. 'Take them to that clearing about half a mile back,' he said. 'I'll call and tell them it's a colonel. Those *puercos* will get a chopper there with no shit asked.'

" 'What about you?' I asked. He nodded at Dewey and the colonel. 'They're out, man. I can still protect myself.' He held up his rifle. So I did what he said. I carried Dewey out first, then the colonel. I had to drag him, he was so big.

" 'Don't forget me, man,'' Sal said when I came back for the colonel. 'Don't let that chopper fly without me.'

" 'I won't,' I said.

"The chopper was waiting when I got the colonel there. Sal was right; because it was a colonel, we got service on a silver platter. They yelled at me to get in, and I screamed, 'There's one more.'

" 'No time,' the medic yelled back. 'They've spotted a mess of Vietcong advancing. Orders are to fly with what we got.'

"I jammed my rifle in his throat and told him I'd hunt him down and kill him if he was gone when I got back. I ran back for Sal. That's when I got this." He touched his right hip.

"It slowed me down, and by the time I reached Sal, they'd already gotten him. He took a round right in the skull. There was skin and blood and pieces of bone everywhere. There was so much blood. I swear I couldn't believe a human being had that much blood inside him . . ." His voice caught. "There was one of them left scavenging. He was pocketing the gold Saint Christopher's medal that Sal's grandmother had given

him. I told him to *didi mau*. Get out. This kid couldn't
have been more than sixteen years old. He just stared at
me with these black empty eyes. Then he held up his
hands to show he was unarmed. I pointed to the medal
he was holding. He threw it back down on Sal's body,
turned around, and started walking into the bush. Then,
without thinking twice, I fired a round into him. I threw
Sal over my shoulder and carried him to the chopper.''
He took a ragged breath and looked back out over his
father's headstone. ''So Señora Quintera got her son's
body, an unarmed Vietnamese boy got shot in the back,
and I got a Silver Star. Like Dewey said, a regular John
Wayne movie.''

I laid my hand on his arm. ''It was a war, Gabe. They
had just killed your friend. What you did was . . .'' I
paused, trying to think of the right word, remembering
how I felt when Dewey pointed that gun at Gabe.
''Understandable.''

He shook me off. ''*I shot a kid in the back*, Benni.
And I was given a medal simply because the person I
happened to save was a colonel. Do you realize how
political those medals are? Do you think I would have
gotten it if I'd left him there and saved Sal first? Do you
know how many times I've wondered if what I did was
the right thing?''

''What you did was right, Gabe,'' I said. ''I know
you. You didn't save the colonel because he was ranked
higher. You saved him first because he was the most
helpless. What Sal told you was right. When you left
him, he was still able to protect himself.''

He turned hard eyes on me. ''That's why I don't care
about that medal. It's just a fancy way of saying you
killed people. That's all.''

We stood for a moment staring at each other. ''One
more thing,'' he said.

''What?''

''About my drinking.''

I took a deep breath, wondering what other revelations

he was about to pour out. I had said I wanted him to open up to me, and like a dam's overflowing floodgate, it appeared to be coming out all at once. "What about it?"

He leaned over and ran his fingertips over his father's engraved name. "You know my father died of a heart attack."

"Yes."

"A couple of years ago I went in for a physical exam. The doctor jumped all over me because my cholesterol and triglycerides were so high and my blood pressure was in another stratosphere. After reading my medical history, he said if I didn't quit living on junk food, start exercising, and learn to handle stress better, I'd be visiting my father sooner than I'd probably prefer. That's all it is, *querida*. Nothing earthshaking. I just want to live a longer life than my dad."

"Diet, exercise, and stress. Well, two out of three isn't too bad."

He pulled me to him, laughing softly under his breath. "I was doing fine on handling stress until I came to San Celina."

"Experts say that certain kinds of stress can actually prolong your life."

"Well," he said, nuzzling the top of my head, "it may not prolong it, but it certainly makes it more enjoyable."

I kissed his neck and asked, "Are you ready to go back to the party now?"

"Not quite yet. I've got one more place to show you before we leave Kansas."

We drove out of Derby on a small southbound highway. The sun had already set, and everything was that soothing lavender color that makes dusk my favorite part of the day. The humidity, for a change, was low, and though the air wasn't as crisp and fresh as San Celina's, for the first time since arriving in Kansas, I didn't feel as if I were suffocating. Of course, the events and revelations of the day might have had something to do with it, too.

He pulled up in front of a red pipe gate that led into a heavily wooded area. A square, hand-painted sign said "Picnic Grounds—VFW Post 7235." The gate was closed with a huge metal padlock. Gabe hopped out, went over, and studied it closely.

I rolled down my window. "What are you doing?"

"I wanted to show you the picnic grounds. We used to sneak in here when we were teenagers. You can drive down to the river."

"It looks like we're locked out."

He continued studying the lock. "We used to be able to pop this open when we twisted it the right way."

"Gabe, that was twenty-five years ago. It couldn't possibly be the same lock."

He gave it a sharp twist, and it popped open. He grinned at me. "This is Kansas, Benni. People here don't throw out things as long as they still work."

We drove through a small clearing where we passed some redwood picnic benches, a replica of a covered wagon, and a faded hand-painted sign stuck in a moldy hay bale that said "Haunted Valley." In the tall grasses surrounding us, the pale glitter of fireflies sparkled like a tiny Disney parade.

"I think they used this for some kind of Halloween fund-raiser," Gabe said, driving deeper into the trees. We came to another, smaller clearing where he turned off the engine. "The river's not much further, but the ground's a little soggy. I don't want to take a chance on getting stuck."

"So," I said, unbuckling my seat belt, "you seemed very proficient with that lock back there. Am I right in guessing I'm not the first girl you've brought here?"

He leaned over and kissed me. "How about if you're the last?"

"I could live with that."

"Actually, you're the first girl I've ever brought here

in this truck. My dad would never let me drive it.''

"This is the first time you've ever driven it?"

He gave an embarrassed smile. "Actually, the second. The first time was the October after my dad died. I took the keys out of Mom's purse, and Rob and I and two six-packs of beer went dragging Douglas."

"Dragging Douglas?"

"Douglas Street in Wichita. Back then, it was the place to cruise your car and be seen. On the way back, I hit a slick spot out on the highway and drove it into a ditch. That's the thing that finally convinced my mom I might be better off staying with my uncle Tony in California."

I ran my hand down his thigh. "Fate. If that hadn't happened, we probably wouldn't be together right now."

He covered my hand and pressed it into his leg. "Probably not."

"We should get back. Everyone's going to wonder where we are."

"Let them wonder." He brought my hand up to his lips and nibbled on the back of my wrist. "I think I'd like to sit here a little longer."

"Oh, I see your hidden agenda now." His lips moved higher, to the crook of my elbow.

"Nothing hidden about it," he murmured.

"Well, I always did have trouble resisting a good-looking cowboy in a pickup truck."

He made a disgusted sound in his throat, pulled off his hat, and threw it to the floor. "I meant it when I said I wouldn't be wearing these clothes after tonight, so you can just put that thought right out of your head. I might own a truck now, but I am not a cowboy. I don't think like one, don't eat like one, don't walk like one, and certainly don't talk like one. Never have. Never will."

I ran my fingers through his coarse black hair. "Gee, that's too bad, 'cause where I come from there's this sort of tradition."

"What's that?" he asked suspiciously.

"When a cowboy gets a new truck, it's not officially his until he makes love to his woman in it. What do you say to that, Friday?"

"Yeehaw," he replied.